Robin Cannon obtained both her bachelor's and master's degrees from Fordham University in New York City before embarking on a teaching career. She has traveled extensively throughout the world and is an avid reader of Russian history as well as an antiques junkie. She wrote *Tilly Fig*, *Rye Hill*, and *Fireflies at Nightfall*, a trilogy that went on display at the 2017 Book Expo in New York City, as well as *The Vanity of Robbers* and *Pignoli and the Chocolate Thief*. She lives in Connecticut with her husband, Bob, where she enjoys walking on the beach and tending to her gardens.

For Diane, who on numerous occasions graciously allowed me to steal away into her attic where all inspiration dwells.

Robin Cannon

Into the Attic Darkly

Austin Macauley Publishers™
London * Cambridge * New York * Sharjah

Copyright © Robin Cannon 2024

All rights reserved. No part of this publication may be reproduced, distributed, or transmitted in any form or by any means, including photocopying, recording, or other electronic or mechanical methods, without the prior written permission of the publisher, except in the case of brief quotations embodied in critical reviews and certain other non-commercial uses permitted by copyright law. For permission requests, write to the publisher.

Any person who commits any unauthorized act in relation to this publication may be liable to criminal prosecution and civil claims for damages.

This is a work of fiction. Names, characters, businesses, places, events, locales, and incidents are either the products of the author's imagination or used in a fictitious manner. Any resemblance to actual persons, living or dead, or actual events is purely coincidental.

Ordering Information
Quantity sales: Special discounts are available on quantity purchases by corporations, associations, and others. For details, contact the publisher at the address below.

Publisher's Cataloging-in-Publication data
Cannon, Robin
Into the Attic Darkly

ISBN 9798891551824 (Paperback)
ISBN 9798891551831 (ePub e-book)

Library of Congress Control Number: 2023920994

www.austinmacauley.com/us

First Published 2024
Austin Macauley Publishers LLC
40 Wall Street, 33rd Floor, Suite 3302
New York, NY 10005
USA

mail-usa@austinmacauley.com
+1 (646) 5125767

I would like to thank Pamela for our field trips to the attic whenever I needed them.

I would also like to thank Sam for keeping a watchful eye as I worked. It was a comfort knowing that he was always there.

Finally, I would like to thank my husband, Bob, and my children; Haley, Molly, and Colin for their enduring support. They are my heart.

Chapter 1

The doorbell rang out its familiar baritone chime, dignified and solemn as though it were a call to church. I felt edgy as I walked toward the front door, my own apprehension pursuing me like a rabid dog. Intent upon eroding what little composure I had left, it was succeeding in sending me into a full-blown panic. There's a lot to be said for composure, especially when you're no longer able to maintain it. I had yet to shake my recent encounter in the attic, the reason for my lack of all self-possession. It was a jarring ordeal, both gruesome and bizarre, and I wonder what my dead mother would think of it if she were alive today.

Can you hear me, Mother? I continued toward the front door, focused on the doorknob just beyond my reach, before falling victim to overriding anxiety. I staggered and fell onto the overstuffed chair in the front hall, reduced to a crumpled heap. My landing was exaggerated, I know but, after all, I had been swallowed up and spit out by my own dread before being tossed like an unwanted ragdoll. More's the pity. But I won't apologize for being overwrought. Not now. Not after what happened in the attic.

Coming around after what seemed an eternity, I was lightheaded but deeply aware that someone was still at the front door, eager to get in. No longer ringing the bell, the persistent visitor now knocked while calling my name out loud. I immediately recognized the unmistakable voice, my gut twisting like old times. What was he doing here?

"Tom, it's Officer Dunnegan! Are you in there?" I quickly shook the cobwebs from my brain and stood up on my feet. "Open the door, Tom!"

"Coming!" I managed to croak. Taking in a deep breath, I walked steadily toward the door and took a firm hold of the old glass knob, forcibly turning it to the right before giving it a good yank.

"Hello, Tom," said the officer standing there, "it's good to see you again. May I come in?" I rubbed my eyes as if to be certain it was Dunnegan.

"You know the way," I said flippantly, stepping aside while gesturing for him to cross what was now a familiar threshold. A shiver ran down my spine. "What's going on?" I asked, glancing up the center hall staircase toward the attic as though I were expecting to see someone at any moment. Did he notice that?

"Do you recognize these things, Tom?" asked the officer, pulling a large pocketknife and an old photograph from his black leather jacket. I briefly put a hand to my throbbing neck.

"Yes, I do," I said, my heart now pounding in my ears just as it had done in the attic earlier that morning.

"I'm afraid I have some bad news about your brother, Eddie," he said, ushering me to the overstuffed chair where he sat me down, assuming that I would need to be off my feet for the news. I found it pointless, though, to be seated for something I already knew, my brother's fate a forgone conclusion.

Just then, Dulcie walked into the center hall from the kitchen, a girl who had brazenly waltzed into our lives and stayed, altering everyone and everything forever.

"Oh, hello, Officer Dunnegan," she said, her demeanor a bit aloof. "I never expected to see you again, now that the trial is over. Is there a problem?" She watched curiously as I stood up from the chair, regretful for not having spoken to her sooner about the trauma I had endured in the attic.

My story is as much about Dulcie as it is about Eddie. From the moment we met her, life had become both bright and dreary, truthful and deceitful, loving and hateful…found and lost. Not even time could erase those memories but today an unexpected, menacing turn of events would overshadow the past, another dark chapter to add to the others. It all began what seems a lifetime ago, but nightmares have a way of haunting you forever. Don't they?

***

Eddie and I grew up privileged thanks to our father, Daniel J. Biggs, who was a high-profile attorney-at-law in an upscale New England town. He didn't come up easy himself though, having been the son of an itinerant laborer who had to follow the work. Moving his family around the northeast often, food on the table could be scarce if the old man, as father liked to call him, decided to stop at a bar on pay day. Yet, father never had a cross word to say about him.

Only the sad smirk on his face allowed us a peak into his true emotions whenever he mentioned the old man. I never knew my grandfather, but I would say it was to his credit that my father was always so determined, not only to make a lot of money, but to climb the social ladder as well. He managed to do both, putting us Biggs in the catbird seat for as far back as I could remember.

"My mother was never really accepted by the neighbors or even the Ladies Guild at the church," my father would say with a tinge of melancholy in his voice. He promised himself that if he were to have a family of his own one day, it would never be subjected to such shabby treatment.

Once father graduated from junior college his family moved again, but he stayed behind with a friend to continue his college career while clerking for a small-town lawyer. He liked the job and decided that one day he'd like to become a lawyer too, eventually being accepted into his last pick from a long wish list of law schools. But that didn't bother him. He had come a long way, nevertheless. It was 1955 and Daniel J. Biggs was right where he wanted to be, the master of his own destiny with a swagger that could put James Dean to shame. He would proudly say later on that his relentless burning of the midnight oil and a few well-placed scholarships got him over the finish line.

It was in law school that father met mother. Oh, she wasn't a law student. Father always said that she was too much of a 'flutter budget' to ever study law. No, she was a secretary to one of the deans; pretty, blonde, slim and, to top it all off, originally from Baton Rouge. "She had this sexy little accent that I couldn't resist," father would say. To him, mother had it all and he fell madly in love with her. It was as though she had come up north just to meet him. Mother liked to call it kismet.

After father passed the bar, they married. Drawn to a life of ocean breezes and salty air, they moved to Old Windsor Cove where father got a job with Chesterman, Hanson, and Mink, a reputable law firm that eventually made him partner. It didn't take long for him to gain notoriety as a shark in the courtroom…and a ladies' man about town. Mother just spent the money with relish and, at the time, turned a blind eye to the rest.

I suppose, to keep father in line, she decided it was time to start a family. I was born first and then after three years came Eddie. We grew up close at first. He was my constant companion and playmate. Father was busy building his law practice back then and spent little time with Eddie and me during those early growing up years, content to remain a background figure who occasionally tucked us into bed or threw a football.

My fondest memories, though, are of the times when mother took us to the beach, and it was often. She would occasionally walk with us along the shore to collect shells or sea glass, but it was here that she took time for herself and completely relaxed, digging her toes into the sand and burying her nose in a good book. Here she was away from father's philandering and the late-night suppers he used to make her sit through with clients or the other lawyers' wives. Eddie and I were free to run, jump and skip flat rocks on the water without having to be under her normally watchful eye. We fished and collected hundreds of tiny crabs for our yellow bucket, only to be made to dump them out before we left for home.

An old shack that stood on the sand near the bait and tackle shop, having held up amazingly over the years against the New England winds of summer, provided us with a great hiding place. It was our own little club house away from home where we'd discuss matters most important to little boys and hide our beach treasures. Eddie loved that shack along with everything else about the beach where he enjoyed himself with reckless abandon.

There, he was a wild child who simply lived life without staying in the margins so to speak. All in all, life at the beach was a paradise, easy and carefree, and my brother was a good friend and companion with whom to share it. But I would eventually conclude that I was wrong about Eddie.

One day, on one of our much-anticipated trips to the beach, his behavior suddenly moved beyond reckless. He repeatedly threw sand at mother and wouldn't stop until I tackled him, the two of us rolling around the sand in fits and shrieks.

"Leave mother alone," I said with a smile while pinning him down, wanting to believe at the time that he was using poor judgment but not being intentionally malicious.

"Make me!" he shouted as he escaped my restraint and ran down the beach. That was the first time Eddie had ever defied me. I felt wounded.

He acted with disregard toward other people that day too, kicking sand onto their blankets when he walked past and calling them names. He threw rocks willy nilly, not caring who or what he hit. Even though I was young, I thought Eddie couldn't be right in the head that day. Nevertheless, unable to help myself, I laughed at some of the things he did, even when mother was upset and perplexed beyond words, powerless to reprimand him.

"Don't encourage him," she would caution in a trembling voice. "I just can't imagine what's gotten into this boy." Poor mother. Poor helpless mother. From that day forward, my eyes became wide open to Eddie.

Now I began to see things more clearly, see Eddie for what he really was. He was certainly wild, almost animal-like, which always caused problems. The grocer in town called Eddie crazy when he decided to throw an apple at another customer, forcing mother to grab him by the hand and leave the store in shame. His teachers said he had no self-control, a gross understatement, often sending Eddie home early from school which would invariably cost him a trip to bed without supper.

If we were in a store, he'd pull merchandise off the shelves and onto the floor, broken items drawing unwanted attention and dirty looks. When he held mother's hand during a stroll, he'd refuse to walk a straight line, sometimes pulling and twisting her arm purposely until she cried out in pain. Father would spank him for that, leaving Eddie unphased. The boy had no regard for anybody or anything, not even himself. Still, father was oblivious to the big picture.

"Boys will be boys," he liked to say, turning a blind eye and sweeping Eddie's behavior away with that one offhanded remark, but I knew it was more than that. Everyone knew. It just proved how indifferent father could be, but it was only a preview to how distant he would become.

As Eddie got older, though, his behavior got worse and clearly more violent. One day he went to the stream behind our house to hunt for frogs. After catching one he immediately threw it hard onto the jagged rocks, killing it.

"Why did you do that!" I screamed at him.

"No reason," he said without emotion, shrugging his shoulders. I was disturbed by the incident but never told mother. Eddie made me promise.

Then, of course, there was the time I caught him striking our dog Tinker, a small terrier that had stolen a cookie from his hand. When the poor little animal yelped in pain I punched Eddie right in the gut, knocking the wind out of him. That was the last straw for me. I distanced myself from my brother for a while, too angry to be associated with him, and kept a good eye on the dog from then on, never telling mother why. Eddie was crazy enough, but at my tender age, I couldn't foresee just how unbalanced he would become. I was eleven and Eddie was eight.

One mid-autumn Saturday, father called mother and told her to meet him for lunch at Webster's Soda Fountain on Kimball Avenue, the main street in the center of our town. It was an easy walk from our house.

"Bring the boys," he told her.

"Does Eddie have to come with us?" I asked.

"Of course, he has to come," mother said. "Do you think I would leave him home alone?"

It was a fair question, silly of me to even ask. Her face showed disappointment in my disregard for Eddie, but she didn't know that I kept his dark secrets about the frog and the dog.

"No, I don't suppose you would," I said softly, mother taking that as a sign of remorse for my asking the question. But I wasn't sorry in the least and made sure to walk five steps ahead of them as we headed down the center, as everyone liked to call it, to Kimball Avenue.

I guessed I should just be grateful that father had invited us in the first place because lunching with him was rare and a trip to the center was always an adventure. There were so many stores to visit, including Taylor's Drugstore, Mrs. Plumb's Dress Shop, The Clock Emporium, Television City, Chamberlain Jewelers and, my favorite store of all, Jack's Toy Workshop. Most of our Christmas presents came from there and starting every November, mother would walk us past the shop window once a week where Eddie and I would excitedly point to the toys on display.

Unbeknownst to us, she'd later write down every toy we coveted, and it was as if by magic that Santa Claus always knew what to leave the Biggs boys. "How did he know I wanted this?" I would gasp, my eyes wide with surprise after unwrapping each gift. Mother would just chuckle as she sipped her Christmas morning cabernet.

There was also Old Windsor Cove Bank and Trust, the Town Hall, Andy's Barber Shop where Eddie and I got our haircuts, and Dave's Spirits and Tackle Shop. I wasn't allowed to go in there because of the spirits, so my fishing gear always came from a small bait and tackle shop on the cove. I liked going there because it was the only place where mother would let me go in alone. "Bait and tackle shops are for boys," she would say before drawing deeply on her cigarette holder.

Most important to us, I suppose, was that father's law office was down the center too. Sometimes I would surprise him if mother was at the bank or buying a dress from Mrs. Plumb. "Don't stay too long," she'd say. Father would tolerate me for about ten minutes before he would have to get back to work, at which time I'd leave. Eddie was never allowed to go there with me though, an unnegotiable rule laid down by father.

On the way to the center, Eddie was pretty good, mother having to reprimand him only once for running into someone's flower garden and tearing out a fistful of yellow daisies before she could grab him by the hand and yank him out of there. I ignored them both as I walked ahead, thinking about what I was going to eat at Webster's, my usual burger, fries, and strawberry shake. When we got there, we saw father sitting at the counter talking to the waitress, a pretty young girl I had never seen before. He was patting her hand while clearly flirting, so typical of father. Mother smirked as she took Eddie by the arm and headed over there. I followed, unable to take my eyes off the waitress.

"Ah, here they are," said father, giving mother a small peck on the cheek as we all took our seats at the counter. "I'd like everyone to meet Dulcie Jackson, the new waitress here."

"Hello," mother said brusquely without even looking at her. "A cup of coffee, please."

Mother picked up a menu immediately, not wanting to get into a conversation with father or Dulcie about anything just yet. She always knew when he was smitten with another woman and ignoring him for a few minutes was her usual punishment.

Eddie and I picked up menus too, even though mother usually ordered for us. My brother began to spin around and around on his stool until he nearly fell off. When mother told him to stop spinning, he swept a glass jar full of sugar off the counter, sending it crashing to the floor where it shattered into a million pieces. Everyone around us fell silent.

"Can't you ever control him?" father commented to mother in a low voice, half smiling at the people sitting around him as he got off his stool and began to pick up the larger chunks of glass off the floor. It was never good when Eddie embarrassed father.

"Oh, don't bother with that," Dulcie said, snapping her gum. "I'll take care of it."

Father quickly obeyed and stood back. She came from around the counter with a dustpan and broom, ready to sweep up the scattered sugar. Unexpectedly, and to father's delight, she commanded Eddie to help. Mother rolled her eyes.

"Let's go, little man. You made the mess, now you help clean it up." Surprisingly, Eddie jumped off his stool and quickly took the dustpan from Dulcie, holding it wherever she told him to. Mother resented this, but it was the first time I had seen Eddie smile in a while…and follow directions!

As the two of them were on the floor cleaning up the sugar, I couldn't take my eyes off Dulcie. About twenty years old, she was tall and thin with long, dark brown curly hair and strikingly beautiful green eyes. She had a nice smile too and walked with a confident strut. This boy of eleven took notice, unexplained butterflies suddenly fluttering in my stomach. Eddie was responding to her better than I had ever seen him respond to anyone before, even mother. And father…well…he had his own agenda.

We ate our lunch quickly, joylessly and mostly silently before heading straight home. Mother seethed with anger as she pulled Eddie by the hand along the sidewalk, not allowing him to twist her arm like he sometimes did, while he hurriedly ran alongside to match her feverish pace. That night she and father had a big argument in her bedroom with the door closed, but I heard everything they said. They argued about Dulcie and father's wandering eye, and he told her that she was wrong and being unreasonable. They also argued about Eddie and the fact that she couldn't control him at Webster's or anywhere else for that matter.

"Let's face it, Ellen!" father shouted. "You can't control Eddie anymore! We need help around here!"

"Not her!" mother shouted back.

"Yes, her! You saw how Eddie responded when she told him he had to help clean up his own mess! You've never been able to rein Eddie in like that!" Father then did what he always did to mother; he made a monumental decision without her. "She and I have already discussed it and she's clearly interested! My mind is made up!" he shouted as he left mother's bedroom, slamming the door behind him.

"Interested in what, the job or you!" she shouted back through the closed door.

I could hear mother crying, but she stopped after a few minutes and went down to the kitchen where father was now making a bologna and mustard sandwich. I stood at the top of the stairs and listened to their conversation.

"You're right, Dan. You're always right. I'll leave it to you to take care of all the arrangements." Poor mother. Poor pathetic mother.

"I'm glad you finally see things my way," father said before biting into his sandwich. "It's only to help you, Ellen. You'll have more time for yourself and be a better mother too. You won't always be so tired."

Father then went about his business without saying another word, putting the bologna and mustard back into the fridge while mother walked out of the kitchen and into the living room where she turned on the television set. I came downstairs to see her reclining on the couch, cigarette holder in hand, flipping through her magazine as though nothing had happened. But something did happen. Eddie and I wouldn't officially be told until the next day but apparently, we now had a nanny.

Chapter 2

It took a little time for me to get used to the idea of having a nanny. I was eleven when Dulcie first came into our lives and felt embarrassed at the thought of someone having to watch over me, but I also recognized that she was really hired to keep an eye on Eddie. I just so happened to be a part of the package. I thought Dulcie was the prettiest girl I had ever seen, even prettier than mother. Eddie thought so too, and he hung on every word she said. It was amazing how she was able to keep him in line for the most part. He still had his outbursts, but Dulcie had a way of calming Eddie, something mother could never do because he could always sense her weakness and took advantage of it. Dulcie had a command over Eddie that he respected and gave my parents his usual hard time when she wasn't around.

Dulcie was waiting for us at our house every day when we got home from school and stayed until bedtime when mother would come in and kiss us goodnight, the only real interaction we had with her now. We even ate our dinner with Dulcie, giving mother and father time to be alone and talk over their day. If we were having dessert, we could bring it into the dining room and sit with our parents if we wished, but we mostly stayed with Dulcie. She entertained us, but more importantly she listened to us.

Weekends were the best because she was with us from ten in the morning until we went to bed. She took us shopping, to the beach, and watched television with us on rainy days. She seemed to like her job as nanny, now only waitressing at Webster's Soda Fountain now and then. Father appeared to be on his best behavior and paid Dulcie a good salary for her faithful attention to Eddie and me, but it was more than just the salary. I also knew that she liked our house and didn't mind being there. She often said so.

"I like this place," Dulcie would say as she looked around. "So rich, so fancy. I wish I could live here." It was a foreboding statement.

As a matter of fact, I didn't really appreciate our house until Dulcie came along. It *was* grand and filled with many of the finer things, father having always been a good provider, but I took it all for granted, figuring that's just the way it was supposed to be. Now that Dulcie was here, I looked at the house through her eyes, a boy's awakening to his good fortune and I got to share it with a pretty girl! I decided that I had a crush on Dulcie, but never shared that feeling with Eddie. He would have exploded. In his mind, Dulcie belonged only to him.

The house was a center hall colonial with a lot of character. Both the living room and father's study had large fireplaces and floor to ceiling windows, one of which in the living room was made of leaded stained glass. There was a winding staircase, plushily carpeted, that started in the front hall and led to the second-floor bedrooms. The kitchen had a butler's pantry where Eddie and I would hide in the large cabinets when we were little, and another staircase leading to the second floor as well. This was the staircase we boys would use to come down for breakfast before school. The second floor had five bedrooms, plenty of room for all of us. Eddie and I each had our own room, while mother and father each had theirs. Mother used the fifth bedroom as a small sitting room.

Above the second floor was a walk-up attic, a beautiful large room of dark wide-plank flooring, dark paneling all around, and wide window seats under each of the two large windows that faced the street. The ceiling was incredibly high, making this the most spacious room in the house. It was a strangely soothing place too and exceedingly private, second only to our treehouse. Mother kept mostly old things in the attic like clothing, furniture, father's first set of golf clubs, and the stuffed head of a deer that he had once shot and killed during a long-ago hunting trip.

Occasionally, I would go up there to get away from everyone, especially Eddie if he was having a particularly bad day, but it was a place where he'd go more often than I for seclusion and calm. The darkness of the attic soothed Eddie and gave him a place to hide from trouble. That would all change when Dulcie's arrival put an entirely different light on the attic for both Eddie and me.

The one room in the house that was off-limits to us was our father's study, a place where even mother was unwelcome. Father said he didn't want us to see or touch any of the important papers containing private client information that were usually strewn all over his desk. That was probably true enough, but I also knew for a fact that he kept a gun in his top right-hand drawer. I snuck in there one day before school to take a cigarette from the tobacco box that sat on top of the desk, having bragged to my friends that I could get my hands on one at any time.

When I found that the box was empty, I opened the top right-hand drawer, surprisingly unlocked in retrospect, and found a handgun with a white bone grip and several cartridges that were now rolling around, just the way my marbles did whenever I opened the drawer where I had them stashed. The hair on the back of my neck stood on end as I quickly slammed the desk drawer shut, a sudden spike of adrenaline causing my heart to race uncontrollably, before running out of the room. I never told anyone what I saw that morning, especially father.

Now that Dulcie was watching over us, mother had more time to do all the things she liked to do. She lounged around while reading her favorite magazines and news rags, including The Baton Rouge Cable. She still liked to keep up with the latest information from her hometown, but it was mostly society tittle-tattle and other gossip. When she wasn't looking, I'd often flip through it to look at the pictures. It was a constant fixture on the living room coffee table.

Mother also enjoyed entertaining her friends a couple of times a week when they would play bridge, drink wine, and gossip about whoever wasn't there. Eddie and I would be occupied by Dulcie in one way or another during those frequent gatherings, but I remember one time when she came late and wasn't there to take charge of Eddie before company arrived. He ran into the dining room where all of the ladies were smoking their cigarettes and having their usual chit chat.

Plunging his hand into the fancy bakery cake that sat handsomely on the table he scooped out a large handful, not only destroying the cake, but shocking the ladies too. As he shoved it into his mouth, frosting all over his face, mother grabbed his other hand and pulled him from the room. A trail of cake crumbs led into the kitchen where she began to clean Eddie up with a wet cloth, but he soon broke free of her grasp before she could finish. Running to the stream in the backyard, he picked up a frog that had just emerged from under a wet rock.

I ran after him, knowing that his uncontrollable behavior was about to lead him to a dark place, grabbed him by the shirt and dragged him over to the treehouse where we climbed together and stayed until he calmed down. From the treehouse I watched the frog he had dropped hop back under the rock, while the faraway look in Eddie's eye took him to a secret place in his head, fiercely guarded by him. No one ever knew what he was thinking when he had that look in his eye.

"Why did you do that?" I finally asked, snapping him out of his contemplation.

"I wanted cake," he said with a vacant look, frosting still smeared over one cheek.

"You could have asked," I said. Eddie stared at me coldly and shrugged his shoulders.

He remained silent until he could hear Dulcie's car pull up. Quickly scampering down from the treehouse, suddenly bright and airy again, he ran toward the driveway.

"She's here! She's here!" he shouted as he jumped and ran, Dulcie awaiting him with her usual smile, unaware of what had happened. I followed, always perplexed but never surprised by Eddie's mood swings.

The ladies left early that day, leaving mother embarrassed and in tears. She would never get any support or empathy from father, that was for certain, as he usually refused to listen to her whenever she tried to tell him about Eddie's latest transgressions.

"I don't want to hear it, Ellen. Eddie is your responsibility when Dulcie isn't here. I've done all I can for you and the boy, haven't I?" he'd say.

"Yes, I suppose you have," mother would say in the demure voice she reserved specially for father. Poor mother. Poor delicate mother.

In the meantime, she still entertained the few ladies who were undeterred by Eddie's behavior and still willing to come, only after she made certain in advance that Dulcie was going to be there. I never felt, though, that these women were really mother's friends, just hangers-on, trying to claw their way up the town's echelons of society. That was when it was particularly evident just how much clout father had around town. Besides, mother always put out a good spread, plenty of fine wine included.

Now on days when Eddie wanted to go up into the attic, he dragged Dulcie along with him, and it wasn't to hide. The attic became a pleasurable room for Eddie, a place to explore and look for long-lost treasure, as long as Dulcie came along to hold his hand. They'd walk around and look at things, or sometimes just sit and talk. I'd go up there too, not because I was particularly interested in what they were doing or talking about, but because I wanted to be with Dulcie too.

I watched her every move, hung on her every word. I watched the curls in her hair bounce when she tilted her head, and her green eyes sparkle like stars whenever she looked at Eddie or me. Being with Dulcie was better than watching television, reading comic books, or sneaking a smoke behind the gym, although sadly for me most of her attention had to be concentrated on Eddie. I briefly thought in my pre-adolescent mind that if I perhaps stirred up enough mischief, just the way Eddie did, she'd then have to pay me some special notice too, but that was a fleeting notion. I would *never* want to act like my brother, an idea that repulsed me, even if it meant gaining all of Dulcie's attention, leaving Eddie in the dust.

One day the three of us went up into the attic as usual to see what we could see. Having pulled the long chain that turned on the overhead lightbulb, Eddie grabbed Dulcie by the hand and brought her over to a trunk where mother kept old family photos. He liked to look at these faded black and white images from long ago of unsmiling grandparents, great grandparents, and cousins who wore funny clothes and posed as though they were stiff and scared. Eddie somehow identified with the relatives in these photos, getting a kick out of their apparent misery and their seemingly drab lives.

"Look at this man," Eddie said to Dulcie, pointing to my father's grandfather. "He looks scary."

"He was probably a very nice man," Dulcie commented.

"Maybe he was an axe murderer," Eddie contradicted, his eyes wide with pretend terror.

"Don't be silly!" she laughed. "I think you watch too much television." Eddie laughed too, Dulcie being the only one who could ever contradict him without causing an outburst.

"I like this photo the best," he said, handing her the image of a distant cousin who had lived a lifetime ago. Smartly dressed in a three-piece suit and tie, he was sitting on a chair with his eyes closed and his hands folded neatly in his lap. Dulcie turned the photo over and read the words scribbled on the back out loud—Cousin Leo Biggs, postmortem. "What does that mean?" Eddie asked.

"It means he's dead, dummy," I interjected. Taking the photo from Dulcie, I studied it intently, my morbid curiosity getting the best of me, but Eddie soon snatched it from my hand.

"I'm going to put this one in my pocket."

"Oh no you're not," Dulcie said, gently taking the picture away from Eddie. "We're going to let the dead man stay in the trunk, and you're going to find something else to look at right now." Eddie reluctantly obeyed, but he would look at that photo time and again.

Walking to the other end of the attic, we found a checkers game that belonged to father when he was a boy. There was still an old Christmas card inside the box that sparkled with loose glitter and smelled like must. *To Daniel from Auntie Marie. Merry Christmas.*

"Let's play! Let's play!" Eddie shouted as he jumped up and down.

Dulcie obliged, the three of us sitting on the floor while she gave instructions. It was funny that Eddie and I never learned to play checkers, but not surprising. For as far back as I could remember, father lacked the patience to sit with us long enough to even play a game while mother only played cards with her lady friends, but Dulcie taught us both that day. Of course, she played with Eddie while I watched and listened.

"All right, jump over my piece. Now you can take it!" Dulcie was a good teacher.

I watched her every move. I watched her hands, her face, her lips. I drank in every word, every expression. I studied the colorful buttons on her blouse and the blue necklace that disappeared into her cleavage whenever she moved. I longed to touch her hair, place a gentle hand on her arm, steal a kiss. I melted whenever she…

"Did you hear that, Tom? Are you paying attention?" Dulcie asked, snapping me out of my fantasy. "The object is to work your way to the other end of the board where your opponent will have to king you. After that you'll be able to move forward or backward." I was embarrassed and felt my face flush.

"Yeah, I heard," I said with a shy smile.

"Are you feeling all right?" she asked. "You were a million miles away." Eddie banged his fists on the floor.

"C'mon, let's play!" he shouted, never liking it when Dulcie gave me the least bit of attention.

Eddie and Dulcie played checkers for another twenty minutes, but eventually we all got tired of it and put the game away for another day. It was time to go back downstairs for lunch, but Eddie didn't want to go.

"Can't we stay up here?" he whined. "I don't want to eat right now."

"I will make you your favorite sandwich—peanut butter and grape jelly with sprinkles," Dulcie cajoled, placing an arm around Eddie's shoulders. I was jealous. "Does that sound good to you, Tom?" she added.

"I can do without the sprinkles," I grimaced, "but I *am* hungry." Then something unexpected happened, keeping us in the attic a little longer.

As we made our way to the other end of the large room, a bird suddenly flew over our heads, panicking as it flew into the windows, looking for a way out. I couldn't imagine how it got in, and it startled me. I had visions of the bird flying circles around my head, becoming entangled in my hair, and pecking my eyes out.

"How did that get in here?" Dulcie wondered out loud, slightly ducking when it flew near her. She appeared to be amused, a faint smile on her lips. I didn't answer for fear of sounding as alarmed as I felt in front of Dulcie and froze up like a statue. Eddie, on the other hand, became excited and chased the bird, trying to catch it whenever it swooped in his direction.

"Don't chase the bird, Eddie," Dulcie directed, "and it will eventually land on something."

She was right, the bird having landed on the trunk of old photos after she took Eddie by the hand, forcing him to stand still. Quickly making her way over to one of the windows, Dulcie opened it, and the bird made its escape. Eddie ran to the window seat and watched as the bird flew away. He was fascinated, but I was relieved. A bird in the attic was not my idea of entertainment.

Just as we came down for lunch, father arrived home from his law office with some exciting news, making our bird story seem trite and not worth mentioning.

"Chesterman, Hanson, Mink, and Biggs has a new client!" he exclaimed as he sat down at the kitchen table, mother pouring him a hot cup of coffee.

"Who is it, Dan?" she asked. "I haven't seen you this excited since your last criminal case."

"It's a big company out of New York called Pallincot. They manufacture furniture." Father sipped his coffee, always Columbian roast with a splash of cream, from a teaspoon. "There's big money in this, Ellen, and I mean big. They want our law firm to oversee the legal aspect of all their accounts. The president of the company met with us this morning."

"Why would a big company out of New York come all the way up here to look for a law firm?" mother asked. "Couldn't they find one closer to home?" Mother smiled at her own salty comment and lit a cigarette.

"They were promised a good tax break if they agreed to move their plant up here. They have big plans to expand the company and broaden their account base. That's where we come in. There will be some long days over the next eight months or so, but I swear, Ellen, it will be worth it," father gushed, slapping his hand on the kitchen table. Mother always delighted at the prospect of becoming richer.

Dulcie, Eddie and I stood in the doorway to the kitchen while father was telling mother the good news. We hesitated to walk in, knowing that father never wanted us under foot when he was talking business, but surprisingly he waved us in.

"Come here, boys! Come here! You too, Dulcie!" Father was downright jovial. "I suppose you heard!"

"We heard, Mr. Biggs. It's wonderful news," said Dulcie as she took the peanut butter and grape jelly from the cabinet. Father gave her a wink that mother thankfully didn't catch.

"Don't forget the sprinkles. You said I'd get sprinkles," Eddie frowned, oblivious to all else.

"I didn't forget, little man." Dulcie grabbed the sprinkles, a loaf of white bread and started to walk us into the dining room where she could make our sandwiches and keep us out of father's hair.

"No, no come back!" he beckoned. "You all need to hear what I have to say because it's important and I'll need everyone's help." I wondered at that point if father had been drinking. He was never one to ask for our help with anything. Even mother looked at him strangely.

"What is it, Dan?" mother asked. "What kind of help are you talking about?"

"Well," he began slowly, "the partners and I decided that we should throw the Pallincot executives a big party, a sort of thank you for choosing our firm to handle their accounts."

"And you want us to help at the party?" I happily asked in disbelief.

"Oh no, quite the opposite," said father, waving his hand. "I want you and Eddie to go out with Dulcie that night, maybe to dinner and a movie, or maybe even to a hotel in town for the night. That's how you'll help. Wouldn't that be fun?" My heart sank. I should have known that father wouldn't want us at a party he was throwing for an important client.

"Dan, are you saying the party is going to be here at the house?" mother asked, surprised and delighted.

"That's what I'm saying!" father beamed, slapping his hand on the table again. "You're a great one for throwing parties, Ellen, and we've got the biggest and nicest house, so I volunteered to do the honors right here!" He was trying to sell the idea, but mother never needed much coaxing when it came to hosting a party.

"What kind of party are we talking about?" she asked.

"The full boat. Hors d'oeuvres, lobster, caviar, champagne. A nice sit-down affair that will dazzle everyone. Maybe we can even have dancing and cards afterwards. We'll spare no expense." Father's mind was racing with the excitement, while mother began to write down her ideas on a piece of paper.

Dulcie, Eddie and I slipped into the dining room while father and mother continued to plan out the party, neither of them even noticing that we had left the room. By then, I was mighty hungry so I didn't mind getting on with lunch, but I couldn't help but feel hurt. For once…just once…I wished father wanted me around. But for now, Eddie and I had a date with Dulcie.

"It looks like we have some planning to do of our own," she said. "Dinner and a movie, that sounds like fun."

"I want to go to Captain Jack's Clam Shack!" my brother shouted, a little restaurant near the beach where mother sometimes took us for lunch before Eddie's outbursts began. I was surprised he remembered the place.

"That's a possibility," said Dulcie. "Or we can go to a hotel where we can eat, swim in the pool, and crash in a room to watch television."

"And play checkers!" Eddie added. I was feeling less and less hurt about father not wanting us at the party.

Preparations were under way, father and mother making their plans while Dulcie, Eddie and I made ours. The big event would take place in only three weeks, not leaving mother much time, but she was always up to the challenge of planning a good party. Father entrusted her with all the arrangements and minute details, repeatedly telling her to spend as much money as was necessary to make this the best party of the year. Mother would have goose bumps for the next three weeks; the responsibilities father had bestowed upon her causing constant chills of excitement. This party promised to be her finest hour.

"We'll write it off as a business expense!" he said, snapping his fingers in the air.

"I'll even have Mrs. Plumb make me a new dress!" mother declared, her eyes twinkling with anticipation. "After all, I'll need to look my best."

"We'll write that off too!" father quipped. Of course, he would remind her more than once that part of her planning was to make sure we were out of the house that night, but I didn't care. The hell with father. Being on the town with Dulcie promised to be a boy's dream come true, even if Eddie was going to be there. The next three weeks would crawl by at a snail's pace...while I continued to dream.

Chapter 3

The three of us went into the attic and sat around the trunk of old photos, the best place to make our plans without distraction. Dulcie wrote down everything we were going to do on the night of the party.

"Okay, so the two of you agree that we'll leave here at four o'clock. We'll head on over to Captain Jack's Clam Shack where we'll have ourselves a nice seafood meal before going to…" Dulcie was cut short, interrupted by Eddie.

"I want a hot dog, French fries, a lobster roll and shrimp!" Eddie declared. "And a chocolate milkshake! Don't forget that! Write it down, Dulcie!" It was obvious that Eddie was getting overly excited.

"That's a lot of food for a little man," Dulcie warned.

"It isn't!" Eddie contradicted, pounding his fist on the trunk.

"We're going to get ice cream after dinner," I chimed in. "How will you be able to eat ice cream with all that other food in your stomach? You'll puke in Dulcie's car for sure." I gave Eddie a dirty look.

"No, I won't," he sulked, lowering his head and playing with his shoelace.

"Let's not worry about what we're going to eat right now. And remember, any food that you boys are unable to finish can always be taken home in a doggie bag," Dulcie said gently, placing a hand on Eddie's shoulder. She knew just how to handle him.

Eddie brightened back up and punched me in the arm. I would have socked him one, but Dulcie stopped me. If we were going to finish our plans, we had to pay attention and not interrupt. Dulcie had to let mother know just how much money she'd need to take us out that night.

"I'll require a budget from you, Dulcie," mother told her. "The cost of everything you'll be doing with the boys that night—food, entertainment, etc." This was a part of mother's meticulous planning. Maybe father would try to write our evening off too.

"So, after Captain Jack's Clam Shack," Dulcie continued, "we'll go to The Farmer's Creamery Barn for ice cream sundaes."

"No, Dairy Delight," Eddie interrupted again, "and I'd rather have an ice cream cone with sprinkles."

"All right, Dairy Delight it is," Dulcie said. "Is that okay with you, Tom?" I preferred the other place for its jukebox and leather booths, but I didn't want to throw Eddie into a frenzy and ice cream, no matter where it came from, was all the same to me.

"Sure, that sounds okay," I said.

"After we're done with our ice cream, we'll go over to the Seaside Hotel and check in; one room for you boys and the one right next door to it for me." Dulcie was scribbling all this down quickly.

"Wait a minute. Why can't we be in the same room?" Eddie asked, looking as though he were about to cry.

"Now, that would never do, would it?" Dulcie said, furrowing her eyebrows in reproach. "Don't worry little man, I already checked it out. There'll be a connecting door between the two rooms, so I'll be right there if you need me." This calmed Eddie down, but he still had a smirk on his face. "We'll be able to use the hotel pool and…" she tried to continue.

"Can I still bring the checkers game?" Eddie cut in.

"Sure, you can," Dulcie said, "and we can watch television too, but I thought we'd catch the eight o'clock movie at the Rivoli Garden Theater first called *Ghosts in Another Dimension*." Eddie was so excited he could barely breathe. As usual I just sat and listened, but it actually sounded like a perfectly good evening to me. Dinner, ice cream, swimming, and a movie…there was nothing to complain about.

"You mean we can stay up past our bedtime too?" Eddie asked in disbelief.

"Of course," Dulcie said as we headed downstairs. Eddie threw his arms around her waste from behind and squeezed her tightly.

"I love you, Dulcie!" Eddie said loudly. I murmured the same thing…to myself.

The next day, Dulcie gave mother our itinerary and a close estimate of the cost, having already made the hotel reservations, looked at the menus from Captain Jack's and Dairy Delight, and stopped at the Rivoli Garden to inquire about ticket prices for that night. Dulcie was as good a planner as mother, who was quite pleased and approved of all the money we needed before going back to her own ideas, calculations, and dress fittings.

"Dan, Mrs. Plumb made me the most beautiful satin dress, powder blue with a large bow in the back, and I found matching shoes this morning. I'm going to look perfect."

"I'm sure you will, dear," father said while hurriedly stuffing papers into his briefcase. "I'm late for the office. Did you hire the caterer and waitstaff?"

"Yes, I did, and the menu is all set," mother assured him, "just the way we planned it. The invitations have gone out and the flowers have been ordered too." Mother had everything under control.

The first two weeks flew by and now there was only one week to go before the party, numerous details fitting into place nicely like pieces of a puzzle, except that Dulcie had developed a nasty cold. I felt sorry for her, everyone did, but there was no time for mother or father to think about Dulcie's cold. Last-minute preparations were still being made as the phone rang off the hook all week long with people who wanted to confirm this or discuss that.

With only two days left to go, mother ran around the house doing last-minute chores, setting the dining room table with her fine porcelain china, polishing the silver, setting up the bridge table, and picking out all the best music records to play on the hi-fi. The house dazzlingly ready, this was sure to be a party that no one would soon forget, and it was all because of mother. Unfortunately, Dulcie wasn't getting any better. In fact, she was feeling much worse.

The day finally arrived, and the excitement was palpable. Being a Saturday, Dulcie should have arrived by ten o'clock, but she hadn't shown yet. She was usually punctual which caused me to worry, especially since she had been sick all week.

"I'm sure she's just running late," mother said as she fluttered from the kitchen to the dining room to the living room and then back again. Over and over, this room to that one, these dishes with those, this fork with that spoon, these champagne flutes with those wine glasses, a different color cloth napkin for each course, and it went on and on. Her hair was in curlers, and she was wearing the housecoat she usually wore when she was busy doing chores while father had gone to the office to check on last-minute details of his own.

"If I want to engage the Pallincot executives in conversation at the dinner table, I'll need to know what I'm talking about," he muttered, spending most of the morning and early afternoon pouring over documents, brochures, and sales receipts of the company. He couldn't be bothered, though, with the minutiae that always presented itself on the day of a party.

That was mother's job. His plan was to come home in the afternoon, have a quick bite to eat, and then slip into his tuxedo. He would watch the waiters walk from one room to the next, tell so and so where to place the ice sculpture, and maybe fidget with some of the silver on the dining room table, but there would be nothing for him to *really* do. Mother had outdone herself.

Since Eddie had gone up into the attic for some private time, the excitement of our impending evening with Dulcie having given him overwhelming anxiety, I was able to walk around the house and see all of mother's lovely touches without him tugging at my sleeve. The table looked spectacular, better than I had ever seen it look before. The lace tablecloth from France had been made especially for her as a gift from father on their one-year anniversary, while the tall silver candelabras, one at each end of the table, would give the room a gentle glow. Her grandmother's fine china at each place, a set mother rarely took out of the closet, was designed with red and pink roses, every plate, saucer and cup beautifully refined and delicate.

A classy touch was the menu resting by each place card, written in calligraphy, revealing the various delicacies of the eight-course meal. Dave's Spirits and Tackle Shop provided all of the champagne and fine wine that mother had ordered three weeks prior, while father was prepared to open an old bottle of scotch whiskey that he had been saving for a special occasion.

"There will never be a better time than this," he said, taking it from the liquor cabinet and dusting it off with a soft cloth the night before.

After dinner, the women would play bridge with decks of cards ordered specially from Toller's Stationary and the men would drink their scotch and smoke cigars in father's study, mother never one to like the smell of cigar smoke anywhere else in the house.

"I think I'll play classical music on the hi-fi during dinner, jazz while we're playing cards, and Big Band if anyone wants to dance afterward," she said, pleased with her playlist. How magical everything would be, how perfect! If only Dulcie would get here.

Tantalizing aromas now began to waft from the kitchen, mother having hired both the head *and* pastry chefs from the Epicurean Castle, the best and most expensive restaurant in town, to do all of the cooking. I wandered into the kitchen and stood in a corner, my mouth watering.

"May I help you, son?" one of the chefs asked.

"Only watching," I said, all at once feeling funny about being in this usually familiar place of peanut butter sandwiches and scrambled eggs, now transformed into a busy, unrecognizable restaurant kitchen.

"Just stay out of the way," the chef said in a friendly manner. "I wouldn't want to trip over you." Smiling, he gave me a large shrimp on a napkin. I gobbled it down and smiled back. "Don't tell your mother that I'm letting you watch."

"I won't," I assured him, hoping he'd give me more food to taste.

I had read one of the menus placed on the dining room table which couldn't compare to witnessing the actual preparation of those gourmet delicacies. Captain Jack's Clam Shack had nothing over the food being carefully cooked, arranged, and displayed in my own kitchen. The hors d'oeuvres were nothing I had ever seen before, sitting pretty on their platters, waiting to be heated or chilled when the time was right. From the caviar, baked oysters, and bacon-wrapped figs to the crab cakes, shrimp cocktail, and stuffed mushrooms, each mouth-watering appetizer beckoned to me with its pretty appearance and fancy garnish. The chef was now making delicate crepes in a pan on the stove to accompany the seafood spring rolls, beef skewers, and little meatballs. Salmon mousse and cheese pastries were among the many dishes being slid into the refrigerator for safe keeping.

"What's all that?" I asked, pointing to the bundles of food that had yet to be unwrapped and prepared. I sensed that the head chef was friendly and willing to talk to me.

"You're looking at the main course, son, what we like to call the entrees," he said, looking at me over his shoulder from his place at the stove, sliding each crepe effortlessly out of the pan before making another. "You have your lobsters and steaks over there, your scallop skewers and stuffed clams right there, and finally your sliced duck and lamb kabobs down there," he informed me, indicating with a nod of his head the food on the kitchen counters that awaited his attention. He let me take a peek at the lobsters climbing over and under each other in their bags. "All this will be cooked when it gets a little closer to dinner time. We want it to be piping hot, you know."

The friendly chef would then prepare the green salad and the vegetables for grilling. "This is hollandaise sauce for the asparagus," he told me, noticing my interest as he splashed sherry into a pan. The making of Au Gratin potatoes would later round out his cooking responsibilities, taking him right up to the minute before dinner would be served. "We chefs are used to working under pressure," he quipped, popping an olive into his mouth.

The pastry chef, on the other hand, ignored me completely. Hoping to sample a tart or handmade chocolate truffle, I stood in my corner quietly watching as he briskly walked past me, not allowing his eyes to meet mine. He never had a chance to sense my anticipation, my wishful thinking, avoiding me so as not to feel obligated to feed me. I silently observed as he poured the cheesecakes, prepared the crème brulé, and placed the shortbreads in the oven. Little did he know that I snatched a strawberry tart behind his back, but that wouldn't be enough to satiate my hunger. It was now twelve-thirty and I was starving.

Dulcie still hadn't arrived, and I now began to get really worried, not only because of her tardiness, but because of the way Eddie might react once he realized the time. I quickly reached into the cabinets and took out the peanut butter, grape jelly, sprinkles, and loaf of white bread. Finding a clear space in the pantry I made two sandwiches, one for me and one for Eddie, and quickly exited the kitchen, bored by this time anyhow with watching the chefs and smelling all the good foods I'd never get to eat.

Mother had already decided that all of the leftover food would be donated to a local homeless shelter, not only as a gesture of goodwill but to bolster her standing even more within the community as well, especially now that one of the biggest companies on the east coast was moving into town. She was no fool, my mother, despite what father said sometimes.

Just as I was about to go upstairs to bring the two sandwiches into the attic, she stopped me.

"Dulcie just called," mother said breathlessly, the panic having already set in. "She assured me that she'd be here, but she's at the doctor's office. She's not feeling well at all today, but I made her promise me faithfully that she'd be here. I even promised her a substantial bonus for taking you boys out tonight." Mother was pale, afraid that all of her well-laid plans would unravel causing father to blame her like he always did.

"Don't worry, she'll be here mother," I said reassuringly, but I wasn't sure at all about that.

"Keep your brother occupied until she gets here, will you?" she pleaded.

"Of course, I will, mother," I answered softly and cautiously headed to the attic, not knowing the state of mind in which I'd find Eddie.

Once I got up there, I found my brother exactly where I thought he'd be, sitting next to the trunk of old photos, staring at the picture of our dead distant cousin, Leo Biggs.

"Are you looking at that photograph again?" I asked Eddie, handing him the sandwich.

"Thanks, I'm starving," he said, taking the sandwich from me and biting into it voraciously. Luckily, Eddie hadn't the slightest inkling of time passage whenever he was in the attic, making him oblivious to all matters happening from minute-to-minute downstairs. He didn't ask me about Dulcie, not even the peanut butter and grape jelly sandwich with sprinkles tipping him off as to the time of day.

After we finished our sandwiches, we looked through the trunk of old photos some more because that's what kept Eddie calm, those images of people living in their black and white world. Once I got bored with that, I rolled out an old rug and placed a dirty pie plate that I had found in a box of junk at one end of it. Using father's first set of golf clubs, I hit golf balls down the rug and into the pie plate over and over again, walking down to retrieve them and then back again to start over. At first, Eddie ignored what I was doing, but after a while he left the trunk and chose a club of his own from the worn leather bag.

I showed him how to hold it and he began to hit golf balls down the rug too, hard and fast at first. He became easily frustrated, unable to sink any of his balls into the plate, but after a while and with a little encouragement, he got pretty good at it. Eddie and I did that for a good half hour.

"Let's play checkers," I said to my brother foolishly, making him suddenly aware that his usual checkers partner was absent.

"Why isn't Dulcie here yet?" he asked.

"Don't worry," I assured him, "she'll be here soon enough. Let's just have a good time up here and before you know it, we'll be going out on the town with Dulcie." That seemed to calm him, but even I didn't believe my words.

As we played checkers, I could hear a car door slam in the distance. Was it Dulcie? "King me!" Eddie demanded, unaware of any such sound, wholly concentrating on the game.

I was dying to go downstairs, but I promised mother that I would keep Eddie occupied, and I would never go back on a promise I had made to mother. I kept my ears perked but couldn't hear anything else from outside or downstairs. Eddie's eyes stayed glued to the board.

All of a sudden, it became apparent that another bird had gotten into the attic, the point of entry still a mystery, as it flew freely above the rafters. Eddie watched it fly overhead and jumped up from our game, upending the board and sending red and black checkers into the air, only to fall back to the ground like loose change, scattering and rolling every which way.

"Come here! Come here!" Eddie screamed. He chased the bird up and down the attic, cornering it at one end. It landed on the back of an old chair and, unbelievably, Eddie got his two hands on it. I held my breath as he gently held the bird, walking it toward me.

"Isn't it pretty, Tom?" he asked me. I backed up.

"I'm not crazy about birds, Eddie," I reminded him. He looked at the bird thoughtfully which was so unlike him, given his treatment of other animals.

"Then open the window and I'll let him go." I stared at Eddie, stunned by his sensible solution. "C'mon, hurry up!" he ordered as I quickly ran over to the window and opened it, stepping aside for Eddie who gently tossed the bird out into the fresh air and watched it fly away as he smiled with satisfaction. I was perplexed as to why Eddie so loved when birds flew into the attic, but I wasn't about to question him. Other than Dulcie, Eddie loved little else.

Sounds of intense yelling unexpectedly drifted up the stairs, causing Eddie and me to freeze. We looked at each other with wide eyes for what seemed an eternity, not moving a muscle or making a sound. Feeling my feet again, I quickly darted downstairs, Eddie duly following me, to see father standing in the middle of the dining room in a full-blown rage, mother standing there too, listening patiently while waiting for him to finish his tirade. It was then that I knew that the car door I had heard slam in the distance earlier was father's. The grandfather clock in the hall chimed two-thirty.

"What do you mean she's not coming!" he bellowed.

"She's got pneumonia, Dan," mother explained. "She's too sick to come. There's not a thing we can do about it." She was calm, but firm, her voice surprisingly unwavering.

"What about the boys, Ellen? What are we supposed to do with them? Suppose Eddie decides to…" Mother quickly interrupted, seeing that Eddie and I were standing there.

"Mrs. Joffrey up the street has agreed to take the boys for the night," she said, having already found a solution to the problem in the middle of all her last-minute busyness. Her hair still in curlers while never having changed out of her housecoat, mother had taken full command of the day without even once stopping to look in a mirror. She had yet to tease her hair, paint her nails, and put on her makeup. The guests would arrive at five o'clock for cocktails.

"Just see to it that they're well out of the house before five o'clock," father seethed before storming up the stairs, slamming the door behind him once he reached his bedroom. I don't think he even noticed Eddie or me standing there as he stalked past us in a fit of rage. Mother took in a deep breath before gradually looking our way, embarrassed by what we had heard.

"I'm sorry boys," she lamented, her heart seeming to break for us, especially Eddie. But mother was fearful too, my brother not having yet reacted to the news about Dulcie. That wouldn't take long.

It took Eddie only seconds to realize what was happening and for the first time I felt really sorry for him, knowing how much he adored Dulcie, a feeling to which I could easily relate. His eyes quickly pooled with tears, but to his credit not a single one fell. It was hard to tell what he was more upset about—Dulcie, or my father's usual lack of regard for us. He twisted his mouth, working hard to keep himself from crying, and clenched his hands tightly into fists. As he rocked from one foot to the next, I could sense that Eddie was a steam boiler about to blow.

"Go upstairs and pack a bag, boys," mother directed with a sigh. "Be ready to go to Mrs. Joffrey's by four thirty." Problem solved. Nothing would stand in the way of her dinner party that evening. Her reputation…and father's…had to come first, even if it meant our feelings, Eddie's and mine, were trampled in the process.

"We're already packed, mother," I assured her. "Dulcie helped us do that the other day."

Suddenly and calmly, Eddie spoke, "I'll go up into the attic and get the checkers game," he said somberly. Mother and I looked at each other in silent surprise. No outburst? No tantrum? It wasn't like Eddie, who had already run up the stairs, to be so understanding.

Mother walked around the dining room table once more, making sure that everything was perfectly in place. She smoothed out the pretty lace tablecloth once again and touched every plate, glass, and piece of silver as though she were giving them her blessing. She adjusted and readjusted each menu and place card. Walking over to the table set up for bridge, she made sure that the decks of cards specially ordered from Toller's Stationary were out of their fancy cardboard boxes, ready for use, while the records she intended to play on the hi-fi were fanned out on the coffee table.

"Now, where are those matches?" mother mused. "I'll need them to light the candles. Is the champagne and white wine sufficiently chilled?" she called out to the kitchen.

"Yes, ma'am!" the head chef affirmed through the open door, all the fine cooking smells deliciously wrapping themselves around me.

In a short time, Eddie reappeared from the attic with one of father's golf clubs.

"What are you doing with that?" I asked. "Where are the checkers?"

"I don't want to play checkers without Dulcie," he sulked. "I don't want to do anything without Dulcie!" He stomped his foot. This reaction was more in character for Eddie, but mother would have none of it, especially today of all days. She was surprisingly firm with Eddie.

"You have no choice, Eddie. Dulcie isn't coming so you and Tom have to go to Mrs. Joffrey's house for the night. That's the way it has to be, and I don't want to hear another word about it." Mother was adamant.

Tinker had innocently wandered into the dining room, unaware of the unfolding family drama. I scooped him up and held him tightly in my arms, waiting for Eddie to react to mother's strong approach which was so unlike her. I thought it would set him off for sure, but to my astonishment he simply looked at her with an icy stare before turning on his heels and leaving the room, still clutching the golf club.

"Fine, I'll go get the checkers out of the attic," I could hear him mutter. Breathing a sigh of relief, I put Tinker back down on the floor, while mother turned on her heels and walked into the kitchen. She was proud of herself.

Nothing would prevent this evening from coming off now, not even Eddie. Everything was back on track.

I heard my brother thundering back down the stairs with the checkers game, I assumed, but he ran into the dining room without it, still clutching the golf club. I became suspicious, wondering what he was up to, but before I could even speak, he swung the club across mother's beautifully set table. I stood frozen and watched in horror as he wielded the club back and forth, swinging and pounding, smashing the plates, breaking the glasses, and sending the silverware flying through the air.

In addition to the two candelabras that had been knocked clear across the room, there were shards of broken glass everywhere, the table having been laid to waste. It had all happened so quickly that I couldn't even grab him before the damage had been done, even the two chefs and mother frantically running from the kitchen only after it was too late.

Finally dropping the golf club, Eddie started to run around the table, grabbing the lace tablecloth as he went while pulling it behind him, sending more pieces of broken china and glass crashing to the floor. Now, the two chefs began to chase him, one running this way around the table while the other ran that way. Eddie tried to make a break for it, but the head chef grabbed him and brought him to his knees, finally subduing him. Stunned by what had happened I stood there motionless, my feet still unable to move after having witnessed the horrific scene my brother had caused.

While Eddie remained on his knees, sobbing uncontrollably, I came to my senses and grabbed Tinker from behind a chair in the living room. I ran out the back door with my dog and headed straight for the treehouse, afraid to be in the room when father came downstairs, knowing that his reaction would be explosive. The party was over before it began. Unexpectedly thwarted in what should have been her finest hour, mother fell to pieces, all of her hard work having been in vain just because Dulcie was too sick to watch us, but really because Eddie was crazy. I felt such sorrow for her, such pity, as the consequences of my brother's actions would soon unfold. Poor mother. Poor betrayed mother.

Chapter 4

Too morbidly curious to remain in the treehouse, I gathered my courage and ran back to the house, leaving Tinker wrapped safely in a blanket. My legs trembled as I slipped in through the back door of the now empty kitchen where all the good smells still hung in the air. Grabbing several strawberry tarts off the counter, I hid inside a large cabinet where I pressed my ear to the wood, straining to hear what was going on. It seemed that Eddie had surprisingly wriggled his way out of the head chef's grasp and ran straight into father's study, slamming the door shut before locking it from the inside. I could hear mother crying as she banged on the door, imploring Eddie to open it.

"Open the door this instant, Eddie!" she begged, sobbing pathetically. "Please, open the door for mommy!"

There was no response from Eddie, and I didn't think there would be, other than the sounds of slamming drawers and stomping feet. The head chef then gave it a try.

"Open the door, son, or we'll have to break it down! You'll have to come out sooner or later!" Drawers continued to slam, and the sound of broken glass indicated to me that Eddie had smashed father's Tiffany lamp on the floor. Mother stopped sobbing long enough to try one more time.

"Mommy is getting angrier and angrier, Eddie! You best open this door right now!" The slamming and stomping abruptly ceased.

It appeared that Eddie had either gotten all his frustrations out, or simply ran out of steam because the house fell eerily silent. Something awful occurred to me though, something more dreadful than what Eddie had done to the dining room table. Suppose when he was rifling through father's desk drawers, probably looking for nothing more than the ability to slam them shut again, Eddie stumbled upon the gun. A chill ran up my spine. In comparison a busted dinner party now seemed trivial.

Suddenly, I could hear the sound of father's footsteps thundering down the stairs. Even though I trembled in fear of what he might do, I decided to crawl out from inside the cabinet and peek through the open kitchen door without being seen. After all, he wasn't coming after me. Apparently having just gotten out of the shower, father was in his robe, still dripping wet. Now, all the adults were standing in front of the study door, Eddie still locked inside.

"What the hell is going on down here!" he shouted. "Ellen?" Mother sobbed continually into a handkerchief, the head chef answering for her.

"It appears that your son was angry about something," he understated, pointing toward the dining room. Father icily stared at him and then at mother with piercing eyes before storming into the dining room.

"Jesus Christ!" he roared. "I'm going to kill that boy! Does he realize what he's done?" Father stalked back to his closed study door, his gait as threatening as his words.

"Are you in there, Eddie?" father bellowed as he banged on the door hard with his fist, causing it to quiver. "You open up this door right now! If I have to go upstairs to get my key, I will tan your ass raw! Open up now!" Mother visibly shuddered.

Father banged on the door a few more times before Eddie opened it, calm and collected. No expression of anger or terror on his face, he was apparently unmoved by father's threatening presence. Looking at everyone with a vacant stare, Eddie was silent and, seemingly, unrepentant. Nonchalantly attempting to walk up the stairs as though nothing had happened, father seized him by the collar with a vengeance, dragged him into the living room, and threw him on the couch.

"What the hell is wrong with you!" he shouted, raising his hand to thrash Eddie but good before the head chef intervened, grabbing father by the arm.

"Take it easy there, Mr. Biggs, he's only a boy. Don't do anything you're going to regret later on," the chef said, gently warning father with a thinly disguised reprimand.

"Unhand me," father spat, pulling away from the chef. Out of breath and wild with rage, he cinched his robe closed before pulling the terrycloth belt tighter. "Who the hell are you to tell me what to do in my own house? You're the hired help, you know, so back off!" he shouted again, ready to have another go at Eddie.

"And you're a lawyer who should know better than to assault a boy who's obviously not all there," the chef said sternly, stepping in between father and Eddie. "I don't want to have to grab you again." The two men stared each other down until father blinked first.

"This isn't over yet, Ellen!" father screamed at mother, by now a whimpering bundle of nerves, before retreating into his study, demanding that both chefs follow him.

Mother gently pulled Eddie off the couch and held him closely, almost protectively, an unseemly show of affection under the circumstances.

"What is wrong with you, child?" mother asked him, the tears streaming down her cheeks. "What on earth is wrong with you?" My brother was limp in her arms, left weak by his rampage. She walked Eddie out of the room and up the stairs without saying another word. Thankfully, I hadn't been noticed by anyone.

As I ran back to the treehouse to retrieve Tinker, father made a desperate conference call to his law partners to try and salvage the dinner party, the two chefs having guaranteed him that they'd be able to pull it off at someone else's house as long as they could finish all the cooking in our kitchen.

"Once everything is cooked, I can get the catering truck from the restaurant to transport all the hot and cold food to the new location," the head chef assured father, confident that the change of plans could work, "but of course the new host will have to set a fine table ready to accept all eight courses of food."

"Don't you worry about that," father whispered, one hand over the phone, "just do your job and Chesterman, Hanson, Mink, and Biggs will take care of the rest. There'll be a hefty bonus in it for you too."

With the excuse that one of his boys had fallen seriously ill, leaving him and mother no other choice but to make an unexpected trip to the emergency room that afternoon, father persuaded one of his partners to host the party at his house. I didn't know at the time just how incredibly devious my father could be.

"I suppose we could do it here, Dan," said Andrew Mink, father's best friend, "as long as everyone understands that it won't be as fancy an affair as the one Ellen had planned for your house. The wife will have to set a quick table, although I know all the good china is packed away and time is short," he said, thinking out loud. "Well, I suppose we can make it work with a different dinner service." Mink didn't sound all that confident, having agreed to the new arrangement for the sake of the firm, but with obvious reluctance. "Hope your boy's okay," he added.

"Thank you, Andrew, he'll be fine, but we were at the hospital all afternoon, thinking it was the boy's appendix, you know," father lied. "Turned out to be just a bad case of the stomach flu that's been going around but, nonetheless, the boy is quite indisposed. Don't you worry, though, because our nanny will be looking after both boys tonight. Ellen and I wouldn't miss this party for the world, knowing how important it is to the firm. And Andrew, don't sweat over which dinner service you use," father reassured his partner. "As long as the Pallincot executives retain their strict confidence in us, you can use paper plates for all I care!"

It was now up to father's secretary to call all of the guests and inform them of the last-minute change in plans, but mother would refuse to play along, too humiliated to show her face. After instructing Eddie to take a hot bath and get into bed she came downstairs, not only to get him a bowl of soup, but to break the news to father that she had no intention of going anywhere that evening. When I walked into the kitchen with Tinker, she didn't even ask where I had been or if I was alright.

"I'm sorry, mother," I said gently. "Is there anything I can do to help?" She smiled weakly.

"Take this bowl of soup up to your brother. Soup always seems to comfort him after he's suffered an outburst," she said, her voice trailing off. "And Tom, keep a good eye on him for me while I tell your father I can't possibly go out tonight."

"Yes, mother," I said, curious as to what would happen next. Just how would she break the news to father, and how would he react? More importantly, what might he do to Eddie once the head chef was no longer there to protect him?

When I got upstairs, Eddie was already in bed, exhausted by what had happened.

"Here's your soup," I said, placing it on the nightstand. He looked at me with big, sad eyes, no longer vacant, but now filled with stormy tears of emotion.

"Dulcie didn't come for us like she was supposed to," he lamented, wiping the sniffles from his nose.

"I know," I answered, not wanting to get too deep into a conversation about Dulcie with Eddie. The both of us were emotionally drained, each in our own way.

"I hate father, you know," he said, a single tear rolling down his cheek.

"Right now, he hates you back," I cracked, causing Eddie to smirk.

"I don't care if he hates me back." But clearly, he did. Sensing that he could get agitated again, I changed the subject.

"How about if you eat your soup now, and then tomorrow you and I will build a bird's nest and bring it up to the attic. Maybe one of your birds will visit and lay an egg in it. Would you like to do that?" Eddie giggled.

"I like that just fine, but you hate birds," he remembered.

"You're right, I do," I agreed, "but I'd be up to the challenge of making a good nest, you know, tight and strong just the way birds make them. Well, how about it?"

"Okay, Tom," he said brightly while reaching for his soup, his dark mood having lifted. I watched Eddie eat, but my mind was really on the conversation going on downstairs between mother and father.

"I'll be right back," I told my brother. "Stay in bed." He continued to eat his soup, still snuggled under the covers, while I crept down the hall to the top of the stairs where I could eavesdrop on the conversation going on between my parents in father's study, the door having been left wide open.

I could easily hear the waitstaff that had been hired to serve the eight-course meal at our house that evening now cleaning up the mess in the dining room. It's my guess that father had offered them quite a bit of money to do the job before they headed over to Andrew Mink's house. If he knew what mother was about to say he probably wouldn't have bothered, leaving the awful cleanup entirely to her.

"What do you mean you're not going!" I could hear father shout while obviously shuffling papers. "Are you crazy, you have to go!"

"I can't send Eddie to Mrs. Joffrey's tonight, Dan," mother said, "he's in no shape, and I don't want to put the responsibility of watching him on Tom, either, because that wouldn't be fair. Not tonight, not after this outburst." Mother was adamant, but her trembling voice indicated that she was still pretty shaken up by what had happened. "Besides, Mrs. Joffrey will question me as soon as I give her Andrew Mink's phone number in case of an emergency, wanting to know why we're not throwing the dinner party at our house as originally planned. I just can't face that tonight. As it is, my reputation is probably already ruined."

Father was clearly agitated by mother's decision, the sound of the shuffling papers getting louder followed by a pound of his fist on the desk.

"Suit yourself, Ellen, I don't give a damn, but your determination to stay at home tonight better not affect my standing with the Pallincot account in any way, or I'll place the entire blame squarely on you," he raged, probably pointing a finger in mother's face the way he always did when he was angry. "I told Andrew that you'd be there, you know," he said, sadistically rubbing salt in a very deep wound. "I told him the boys would be with their nanny, thinking you were going to send them over to Mrs. Joffrey's anyway. I told him you wouldn't miss this party for the world because you knew how important it was to the firm!" father shouted, his voice having reached a manic crescendo. "So much for that!"

"Well, you shouldn't have done that, Dan!" mother stated, loud and clear. "And I resent your callousness toward me," she added with disgust. Turning on her heels, she walked out of the study and headed upstairs. I quickly ran back into Eddie's room unnoticed before she would briskly walk by, go into her bedroom, and slam the door, only to weep bitterly.

I stayed with Eddie until he fell asleep. I could hear father stomp up the stairs and head into his own bedroom, still clearly agitated by his conversation with mother. The slamming drawers told me that he was dressing for the dinner party, probably in his tuxedo. It didn't take him long because he left his room quickly, never checking on Eddie or me, and stormed out of the house. I would hear his footsteps again late into the night when he arrived back home from the party and stumbled up the stairs, obviously drunk. Poor mother. Poor neglected mother.

The next morning, mother sat at the kitchen table, drinking a cup of coffee while smoking her first cigarette of the day. I checked on Eddie who was still asleep before going downstairs to join her.

"How are you feeling today, mother?" I asked.

"I've been better, Tom," she said, her smile still weak. "Thanks for watching Eddie last night while I spoke to your father." I looked at her, searching for something to say, not wanting her to know that I had heard the whole thing.

"What's going to happen, mother, to Eddie I mean?"

"I'll tell you what's going to happen," father said as he walked into the kitchen, the odor of liquor from last night's dinner party still on his breath. He was obviously hung over too. "Tom, would you please leave your mother and I alone for a little while." Mother stiffened her back as though she were preparing for a fight, but she was weak, too weak to fight father.

I looked at mother as I slowly got up from the table and left the room. If I'd had the presence of mind, I would have grabbed something from the fridge. I was starving, having eaten nothing more than several strawberry tarts the night before. Even Eddie got to eat a bowl of soup. Boldly, I listened outside the closed kitchen door, not moving a muscle or making a sound.

"Ellen, I've come to a decision," father started. "Eddie can no longer live here. You may send him to any psychiatric hospital you want, you don't even have to tell me where, and I'll pay for it no matter what the cost."

Mother gasped. "Do you realize what you're saying, Dan?" aghast at father's radical solution.

"I mean every word of it, Ellen," he said adamantly. "Eddie needs to be in a place where he can be helped. He's too violent now and besides, my firm could have lost the biggest account it ever had if just one Pallincot executive caught wind of what happened here yesterday. As it is, I can't even tell my own partners the truth for fear they'd boot me right out the door!" Father was not only angry, but he was now nervous.

"That's what it's really about, isn't Dan? Not Eddie's need for help, but your reputation with the firm, and Pallincot." Of course, mother was right. Father couldn't give a hang about Eddie.

"Don't forget, it's your reputation too, Ellen," he reminded her. "We came this close to being laughing stocks yesterday, to losing everything we'd ever worked for. No, my mind is made up. Eddie needs to be put away. We can't chance any more violent outbursts here in the house, and I can't keep lying and making excuses to my partners and clients. We'd eventually be found out!"

"Maybe it won't happen again," mother said, grasping at straws.

"Let's not kid ourselves, Ellen. Sooner or later, it *will* happen again." I hated to admit it to myself, but of course father was right about that. "You pick a hospital, near or far, and all I need to know is how much money to fork over. Beyond that, I don't need or want to know anything more about it," he finished coldly.

At that point, I sadly walked away from the door, stepping on a shard of glass that had been left undetected. My brother was being put away like an old sweater, like all the things from days gone by, no longer wanted or useful, up in the attic. This day was off to a bad start.

In keeping with our plan, I went upstairs to awaken Eddie. "Wake up, lazy bones. It's time to build a bird's nest."

My brother opened his eyes and stretched. "Will Dulcie be here today?" he asked.

"Probably not," I said. "She's pretty sick, but don't worry she'll be back." The question was, would my brother still be here?

Eddie and I went into the backyard and gathered up all the leaves and twigs we could get our hands on. We twisted, bent, and wove all the pieces together as best we could into a messy hodge podge of brush before slathering it with thick mud. Each in turn, we pressed down hard on our creation to form a deep indentation that any bird would appreciate. Once again, we coated it with mud on the inside and all around the outside before placing it in the sun to bake.

In the late afternoon, after the sun had made its swing around the house, we carefully lifted the dirty mess and brought it up to the attic, dropping chunks of dirt along the way. We had no idea what we were doing, but this little project between the two of us made Eddie happy, as though nothing disturbing had happened the day before.

Mother was obviously making plans to send Eddie away, just as father had demanded. She said nothing to me about it, not knowing that I had already overheard her conversation with father, and of course said nothing to Eddie. She made a good many phone calls, speaking to all sorts of people, but I was never able to discern what they were saying, picking up on only random words here and there that meant nothing in and of themselves.

Mother had a habit of waving me out of the room whenever she was on the telephone, so it was difficult to listen in on a conversation but more so whenever it pertained to Eddie. Her voice would invariably become low and quiet as she arranged my brother's fate, but I knew what she was up to. After three or four days, though, I was able to determine that most of her telephone calls were being made to a woman named Louise.

Two weeks passed and Dulcie was set to return. Mother had kept telling Eddie that if he behaved like a good boy maybe our nanny would come back. That kept my brother on his best behavior for the entire two weeks, the longest he had ever gone without an outburst. This made it all the more piteous to me that, despite the impeccable manners he had struggled to maintain, Eddie was about to be sent away anyhow. Mother still had no idea that I knew, and father just went about his business, leaving all the arrangements to her regarding my brother's exile.

Upon Dulcie's return, mother took her aside in the kitchen and filled her in on what had happened the day of the dinner party. Dulcie was shaken, feeling both guilty and responsible for the whole mess, as mother recounted the horrible saga. I stood in a dark corner of the pantry, hidden throughout their conversation.

"I should have been here," she lamented. "If only I had taken the boys out as planned, none of this would have happened."

"Don't be silly," mother said, "you were awfully sick."

"It wouldn't have hurt me to take care of them for just one more day," Dulcie answered, her eyes filling with tears. She had a genuine affection for us boys, especially Eddie, and that's why it wounded her so when mother informed her of what she and my father were planning to do. Dulcie had no words and probably thought, as I did, that what they were doing was unfair and downright cruel to Eddie. Struggling to gather herself, she took in a deep breath and spoke again.

"What if I promise to keep a very careful eye on him every minute that I'm here," she proposed.

"That's impossible," father chimed in after suddenly walking into the kitchen, obviously having heard through the door what Dulcie had just said. "You can't possibly keep an eye on him every minute. There'll be instances when you can't be with him, or you show up late, or you get sick again. What if he gets it into his head to turn violent in your absence. We can't take that chance. Our reputation would be damaged for good. He cannot live here anymore, Dulcie, and that's final," he emphasized coldly, grabbing an apple out of the fridge. "No, he's going to a hospital where he belongs."

Father stalked back to his study, giving me the distinct impression that he was holding a grudge against Dulcie for not showing up that day, but mother was obviously embarrassed by his candor.

"I'm sorry," mother said after father left the kitchen, actually consoling the nanny when it was her who should have been consoled. "It wasn't my decision, but it's probably for the best," she sighed with an ache in her voice. It was then that Dulcie realized the lengths to which my mother would go in deference to my father, even if it meant sending Eddie away, maybe for good. I had to believe that this decision would, in the end, rub mother the wrong way and tear at her very soul, otherwise what kind of mother would she be?

"Well, perhaps I'm overstepping my bounds, but what if I lived here, you know, took a room," Dulcie suggested. "I could be here all the time, even if I got sick." Mother looked at her and gave pause.

Now, even at a young age I knew my mother who probably thought this was a pretty good idea, a most sensible solution to curbing Eddie's behavior if she were to keep him at home. But I also knew that she was, in all likelihood, much too insecure in her marriage to allow such an arrangement, knowing that father might just go for the suggestion. Having another woman live under her roof, especially one as young and pretty as Dulcie, was out of the question given father's tendency to, let's say, stray.

So, I wasn't surprised when she said... "Oh no, dear, that would never do. I couldn't possibly accommodate you here." And with that, mother turned away from Dulcie, effectively ending the conversation.

Over the next week, mother took Eddie out of school and packed his bag, telling him he was going on a great adventure. Dulcie was compelled to play along, keeping my brother on an even keel. Although she was given strict instructions by mother not to tell him anything specific, even she was in the dark as to where he was actually going. Eddie was glad to have Dulcie back, not knowing that after he was gone, he'd probably never see her again.

At first, Eddie liked the idea of being out of school, feeling more and more excited about his trip.

"The other kids are going to be so jealous. Are you going on a great adventure too, Tom?" he asked me.

"No, not this time," I answered as I watched him put a yo-yo into his duffle bag.

"As soon as I get home, we'll check on the bird's nest together," he said, zipping up the bag again.

"Yeah, sure, as soon as you get home," I agreed. "Behave yourself so you can come home soon, okay?" I turned and walked out of Eddie's bedroom feeling sad, confused, and, most of all, angry at mother and father.

What I had just said, along with my somber mood, didn't sit quite right with Eddie as though he had suddenly realized that this great adventure could possibly be a punishment. He followed me into the hall, looking a little apprehensive. Eddie could be crazy, but he wasn't stupid.

"Tom, mother said that Dulcie would be going with me on the trip and if not, she'd meet me in a few days. Is that true?"

"I don't know," I lied, shrugging my shoulders, not wanting to get involved. "Good night, Eddie, get some rest. Tomorrow is a big day for you." My brother stood there with a disappointed expression, not having gotten the answer he was looking for.

I turned away with slumped shoulders, knowing straight away that mother had only pretended with Eddie, saying that Dulcie would be joining him on his great adventure only to keep him calm before his departure. How could she? I looked back to see my brother still standing there, looking scared and vulnerable as he watched me walk down the hall. The entire situation was suddenly more than I could bear. Once I reached my bedroom, I fell into bed and cried myself to sleep.

The next morning, I went into the kitchen to grab a little breakfast before school and found mother sitting at the table with Eddie, eating bacon and eggs. She was dressed in her light green suit and matching hat, while Eddie wore his blue suit and tie.

"Sit down and have breakfast with us, Tom," mother said quietly. "Eddie and I will be leaving shortly for his great adventure, but we'll be back before you know it, isn't that right, Eddie?" she said feebly, her trembling hand bringing a cup of splashing coffee to her lips. Lies, lies, and more lies.

"No thanks, I'm late." I grabbed a piece of toast off the table, unable to look my mother in the eye. She had never bothered to tell me the truth about what was going on, or even pretend with me, the way she was with Eddie.

"Guess what!" my brother exclaimed brightly. "Mother and I are going to take a train to my great adventure, but she won't tell me where it is yet because it's supposed to be a surprise! The best part is that Dulcie's going to meet me there in a few days, just like mother said she would!" he shouted, shoveling the eggs into his mouth, not wanting to be late for his train. The lies just kept mounting up.

Father walked into the kitchen with his usual gruff morning manner and poured himself a cup of coffee. Dressed in a suit and tie, ready to leave for the office soon, he briefly sat at the table.

"Here's a couple of bucks for your pocket, Eddie," he said. "Buy yourself a comic book at the train station."

"Thanks! I never had two whole dollars of my own before!" Eddie shouted, stuffing the money into his pocket.

"Now be a good boy and run to the living room window to see if your taxi is here," father instructed. "Tom, you go with him." I knew that I was being asked to leave the room so that the adults could talk alone. More secrets, more lies.

After Eddie and I left the kitchen, father spoke quickly and quietly to mother before our return.

"Have all the necessary arrangements been made at a good psychiatric hospital, Ellen? A place where he can live and get treatment? A place where he can grow up? Do you understand what I'm saying, Ellen?" She understood perfectly well what he was saying.

He didn't want Eddie to come home, ever. "Here's the five thousand dollars you requested in cash. Thank you for not burdening me with the details but like I said, I don't need or want to know anything more about it."

My brother and I ran back into the kitchen and sat at the table.

"Not here yet!" Eddie shouted with excitement, eager to begin his great adventure.

"Don't worry, it'll be here soon enough," father assured him, giving Eddie a quick pat on the back. "Be a good boy, and we'll see you soon." I looked away and rolled my eyes. Kissing mother on the cheek, father quickly rose from his chair without saying another word, went to his study, and closed the door. Of course, he never even looked my way.

Suddenly, a honking sound signaled to mother that their taxi really was here. Eddie jumped up again from the table and quickly left the kitchen. Mother put the overstuffed envelope on the table into her purse.

"So long, Tom!" he shouted as he ran to the front door.

"So long, Eddie!" I yelled after him. "Remember, behave yourself!" Mother and I locked eyes for the first time that morning as we both got up from the table to follow Eddie.

"Mother, where is Eddie *really* going," I asked her, "and when will he be back?"

"That's a conversation for another day," she said with a shaky voice, placing her hand on my shoulder.

“When will *you* be back?” I asked quietly.

“I’ll be back by the end of the week. Have a good day at school,” she said, cupping my cheek. She walked out of the kitchen and never looked back. I stood for a few seconds in frozen silence before following her.

I quietly watched through the living room window while Eddie and mother got into the taxi. My brother smiled and waved as they pulled away, so full of excitement and anticipation, off to his great adventure. Thinking that Dulcie would eventually meet him there, it was the greatest deception I had ever witnessed, perpetrated by my parents, especially mother. As I watched the taxi go around the corner, I shuddered to think what my brother would do, how he would eventually react once he realized it had all been a ruse. With a pit in my stomach, I left for school. And just like that, Eddie was gone.

Chapter 5

Eddie was nine and I was twelve when he left, causing in me a feeling of abandonment difficult to shake off. At least I now had Dulcie all to myself, mother having had the good sense to keep the nanny on as usual in her absence, even though she was in the midst of making senseless plans to send Eddie away. I was gratified and relieved that I wouldn't have to fend for myself but, at the same time, a little surprised by my mother's thoughtful arrangement now that my brother was gone. I wouldn't allow myself to believe that she was being considerate of me, instead supposing that she had to give Dulcie something to do, at least temporarily, probably at father's insistence. After all, she never really intended for her to meet Eddie in a few days, or ever again for that matter.

Every day after school was spent with Dulcie, and it turned out to be the greatest week of my life. She was sympathetic about Eddie, still feeling badly about the circumstances herself, giving me the support and understanding that I should have gotten from mother, and would never get from father. We talked about Eddie a lot and shared our thoughts about the situation. Even though my brother was troubled, neither of us liked the fact that he had been sent away and Dulcie wasn't afraid to say so. She especially didn't like that my mother lied, using her name to keep Eddie calm.

"When your brother finds out that I won't be meeting him, wherever he is, he'll hate me, maybe for the rest of his life," she said, shaking her head sadly. "He'll think that I let him down."

"It's my parents who let him down," I said as if to console her.

"We have to trust that it was the right thing to do," she stated, "that they were acting in Eddie's best interest."

"They were acting in their own best interest," I said brusquely, unaccepting of any other explanation and unwilling to validate their solution to Eddie's problems. As far as I was concerned, they had thrown my brother away like a piece of trash. We sat silently after that, neither of us having anything more to say.

Dulcie and I had lighter conversations too and we did some fun things together, uninterrupted for the first time by Eddie's demands. She taught me how to cook, something mother never did, allowing me to cut up vegetables and measure out ingredients. Together we made stew, shepherd's pie, and tuna casserole, leaving a different dish for father every night. He would eat whatever he found on the kitchen table after coming home from the office, but never said a word about the food. Actually, we didn't see much of father until the end of the week, but I didn't care. That meant I still had Dulcie all to myself.

One late afternoon, we roasted hot dogs and marshmallows over the old barbecue pit in the backyard that had been built by the previous owners of the house years ago. It was the first time I had ever seen it put to use, my parents never having roasted anything with Eddie and me. We climbed into the treehouse and ate what we cooked while talking about all sorts of things.

"So, do you have a girlfriend, Tom?" she asked. I laughed and felt my face flush.

"No, do you have a boyfriend?" I shot back quickly.

Dulcie laughed too. "No, I don't, but I don't mind," she said. "It gives me the freedom to do whatever I want. If you have a boyfriend you're tied down, know what I mean?" I knew what she meant, after having thought about it. "Anyway, enough of that. How's school going?" Dulcie asked. "Are you getting good grades?"

"Yeah, I'm doing okay, but I got a D on a math test the other day," I said reluctantly.

"That's not doing okay," she laughed. "I can tutor you in math whenever you want!" Dulcie had a way of coming up with a solution for everything, always in an unthreatening, light and breezy manner. If father had ever found out about the D, he would have tanned me. "And don't worry," she said, "I'll never tell. So, what do you want to be?" she asked, changing the subject. "A lawyer like your dad?"

"Hell no!" I shouted. Never liking my father much I didn't take a shine to his profession either, part of the reason why Eddie was sent away in the first place. Dulcie laughed.

"Well, if you don't want to be a lawyer, then what *do* you want to be?" she asked, standing up to stretch.

"A photographer," I answered right away, that having been a secret dream of mine for as far back as I could remember. "I'd like to take pictures of things all over the world—people, places, animals, whatever I see that looks interesting." I wasn't at all sure if Dulcie had heard me, her thin body now bent over the railing of the treehouse, watching the squirrels scamper down below. Nevertheless, it was nice to finally have someone to whom I could say my dream out loud.

One day, she surprised me by picking me up from school. We got into her beat up Chevy and drove over to Captain Jack's Clam Shack.

"I feel bad that we never got to do this, so here we are!" Dulcie said, the trip easing her guilt a bit, although we both agreed that it was a shame Eddie couldn't be there too. I ordered a lobster roll while Dulcie had fried shrimp. We both shared a large order of onion rings and I even got to have a Coca Cola, despite the fact that mother never allowed us to drink soda, one of her strictest rules. "Well, your mother isn't here now," Dulcie said with an impish grin.

After Captain Jack's, we drove to The Farmer's Creamery Barn where we sat in a worn out, brown leather booth which was extremely cushy and comfortable. Dulcie gave me a dime to put in the juke box, so while we talked about this and that I drummed my fingers on the table to *The Girl from Ipanema*. We both got large hot fudge sundaes with extra whipped cream, sprinkles, and plump red cherries on top. I knew that Dulcie had specially tailored this outing just for me and it was the best time I ever had. It was then and there that I knew for sure I had fallen in love with her.

By the end of the week, father had warmed up to Dulcie being in the house again, even taking the two of us out to dinner. He was a real gentleman, pulling out her chair and ordering for her from the menu.

"The lady and I will have the chateaubriand for two," he told the waiter, his penetrating stare fixed on Dulcie. "You get whatever you want, Tom."

"Yes, sir," I sulked, feeling like the obvious third wheel at the table, the tag-along, the afterthought.

Taking my cue from father I ordered the chicken cordon bleu without consulting either of them, eating it silently while they softly spoke to one another, mostly about Dulcie's background—her upbringing, schooling, and things like that. Father patted her hand more than once, clearly flirting with her.

To my great surprise, Dulcie flirted back, coyly smiling, her beautiful green eyes settled on father in a piercing gaze while tossing her long, dark brown curls over her shoulder. I was furious. Excusing myself from the table, I went to the men's room, so agitated that I nearly threw up my dinner. This little outing of father's meant that I no longer had Dulcie all to myself. Truth be told, I was jealous.

In a bad mood, I walked back to the table and sat down with a thud, folding my arms across my chest.

"Did you enjoy your dinner?" Dulcie asked, sensing that something was wrong.

"I suppose so," I said with a shrug, obviously brooding. "I'm ready to go home now. I have a test to study for."

"On a Friday night?" father asked. I was surprised he had even heard me, his stare still fixed on Dulcie.

"Yeah, well, it's a hard test," I answered.

"Dulcie just asked me if she'd still have job with us after your mother gets home," father said, cluing me in on what they had discussed in my absence.

"And what did you say?" I asked, as if I didn't know.

"I told her she definitely would," he said with a wink and a nod, smiling broadly at Dulcie. "Would you like that, Tom?" Just how naïve did he think I was?

"I guess so," I shrugged.

No longer feeling happy to be there, or charitable toward either Dulcie or my father, I decided to break up our little three-way dinner date with a question sure to destroy father's amorous disposition.

"So, father, where's Eddie," I asked in a firm voice, staring at him unflinchingly, "and when will he be coming home?" My glare dared him to answer the questions, but he wouldn't.

Brushing me off quickly, father said that I'd have to talk to mother about Eddie because he had no idea *where* he was, which I found hard to believe. How could he not know? Of course, the question made him uncomfortable as I knew it would, even Dulcie shifting in her seat. The kid at the table had shattered the romantic ambience. What a pity. The only other thing father could say was…

"Check please!"

We drove home in silence, and I went straight to my room, unsure of how I'd feel about Dulcie the next morning. The following day promised to be a strange one, causing a pit in my stomach. Perhaps it was the chicken cordon bleu or father's shameless flirting, but I really think it was the anticipation of seeing mother again. Should I press her about Eddie's whereabouts? Would she be ready to have that conversation? Dulcie would be at our house by 10:00 am, father suggesting with a smile and a wink that she drop by his study to say hello. Mother would be home by noon. Poor mother. Poor unsuspecting mother.

Mother most certainly had a different sort of week than I did, wherever it was she and Eddie had landed. Probably tiring and difficult, as time spent with my brother was rarely easy, but definitely tragic. How did she handle it? The lies, the deceit…allowing father to talk her into erasing Eddie from our lives. Did she grapple with her conscience at all? Maybe she was glad to be rid of Eddie, the devil having already taken her soul. I could only imagine at night when I closed my eyes what had gone on, my feelings for mother jumbled and torn. I could only imagine.

***

"Well, come in, Ellen. So nice to see you again, dear," said Louise. "I remember you when you were just a little girl. And who do we have here?"

"This is my son, Eddie," said Ellen as she hugged her old neighbor. "Say hello to the nice lady, Eddie."

"Hello," the boy said sullenly. "I'm just waiting for Dulcie to meet me here in a few days." His eyes looked to the floor as he rocked from one foot to the other.

"Dulcie? Who is that, dear?" Louise asked Eddie who continued to look down and rock. Not getting a response, she looked at Ellen.

"She's Eddie's nanny back home," said the boy's mother. "I told him that Dulcie would meet him here in a few days," she said, imploring the old neighbor with her eyes to nod in agreement. "Remember we discussed that?"

"Oh yes, I remember now," said Louise, sensing that this lie would keep the boy calm for a few days, buying her some time. After that, she'd figure out how to handle him.

She always figured it out. Old Louise was a pro at managing wayward, troubled, boys. She had been doing it for as far back as Ellen could remember. A nurse and self-proclaimed psychologist, she was a tough broad with a heart of gold, and everyone knew it. Louise's house was modest, but it was a safe place where boys like Eddie could live without judgement or fear. They could be themselves, have their tantrums, and move on to the next day. Most importantly, they'd be loved. Ellen brought Eddie there for all those reasons and more, unable to bear the thought of leaving him at a sterile, psychiatric hospital.

"When I was younger and lived down the road from here, my mother always talked about how good you were at handling disturbed boys like my Eddie," Ellen said, her son having walked his way over to a window in the adjoining room, curiously looking out on the backyard.

"Your mother was correct. With discipline and love I've been able to keep troubled boys of all sorts in line. Did you bring me the money we talked about, in cash?" Louise asked.

"Yes, I did, five thousand dollars, just as we discussed," said Ellen, taking the overstuffed envelope of money out of her purse and handing it over to the old woman. "When that's gone, you can contact me at this post office box and I'll wire you another payment," she said, handing Louise a piece of paper with the address that she had taken under an assumed name. "My husband must never know that Eddie is with you."

"Why ever not?" Louise questioned, bewildered by Ellen's deception.

"He thinks Eddie has been brought to a hospital. That's where he feels our son belongs. Truthfully, I was too afraid to leave him in a place like that. I don't believe my husband wants Eddie to come home ever again, and I just couldn't leave him to languish in a setting full of…well…I'd rather he be here with you." Ellen was pale and felt weak.

"Don't worry, my dear," said Louise, patting her arm. "Eddie and I will be just fine together." Ellen smiled feebly before sitting in a chair.

"You'll have to excuse me," she said, "but I'm not feeling very well."

"That's understandable, considering that you're about to leave your boy behind," said the old woman, "but try not to worry about him. He's in good hands here. As far as your husband is concerned, he'll never find out who I am or where you've left Eddie. I'll communicate with you, and you alone, through this post office box," she said, looking again at the piece of paper Ellen had given her, "and I'll never put a return address on the correspondence I send you; I'll even mail everything out of Mississippi if you wish. Eddie's whereabouts will remain a secret between you and I until you instruct me otherwise."

"That all sounds fine," Ellen sniffled, wiping her nose with a tissue. "You'll let me know how he's doing, won't you?" she asked soberly.

"Yes, of course, and when I require more money, but what you've brought me should last a good long time," Louise assured her, "probably the better part of a year." Ellen was dizzy and felt faint.

"Could I bother you for a cup of tea?" she asked, gently rubbing her temple.

"Oh, forgive my manners. I'll put the kettle on the boil right away, my dear." Louise went off into the kitchen while Eddie walked back to where his mother was seated and began to kick her chair.

"Please don't do that, Eddie, mother has a headache," Ellen pleaded softly. As he was about to kick the chair again, another boy walked into the room, several years older than Eddie.

"C'mon, kid. I'll show you where you'll be sleeping," said the boy. Eddie immediately complied, looking over his shoulder at his mother as he left the room. It seemed as though he was starting to get a sense of the finality of it all.

"Oh, did Richard take Eddie to his room?" Louise asked as she came back with a tray of refreshments. "Be sure to have a chocolate chip cookie, my dear. I baked them fresh this morning." Ellen wasn't in a chocolate chip cookie kind of mood, but she ate one anyway.

She didn't know what was bothering her most, the downright lies she had told Eddie, the fact that she was shamefully relinquishing her motherly duties to someone else, or the wool she had pulled over her husband's eyes. Ellen would later say goodbye to her son stiffly, as though nothing were out of the ordinary, as though they'd see each other again soon, so as not to upset him. And, of course, Dulcie would be there to meet him in a few days, she reminded him.

"Are you ready to start your great adventure?" Ellen said, forcing a nervous smile.

"I suppose so," said Eddie, "but I think I'll wait for Dulcie." Grabbing a couple of chocolate chip cookies, he gave his mother a limp-wristed wave of the hand and left the room. Ellen would watch him as he went, a single tear falling down her cheek.

The next morning on the train ride home, Ellen sat in the dining car with a cup of coffee, feeling sicker than she had the day before. Her head throbbed, her bones ached, and she was nauseous too, finding it difficult to watch the rapidly passing trees and small towns through the dining car window. She wasn't at all sure that her body would be able to withstand the rattling and side to side motion of the train on her long journey home. Alone with only her own thoughts to occupy her, she would think of Eddie, her mind now sickened too. What had she done?

After taking the two aspirin she had found in her purse with the last gulp of coffee left in her cup, Ellen retired to her compartment and tried to get comfortable. She would fall in and out of one unsettling dream after another, her guilt over leaving Eddie having caught up to her. She was in agony, tormented by demons, her brain playing tricks as her dreams turned into nightmares. Would Eddie ever forgive her, and would she ever be able to forgive herself? Finally, she fell into a deep slumber, black and dreamless, as she headed toward home, and the fate that awaited her there.

***

The next morning, I got up early and went into the attic with Tinker to avoid seeing Dulcie when she arrived. At first, I sat on one of the window seats and stared out onto the street for a good long time, watching the cars go by. As the squirrels walked the telephone wires and the birds flew from one tree to the next, I mulled over what had happened the night before at the restaurant between Dulcie and my father. It was a disappointing evening for me, erasing from my thoughts the great week she and I had spent together, replacing it with the overwhelming notion that she had probably considered me a mere child all along.

Even if that were true, I had always tried to act like a man around Dulcie, so it was a blow to my fragile, pre-adolescent ego to know that she didn't think of me as one. Is if that weren't bad enough, she and father were doing something deceitful behind mother's back, just as mother had done to Eddie. It seemed to me that the adults were acting childish, while I was trying to be so adult.

I pulled the long chain that turned on the overhead lightbulb and opened the trunk of old family photos. Becoming strangely absorbed in the black and white world that Eddie always found so soothing, I looked through one photo after another, stopping when I came to the one of our dead cousin, Leo Biggs. I stared at it for a long time, not because I was interested in Leo, but because I was thinking of Eddie. Why was he so fascinated by this photo? Was it because he somehow saw himself in Leo Biggs, a dead man sitting on a chair, dressed in a three-piece suit and tie to look alive when he really wasn't? It was all too ghastly for me to think about but then again, Eddie could be pretty ghastly sometimes.

After a while I got tired of looking at family photos and rolled out the old rug. On my hands and knees, I felt for the dirty pie plate I had previously shoved under a chair and placed it down at the far end of the rug so that I could hit golf balls into it, using one of father's clubs. Whereas Eddie always found comfort in looking through the trunk of old family photos, this was the activity that pacified me most whenever I needed to spend time in the attic.

I hit the ball and retrieved it, hit the ball and retrieved it, back and forth, back and forth until I realized that the club I was using was the same one my brother had used to destroy mother's table. I threw it down in disgust, walking over to the corner where he and I had placed the bird's nest we made together, chunks of dirt and pieces of grass having fallen to the floor all around it. There was nothing I could do in the attic that didn't remind me of Eddie. Perhaps I could go out to the treehouse, but thoughts of my brother would follow me there too. Eddie was everywhere I looked.

Deciding that the privacy of my own bedroom was probably the best place to hide out if I wanted to avoid Dulcie, I turned to leave the attic when suddenly she appeared, her footsteps light and silent. She carried a box wrapped in pretty paper and handed it to me.

"What's this?" I asked quietly, unable to look her in the eye.

"Open it and find out," she said, sensing my discomfort.

I unwrapped the box to find a brand-new Polaroid camera. She *had* heard me, this mere child who so wanted to be a grownup for Dulcie.

"Thank you," I stammered, unable to prevent a smile.

"Well, you told me that you wanted to be a photographer when you grow up," she said. "I thought this would get you off to a good start."

"I don't know what to say." I suddenly felt ashamed and embarrassed. Perhaps I should be angry with father alone and leave Dulcie out of it.

“Don’t be silly, you’ve already said it,” she remarked, her voice a little lighter. “I’m sorry if you didn’t have a good time last night. Sometimes adults get to talking and…”

“I get it,” I blurted out. “You know, this past week has been difficult for father because he’s missed mother so much since she’s been gone,” I lied. “I understand that he just needed someone else to talk to, but today mother will be back,” I reminded her, “and he’ll no longer need someone else to talk to.” My words were deliberate and I’m sure Dulcie got the point, but I decided to definitely let her off the hook. “Want to play checkers,” I asked, changing the subject quickly, “maybe outside on the grass?” I couldn’t wait to get out of the attic, shake Eddie’s cobwebs off of me, and think of something else other than my brother, if only for a few minutes. But, from here on in, even during a simple game of checkers, Eddie would be sitting on my shoulder.

“Sure, and then maybe you can take some photos with that new camera of yours,” Dulcie said as she followed me down the stairs and out of the attic. We would play checkers and take photographs of nature in the backyard until mother’s taxi pulled up at noon, the beeping horn bringing back the pit in my stomach.

I ran out to the front drive to greet mother as she got out of her taxi. Dulcie went into the house through the back kitchen door, allowing me to be alone with mother who had been gone for a week. When she left, mother was anxious about taking Eddie on his great adventure, knowing that she’d be leaving him there, wherever that was, for good. Today, she still seemed anxious, but she was sick too, her eyes puffy, her skin shiny from sweat, and her shoulders stooped. She was so weakened that she couldn’t even carry her pocketbook.

“Let me help you, mother,” I said, placing a gentle arm around her shoulder. “You don’t look like you’re feeling too well.”

“I’m not,” she said weakly. “Take me straight to my bedroom.” As I walked mother into the house, father was on his way out to get the bags and pay the taxi driver.

“Mission accomplished, Ellen?” was all he could say as we passed each other in the front hall, mother’s head bowed low with fever.

“Yes, Dan, mission accomplished,” she said softly, not even looking at him. Poor mother. Poor sick mother.

I took her straight to her bedroom like she asked. Sitting in her comfy chair by the window, mother took off her shoes, dropping each one to the floor with a sigh of relief. She gently massaged each foot before putting on her slippers.

"Get mother's robe out of the closet, will you, Tom?" Her eyes were now glassed over with sickness, and she clearly had a headache. I walked over to her closet slowly, almost on tiptoe, so as not to make any noise, fearing that her head would crack and break the way her fine china did the day Eddie destroyed it. Had Eddie now destroyed her too?

"Mother, do you think you should call a doctor?" I asked, handing her the robe.

"I'll be fine, Tom. I just need to take a hot bath and get into bed," she said, leaning her head back against the chair. I decided to ask her, flat out, all the questions I had about my brother before being inevitably dismissed.

"Mother, where is Eddie? Is he nearby? When can I see him?" She rubbed her temples, the headache obviously getting worse.

"Tom, come sit by mother," she said softly. I sat on the rug by her feet and looked up at her tired, defeated expression. "Eddie is in a place far from here where he'll be happy and well taken care of every day," she said, reaching down and stroking my hair, "but you can't go see him, not now, not yet."

"When then, mother? When will I be able to see my brother?" I asked persistently, causing her to let out a long sigh before standing up from her chair. Walking over to the window, she gently pushed the curtain aside and looked out onto the garden, answering me without having to look at me.

"I'm not sure, Tom. Perhaps never. Seeing Eddie might set him off. I didn't want to tell you these things, but you need to know them, and you're old enough to hear them." She suddenly turned around to look at me. "Eddie is gone, Tom, and you just have to accept that." Mother's face was anguished and pale.

"Do you accept it, mother?" I asked, unwilling to believe that she ever could.

"Just like you, Tom, I have no choice," she said, slowly shaking her head. I didn't want to believe that mother could ever write off her own flesh and blood.

"Well, can you at least tell me where he is exactly?" I implored, my anger rising.

"I'm sorry, Tom, I can't," she said, her voice weak, but her words unwavering.

"You can't or you won't?" I asked, my voice louder now, disregarding her headache.

"He's gone Tom," mother repeated emphatically. "Let him go." She then walked into her private bathroom, directing me to see myself out before shutting the door. I could hear the water running into the bathtub as I turned and left the room.

I walked down the hall and into my own bedroom, slamming the door shut. Sitting at my desk, I decided to write Eddie a long letter telling him all the things I was thinking, telling him not to worry because someday we'd see each other again, maybe soon. Taking pencil to paper, I struggled, feeling saddened and so helpless. Would we *really* see each other again? I didn't want to lie to him, he'd been lied to enough already, and I was beginning to have my doubts. But I couldn't just let him go. He was my brother. I just couldn't.

A knock at the bedroom door startled me, snapping me out of my deep thoughts of Eddie. It was Dulcie who I had completely forgotten was still here.

"I was wondering if you'd like to go see a movie, as long as you're up to it, that is," she said, noticing that I was upset. I didn't have to think about it twice. Perhaps a movie was just what I needed, a strong dose of Hollywood to get me away from real life.

"Sure, let's get out of here," I said. "I'm up to it just fine."

On our way out we ran into father jogging up the stairs to see mother, probably to confirm again that the mission had indeed been accomplished. Beyond that he wouldn't require the details, considering them all too tiresome and unnecessary, while I was dying to know everything, unwilling to let my brother go the way mother wanted me to. Father simply wanted Eddie gone, especially after the dinner party fiasco, but his attitude wasn't surprising.

He had become determined to never let anyone jeopardize his success ever again, especially his own son. When it came to Eddie, father was a cold fish, the kind that ate its young. For now, I'd let the matter rest while I had Dulcie all to myself again, but my thoughts would eventually turn to one day…finding my brother.

Chapter 6

The next day the sun rose, and life went on as though Eddie never existed. Mother laid in bed still not feeling well, her headache and fever not having subsided yet, while her anxiety was obvious. I sat with her whenever I could, if only to seize upon a chance opening that would allow me to ask about Eddie again. Shamefully, I thought I could break her down, but she gave me no such opportunity, remaining tight-lipped about my brother. After three days, father insisted that she call a doctor.

"You're not well, Ellen, and we need to get you back on your feet," he said. "The firm is planning a big get together with the Pallincot executives and their wives at the Ocean Front Resort in four weeks, and we're *both* expected to be there," father said with emphasis, never having gotten over the fact that mother wouldn't go with him to the dinner party at Andrew Mink's house after Eddie's big outburst. Ironically, his insistence that she take Eddie away was what put her to bed, unable to reconcile the position in which he had placed her.

"What's this big get together all about?" mother asked in a weak voice.

"You know, the usual fun, food, and drinks, mixed in with a lot of planning and business talk. I'll need you by my side," father said. It was business first. Always.

The doctor came to the house and examined mother, telling her that she had a nasty virus, and that it would take a week or so for her to get back on her feet. Even at that, she'd still have to take it easy. Moreover, he was concerned about her heart.

"It seems to be weakened a bit," he said, moving the stethoscope around mother's chest while I sat on the bed, and father stood in the doorway. "How long have you felt unwell?" he asked.

"Three or four days, I suppose," she said, mentioning nothing of her trip, the anxiety it had caused, or my brother. A virus and an unwell heart. It seemed like payback, Eddie's revenge.

"I'll be back to check on you in a few days," the doctor said, giving her a bottle of pills. "In the meantime, stay in bed and call if you need me."

Mother followed orders, staying in bed and taking her medicine as directed. The doctor came back in a few days to check on her just as he said he would, listening to her heart once again as he moved his stethoscope from side to side, up and down, and all around.

"Sounds a bit better," he said. "Still, I think I'd like to perform some tests. Make an appointment, sooner rather than later." Mother agreed but wasn't too worried, knowing that the trip with Eddie had taken a lot out of her, mentally and physically. Anybody's heart would have reacted the same.

After a week, mother was out of bed just as the doctor had predicted and moved about the house quietly, not doing much of anything. Her meals were light, and she read her magazines while lying on the couch, unable to resume her smoking habit just yet. One day, she walked into Eddie's bedroom and looked around. It was all in there, sad reminders of his absence; an empty bed, a dresser without clothes, and a toy airplane sitting on the desk, Eddie no longer there to twirl the propeller. I followed her into the room.

"Is there anything I can do for you mother?" I asked as a pretense, assuming that she would be willing to open up about Eddie if we stood in his bedroom long enough.

"No, Tom. Not right now," she answered quietly.

"Eddie's room seems kind of lonely without him, doesn't it?" I commented, but mother remained silent. "I can clean it for you, mother," I said with a bounce in my voice, "maybe dust, vacuum, and straighten things up, so that when Eddie comes home, it'll be ready." Mother took in a deep breath and let it out slowly.

"I'll be turning Eddie's bedroom into a small office, a place where I can have a desk of my own to plan things, write my letters, and whatever else your father needs me to do," she said without much feeling in her voice. "I may even have another doorway cut out here," gesturing to the wall behind Eddie's dresser, "so that I can walk from this room into the sitting room more easily."

It was all mapped out, and so cold. My brother was being further erased, a place to lay his head at night in this house no longer available. Mother's continued recuperation didn't stop me from questioning her about Eddie's whereabouts again, willing to chance her frustration with my persistence.

"Where is Eddie now, mother?" I asked. "If he's never coming home then tell me where he is so that I can go visit him, or at least write." I believed that if I asked about my brother often enough, mother would eventually break down and tell me what I wanted to hear.

"Tom, we've already discussed these things," she said tersely. "No visiting, no writing. Eddie is gone."

"Just like that?" I asked. "You won't even leave his bedroom the way it is?"

"The sooner we all move on, the better," she stated.

"You're being so cold, mother," I blurted out, "like you never even loved him, your own son. Your heart problem is that you have no heart!" I was shocked at myself for having the nerve to say what had been on my mind ever since all the lies, ever since I knew Eddie was being sent away, finding it difficult to believe that mother might be aching too.

I didn't feel sorry, though, not one bit. It felt good to get it off my chest, even though it was a malicious thing to say. I suppose I was trying to be hurtful, my own anguish over Eddie getting the best of me. Naturally, mother didn't take too kindly to it, slapping me right across the face. It threw me backward.

"No heart? You think I have no heart? Sending your brother away was the hardest thing I ever had to do in my entire life," she said loudly, her tears coming quickly, "not to mention the fact that I was told by your father, in no uncertain terms, that I had no choice in the matter. Do you really think my heart didn't break when I had to admit that I couldn't control him, or that he needed more help than I was capable of giving? No, you're wrong about me, Tom. I have a heart but I'm being realistic, and you need to be realistic too." Her emotions were raw and unrestrained.

Mother quickly turned on her heels and walked out of Eddie's bedroom, her chest heaving as each short breath caught in her throat, leaving me no time to respond. I had a difficult time buying any of it. How heartbroken could she be? When she slapped me across the face, I was stunned, but her determination to simply move on without leaving so much as a reminder of Eddie intact, not even his bedroom, was worse than a slap. It proved to me once and for all that she had closed the chapter on her second son, something I was still unwilling to do. It would be a few weeks before I could look mother in the eye again, but that slap would remain with me forever.

As the days passed, mother felt stronger, regaining her sense of purpose and a willingness to get back out there into society. She did make an appointment with her doctor who still wanted to perform some tests on her heart, but that didn't stop her from having a luncheon one Thursday afternoon for the wives of father's partners, women who she knew well and felt comfortable with. She also knew they wouldn't press her about Eddie, despite the rumors circulating around town, by asking intrusive questions or bringing up the ill-fated dinner party that had to be detoured.

They could be caddy, but not to your face. It was an easy, uncomplicated way to get back into the stream of things, enabling her to start slowly and eventually work her way up to the more glamorous affairs she was known for.

"I'd like to have another go at a fancy dinner party at our house within the next three or four months," father told her. "It might make up for the debacle Eddie caused. Can you handle it?"

"Of course," mother said. "You just watch me." She had become like father, all about the business of the firm, all about raising their profile. That's what still kept them together, if nothing else.

Mother also picked up some charity work, arranging fundraisers for various worthy causes in Old Windsor Cove and the surrounding communities. She felt useful again, and appeared to be back to her old self, keeping busy and getting her name back out there as a person of status and social means. All the ladies in mother's circle strived for that, a group of self-important social climbers who did some good things, but spent an awful lot of time patting themselves on the back over a game of canasta, a glass of wine, and a menthol cigarette tucked securely into a long holder.

Mother was no different, making a name for herself and pretentious gatherings her life's blood now, more so than before. She had to make up for lost time and she did it by creating a busy life...in exchange for Eddie. But there were days when she was too tired to get off the couch. It didn't seem normal.

The time came for mother's appointment with her doctor whose office was at Shoreline Hospital two towns over.

"Do you want me to drive you there, Ellen?" father asked. "I have the afternoon off with nothing better to do," he said, as though a good football game on television might have prevented him from making the offer.

"That won't be necessary, Dan," mother said, "I'll be fine to drive myself. The doctor is just being cautious." She felt that her heart had probably gotten back to normal now that Eddie was gone, he undoubtedly having been the cause of her cardiac episode, and that her curious bouts of fatigue were just a leftover nuisance from the virus.

***

When Ellen got to the hospital, the doctor performed a number of tests on her heart, keeping her there for the majority of the afternoon in a medical gown. Two other doctors and several nurses walked in and out of the room, assisting and consulting. Putting their heads together they whispered in the hallway, pointing at this and conferring about that, the long strips of paper with the irregular jagged lines causing them concern. Ellen was surprised by the gravity of it all, but apparently it was no joke.

"Mrs. Biggs, we've performed a number of tests as you know," her doctor began gently, "and we think you have coronary artery disease, advanced enough that it has put you into congestive heart failure. Of course, we're still waiting on the results of one or two more tests to make that diagnosis conclusive, but I believe at this point that we can confidently say you have a serious heart condition." The doctor was grave.

"Are you sure about all of this?" Ellen asked in disbelief. She was just tired, that's all.

"We're sure. It's your heart condition that's making you tired, a tell-tale sign of what's going on," the doctor said.

"Well, what happens now?" she asked.

"We want you to stay in the hospital for several days which will allow us to stabilize you with medication. After that, we'll figure out our next steps." The doctor had formulated a plan, but Ellen wanted no part of it.

"I can't possibly stay here for several days," she said incredulously as though her destiny with high society couldn't wait, not even seventy-two hours. Besides, she didn't want Dan to think that she was now incapable of fulfilling her obligations to him. Attending the upcoming get together with the

Pallincot executives and their wives at the Ocean Front Resort, and organizing the fancy dinner party her husband wanted to throw took precedence over everything else, including some silly heart condition. At that point, the doctor got blunt.

"What you have can kill you, and it most likely will, if you refuse to do as I say. You, Mrs. Biggs, are a walking time bomb," the doctor warned in no uncertain terms, scowling at his skeptical patient. He had made his point. Ellen had no choice but to comply.

***

Early that evening, we went to the hospital to see mother after she had called the house to give father the news. When we got there, she filled him in on what the doctor had said, almost apologetic for having to cease her activities for a little while. I stood there and listened in silence, finding it both tragic and interesting.

"I'll be back up and running before you know it, Dan, don't you worry about me," she said. Father cheered her on because, after all, she had a big get together to attend and a fancy dinner party to organize. But it was then and there that he would make another monumental decision without her, keeping it to himself for the time being so as not to upset her.

The next day Dulcie was there to greet me when I got home from school. Without wasting much time, we drove straight to the public library where I needed to look for books about the Revolutionary War, the topic I had chosen for my history project. The librarian showed me a number of relevant accounts while Dulcie strolled over to a different section in search of a romance novel, each of us taking only thirty minutes to find success.

I checked out three books that afternoon, the first containing Revolutionary War maps, the second a complete biography of George Washington, and the third a reproduction of a soldier's diary about life at Valley Forge. I had plenty of material to write a good paper and make a decent diorama. Dulcie borrowed a thick love story, figuring she'd have to renew it at least once in order to finish it.

"Yeah, this will keep me busy for a month," she said, flipping through the pages on our way out the door, yet she seemed distracted, something else definitely weighing on her mind. "How about we grab a quick ice cream cone on the way home," Dulcie said, still thumbing through her book as we walked to the car. "We'll go to that place your brother likes, Dairy Delight."

I could certainly go for my favorite vanilla ice cream cone dipped in chocolate and rolled in coconut, what I always ordered whenever we went to Dairy Delight, but what I liked even more was that Dulcie hadn't mentioned Eddie in the past tense. That made me happy, taking my mind off the history project right away.

"Sure, I'd love to go to Dairy Delight," I said, sensing that Dulcie wanted to talk to me about something. Whatever it was we'd be alone, and I'd have her all to myself just the way I liked it.

We got our cones and sat at one of the picnic tables outside, the brilliant sunshine warm on our faces, the air crisp and clean, even before the sea breezes shifted our way. At that moment, I thought of Eddie. He would have liked to have been here too. I pictured him clearly, ice cream and sprinkles dripping down his chin, the way it always did whenever we came here, while he would fidget and laugh at nothing in particular. It made me smile.

"Listen, Tom," Dulcie began, "I'd like to run something by you, something that I'll be doing because, well, it involves you too." She shifted in her seat.

"Sounds serious," I said, picking a shred of coconut off my chin and putting it in my mouth.

"Well, it's life changing, for me anyway," she said.

"Sounds like you're moving away to a different place," I guessed. I was partially correct.

"I'll be moving to a different place all right, but it won't be away, it'll be right here," Dulcie said.

"I don't get it," I said, biting a small hole into the bottom of my cone and sucking the ice cream out of it. "Where'll you be going?" She wouldn't bring me all the way to Dairy Delight just to tell me she was moving into a different apartment in town, would she? Dulcie took in a deep breath.

"Your father has asked me to move into your house and I said yes," she answered, searching my face for a reaction, any reaction. I was too stunned to even blink, knowing that this was the one thing mother didn't want. She had already told Dulcie so.

"Why did he do that?" I finally managed to blurt out, clearing the coconut and ice cream I was about to swallow from the back of my throat.

"He thought I could take some of the work off your mother's shoulders if I lived there." I knew Dulcie was looking for my approval, but I wasn't about to give it.

"Mother has already told you that she couldn't accommodate you at our house," I reminded her.

"How in the world did you know that?" Dulcie asked. "Were you eavesdropping on our conversation?"

"What if I was?" I asked in a salty tone, reacting in defense of my mother's position. "Mother isn't going to like this, especially since she's already told you that you couldn't live at our house. You should have told father that."

"Things have changed, Tom," she said, trying to speak quietly, the picnic tables all around us now filled with customers. "Your mother will need help, so I think she'll appreciate that I'm there. I'll cook, clean, do the laundry, and take care of you, all the things she'd have to do if I weren't there. Don't you want her to rest up and get well?"

What Dulcie said made perfect sense, but I would have none of it because I knew better. I knew that she wanted to live in our house way before mother ever got sick, and I knew that she was sweet on father too. I through the rest of my ice cream cone to the ground and clenched my fists under the table, losing my temper.

"Look, I'm not Eddie," I said in a disrespectful tone of voice. "I don't need you to take care of me, I can take care of myself. I'm also old enough to pitch in and help. The last thing mother needs when she gets home is you living in our house. It might give her a heart attack, for Christ's sake!" I was angry, knowing the real reason father had asked Dulcie to move in.

"You're being a little dramatic, don't you think?" she asked. "I would only be there to help your mother, make her load lighter, and hopefully take off some of the pressures of running a household. How in the world would that give her a heart attack?" She folded her arms across her chest and sat back, waiting for an answer. The gloves were off.

"Let's talk about the real reason father asked you to move in," I said, stumbling over the words as they left my mouth, speaking candidly for a twelve-year-old boy, nevertheless.

"And what's that?" Dulcie asked, trying to be stoic, but she knew I was on to father, and her.

"Father likes you and you like him," I started.

"Well, of course, otherwise he wouldn't have hired me in the first place, and I wouldn't have taken the job," she said, trying to dodge my meaning.

"You know what I'm talking about," I said, my eyes lowered to slits, "so don't play dumb with me, Dulcie. Father would like nothing more than to have an affair with you, and how convenient it would be if you lived under our roof. I saw the way the two of you looked at each other the night we went out to dinner. He was flirting, and you were flirting back, so don't try to tell me that you'd only be there to help mother." I was seething with anger, a little girl over at the next table staring at me, but the truth was I felt jealous again. Dulcie was speechless at first, but that didn't last long.

"How dare you," she managed to spew out, "you little ingrate. You've got this all wrong." She was incensed, but I could tell it was a phony reaction. I knew my father so very well and now I had her number too.

"I want to go home," I said, quickly standing up from the picnic table. "This is bullshit."

As I stalked back to the car Dulcie followed, telling me to slow down. I was so angry I couldn't see straight, and I didn't care one bit if she told my father everything I said when we got home. He wouldn't be able to deny a word of it. Mother would be home in a few days or so, and this news would upset her beyond words. More drama. More lies.

"Jeez, if it's going to upset you that much, I won't do it," she said, "I won't move in." We got into the car, slamming both doors.

"Do you really think father would stand for that, you changing your mind?" I asked rhetorically. "He'd fire you first before letting you do that! No, he'll tell you not to worry about some little kid because he doesn't give a damn what I think, then he'll have it out with mother, and it'll all be over. She'll comply, he'll get his way, and you'll be sleeping under our roof before you know it! By the way, where are you supposed to sleep anyway?" I asked, my chest heaving after my little rant.

"In Eddie's room for now," Dulcie said hesitantly, afraid of my reaction.

"Eddie's room!" I shouted. "First, mother says she's going to turn that room into an office, and now you're telling me it's going to be your bedroom! Will anyone be considering Eddie ever again? Is he dead to everyone but me?"

I didn't know what to be angriest at—Dulcie taking over Eddie's bedroom which would scuttle mother's office plans, mother wanting to turn Eddie's bedroom into an office in the first place, or father choosing Dulcie over mother.

Both my parents and Dulcie sickened me for different reasons, but my undeniable jealousy over father's real intentions filled me with rage. After that, we drove home in silence.

When we got home, I went straight to my bedroom and slammed the door, a signal for Dulcie to stay away. I didn't know if she'd tell father about our discussion or not, but at that point I couldn't care less. Now, I wasn't looking forward to mother's homecoming at all, unsure of how her heart would take the news, certain that there would be a bad scene and I didn't want to be around to see it. As it was, father was working late that evening.

When Dulcie called me down to dinner, I grabbed my chicken off the kitchen table and brought it back up to my room, once again slamming the door. I didn't know if anything I said that afternoon would have an effect on Dulcie, or make the slightest bit of difference in her decision to move in. I got my answer the following morning when she showed up with her suitcase.

Dulcie set herself up in Eddie's room, just as she said she would, with father's blessing. Apparently, she didn't tell him about our stormy conversation the day before because he never mentioned a word about it to me, Dulcie probably figuring that my turbulent emotions would subside once mother got home from the hospital. I knew I couldn't stay angry forever but, once again, I had a pit in my stomach as I awaited mother's return. More than that, my jealousy just wouldn't leave me.

At least Dulcie was true to her word, cleaning the house, cooking the meals, and preparing for mother's return with fresh sheets on her bed and clean towels in her bathroom. I stayed out of the way, making myself scarce. Over the next few days, whenever it was time to eat, I took my meals from the kitchen to my bedroom where I could eat in private, avoiding father and Dulcie's table talk altogether. Sometimes I even ate up in the treehouse, the fresh air always clearing my mind of unpleasant thoughts.

Father never said anything to me about my absences from the table, either not noticing or not caring, which allowed him to make his moves on Dulcie without my notice. How convenient. Mother would be home from the hospital late tomorrow afternoon, and I'd have to keep myself busy after school to avoid all of them.

The next day after I got home from school, I decided to use my camera, but I didn't want to take photos of nature in the backyard. Instead, I'd look for something more interesting, more challenging, just like a real photographer.

Dulcie had left a note on the kitchen table saying she'd be out for the afternoon doing the marketing while father was still at the office and mother remained in the hospital, not due to be released until five o'clock. I figured that I had at least an hour to myself before Dulcie got home, and that father would go straight from the office to the hospital to pick mother up. I was wrong.

Not feeling kindly toward my father lately I decided to break his strictest rule and root around his study in search of something that might make for a worthy photo. I went through his desk, seeing the gun in the top right-hand drawer once again, its cartridges rolling around like marbles, once again causing the hair on the back of my neck to stand on end while my adrenaline spiked as it had before, causing my heart to beat uncontrollably. I couldn't imagine finding anything more notable to photograph but I closed the drawer in haste, suddenly frightened at the thought of father finding a picture of his gun in my possession.

Taking in a deep breath, I managed to forget about the gun and decided to look through a stack of legal documents on top of the desk. Careful not to change their order I started to click away, photographing one page after another. I had found something more interesting than the gun after all—a case father was working on involving a husband who allegedly murdered his wife. It would make for fascinating reading if I could get the photos to come out focused and up close.

Satisfied with my amateur photography, I left father's study and closed the door, carefully leaving everything on his desk the way I had found it. I proudly walked into the kitchen and poured myself a glass of milk, having gotten back at father in my own way. The best part was that he'd never know what I did.

Looking through the photos I had taken with my Polaroid, I determined that with the aid of my magnifying glass I'd be able to read those legal documents just fine. After I drank my milk, I grabbed a couple of chocolate chip cookies and ran up to my bedroom, closing the door and locking it behind me. It was time for some interesting reading.

I placed my camera on the nightstand and spread the photographs all over my bed, arranging them in the correct order. Slipping my magnifying glass out of its silk pouch, I began to read father's legal documents, one photo at a time. The key words flooded my brain—poison, heart attack, premeditated murder. I was immediately fascinated by the intrigue, keenly reading over every detail more than once before the slamming of car doors in the driveway stopped me cold.

Quickly gathering up the damning photos, proof that I had been in father's study, I threw them into my top dresser drawer with shaking hands as though the locked bedroom door weren't enough to protect my privacy. Looking out of my window onto the driveway, I could see father helping Dulcie into the house with the groceries after he had pulled his car in behind hers. Back and forth they went, several times until all the groceries were in. Just as I was about to turn away from the window, they came back out again, Dulcie closing the trunk of her car while father stood and watched.

As she started to walk back toward the house, he took her by the hand and drew her near, putting his arms around her waist. He kissed her gently on the lips and she kissed him back, the branches of the oak tree throwing cascading afternoon shadows over their embrace. I immediately grabbed my camera off the nightstand and took the most notable photo of the entire afternoon. It wasn't only proof of what I had seen, but it would validate what I already knew. I was so racked with jealousy that I wanted to scream, punching the wall instead. I shoved the photo into my top dresser drawer with all the rest and covered them carefully with a shirt.

Running down the stairs, I headed straight out the front door and didn't stop until I reached Kimball Avenue. I walked aimlessly, my pride wounded, Dulcie having taken my heart and torn it in two. Eddie once said that he hated father, and now I hated him too. Mother would be home soon, and things couldn't be messier. I put my hands in my pockets and reluctantly turned around, knowing I had to go back. I felt all alone with no one to turn to, nothing left but a house of deceit. Poor me. Poor mother. Poor bamboozled mother.

Chapter 7

As Ellen and Tom contended with fractured hearts, each battered and torn for different reasons, Eddie acclimated himself to living with Louise and Richard after having grasped none too easily that his great adventure was permanent, and that Dulcie was never going to come. He raged and howled at first and refused to eat, but Louise wouldn't allow that in her house, calming him down each time with her tough but respectful approach which was something new to Eddie. He eventually came to appreciate Louise, not only for the boundaries she set but for the way she took care of him, immediately enrolling him in school, buying him a new set of clothes, and even giving him an allowance for the chores he did.

Of course, Eddie didn't know at the time that the generous amount of money Ellen had left with Louise was supporting every aspect of his life away from Old Windsor Cove. But it was Richard who took Eddie under his wing, a new big brother who spent time with him, gave him advice, and grabbed him by the shirt collar whenever he sensed that an outburst was imminent. Richard always knew when Eddie's moods were about to turn volatile because he was familiar with the signs, behaving in much the same way at one time, especially when he first came to live with Louise.

Orphaned at a young age, Richard was a petty little thief, a dirty tough talking pocketbook snatcher who always managed to stay two steps ahead of the law, barely scraping his way through life until Louise took him off the street and gave him a home. She eventually went to court and made it legal, adopting Richard as her son, the two of them officially becoming a family.

At first, he was full of anger just like Eddie, having been unaccustomed to following the rules, but in time he would settle into his new life, appreciating the roof over his head and the food in his belly. Louise had saved him from himself.

Now, Eddie had unofficially joined the family and Richard liked him well enough, glad to finally have the companionship of another boy in the house, someone who could be like a little brother as long as he behaved himself. "Do what I tell you," Richard would say to Eddie, dangling him by his shirt collar, "and everything will be just fine between us." Eddie never felt bullied, though, seeing Richard as a mentor, hanging on his every word while looking up to him in a way he never did his own brother.

Things were copacetic between them, two misfits who had finally found security and Richard had no doubt that Eddie would grow to like it there. He became protective of Eddie who liked having someone to look out for him now that Dulcie was no longer around. Louise may have set the rules, but it was Richard who Eddie turned to for heart-to-heart talks, boy stuff he'd never say to a woman.

"I bet Dulcie is thinking of me right now," Eddie said, revealing his wishful thinking.

"Who is this Dulcie girl anyway?" Richard asked, whittling a branch with his pocketknife.

"A pretty girl back home," Eddie lamented.

"What, are you in love with her or something?" Richard wanted to know, making a face as he looked up from his whittling.

"Yeah, I think so," Eddie said, his voice breaking a bit.

"Don't you dare cry over some dumb girl," Richard warned, "she isn't worth it."

"But I miss her," Eddie snapped, "and she's not dumb!"

"Stop it or I'll knock you from here to across the street." Richard closed his knife and shoved it into his pocket, throwing the branch he had whittled to the ground. "There are other things more important to think about, like the math homework you haven't done yet. I don't want to be waiting around for you after school tomorrow because you've gotten a detention."

"Haven't you ever liked a girl, Richard?" Eddie asked.

"Nope, never have, they're too much trouble. Besides, do you think I want to be walking around like you, pining over some girl who's never going to show up?" Richard stuck his nose in the air and sniffed. "I smell biscuits. Let's go inside and grab a couple before supper, then you best do your homework."

"She might still show up," Eddie pouted, not really believing his own words. Richard grabbed him by the collar and walked him toward the house.

"Aw, quit your sulking. I'm telling you she isn't worth it." Eddie took Richard's advice as usual and immediately changed the subject. "Will you help me do my division then?" he asked.

"Now you're talking," Richard replied happily, giving Eddie a pat on the back and a gentle kick through the door.

Eddie missed Dulcie and Tom less and less as the days passed while he never really missed his parents at all, but for some unknown reason he still had a yearning for the attic, that strangely soothing, dark place of solitude with its trunk of old family photos. He sometimes longed to see the picture of Leo Biggs, postmortem, something he thought he would surely see again until he realized that it would be lost to him just like everything else in his old life.

The attic in this house didn't hold the same charms, but there were other things to keep him busy now, hard work the remedy for a lost soul according to Louise. Besides school, where he was actually making friends for the first time in his life, Eddie was expected to do chores at home every day which he didn't mind doing because he and Richard usually worked together to get them done.

Eddie needed to learn how to take on his newfound responsibilities, both Louise and Richard showing him how to vacuum, dust the furniture, and properly wash a dish, among other things.

"No, hold the vacuum handle like this, then go back and forth, back and forth, until the entire rug is clean," Richard would tell him. Eddie liked vacuuming because it was mindless, allowing his thoughts to wander aimlessly and privately. This was when he sometimes daydreamed about Dulcie, precluding Richard from teasing him about his secret little longings to see her again. At other times he liked to recall the days when he would endlessly twirl the propeller of his toy airplane, or climb into the treehouse where he could feel the cool breeze on his face, or play checkers and hit golf balls in the attic.

It was gone, all gone, giving Eddie an idea that he eagerly shared with Richard one Saturday afternoon when they were in the backyard, taking turns with the lawn mower.

"We should build a treehouse," he said, pointing to a large tree in the backyard. "That would be the perfect tree for it too."

"I have to admit that building a treehouse might be fun," Richard said. "We'd have to save up our allowances to buy the nails, but I bet we could salvage the lumber we need from the back of that old sawmill on Decatur Road. It's all scrap anyway. They'll never have another use for it."

"I'm good at hitting nails with a hammer," Eddie said. "My brother showed me once. I bet you're good at it too."

"I've never used a hammer before, but I probably could," said Richard, staring up into the branches of the old tree. "Yeah, this tree would be perfect, but we have to ask Louise first."

"She'll say yes. Remember, hard work is the remedy for a lost soul," Eddie said, half-heartedly mocking Louise. The boys laughed, but they both knew she was right. "I can teach you how to use a hammer, Richard," Eddie said proudly, this time he being the one to show someone how to do something.

"I bet you could, kid," Richard said, tussling Eddie's hair, "but for now, let's just finish cutting the lawn." Eddie was content to leave it there for now, Louise bringing them two glasses of ice-cold lemonade.

"It's my turn to use the lawn mower next," Eddie reminded Richard.

"Use it all you want," he chuckled, sitting back in a chair with his feet propped up on an overturned bucket as he drank his lemonade. "I never saw anyone who liked to do chores as much as you do." Richard watched as Eddie struggled to push the mower in a straight line across the backyard. His lost soul was healing.

While Eddie liked vacuuming and cutting the lawn, Richard enjoyed washing and waxing Louise's car, hoping that perhaps one Sunday morning she'd take him to an empty store parking lot to drive it around. He dreamed that eventually the car would be his, an old Chevy Impala with leather seats and a radio that worked.

"Fat chance," Eddie commented, "but if she ever does take you to an empty store parking lot on a Sunday morning I want to go too."

"What for?" Richard asked while polishing the driver's side fender. Eddie was now gazing through the window at the roomy backseat.

"Maybe she'll let me drive it after you," he casually replied as he continued to look over the car's interior. Richard threw his rag to the ground and grabbed Eddie by the collar.

"Don't you dare spoil this for me," he barked. "You're far too young to drive."

"So are you," Eddie grumbled, wiggling out of Richard's grasp before straightening his collar.

“Not as young as you are. If you whine to Louise that you want to drive too, she won’t take either of us.” Richard made a good point.

“Okay, okay,” Eddie said. “I’ll stay at home when you and Louise go to the empty store parking lot to drive this heap around.” Eddie knew, though, that it would never happen, that Louise would never allow Richard to drive her car. It was Richard’s own secret little longing, just the way he sometimes daydreamed about seeing Dulcie again. Eddie figured that everyone should have something to dream about once in a while, but for boys like Richard and him dreams rarely came true.

Eddie never enjoyed doing a chore more than when Louise asked Richard and him to paint the back porch. He felt like a real grownup as soon as he picked up the brush, something that would have been unthinkable back home.

“This is the best chore I’ve ever had to do in my whole life,” Eddie said as he and Richard set out to scrape off the old paint and slap on the new, Louise keeping a close eye on the both of them.

“Be neat about it, boys, and there’ll be a fresh apple pie in it for dessert,” she said, finally walking back into the house. It took them the entire afternoon, three little steps and a handrail, but they did it.

“Not a bad job, if I say so myself,” Richard said, admiring their work.

Eddie and Richard not only did chores together, but they enjoyed mucking around too. Richard liked to take Eddie to a river channel near the sawmill where they would go fishing. He taught him how to bait a hook, something Tom would never do, and they’d catch one catfish after another. Pretty big ones too.

“Now you have to take it off the hook and clean it,” Richard would say, showing him how to go about the smelly deed, but Eddie never minded because Louise would always praise him for a job well done before cooking up the day’s catch for dinner that night.

“You’ll make someone a good provider one day,” she’d say. Eddie didn’t know what that meant, but he knew it was a compliment.

Richard also taught Eddie how to do magic tricks which he would perform for Louise after supper in the living room.

“Watch my hand carefully, Louise,” Eddie would say during his sleight of hand trick, but the penny would usually fall to the floor and roll under the couch. Louise always clapped anyway, but Eddie would perform the trick over and over again until he got it right. That was almost as much fun as stopping at the corner candy store after school to buy himself a lemon lollipop while Richard always preferred a jaw breaker.

"Want a lick of my lollipop?" he'd ask, slobbering all over it before shoving the yellow ball on a stick in Richard's face, prompting him to back away and give the same response every time.

"That's gross! I'm not licking anything you drooled on first!" he'd shout, grabbing Eddie by the collar and giving him a gentle shove down the sidewalk. It was all in good fun, and the two of them would sometimes laugh all the way home while eating their treats. That was also something new to Eddie. Laughing.

One Saturday afternoon, Richard took Eddie to a local baseball game.

"Get yourself a jacket," he told him. "You and I are going to walk over to the charity baseball game at the town diamond."

"Really? Just you and me, Richard?" Eddie was so excited he could hardly contain himself, never having been to a real baseball game before.

"Are we going to sit in the stands?" he asked.

"Where do you think we're going to sit, knucklehead?" Richard laughed. Sometimes Eddie was so simple that he just couldn't get mad at him.

Louise gave them each two dollars to get into the game and a sack of homemade shortbread cookies baked fresh that morning. "Come home directly when it's over," she instructed. "Supper will be on the table."

When the boys got there, they walked up into the stands, Richard telling Eddie to pick out the two best seats. It proved to be an exciting game. The crowd was boisterous, cheering loudly at every hit while Eddie joined in as he ate his shortbread cookies. He even caught a foul ball. When the game was over, Richard took him down to the dugout where he had the ball signed. It was the most thrilling day of Eddie's life, and he left the town diamond with something to show for it.

"I want to be a baseball player when I grow up," he commented as he and Richard walked home, throwing his ball up in the air and catching it before it hit the sidewalk.

"Try out for the team at school," Richard suggested. Eddie made a face.

"I don't have a glove," he said. "Oh well. It was just a thought." Eddie's mood was light and relaxed, and he didn't really mind not having a glove. He continued to throw his ball up in the air, satisfied with just having had such a fun afternoon with Richard, knowing deep down inside that he'll never be a baseball player when he grows up. But it was something new to dream about.

Eddie brought his baseball to the kitchen table the next morning, placing it down next to his glass of orange juice where he could easily admire it. Richard rolled his eyes and laughed, but not for long as Louise gave them both some good news.

"I understand you boys want to build a treehouse," she said, putting a plate of scrambled eggs and toast in front of each of them. Eddie's eyes lit up.

"We sure do!" he shouted, so excited that he knocked his baseball to the floor where it rolled behind the refrigerator. Richard laughed.

"It was really Eddie's idea," he said, giving credit where credit was due.

"Well, I've decided to let you build one, but there'll be a few rules." Eddie flew from his seat to retrieve the ball, returning quickly to give Louise his undivided attention.

"I'm listening, Louise," he said eagerly, sitting up straight in his chair, his hands folded, looking as though he would burst with excitement.

"At ease," Richard whispered as he leaned over toward Eddie, gently taking him by the collar. Eddie relaxed, letting out the deep breath he was holding. Richard then looked over at Louise and nodded. They were ready to listen. "Alright, Louise, what are the rules?"

"Well, Mr. Hewitt, the owner of the old sawmill on Decatur Road has agreed to supervise, so you'll have to listen to him. If the two of you are going to build a treehouse, then I'll want to know that it's safe. Tomorrow is Saturday and he'll be here bright and early."

"I can live with that," Richard said, grateful for the help.

"Then I can live with it too," Eddie nodded, but not without saying, "as long as he lets me hit nails with a hammer."

"Oh, I'm sure he will," Louise assured him while buttering her toast.

"I'm going to teach Richard how to hit nails with a hammer too," he added, nodding his head again. Louise smiled.

"Let her talk," Richard told Eddie, "I want to hear the rest of it."

"So do I," Eddie agreed. Richard let out a sigh.

"The next thing," Louise quickly interjected, clearing her throat, "is that the two of you will have to reimburse Mr. Hewitt for the nails and the lumber out of your own allowances."

"You mean he's going to charge us for that splintered, worn out scrap wood behind the sawmill?" Richard asked. "That's a gyp. He should be paying us for hauling it away. It's junk."

"Exactly," said Louise. "That's why I've asked him to sell you whatever new scrap he finds in his possession, sturdier scrap, at a discounted price of course."

"How discounted?" Richard asked.

"Yeah, how discounted?" Eddie mimicked before Richard could take him by the collar again to keep him quiet.

"Oh, I think you'll be pleased. How does a nickel a piece sound?" Louise asked, finishing her toast. Richard smiled.

"I think we can handle that," he said.

"Yeah, I think we can handle that," Eddie repeated, gulping down the rest of his orange juice.

"You're such a copycat," Richard whispered. Eddie made sure to open wide so that Richard could see the scrambled eggs he had just shoved into his mouth.

"Now, none of that!" Louise scolded. "Eat up and be off to school, the both of you, and leave that baseball behind, Eddie," she ordered. The two boys quickly finished their eggs and toast before Richard grabbed Eddie by the collar and pulled him out the door, headed for school. The treehouse Eddie had wanted would soon become a reality, and the best part was that he would get to build it with his own two hands right alongside his best buddy Richard. He could hardly contain himself, Louise actually calling the school that morning to warn that he'd be more excitable than usual that day.

"Please be patient with him," she requested. "He's thrilled over this treehouse project and I'm afraid you might find it difficult to curb his excitement today." She already knew Eddie all too well.

Over the next two weeks, Mr. Hewitt helped Eddie and Richard build their treehouse every day after school and on Saturdays. Eddie got to hit nails with a hammer, showing Richard how it was done, although he really didn't need the instruction, having been perfectly capable right from the start. The treehouse was grand with three windows and a sturdy ladder. Louise had no doubt that it was safe.

"Well now, boys, the nearest I can figure is that you owe me three dollars and fifty cents for both the lumber and the nails," Mr. Hewitt calculated, a toothpick wedged in his teeth. He gave Eddie a wink as the two boys gladly paid him, each digging into his own pocket for a dollar and seventy-five cents.

Eddie wasted no time in scrambling toward the ladder, but Richard grabbed him by the collar and pulled him back.

"Hold on there, kid," he started, "there's one more thing." It was then that Louise came out of the house with a cake topped with one lit candle, singing happy birthday to Eddie.

"It's my birthday!" he shouted. "I forgot! It's my birthday!" Eddie quickly blew out the candle and ran around the yard, jumping up and down.

"I figured you'd want to eat it in the new treehouse!" Louise laughingly shouted after him. Richard had disappeared into the house for plates and forks.

"Will you be eating it with us, Louise?" Eddie gushed, full of affection for his thoughtful caretaker.

"I will, dear, if you'd like me to." He took Louise by the elbow and walked her over to the tree where she handed Eddie's cake over to Mr. Hewitt before slowly climbing the sturdy ladder.

"Don't you worry, I'm right behind you!" Eddie called up to her as he began to climb. Richard followed with the plates and forks while Mr. Hewitt went up last, balancing the pretty cake with one hand. The four of them sat in the roomy treehouse and ate most of the double layered chocolate fudge confection, Eddie's favorite. It was the only birthday party he had ever been thrown, so it was no surprise that even on his special day there had been no word from home.

That night, right before bed, Eddie received his birthday presents from Louise and Richard—a leather baseball glove and a wooden bat carved with his initials.

"Use them in good health, dear!" Louise exclaimed as she wrapped up the rest of the chocolate fudge cake and put it in the refrigerator for the next day.

"Now you can try out for the team at school," Richard suggested again. "I'll help you practice. We can have a catch every day, and I'll pitch to you so that you get used to batting a ball. What do you say?"

"I say thank you!" Eddie shouted, throwing his arms around Richard's waist before squeezing him tightly.

"Don't get sloppy on me now," Richard said quietly, gently hugging Eddie back. "I'm glad you like your presents. I almost got you a checkers game, you know."

"I used to play checkers, but not anymore," Eddie said. "Checkers is for little kids." Clearly, he was ready to move on.

Everything the boys did brought them closer together as though they were really brothers, caring and protective of one another just the way family ought to be. Eddie felt safe with both Richard and the steadfast Louise, someone he now looked to as a mother. He was finally being cared for and loved for who he was, embraced by this new family even after having what were now only occasional outbursts. Most importantly, they listened to him and considered his feelings, just the way Dulcie used to do. But Eddie was living a good life without her and never wanted to leave the home where he now belonged.

At night, though, he would sometimes fear that his mother would one day come back for him. Let her try, he'd think to himself before closing his eyes, confident that Louise would never let him go. Unfortunately, Eddie was naïve in this regard and as the future unfolded, a happy ending to his story would remain elusive.

Chapter 8

While Eddie was living his best life in Baton Rouge, his father was about to tackle one of the greatest court cases of his career, his son's progress the furthest thing from his mind. Although the law firm of Chesterman, Hanson, Mink, and Biggs immersed itself primarily in corporate law, Daniel J. Biggs was a criminal lawyer by trade, giving his firm the range for which it was highly regarded. The Pallincot account may have raised the firm's profile and boosted its earnings by a wide margin, but a good criminal case always proved to be much more interesting to Dan Biggs than any corporate account could ever be, especially the one he was working on now. Case in point: the husband who allegedly murdered his wife.

Michael Kainor, the defendant, was a biochemist at the New England Treatment Laboratory, having worked there for fifteen years. A handsome and distinguished man of forty-five, he was married to his high school sweetheart, Elizabeth, and they lived in an upper middle-class neighborhood near the shore. He was renowned for his research on the treatment of heart disease, having been honored several times for his efforts, and sat on the Board of Directors of the Biochemistry Caucus and Seminar Association.

Michael Kainor's rise to prominence placed him in important and varied circles where he met other researchers from all over the world. His numerous work-related travels and lectures took him away from home often, allowing him to lavish the many women he encountered with food, drink, and a little pillow talk if they so desired. His wife would find out through the grapevine that he was behaving less than honorably when he was away, this to her smacking of intolerable conduct. Threatened with divorce he capitulated, promising her that he would never engage in such dalliances again.

Of course, that wasn't true, and he figured that what his wife didn't know wouldn't hurt her. So, Michael Kainor was careful to save his wandering eye for places far away and continued to enjoy himself, this time succeeding in his amorous pursuits while his wife was never the wiser.

Unfortunately, fate would play a cruel trick on her, a cheating husband the lesser evil, when she was diagnosed with advanced heart disease. Her chances of survival were minimal at best without a heart transplant, a new and delicate procedure that was uncommon and without significant history in the medical journals. How fortunate that it was the disease in which her husband was so well informed, treatments and procedures familiar to him, although she was so fragile that the least mistake in her care could be lethal. Of course, he knew this as well.

After Elizabeth Kainor's eventual massive heart attack, she was found at autopsy to have an acute amount of potassium chloride in her system, so abnormally elevated as to pique the interest of the medical examiner, bringing about a suspicion of either foul play or suicide.

Did Michael Kainor murder his sick wife by overdosing her with high amounts of potassium chloride, a known toxin to a severely diseased heart, or did she kill herself knowing that she was living on borrowed time, her life expectancy negligible? Prosecutors argued that it was the defendant who had both the motive and the means to kill his wife.

"The prosecution contends, your Honor, that Michael Kainor murdered his wife, having both the motive and the means. He was highly motivated to murder Elizabeth Kainor who constantly nagged him to put an end to his extramarital affairs, and who threatened him with divorce once she found out he was cheating on her. This he could never allow as his reputation would be sullied in court, Elizabeth Kainor certain to expose his various exploits with a number of women, possibly endangering both his job at the New England Treatment Laboratory and his membership on the Board of Directors of the Biochemistry Caucus and Seminar Association."

"He had fallen in love with at least two other women who are here today, and rendezvoused with countless others throughout his travels, but Elizabeth Kainor's efforts to prevent him from seeing these women were tireless, inasmuch as her physical and emotional strength would allow, thwarting the lifestyle to which he had grown accustomed."

"Michael Kainor felt as though he had an albatross around his neck, continually feeling the need to succumb to her demands because of her illness, but we contend that he no longer loved her and wanted her dead. He resented her for being sick which tethered him to their home for longer periods than he wished, keeping him from doing what he really wanted to do and that was to travel around to see his varied mistresses. He was disgusted by the sight of her, this woman who was once beautiful, but was now so ravaged by disease that he couldn't even look at her.

"No, Michael Kainor didn't even feel sorry for his wife, on the contrary he was repulsed by her. He no longer felt the need to be loyal to someone who he thought of as no more than a sickly creature who needed to be put out of her misery. She was cramping his style, a jagged pebble in his shoe who was causing discomfort and needed to be thrown far, far away so as to never get into his shoe again."

"Michael Kainor also had the means to murder his wife because he was a biochemist who had access to all kinds of drugs and other elements that would go into drug compounds. We know that Elizabeth Kainor died of potassium chloride toxicity, high levels of the mineral causing her to have a massive heart attack."

"Any biochemist would know that a patient with a diseased heart, especially one as fragile and barely functional as Elizabeth Kainor's, should never take high doses of potassium chloride without the specific consent or guidance of a doctor for fear that it would cause a massive heart attack, just as it did to Elizabeth Kainor. Her doctor assures us that he never gave any such consent, and had no knowledge of her use of the mineral that, in her case, would serve no purpose."

"The prosecution believes that Michael Kainor, due to his biochemistry background, was well aware of the deleterious effects high levels of potassium chloride would have on his wife, and purposely gave her a high dose of the mineral after obtaining it through the laboratory where he worked, knowing that it would kill her."

"The prosecution contends that on the day in question, Michael Kainor gave his wife an overdose of potassium chloride, having mixed it into a batch of chocolate pudding, Elizabeth Kainor's most tolerable form of nutrition during the last stages of her illness. He then went on a business trip that kept him away for twenty-four hours. When he left, his wife was alive but by the time he got home the next day, Elizabeth Kainor was dead, having had a massive heart attack overnight due to the high levels of potassium chloride in her system fed to her by Michael Kainor."

"It was significant that he served her the toxic pudding just minutes before leaving for his business trip, knowing she would die somewhere within the span of his twenty-four-hour absence, the perfect alibi. He would then come home to find her dead, thinking it would look like a natural occurrence to the police given her condition, a cardiac event expected to eventually happen anyway, but an unanticipated autopsy would foil what he thought to be the perfect murder. It was nothing less than cold and calculated. For these reasons, the prosecution asks for a guilty verdict."

The defense's opening statement was typical Dan Biggs, simple and brief. He proceeded to dispute the prosecution's accusation with a most reasonable line of defense, contending that suicide was more likely the cause of Elizabeth Kainor's unfortunate death. An extremely ill woman with no hope of recovery, her final act would be to end her own suffering in the absence of her husband so as not to upset him, one last gesture of love.

No, Michael Kainor was not at home at the time of his wife's death and, therefore, was incapable of murdering her. Dan would go on about Elizabeth Kainor's selfless act and the husband who grieved his loss, while the case would eventually evolve into something different for the defense, something unexpected, as new details and an unexpected witness would later emerge.

The prosecution called a number of witnesses to the stand at trial. Their first witness, Penny Morgan, was a secretary from Des Moines, Iowa who met the defendant when he toured the chemical plant where she worked. She was questioned about her relationship with the defendant and if he had ever brought up the subject of his wife.

"We were lovers for six months," she said. "He was unhappy at home and needed someone to quench his desires, if you know what I mean. He said his wife was a drag, a very sick woman who he hoped would die soon to put an end to both their suffering. He came to my apartment whenever he was in town. We'd go out to dinner and then wind up in bed. I saw him two, maybe three times a month. After a while, I started to really fall for the guy."

"I asked him to leave his wife and, you know, make a commitment. He said he'd do that soon, but that he had to take care of an issue at home first. He made it seem as though the issue was his wife. After that conversation I never heard from him again. I knew he hadn't gone back to his wife because all he ever tried to do was ditch her. I had to face the fact that he probably got himself another mistress, someone who wasn't pressuring him to make a commitment."

Their next witness, Jessica Ward, was a biochemist from Gary, Indiana where she and the defendant met at a biochemistry conference. She was questioned about her time spent with the defendant during the conference and if he had ever mentioned his wife.

"We met at a luncheon that the conference was sponsoring and wound up in a hotel room on his last night in town. I could tell he was a player. He talked about how he couldn't stand his wife," she said, "and that he would like nothing better than to be free of her. I told him he wasn't being very nice and that he shouldn't talk about his wife that way to a relative stranger. He said she wasn't long for this world anyway, having advanced heart disease, and asked me if we could meet again the following month. He said he'd come back to Gary to see me, and I told him that I didn't think it was such a good idea. The next morning, I gathered up my clothes and got out of there fast."

Their third witness, Sara Jessup, was a waitress in Washington, DC, much younger than the other two witnesses, just having graduated from college. She was asked how she knew the defendant and if he talked about his wife at all.

"He came into the restaurant where I worked, saying he was in DC on business. I thought he was cute, so I flirted with him but that was nothing unusual. I often flirted with patrons and usually got big tips out of it, but he flirted back in a big way, really coming on strong. He asked me if I'd like to meet him for a drink after my shift. I said yes and we went to a bar at the Tunxen Hotel, a real fancy place. We sat there and had a few drinks, and it wasn't too long before he put his hand up my skirt."

"I asked him if he was married and he admitted he was, but that he didn't love his wife anymore. He said she weighed him down, and that he hoped the illness she had would take her life soon. He said he didn't want to talk about her anymore, or even have to think about her. We took a room for the night and had sex until dawn. When I woke up a few hours later, I got dressed and left him there snoring. I know that over the next couple of months he came looking for me three or four times, but I made myself scarce."

An expert witness called by the prosecution was the medical examiner. He confirmed that Elizabeth Kainor had died from potassium chloride toxicity, high levels of the mineral causing her to have a massive heart attack.

"Yes, it was potassium chloride poisoning that killed her. When I did the autopsy, I found that Elizabeth Kainor had a significant case of hyperkalemia. This stopped her heart, remnants in the form of three empty potassium chloride capsule shells in her large intestine serving as tell-tale evidence that an intentional overdose caused the toxicity. Her serum potassium level was 12 milliequivalents per liter which is acutely high, the normal range being 5 to 5.5 milliequivalents per liter, causing her to have the massive heart attack."

"This high level of potassium weakened her muscles to the point of paralysis, rendering her incapable of summoning help. Her heart condition being what it was, the potassium overdose killed her within twenty-four hours of ingestion."

Following the medical examiner was the director of the New England Treatment Laboratory, Michael Kainor's boss. Only two questions were asked of the director, and he wasn't allowed to expand upon his answers. The prosecution simply wanted to know two things, and they got the answers they were looking for.

"Yes, we had quantities of potassium chloride shipped to the lab on a weekly basis and, yes, Michael Kainor had access to all of it."

The prosecution's final witness was Elizabeth Kainor's personal physician. He was an older gentleman who had known Elizabeth for twenty years. He defended his medical management of Elizabeth, potassium chloride never a part of his regimen.

"I never prescribed potassium chloride for Elizabeth Kainor. It would have been inadvisable, given her specific heart condition which was advanced beyond repair. Her kidneys were a factor in my decision as well, her latest bloodwork indicating that she was in the early stages of kidney disease. This can prevent the body from properly filtering out potassium chloride, allowing for a potentially dangerous buildup in the system. I would have never prescribed additional potassium on top of that."

The prosecution rested, certain that it had a tight case against Michael Kainor, proving beyond what they considered a reasonable doubt that the defendant despised his wife so much that he wished her dead to more than one paramour. In addition, he had access to the potassium chloride that killed her.

They were confident that the picture they had painted was convincing, portraying Elizabeth Kainor as the long suffering and pitiful wife who was victimized with a bowl of pudding by her callous husband, a villain who thought he could get away with the perfect murder. Furthermore, what seemed to be unassailable witness testimony depicted the defendant as a rogue, a decidedly unsympathetic character who would not be easy to defend. Dan Biggs had his work cut out for him.

The defense would call a number of witnesses to the stand as well, Dan Biggs scrubbing his suicide argument in light of new evidence that just might disarm the prosecution. He had hired a private investigator to sniff around and ask a lot of questions, the cunning sleuth traveling the country before hitting paydirt, granting him the sort of critical information he had been hoping to uncover. Attorney Biggs was now left to find just one final piece to the puzzle that would tie everything together with a pretty red bow.

One day before the trial began and quite surprisingly, Elizabeth Kainor's neighbor, a Mrs. Stanton, walked through the doors of Chesterman, Hanson, Mink, and Biggs to tell her side of the story. Yes, the private investigator had been sniffing around her as well, but she claimed to have seen nothing on the day before Mrs. Kainor was found dead, not sure if she should share her tittle-tattle with a gumshoe. On a certain level she was eager to get involved while on another she thought it best to hide her meddlesome nature.

After much thought, she reconciled her feelings and decided to come clean with Dan Biggs, the known lawyer on the case, and share what she had seen the day before Elizabeth Kainor was found dead in her bed of a potassium chloride overdose. He had finally found that one final piece to the puzzle or, rather, it had found him, becoming the ace up his sleeve. Mrs. Stanton was, indeed, that pretty red bow.

Dan Biggs's questioning of witnesses was initially swift and straightforward. For his first witness, he recalled the director of the New England Treatment Laboratory for cross examination.

"No, I have never found there to be potassium chloride missing from the laboratory. I know because we have strict protocols that keep an accounting of every drug that goes in and out of the lab. If we ever received anything extra, I knew about it. If anything ever went missing, I knew about that too. We have cameras based at every station in the lab, affording no one the opportunity to steal anything. No, I don't believe that the potassium chloride that killed Mrs. Kainor came from the New England Treatment Laboratory, especially given the fact that potassium chloride capsules aren't produced there."

"The potassium chloride that killed Mrs. Kainor came in capsule form, leaving remnants in the form of empty shells in her digestive tract, a common occurrence when taking capsules. Those types of capsules are typically produced for over-the-counter consumption and can easily be obtained by the consumer. At the New England Treatment Laboratory, we turn our potassium chloride into a liquid serum that is used for varied purposes throughout the medical field. It is not used to make capsules for over-the-counter consumption, nor is it obtainable through a pharmacy or any other type of store."

After the director had testified, Dan Biggs then recalled the medical examiner for cross examination as well.

"As I stated before, I found remnants in the form of three empty capsule shells in her large intestine. All of those shells were imprinted with the same lot number down the side, indicating that they were manufactured for over-the-counter consumption. I have no specific knowledge as to where they may have been produced or sold."

The next witness called to the stand was the Kainors' pharmacist, a witness for the defense, who would enlighten everyone as to the information the medical examiner couldn't provide.

"No, neither Mike nor Elizabeth Kainor ever purchased over-the-counter potassium chloride supplements from my pharmacy but even if they had, my inventory of supplements wouldn't have been the ones to kill her. In other words, the potassium chloride capsule shells found in Elizabeth Kainor's large intestine were from supplements produced and sold in a different state or region of the country. The lot number imprinted on their sides as reported by the medical examiner is an indication of that."

"Once over-the-counter dietary supplements are manufactured, they are sold in only specific states or regions so as to simplify any recall efforts, should they arise. The potassium chloride supplement ingested by Elizabeth Kainor was neither manufactured nor sold in this state. I'd have to do a quick look up in my catalogue to pinpoint its exact origin, but someone brought it into this area from somewhere else."

So far, so good. Dan Biggs was putting on a worthy defense and he was confident that his new approach was steering the jury in the right direction. He asked the court to allow a recall of the pharmacist the following day to testify further, and the judge readily agreed. At that time, he would prove that Michael Kainor didn't murder his wife.

The next morning, trial began at ten o'clock sharp. His adrenaline pumping, Dan Biggs first recalled one of the women who had been questioned by the prosecution, the youngest one in fact, Sara Jessup.

"Miss Jessup, where do you live?" he asked after taking in a deep breath.

"I live in Bethesda, Maryland," she confirmed.

"And where do you work?"

"I work at The Eatery Café in Washington, DC as a waitress."

"Is that all you do there? Waitress?" Dan asked, raising a brow.

"Yes, that's what they pay me for," she said flippantly. He liked her moxie.

"Is there anything else you do in the restaurant that they don't pay you for?" he probed with a smile.

"I don't think so." The waitress furrowed her brow, now wondering what Dan Biggs was up to.

"Are you sure?" he asked, giving her another chance to answer the question.

"Well, from time to time the chef in the kitchen asks me to make desserts for the dinner menu when I'm off shift. My desserts have a good reputation, people love them. Is that what you're referring to?" Miss Jessup hadn't considered this information to be relevant to the case.

"What kinds of desserts?" Dan asked.

"Everything. I make cakes, pies, cookies, you name it." Miss Jessup shifted in her seat.

"How about puddings? Have you ever made puddings?" asked the defense lawyer, knowing full well that she did.

"I make both butterscotch and chocolate pudding cakes for the dessert menu," answered the waitress.

"So, you know how to make pudding?" he asked, wanting to make sure.

"Yes, of course. You have to know how to make pudding if you want to make those kinds of cakes." What silly line of questioning was this anyway, she wondered?

"Has the chef in the kitchen ever asked you to make pudding so that the restaurant can sell it as simply pudding?" Dan probed further.

"Once in a while I'll make extra dark chocolate fudge pudding when I make a chocolate pudding cake, and that's put in containers and sold at the takeout counter. Customers seem to like it."

"So, people come into the restaurant, buy your dark chocolate fudge pudding at the takeout counter, and then take it out of the restaurant?" the lawyer inquired, wanting to verify what Miss Jessup had just said.

"Yes, that is correct," she affirmed.

"Has the restaurant sold a lot of your chocolate fudge pudding at the takeout counter?"

"When containers of my pudding are marketed at the takeout counter they usually sell out. Like I said, customers seem to like it." Dan was making great headway.

"So how many containers of the dark chocolate fudge pudding would you say have been sold at the takeout counter thus far, to the best of your knowledge?"

"I would say somewhere between twenty and thirty containers," the waitress confirmed. She was proud of her desserts and kept close tabs on them.

"And who works at the takeout counter?" Dan asked.

"I do, along with all the other waitresses on my shift. It's part of our waitressing duties. We take orders from customers, bring them their food, bus their tables, and take turns waiting on people at the takeout counter. It's a small restaurant, so our system works out well."

"Do you recognize any person in this courtroom as having purchased a container of your dark chocolate fudge pudding from the takeout counter at The Eatery Café in Washington, DC?" Dan inquired. His heart was racing. There was nothing like a good adrenaline rush in the courtroom.

"Yes, I do," the waitress said, once again shifting in her seat.

"You're doing fine, Miss Jessup," Dan said, sensing her discomfort. "Can you point out that person to the court?"

"Yes, that woman with the blue blouse sitting in the second row," said the young waitress, her lips quivering as she pointed her shaky finger.

"Let the record show, Your Honor, that the witness has just identified Jessica Ward, the biochemist from Gary, Indiana, as having purchased a container of dark chocolate fudge pudding from the takeout counter at The Eatery Café in Washington, DC."

"Duly noted, counselor," said the judge.

"Thank you, Miss Jessup. That will be all." The young waitress stepped down, her legs weak. She now understood the relevance of her desserts, especially the dark chocolate fudge pudding. The attorney's line of questioning hadn't been silly after all.

With the permission of the court Dan Biggs then recalled the Kainors' pharmacist. Having further information to divulge that was highly relevant to the legal proceeding, the pharmacist would be one of the most important witnesses in the courtroom that day besides Mrs. Stanton, the Kainors' neighbor who the defense was confident would break their case wide open.

"Can you once again tell me the significance of the lot number imprinted on the capsule shells found in Elizabeth Kainor's large intestine?" Dan asked.

"They indicate exactly where the capsules were manufactured and sold," the pharmacist repeated.

"Can you tell me then exactly where the capsules ingested by Elizabeth Kainor were manufactured?" Dan questioned, looking to pinpoint their origin.

"Yes, they were manufactured in Prince George's County, Maryland," the pharmacist confirmed.

"And where were they sold?" Dan continued.

"That lot was sold in the states of Delaware, Maryland, Virginia, and in Washington, DC." The pharmacist had clearly researched the matter in his catalogue, knowing he would be recalled to the witness stand.

"Thank you, that will be all." The pharmacist stepped down. The defense was almost there.

Dan Biggs finally called Mrs. Stanton to the stand. She was a middle-aged woman, a busy body who kept close tabs on everything that went on in her neighborhood. She knew everyone's comings and goings, a typical day having her walk from one window to the next where she watched the traffic, investigated slamming car doors, scrutinized people walking their dogs or mowing their lawns, and saw neighbors off to work and arriving back home again. Having lived next door to the Kainors for ten years, she was familiar with every intimate detail of both their lives, knowing that Elizabeth was gravely ill while Mike's business-related travels were numerous and extensive.

This appalled her, given his wife's condition. Now keen to tell her side of the story in court, assured that her snooping would bring Elizabeth Kainor's real killer to justice, Mrs. Stanton raised her right hand high and steady to take the oath and then sat in the witness box, her back ramrod straight. After giving her a glass of water, Dan Biggs proceeded.

"How long have you known the Kainors, Mrs. Stanton?" he asked.

"I've lived next door to them for ten years," said the nosey neighbor, now anxious to describe what she saw.

"Did you know that Elizabeth Kainor was very sick?"

"Oh, yes, it was general knowledge at our end of the street," she said, nodding her head.

"Did you know that Michael Kainor traveled extensively, leaving his wife home alone?" asked the confident attorney, knowing that Mrs. Stanton would be a wealth of exactly the kind of information he needed.

"Yes, I knew that," she said, her back still ramrod straight while her hands were folded in her lap.

"On the day before Elizabeth Kainor was discovered dead by her husband, did you see him leave their house?" Dan asked.

"Yes, I did, he left the house at eleven o'clock in the morning. I know the exact time because I had intentionally glanced up at my kitchen clock when I saw him leave." She was quite sure.

"Then what did you see?"

"I saw that woman over there come to the house at eleven fifteen, exactly fifteen minutes after Mr. Kainor had left." Thank goodness for nosey neighbors Dan thought to himself.

"Let the record show, Your Honor, that Mrs. Stanton has just identified Jessica Ward, the biochemist from Gary, Indiana, as someone she saw come to the Kainors' house at eleven fifteen, only fifteen minutes after the defendant had left the house."

"Duly noted, counselor," said the judge.

"And how did you know it was exactly eleven fifteen, Mrs. Stanton?" the attorney continued.

"I had glanced at the clock again. I like to know the exact times when people come and go. It's just a part of my nature," she admitted.

"Did she drive up in a car?"

"No, a yellow taxi dropped her off down on the corner which caught my eye." Mrs. Stanton was a gem.

"Why so?" Dan asked.

"Wouldn't a big yellow taxi catch your eye?" Laughter from the courtroom elicited a swift gavel and an order from the judge to be silent.

"Was the yellow taxi the only thing that caught your eye?" asked Dan Biggs, getting the testimony back on track, although he couldn't prevent a vague grin.

"No, it wasn't. I found it odd that she didn't have the taxi driver drop her off right at the house," said the observant neighbor. "She walked the rest of the way from the corner."

"Was she carrying anything with her when she walked up to the house?"

"Yes, she was carrying a pretty green bowl with flowers on it, covered with aluminum foil like it was some kind of food." Mrs. Stanton was a stickler for details.

"Did you see her leave the Kainors' house?" Dan asked.

"Yes, an hour later."

"So, twelve-fifteen?" he asked.

"Yes, it was exactly twelve-fifteen," said the neighbor who was relishing her role as a witness in court, a snoop's dream.

"Had you glanced up at your clock when you saw her leave?" Dan just wanted to make certain of this for the record, even though he knew she had.

"Yes, I glanced up at the kitchen clock again and saw that it was twelve-fifteen," she confirmed.

"Did she have the pretty green bowl with flowers on it with her?" the attorney continued.

"Yes, she was carrying it with her by her side."

"Did it still have the aluminum foil on top?"

"No, the aluminum foil was gone, and the bowl appeared to be empty. It looked as though it had been washed too." Dan could see that the jury was taking feverish notes.

"Was there a taxi waiting for her?" he asked.

"Down on the corner. I watched her get into it," the neighbor affirmed.

"Thank you, Mrs. Stanton, that will be all."

Dan Biggs then called the taxi driver to the stand who identified Jessica Ward as the woman he had dropped off on the corner of the Kainors' street at approximately eleven thirteen in the morning on the day in question, only to pick her up on that same corner at twelve seventeen in the early afternoon. He then brought her to a commuter parking lot three blocks away where he saw her get into a red Pontiac with Indiana plates. He still had his copy of her receipt, proving that he had picked her up at the commuter parking lot, dropped her off on the Kainors' street, picked her up on that same street an hour and four minutes later, and then brought her back to the commuter parking lot.

And yes, she had in her possession a pretty green bowl with flowers on it, covered with aluminum foil when he dropped her off, but uncovered and washed when he picked her up an hour and four minutes later, confirming Mrs. Stanton's testimony.

Now, there could only be one witness left. Dan Biggs recalled Jessica Ward to the stand.

"Miss Ward, were you in Washington, DC four months ago?" Dan asked.

"Yes, I was," she replied nervously.

"Why did you go to Washington, DC four months ago?"

"Because I knew Mike Kainor would be there on a trip with the Biochemistry Caucus and Seminar Association as a member of its board of directors," she stated.

"Why were you so interested in seeing Mike Kainor again?" asked the attorney, giving the witness his best quizzical expression. "According to your testimony you said, and I quote, '*I told him he wasn't being very nice and that he shouldn't talk about his wife like that to a relative stranger...asked me if we could meet again the following month...I told him that I didn't think it was such a good idea. The next morning, I gathered up my clothes and got out of there fast.*' You gave the unmistakable impression that you weren't too keen on seeing Mike Kainor ever again. What made you change your mind?" Dan furrowed his brow, feigning confusion.

"I found out that I was pregnant. I wanted to tell him that he needed to take responsibility, that maybe if he was so miserable with his wife he should make a commitment to me, now that I was carrying his child. I was scared to death of being alone," she admitted before shedding a single tear down one cheek. Dan gave her a tissue as Mike Kainor smirked.

"What did he say to that?"

"He said that he couldn't leave his wife or even think of making a commitment to me until she was dead. He said that maybe we could talk again the following week, that he'd be leaving home for an overnight business trip, and that maybe I could meet him at his hotel."

"You never met him there, did you, Miss Ward," Dan argued.

"No, I didn't. I knew he was just stringing me along." Jessica Ward blew her nose.

"After his rejection, did you buy potassium chloride supplement capsules from the Cherry Blossom Pharmacy in Washington, DC?"

"I don't recall," the witness stated, staring straight ahead.

"Remember you are still under oath, Miss Ward. A copy of the receipt from the day of your purchase in the record book of that very pharmacy tells me otherwise." Dan had forced her into a corner.

"I may have," she finally acknowledged, nodding her head.

"Did you then purchase a container of dark chocolate fudge pudding from the takeout counter at The Eatery Café in Washington, DC, Miss Ward?" the lawyer continued.

"Yes, I did," she replied.

"And did you mix the contents of the potassium chloride supplement capsules and the dark chocolate fudge pudding in a green bowl that you had also purchased in Washington, DC?" Dan asked, the walls now closing in on this witness just as he had planned.

"Yes, I did," she admitted, locking eyes with Michael Kainor for the first time. "When I emptied the contents of the potassium chloride capsules into the pudding earlier, three of them must have escaped me and wound up in the bowl without having been broken open, and that's why the empty shells were found in Elizabeth Kainor's large intestine."

"Did you then drive up north to the hometown of Mike and Elizabeth Kainor where you took a taxi to the Kainor household, presented the deadly mixture to Mrs. Kainor and then, having made sure she ingested it, left her there to die?"

"Yes, yes, yes. After leaving Washington, DC, I began to drive up north, biding my time, seeing the sites, so that I could coincide my arrival at Mike's house within minutes of his departure for his business trip the following week, knowing that my timing meant everything. I went to the Kainor home and knocked on the door. When Elizabeth answered, I told her that I was a colleague of Mike's from the New England Treatment Laboratory, and that he had asked me to check in on her in his absence. I told her of his concern that she was alone, and that he wanted me to make sure she was eating.

"When we were together at the biochemistry conference in Gary, Indiana, Mike had mentioned to me that chocolate pudding was all her stomach could tolerate as of late, so I presented her with the bowl of dark chocolate fudge pudding mixed with the contents of the potassium chloride capsules that I had packed with dry ice in the trunk of my car, telling her that Mike had requested I bring it to her, knowing she could eat it. He wanted her to keep her strength up, that he'd be home soon, I said, and that he loved her. I insisted that she get back into bed where she'd be more comfortable, and I watched her eat the entire bowl of pudding."

"You watched her eat the entire bowl of chocolate pudding mixed with potassium chloride?" Dan repeated, her deed so cold and calculated.

"Yes, I did," the witness confessed.

"Did she actually find the taste agreeable?"

"Being a biochemist, I knew that the taste of the potassium chloride I had mixed into the pudding would be too salty to tolerate, so I added a few ingredients of my own to tone that down and enhance the chocolate flavor before I even arrived."

"So, she ate it all on her own?" Dan confirmed.

"Yes, she did," Jessica Ward said. "Every last bit of it."

"Then what?" Dan lowered his voice for affect as the jury looked on in shock.

"I tucked her in, washed the bowl clean in the kitchen sink, and then left."

"Why did you do it, Miss Ward? Was it that you wanted Elizabeth Kainor out of the way so that Michael Kainor would marry you, or were you trying to frame him for rejecting you?" The prosecution, made speechless by this turn of events, remained silent. They would have their culprit, but it wouldn't be Michael Kainor. The trial was all but over.

"Both, I suppose," the witness continued willingly, having answered everything else. "I did want her out of the way because then maybe I'd be able to talk Mike into being with me, with his child. I never thought there would be an autopsy, but I also knew deep down that if there was an autopsy, he would be the one accused of killing her, given the timing of her death in relation to his departure and, of course, his biochemistry background. I figured he would be deserving of that, especially after what he had done to me, never thinking that I might get caught. As a matter of fact, I felt quite confident that I would get away with it. I was wrong about that wasn't I, Mr. Biggs?"

"A serious miscalculation on your part, Miss Ward. A serious miscalculation."

Jessica Ward wept bitterly as she was quickly escorted from the courtroom, her own legal battle having just begun. She had almost gotten away with it, but that day it would be Michael Kainor who was free to go, having been acquitted of all charges. He hadn't murdered his wife after all, although he was a scoundrel, nonetheless. Sauntering down the steps of the courthouse he lit a cigarette and whistled his way up the street, off to meet his next liaison in a dark gin mill where he wouldn't be recognized. As for Daniel J. Biggs, he would simply call it a good day and go home a winner, his scandalous client…now off the hook.

Chapter 9

On the afternoon that the trial ended, I came home from school to find my parents having a conversation in father's study. I sheepishly walked in to say hello, ever aware that he had placed that room off-limits to everyone a long time ago, even mother, unless he chose to extend one of his rare personal invitations to enter with a simple 'come', or just a wave of his hand if he felt like saying nothing at all. If he ever knew I had been in there, more than once, his wrath would have been sharp and swift. Mother had been home from the hospital for about a month and in that amount of time things around the house had changed drastically, Dulcie having moved into Eddie's bedroom as a permanent resident.

Mother had received strict instructions from her doctor to avoid stress and anxiety at all costs, so to my great surprise she didn't even argue with father when she came home to find Dulcie's suitcases in the room where she had intended to make herself a small office. Once again, she acquiesced, but this time father made some concessions of his own, giving her more of his attention, sharing with her the details of his work every day when he returned home, and providing her with a small desk in his study. Father was clever, all of this to both make mother feel like a real partner, and distract her from Dulcie's constant presence.

Of course, he continued to entrust her with the arrangement of his personal and professional social calendar which he was glad to do, no one able to handle that job better than mother. Giving her a little conversation at the end of the day and a small piece of his study was little recompense for all that she did for him, still it was always a shock to see the two of them in there, gossiping and clucking like two old familiar hens. I made my way unobtrusively over to a small couch and sat, tired from the day. They both glanced at me dismissively, but I stayed put and listened in, curious as to what they found so interesting on this particular day.

"So, you won the case because of the carelessness of a witness for the prosecution?" mother asked.

"Yes!" father said with glee. "She left clues up and down the eastern seaboard! Never underestimate the value of a good private investigator, Ellen. He's a lawyer's best friend."

"Oh, Dan, that's wonderful," mother gushed. "You must be thrilled."

"I am, I am," father answered while pouring himself a glass of sherry from the liquor cabinet behind his desk, "and this little bottle right here kept me focused until the end," he said, pulling a bottle of potassium chloride capsules from his jacket pocket.

"What on earth is that?" mother asked, the alarm in her voice obvious. "You weren't taking pills to stay awake in court, were you?"

"Of course not," father laughed, "don't be silly!" "These are potassium chloride capsules, just like the ones that killed Elizabeth Kainor. I bought these at the pharmacy before placing them on my desk at the office. I stared at that bottle every day; it was my inspiration to stay focused, to get to the bottom of things. The killer thought she was being quite clever when in reality every clue she left behind, and there were many, led me straight back to her. It's been a banner day, Ellen!"

"Your client must have been pleased, Dan," she said, beaming.

"He was. Now he can go back to living his life like the cad he is." Father smiled and shook his head before downing the rest of his sherry. Opening his top right-hand desk drawer he placed the bottle of potassium chloride capsules inside, probably right next to the gun that I had discovered without him knowing. I could hear the bullets rolling around when he opened and closed the drawer as I looked down at my feet, pretending to be disinterested, all the while wondering to myself just who he thought he was, calling another man a cad.

"Well, this calls for a celebration," mother said.

"Indeed. What do you have in mind?" Father was up for anything.

"How about if I plan a small luncheon at The Colonial Saddle Tavern early next week for all the partners and their wives, something intimate and informal," she replied, her wheels already spinning.

"That sounds just fine. I'll leave all the planning up to you, Ellen," he said. "Just let me know when to show up and make sure they have plenty of scotch on hand!" Father was in a good mood.

"Changing the subject," mother began, "I was delighted to have felt well enough to attend that get together between the Pallincot executives and your law firm at the Ocean Front Resort. Interesting people those executives, although I found their wives to be a bit snooty."

Father laughed. "No more than some of the women you associate with," father said, still smiling. "It's all a part of the game, my dear."

"I suppose it is, but did you see some of the outfits those women were wearing? I wouldn't be caught dead!" mother exclaimed, pushing a cigarette into her holder.

"No more garish than what their husbands were wearing. They all looked as though they had dressed for a luau in Hawaii." They both snickered while father reached for his lighter. "Should you be smoking again, Ellen?" father asked as he lit mother's cigarette.

"Probably not," she answered, taking a long drag, "but if you're asking me to plan a sizable dinner party, then I'll need to rely on the filthy habit to keep me calm." Mother was nonchalant about it, never giving her health a second thought, especially when she was feeling better. Father had no response, really not caring one way or the other. "Tom, dear," she said, deciding to acknowledge me, "did you have a good day at school?"

"I suppose so," I said, shrugging my shoulders. "What's for dinner?"

"I have no idea, that's Dulcie's job now. Wash your hands and meet us in the kitchen; we'll find out together. Coming, Dan?" Mother had more important things to think about than cooking dinner. She was father's partner now, a real partner, and had a small desk in his study to prove it. He kept her busy to distract her from his infidelity while she used him to gain more prominence in their social circles. But in this way, they worked well together and had a powerful partnership that even Dulcie couldn't destroy.

Taking full advantage of Dulcie's presence mother treated her like a servant, demanding that she satisfy her every want, need, and whim to the fullest. This was her personal brand of retribution in response to, yet, another major decision made by father without her approval. She told Dulcie that she had changed her mind about her living there, that she had consented to the permanent arrangement only because she needed the help, and that she would allow her to remain only if she followed her instructions to the letter.

Of course, none of that was true but by saying those things mother felt as though she had the upper hand, and if that's what it took to make her happy, then father was willing to play along. In the end, Dulcie was there because he placed her there, under his roof, where she'd essentially be at his beck and call too.

Sometimes, he'd feel badly about the way mother treated her, but he never said a word, it being essential that he remain in mother's good graces at all times. It was at night when all was quiet and mother had gone to bed that he'd make it up to Dulcie under the cover of darkness, stirring in me a deep inner rage that I could never suppress. He needed both of them, and he used both of them. I spied all of this through the lens of an adolescent boy, and like father's private investigator I had uncovered plenty of clues that confirmed what was going on in this undeniable house of deceit.

While mother had whole heartedly jumped back into the whirlwind of society, constantly planning her own events or attending one affair after another with father, I had gotten a job for a few hours after school two days a week as a grocery boy for Mr. Laskov at his small neighborhood supermarket.

I delivered phone-in orders and stocked shelves for three dollars an hour plus tips, not much of a salary, but I was only twelve, going on thirteen soon, and Mr. Laskov knew a good bargain when he saw one. Sometimes I made as much as twenty-five dollars a week, though, if my tips were exceptionally generous. He paid me in cash, and by the end of the week I had enough money to keep myself in candy and camera film for another week. Father insisted that I open up a savings account so that I could put some of my pay in the bank too.

"You'll be proud when you see your savings grow," he said, a fair point, although I was surprised that he had any inclination at all to give me financial advice.

I suppose the only reason father allowed me to take the job with Mr. Laskov in the first place was because he had known the old grocer for a long time, having played cards with him and other business owners from Kimball Avenue on many occasions. I guess you could call them friends and father respected him as a successful business owner who had a distinct wisdom that only comes with age.

Mr. Laskov belonged to the Chamber of Commerce as its vice president and now I was in his employ, witnessing first-hand the town politics and intrigue that many of its members would discuss with him when they visited his supermarket, the hub for town gossip, where everyone knew each other's business and the chatter was almost comical. This was much like the world mother and father lived in except these people paid dues which somehow made their brand of gossip more official.

"Always do a good job for him and do nothing to embarrass me," father said.

"I won't," I promised, father always worried about his reputation, probably the real reason he kept a finger on my job. I listened, though, and never did anything to shame him, not wanting to be sent away like Eddie. "I put ten dollars in the bank today, father."

"Good for you," he said, shuffling through some papers on his way into the study. Without even looking up he shut the door behind him, my signal to get lost.

I got used to my job quickly and actually enjoyed it. I now knew what it was like to have money of my own, taking as many pictures as I wanted because I could replace the film on payday. I briefly continued to photograph the usual interesting subjects outside like flowers, birds, and squirrels, but I soon found it more interesting to exclusively capture the comings and goings of people, learning right off that if I strung a number of photographs together. I could come up with a sort of storyline, almost like a television show, demonstrating what people were doing from beginning to end. Once or twice, I brought the camera to school, but for the most part I photographed father, mother, and Dulcie, usually without their knowledge. Some of the images revealing, I felt as though I could be one of father's private investigators, sneaky and undercover, but to whom would I present my case?

Still, my enthusiasm could never match the anger I felt over the interactions I caught on film between father and Dulcie. Nonetheless, I dated each photo, placing them all in my top dresser drawer with the others under my shirt, a neat little compilation that would blow the lid off of father's duplicity if they were ever discovered.

Dulcie continued to wait on mother every day, flying to her side in an instant whenever she was called, ready to meet her every demand whether it be frivolous or not. I snapped photos of Dulcie cooking and cleaning, but I also caught images of her rubbing mother's feet and lighting her cigarettes. These to me were demeaning requests, but in the end, it was Dulcie who had the last laugh.

I photographed her and father at all times of the day and night, their affection for one another obvious even to the casual observer, their smiles and glances easily giving it away. Maybe father attended fancy affairs with mother on his arm, but it was Dulcie who he came home to at night.

They would occasionally go into the attic and sit in the farthest shadowy corner, lit only by a moonbeam, and cover themselves in an old forgotten blanket. Their muted words were shamelessly affectionate as they kissed while I silently clicked away from the dark staircase at the other end of the attic so as not to be seen, my flash purposely turned off. Sometimes when mother would go into town they'd sit on the stone patio out back, casually sipping their coffee while openly flirting, the shade of the large tree gently swaying in the breeze along with the scent of lilacs perfuming the air making it all seem so civilized.

Father snuck in a kiss whenever he could, stroked her hair, and held her hand, all of it caught on film. Sometimes when mother would throw one of those pretentious luncheons at the house, and didn't need her to stick around, Dulcie would meet father at a restaurant a couple of towns away where they would sit for an intimate meal in a private corner, this according to the gossip I overheard at the supermarket. Biting my lip, I would carry on as though I had heard nothing, father's cheating old news to me. What about mother, though? Was she really that gullible?

One morning, I walked into my bedroom to find mother putting away a newly purchased set of socks in my top dresser drawer. I froze, afraid that she might find the damning photographs I had hidden under the shirt. Mother turned to look at me.

"Really Tom, how many times have I told you that shirts don't belong in the top drawer, they belong in the third drawer," she said, "her fingers fumbling around over the shirt as though she were about to pick it up."

"Dozens of times, mother," I said, springing over to the dresser after coming to my senses. I put a gentle hand on the shirt. "I'm sorry, I'll take care of it. You shouldn't have to move my clothes around."

"Well, please do," she said. "If your drawers are disorganized, you'll never find what you're looking for on the first try. Perhaps I should have Dulcie come in here and reorganize your dresser drawers from top to bottom, and your closet too," she said, having moved over to the closet before opening the door.

"No, you don't need to do that, mother. I put the shirt away in the top drawer by accident," I said, lowering my eyes. "It won't happen again." I tried to look as remorseful as possible.

"Remember Tom, you should be able to put your finger on anything you're looking for without even turning on a light." Mother was an expert at organizing more than just social events. Her best parenting advice always pertained to organizing something!

"I'll remember," I answered as I watched her walk out of the room with a sigh of relief. Poor mother. Poor naïve mother.

Now in my fourteenth year, I decided it was time to assert myself without whining, especially during my interactions with Dulcie. Mother's next attempt at throwing a dinner party for the Pallincot executives, father's law firm partners, and all their wives was well on its way to being a smashing success, Eddie no longer there to sabotage it.

A new set of china, father's gift to mother when she got out of the hospital, made for a pretty table and the same caterer took over our kitchen to prepare another spectacular eight-course meal. Dulcie asked me if I'd like to go out to dinner that night and maybe take in a movie afterward, but this time I refused.

"I'd rather stay home," I said, resentful not only of her relationship with my father, but her attempt to be with me as though she had done nothing wrong.

Things hadn't been the same between Dulcie and me for a while, ever since I had objected to her moving into Eddie's room for a couple of reasons, father's desire to have her permanently close to him the most obvious. We hadn't really talked in a long while, my stomach always twisted in knots whenever she came near, in part because of the affair, but also because I still adored her. I would dream of being in father's place, an adolescent boy's fantasy, but the anger caused by the pictures in my possession always had a way of snapping me out of it, even though I was unwilling as of yet to give up my covert photography.

Maybe it was time to step forward, rebuild our relationship, and come to terms. Always being angry at Dulcie made me tired and, besides, mother would eventually become suspicious of my negative behavior toward her, something I didn't want to have to explain, especially to mother. Regretting my knee-jerk reaction, I quickly came up with an alternative, realizing my foolishness in not agreeing to go out with her.

"What if we just take out some Chinese food and eat it up in the attic over a few games of checkers."

"That sounds fine to me," she said as we each wrote down on a single piece of paper what we wanted to order. "You'll have to go with me to pick it up."

"No, you go ahead," I contradicted, no longer willing to be told what to do. "I'll meet you in the attic." My knees were weak, having made my own decision.

"All right," Dulcie said, giving me an odd look, "I'll be right back."

"Be sure to get some duck sauce," I said with a faint smile, shyly attempting to break the ice. Asserting myself wouldn't always be easy.

Dulcie came back quickly and met me in the attic, the checkers game already set up. We ate on the floor and enjoyed our meal, sharing the lo mein and the pork fried rice, using wooden chop sticks.

"Thanks for remembering the duck sauce," I said with a restless sigh. I was clearly preoccupied.

"Sure, no problem," she answered, looking at me funny. "Do you have something on your mind?" If I didn't blurt it out now I never would, this being a good opportunity to take advantage of our privacy in the attic.

"I know about you and father," I said, looking her straight in the eye.

"We've had this conversation before. I'm here to help your mother out and that's all," Dulcie said emphatically.

"No, you don't understand," I started. "I've seen the flirting, the two of you kissing, father holding you, I've heard the gossip, I've even come up here and…" I stopped short, not wanting to admit that I had followed them into the attic.

"What are you talking about?" she asked, feigning innocence, a typical gut reaction I suppose after having been caught.

"Let's not play games. Like I said, I've seen it with my own two eyes," I repeated confidently, shoving the last bite of an eggroll into my mouth. Dulcie looked at me with a blank stare, processing a comeback. I had witnessed what she thought were private moments between her and my father or perhaps she didn't even care that the two of them had been seen, their tawdry behavior so bold and reckless as to deliberately invite scrutiny.

"I don't know what to say," she said, looking down at her feet.

"I do. Tell me that it'll stop," I answered. "Tell me that you'll tell father it's over because it's wrong and, most of all, it's unfair to mother…and me. Tell me those things."

"Does your mother know?" Dulcie asked anxiously, her eyes still studying her feet. Her question had enabled her to avoid telling me what I wanted to hear.

"I don't think so," I said, still waiting for a real response.

"Are you going to tell her?" she asked. Another question. She was only worried about herself, about being exposed, like nothing I had said even mattered. I was getting a little agitated.

"No, I'm not," I answered brusquely, insulted that she'd even think I might snitch. "Look, the only reason I brought all this up in the first place is because I want you to know why I've been so angry with you." Dulcie finally looked up at me. "So now you know. I don't want to be angry anymore, but father's betrayal, and yours, have been difficult for me to swallow." Now it was my turn to look down, my eyes getting a little teary.

"I'm so sorry," Dulcie said, "for anything you've seen or heard." She placed her hand on mine, but I pulled back immediately. Regaining my composure, I straightened my back.

"I want you to know that I'm letting go of my anger toward you for my own sake, but things between us will never be the same as they used to be until you cut my father loose," I said aloofly as though I no longer cared about her but, of course, nothing could be further from the truth. She looked away.

"Maybe I will," she said, the closest I'd get to the answer I wanted to hear, her voice trailing off as she stared out the window that looked onto the street. She fell silent and introspective.

"That would be best," I encouraged, but my gut told me she was giving me lip service, hoping I'd drop an embarrassing subject.

Being in the attic together after having had such an awkward conversation made it feel as though we were trapped like flies in a spider web, motionless, unable to get away. She remained silent, still staring out the window, giving me an opportunity to admire her brown curls and beautiful green eyes without being noticed. In that instant, Dulcie was mine again and I unashamedly gazed at her beauty, the matter of her and father gone from my mind for a fleeting moment. She suddenly turned her stare away from the window, leaving me no time to avert my eyes.

"Tell me what you're thinking," Dulcie said with a furrowed brow, finding my gaze curious.

"I'm thinking that I'd like to kill father," I said, embarrassed that I had been caught mooning over her. Dulcie now sensed that I had a crush on her. I could tell. She tried to giggle but it was halfhearted, both of us knowing that none of this was funny. "I really don't feel like talking anymore," I said after finally looking away from her. "Let's just play checkers."

We both sighed and began to play. It wasn't easy but I said what I had to say, having successfully asserted myself without whining. It sounded as though everyone downstairs was having a wonderful time at the dinner party, echoes of laughter wafting up into the attic. I looked toward the stairs and wondered how it was all coming off, and how everyone looked as they floated from room to room, drink in hand. Did mother and father present as the perfect couple to their guests? I suppose, in a way they were, given their arrangement.

I shook my head as I imagined the pretentiousness of it all, each wife trying to outshine all the others with a classy new dress and eloquent words that were usually no more than irrelevant and shallow utterances, while the husbands were in father's study, smoking cigars, drinking scotch and talking business. Dulcie looked toward the stairs too, perhaps for a different reason. Was she longing for father or wishing, perhaps, that she could be a guest at the party instead of having to contend with the angst of a boy like me? We wouldn't share our thoughts.

"King me," was all I could say in a somber tone, nothing else left to talk about. We remained in the attic and played checkers, slipping back downstairs only after it had gotten quiet. Without looking at each other, we said a quick goodnight before retreating into our own bedrooms, finally closing our doors on what had been a difficult evening. I lay awake pondering our exchange, the words tumbling around my brain like clothes in a dryer. Was Dulcie doing the same? Only tomorrow would tell the impact of our candid discussion.

The next morning when I went downstairs for breakfast, mother was lounging on the couch in the living room, still wearing her robe and slippers while smoking a cigarette.

"How was your dinner party last night, mother?" I asked, after having grabbed a piece of leftover cheesecake from the kitchen.

"It was marvelous, Tom," mother beamed, obviously quite pleased with herself. "It couldn't have gone any better." She stretched and ran her fingers through her hair before taking a long drag on her cigarette.

"You ought to rest today, mother," I said. "You've been working hard ever since you got home from the hospital. Not only must you slow down but you should stop smoking too. It's no good for you mother," I pleaded, "given your heart condition."

"I'm on top of the world this morning, Tom. Don't spoil it for mother," she said, pouting at me. "Be a dear and get me another cup of coffee. Dulcie doesn't seem to be up yet."

As I went into the kitchen to pour mother's coffee, I could hear father walking into the living room where he greeted mother with a morning kiss on the cheek and a thank you for last night.

"That was one of the best dinner parties you've ever thrown, Ellen," he beamed. "Everyone was quite impressed. You really outdid yourself." Father picked up the newspaper off the coffee table and sat down in a chair opposite mother to read.

"Thank you, Dan. It was a job well done if I do say so myself," she replied, putting her cigarette out in the ashtray.

"Here's your coffee mother," I said, carefully handing her the cup I had brought from the kitchen. Father never lowered his newspaper.

"Would you like a cup of coffee too, father?" I offered.

"That would be fine, Tom," he answered coldly, never showing his face. There were times when father could be more distant than usual.

I brought his coffee into the living room and placed it down on the end table next to his chair. Not waiting for a thank you, I turned to leave the room when mother suddenly asked me where I was going, a rare show of interest in what I was doing.

"I thought I'd ride my bike down to the bait and tackle shop on the cove. I have a few bucks left over this week and I need some hooks," I answered, wondering why mother had asked.

"Well, before you go, please take a picture of your father and me sitting on the couch with that camera of yours," she requested. I was surprised. Mother didn't usually like being photographed, especially since her return from the hospital. Whenever I took a picture of her she'd shoo me away, but not before looking at the developed image, of course.

"Oh, come now, Ellen, why would you ever want to do that?" father asked. "Let the boy go," he said over the top of his newspaper.

"It will commemorate a successful dinner party, Dan! Look at the two of us, sitting around the next morning, basking in the glory of our triumph. We need to mark the occasion. Come, sit here close to me," mother said flirtatiously, patting the couch.

"For heaven's sake, Ellen, I'm in my bathrobe," father protested, reluctantly putting his newspaper down before sitting on the couch next to his wife.

"No matter," she said, "Tom will take a close up shot, won't you, dear?"

"Sure, if you'd like," I answered with a smile, secretly gratified to see father so perturbed.

"Besides, it was your triumph, not mine," he reminded mother. "I simply took advantage of it." Father let loose a sly smile.

"Spoken like a true lawyer," she laughed, linking her arm in his.

Before father could change his mind, I quickly ran up to my bedroom and grabbed the camera off my desk. Halfway down the hall, I could hear Dulcie's bedroom door open.

"What's the big hurry?" she called after me, yawning and rubbing her eyes.

"I'm taking a photograph of my parents," I said breathlessly over my shoulder before quickly running back downstairs to the living room, having barely looked at her.

Father and mother were still sitting on the couch next to each other, poised to have their photo taken. He had his arm around her, ready to smile at my command, while I stood in front of them.

"Okay, are you ready?" I asked.

"Oh no," mother said to father, "I don't want a photo of us with your arm around me. I want a photo of us doing this," she directed, planting a kiss on his lips, long enough for me to snap the photo.

I handed the photograph over to mother after it slid out of my camera, the image having yet to appear. She gently waved it in the air while awaiting its development.

"That was quite a kiss, Dan," she said coyly as a compliment to father while he stood there and watched her, curious as to how the photo would turn out.

"You're still the best kisser in town," he said, returning her compliment as he nuzzled her cheek. Mother giggled and pushed him away.

After the photograph had fully developed, even father was pleased with the image that had emerged, a beautiful portrayal of the two of them kissing on the couch. The sunlight streaming in through the front window gave it an ethereal touch, a romantic aura that mother adored.

"Oh, I'm going to frame this and put it on my desk in the study," she said breathlessly, unable to take her eyes off the photo.

"It sure is nice," father said which I took as an indirect compliment, the most praise I'd gotten from him in a long time.

Just then, Dulcie walked into the living room. Father discreetly excused himself while mother continued to admire the photograph.

"Would you like me to make you breakfast, Mrs. Biggs?" she asked.

"Look, a photograph of my husband and me," mother said, practically shoving it under Dulcie's nose. "Isn't it beautiful?" she asked.

"It is, it really is, Mrs. Biggs," said Dulcie, studying the photo before awkwardly looking at me.

"I want you to go out today and buy a small frame for it," mother instructed. "Maybe one day you'll be as lucky as I am," she said in a condescending tone, "but for now all you can do is dream, you poor thing." Mother ran her fingers through her hair again before asking Dulcie for another cup of coffee. "Oh, and dear, I'd like my eggs scrambled soft."

Chapter 10

If father and Dulcie were still carrying on, they were being more discreet about it. My eyes and ears were open as usual, my camera always at the ready, but there wasn't much to look at after my candid discussion with Dulcie in the attic. At least she knew that I had seen them and wasn't naïve to their affair. I hoped she would come to realize, too, that if I had spied so many of their affectionate moments while having gone undetected, then it was probable that mother would eventually spot them as well. How she hadn't caught them by now was a mystery to me.

Over the following months I would set two main goals for myself. The first was to poke around father's study as much as possible. This I found exhilarating, perhaps because there was always the chance of getting caught. He conveniently left his desk unlocked and often unattended, probably figuring that it was safe from prying eyes. The fact was that father deemed his study inviolable, having placed it off-limits to all of us years ago, but I no longer cared about its sanctity, given that he had broken a few rules of his own…with Dulcie.

Shuffling through his papers and snooping inside his desk drawers were now my obsession. On top of his desk, he had an inbox and an outbox, the first containing papers he hadn't read yet, the second comprised of documents that were ready to go back to the office, the court, or a client. When I was sure that everyone would be out of the house for a while, I'd eagerly read the papers in both boxes, drinking in every bit of confidential information, a clear glimpse into father's latest legal pursuits.

After that I'd look through the drawers, knowing that I'd see his gun again, the cartridges rolling around like marbles, and the bottle of potassium chloride capsules he had more recently stored. No matter how many times I saw those frightful objects, the hair on the back of my neck would stand on end as if each instance were my first, a sudden spike of adrenaline causing my heart to beat uncontrollably for what seemed an eternity.

There were other things, too, that fascinated me like his checkbook and bank statements. I read through his finances with great interest, noticing that he paid Dulcie three hundred dollars a month as live-in help while he gave mother five thousand dollars in cash the day before she took Eddie away. I knew that had to mean something. But what? Less serious in nature was the drawer he kept filled with chocolate bars which I dare not touch for fear he would figure out that I had been in there.

In any case, I was always careful to leave the top of his desk and its drawers the way I found them so as not to raise any suspicions, especially if I photographed something of interest like a juicy court case. He had no idea that I was so aware of what was going on in his life, both professionally and personally. I became fixated on knowing his business, fascinated by everything I found, his activities always reading like a dime store novel. What's more, mother's desk was now in father's study as well and, as far as I was concerned, it was fair game.

Mother's desk was usually far less interesting though, but I remained hopeful that it would one day give me the information I needed to achieve my second goal, and that was to find Eddie. Where was he? Damned if I knew, the desk having yet to divulge how mother pulled off her underhanded deed while her lips remained sealed, although I had a hunch that I'd find evidence leading to Eddie's whereabouts in the top drawer, if only I were able to open it. She was smarter than father in that regard, not to assume that her desk would remain private, safeguarding her best kept secret under lock and key.

The other drawers remained unlocked, however, containing items that were far less consequential such as stationary, an address book of friends and acquaintances, and catering menus, among other things, but it was that top drawer that was of particular interest to me. Undeterred, I wasn't afraid to approach mother, choosing my times wisely as I looked for answers that the desk had yet to reveal.

"Mother, where is Eddie?" I asked one morning as she sat on the patio, reading her favorite news rag, The Baton Rouge Cable, while drinking a cup of coffee. Her answer was just as I expected, unwavering in its simplicity, short and to the point.

“He’s gone, Tom,” she said in a calm almost blasé tone of voice, this her usual reply as though she had no other answer to give, but I knew better. Of course, she knew where Eddie was, but continued in her refusal to tell me. I pressed on.

“Why won’t you tell me, mother?” I asked. “I want to know where my brother is!”

“It would do you no good,” she said, “and it would do Eddie no good either. Let it go, Tom. Just let it go,” she repeated calmly without even looking up from her paper.

“But I want to see my brother,” I persisted.

“Impossible,” she said before turning a page, her eyes never straying from the newsprint.

“Mother, where is Eddie?” I asked one more time.

“He’s gone, Tom,” she repeated. Our conversation had gone full circle and for now would go no further. I continued to chip away at mother whenever I could, but at this point I had a better chance of learning Eddie’s whereabouts if I were to pry open her top desk drawer.

One day, I walked into my bedroom to find Dulcie putting away a set of clean socks and underwear in the top dresser drawer. It startled me.

“What are you doing?” I asked with alarm, thinking only of the photographs underneath the shirt I had yet to remove at mother’s request.

“Just putting away your clean laundry,” she said, sounding unsure as to why I was so surprised.

“You don’t have to do that,” I said to Dulcie, “just leave the clean clothes on my bed.”

“If that’s what you want,” she said. “You know, shirts belong in the third drawer.” She closed the top drawer and looked at me long and hard as though she had something on her mind.

“Yeah, so I’ve been told by mother,” I said with a smirk. “I’ll take care of it.”

Dulcie left my bedroom without saying another word, perhaps still feeling a little awkward after our last discussion in the attic. I quickly closed my bedroom door and ran over to my dresser, opening the top drawer again. It didn’t appear that my shirt had been moved and when I lifted it off the photographs, they seemed to be untouched and in the same order in which I had left them.

It was clear to me that they were no longer safe in the dresser, my room not as private as I had thought. I gathered all the photos from underneath the shirt, clear indications of my intrusion into father's business, and shoved them under my mattress for now with the intention of relocating them to the treehouse when the time was right.

Dulcie continued to be at mother's beck and call, performing the most menial of tasks, while mother continued to work for father, planning, scheduling, and kowtowing. Every morning, after he had gone to the office and she had finished her first cup of coffee, mother would retreat into father's study and sit at her desk. On a typical day, she would write letters, extend invitations, talk on the phone, and make reservations, all the while smoking one cigarette after another.

"Dulcie, see that these letters get to the post office before noon," she'd say, then pick up the dry cleaning and do the marketing. "I've left you a list on the kitchen table," mother would order, leaving no doubt as to who was in charge of the household. "And I need a light for my cigarette, dear," she'd say, her holder dangling from her lips.

"Yes, Mrs. Biggs, I'll get it all done," Dulcie would say, lighting mother's cigarette without receiving so much as a thank you. I had it on reliable gossip overheard at Mr. Laskov's supermarket, though, that these were the times when Dulcie would visit father at his law office under one pretense or another. I found it hard to believe that his partners weren't aware of what was going on.

When no one was around to watch me, I retrieved all of the photographs from under my mattress, stuffed them into an inside jacket pocket, and brought them up into the treehouse. I kept a lock box up there with other personal items, such as a pocketknife that a friend at school had traded me for a set of old comic books; a couple of impressive pieces of sea glass; five or six unusable foreign coins; a few pretty rocks; and a rodent skeleton I had discovered in the garage under the car.

This is where the tawdry photos would go, with the rest of my private belongings, locked up and inaccessible just like whatever lay in mother's top desk drawer. It was a relief that they were gone from my dresser and safely hidden elsewhere, making me a full-time player in this house of deceit, just as guilty of duplicity as Dulcie and father. My snooping and sneaking around, always careful to cover my tracks, was proof of that.

One late Saturday afternoon, while mother and father were at a party and Dulcie was out shopping, I went into father's study with my camera to see what I could see, this time intending to pry open mother's top desk drawer with a nail file I had found in the bathroom. I went to father's desk first, though, on the pretense of looking for something new, although that wasn't the real reason. I must admit that I liked it when the hair on the back of my neck stood on end and the sudden spike of adrenaline caused my heart to race uncontrollably whenever I saw the gun, the cartridges, and the bottle of potassium chloride capsules, making my snooping all the more exhilarating.

I opened the top right-hand drawer and was duly jarred before studying the lines of the gun more intently and watching the cartridges roll around more closely, even picking one up and examining the brass sheen of its outer shell, a bold departure from my usual routine. I placed the cartridge back in the drawer and picked up the bottle of potassium chloride capsules, reading every word, direction, and warning on the label. I even opened the bottle to see what they looked like, my curiosity never having been so acute.

After putting the bottle back down next to the gun, I opened up the drawer with father's bank statements, picking up all of them in a single grab while exhaling a sigh of boredom, having previously seen them. For the sake of thoroughness, I shuffled through them once again, this time feeling as though I were wasting precious minutes, never knowing when Dulcie or my parents might come home to discover my intrusion.

As I got to the bottom of the pile, I uncovered two pieces of stationary, one yellow and the other blue, that had been intentionally buried so as not to be seen. To my shock they were both love letters, one written by Dulcie, the other by father. I had hit pay dirt, unexpectedly finding further indications of father's infidelity underneath the most boring of documents in his desk.

I placed both letters on top of the desk with the intention of photographing each of them right away, but I couldn't help but read them first, too impatient to wait, my curiosity getting the best of me. I had been jarred once again, my heart pounding out of my chest, my hands trembling, but this time it wasn't because of the gun. Just when I thought that nothing could be juicier than some of the photographs I had taken, or the gossip about Dulcie and father I had overheard at Mr. Laskov's supermarket, these letters found their way into my hands.

I pushed aside the images in my head of father beating me for having found them, took in a deep breath, and steadied myself, now ready to pour over the scandalous words certainly never meant for my eyes. I only wondered why father hadn't yet given Dulcie the letter he wrote, but I would look at hers first, eager to read of her romantic feelings for him, the adult side of her that she never shared with me.

Dear Dan,

I know that I promised you we'd be together forever, but I should have never made such a promise. I no longer think it's such a good idea. I love you, that's never going to change, and I know you love me too, but you have a family that needs you. Your wife works diligently for you every day while your son is of an impressionable age. He needs a father to help him sort things out and speak to him, which you rarely do. Of course, I still feel pangs of guilt whenever I think of poor Eddie who would have never gone into such a rage the day of the dinner party if I had only been there. I know I was sick, but that wasn't Eddie's fault.

I can't have these things on my conscience any longer. I think I should look for another job soon, but it may take some time. Please know that if you didn't have other obligations, I wouldn't even be writing this letter, but you are already spoken for and because of that, it's high time we realize that our relationship could never work out in the end. I will not and cannot be the one to break up your marriage. I hope you understand. I'll always love you.

Dulcie

I couldn't believe it. Dulcie was taking the high road. Perhaps the candid discussion we had in the attic made all the difference. She was thinking of mother, Eddie, and me when she wrote those words, making me love her all the more. She was obviously trying to do the right thing, but would father be as virtuous? I took a quick snapshot of her letter and pushed it aside, giving my full attention now to father's letter.

Dearest Dulcie,

I cannot believe that you would break off our relationship. I love you more than I've ever loved anyone, including my wife. Don't you ever worry about her or my son. I'll always take care of them but it's you that I want. I can't imagine living a single day without seeing you, holding you, kissing you. What happened to Eddie was not your fault. It was bound to happen sooner or later, so if it didn't happen on that day, it would have happened on another, whether you were there or not.

Please don't leave me. Let me take care of you for the rest of your life and I promise you that it will be a happy one. You'll always live in this house with me, and you'll never want for anything. If I could give you the stars I would but for now please just take me as I am, the man who loves you and kisses you most tenderly. If you insist upon leaving me, then I will...

No wonder father's response to Dulcie was still in his possession. He hadn't finished it yet. I took a snapshot of that letter too and quickly put both pieces of stationary back where I had found them, at the bottom of the pile of father's bank statements which I quickly shoved back into his desk drawer. My breathing became a little easier and my hands shook a little less, but I couldn't wait to get the hell out of father's study, still staggered after having found his affair with Dulcie documented on paper. It was more hard evidence, as father would say, my photographs of the two of them together no longer the only proof.

Grabbing the newest snapshots off the top of the desk, I quickly left the study and ran straight up to my bedroom. Prying open mother's top desk drawer would have to wait for another day, my discovery of the letters enough to satisfy my snooping for now. Besides, it was getting late, and I was sure that Dulcie and my parents would be home soon. Throwing on a jacket, I ran back downstairs and out into the yard where I climbed up to the treehouse, finishing the business I had started before it got too dark to see what I was doing.

I wouldn't feel safe until my images of the incriminating love letters were under lock and key with my other photographic evidence of father's philandering. What did he intend to do if she did, in fact, leave him? This I couldn't even guess, given that his letter was unfinished, leaving his plan unwritten. I scrambled down from the treehouse, unable to think about it any further, and ran back inside. The twilight told me it was nearly dinner time, and I would be sitting at the kitchen table waiting patiently, like a good boy.

The next morning, I woke up to the sounds of loud arguing coming from the driveway. I jumped out of bed and went to my window to see Dulcie and father embroiled in a heated discussion. Father grabbed her arm, but she wriggled out of his grip, storming back into the house and slamming the door behind her. Father jumped into his car and sped away, tires screeching. Damn it! He had been trying to bend her to his will. I was furious at father. How dare he? It wasn't a great way to wake up, the day getting off to a bad start. It was eight fifteen.

I quickly got dressed and ran downstairs, not only to subtly find out what was going on, but to also grab a couple of pieces of fried chicken and a hunk of apple pie leftover from the night before. It was a beautiful Saturday morning and I intended to walk down Kimball Avenue to the town green, a good place to sit under a tree with a picnic lunch while studying for Monday's history test. Right now, though, my stomach was in a knot. Damn that father. When I got downstairs, I found Dulcie throwing some chicken and pie into a paper bag for a picnic of her own. I would have to be discreet.

"Where is mother?" I asked nonchalantly, trying not to show the agitation I felt toward father.

"Off to a charity bizarre somewhere down the center," Dulcie said angrily. "I offered to make her breakfast, but she grabbed some leftover chicken and threw it into the picnic basket along with a couple of pieces of pie and a bottle of wine. She said that she and the other organizer of the bizarre would eat an early lunch before the event started. Now there's a meaningful life for you," she said in a mocking tone, the first time I ever heard Dulcie use sarcasm in mention of mother.

"Well, then good thing you made a lot of fried chicken last night," I said, in an attempt to lighten the mood, but Dulcie was having none of it, giving me a dirty look, which was out of character for her. "Where is father?" I asked, pushing her patience.

"Down at the office," she spat, her fury emanating from every pore. She was in a full-blown rage.

"Where are you going?" I asked, this time sure she would explode.

"You're full of questions this morning, aren't you?" she snapped.

"I was just wondering," I said, innocently shrugging my shoulders.

"I'm going down to the beach. I need to be alone. I have a lot to think about," she said, snatching her paper bag of fried chicken and pie off the kitchen table before storming out the door, not even asking me about my own plans.

Dulcie got into her car and left in a hurry, not knowing that I had seen and heard what had happened in the driveway earlier. When I was sure she was gone I ran into father's study to swipe some change from a large jar under his desk. He'd never miss it, the jar practically overflowing with coins. Everyone was gone and the house was eerily silent, father's study, for the first time, actually giving me the creeps.

Having gotten what I needed, I ran back into the kitchen and took the last three pieces of fried chicken and a large hunk of apple pie, wrapped them tightly in aluminum foil, and placed them in my school lunch bag among other things. Grabbing my history book and the notes I had taken in class the day before, I headed out of the house toward Kimball Avenue. It was nine o'clock.

It was good to breathe in the fresh air as I walked, trying to sort out in my mind what had happened that morning. I was so angry with father, not only because I had witnessed his earlier treatment, Dulcie, but also because it had caused her to become furious, leaving the house in an uncharacteristic fit of bad temper. It was a real lovers spat. Every time I thought about it, I could feel the blood rush to my face and the hair on the back of my neck stand on end as though I were looking at the gun.

I was getting close to the town green, father's office only a stone's throw away, while mother was at her charity bizarre somewhere nearby and Dulcie was at the beach only a mile down the road. The way I saw it, none of us ever strayed too far from one another and the dysfunctional family mess in which we found ourselves, none of us except Eddie.

***

Dan Biggs sat at his desk, shuffling through papers and taking notes. The Pallincot account was always a challenge, but Chesterman, Hanson, Mink, and Biggs was raking in a substantial amount of money because of it. Of course, he was still riding high from winning an acquittal at Michael Kainor's murder trial, a high-profile case that shined a light on both the firm and him personally.

Indeed, everything was going incredibly well for Attorney Biggs, due in great measure to his diligence, the office his fortress where he spent many a day and night grappling with legal issues until they were resolved to his satisfaction. This to him was more important than his wife and children, but lately he was feeling that it could never be more important than Dulcie.

Once he got to his office, he would usually forget about his problems at home but today he couldn't help but agonize over what had happened that morning, this distracting him from his work. He lay down his pen and hung his head, rubbing his eyes in an attempt to get Dulcie off his mind. He had embarrassed himself. He shouldn't have grabbed her the way he did. Would she ever agree to stay with him after that? She had to stay, he needed her to stay. If she insisted upon leaving him then he would…

Dan's thoughts were interrupted by the opening of the squeaky door to the outer office. He had meant to get that fixed a long time ago but, perhaps, it served him well today because he was there to work, not to think about Dulcie, and the squeaky door snapped him out of his haunting personal dilemma.

"Hello? Who's out there?" Dan asked. "Oh, hello, I didn't expect to see you here this afternoon," he said, waving the person into his office. "Is that food from home? I was going to order out in a few minutes. Put it right there on my desk," he directed, moving a large stack of papers out of the way. "Leftover fried chicken and apple pie is fine with me," he said stoically. "I'm starving, so you've come at just the right time. How did you know?" He tried to force a smile, feeling unusually vulnerable.

Looking at his visitor, Dan got up and came out from behind his desk, moving a couple of chairs over to a table in front of the window overlooking Kimball Avenue. Just as they were about to sit down the phone rang, requiring that he go back behind his desk.

"Hello. Oh, hello, Mink. Yes, I've been working on it all morning. As a matter of fact, I should be finished with it by two o'clock. I'm about to take a lunch break with…yes, yes, I understand. It will be ready on time; don't you worry about that. Sure, you can come by and pick it up at two. If I'm not here, it means I've already gone home. Well, I'm about to eat lunch with…what's that? Sure, I can look into that too. I have no doubt this will turn out in our favor. I've got some fried chicken waiting for me, so goodbye for now, Mink," Dan said, hanging up the phone quickly before his law partner and friend, Andrew Mink, could so much as utter another word.

Dan stood up again from his chair, but his eyes were drawn to the scattered papers on his desk, causing him to become absentmindedly sidetracked. The Pallincot account was multi-dimensional. He was preparing for an important meeting with a group of investors who were interested in backing Pallincot. Dan was in charge of teasing out the legal aspects of their investment and if he could entice them with assurances of a substantial financial gain, then Pallincot would stand to bring in enough money to expand the company even further, transforming it from a regional operation into a national one.

Besides the Michael Kainor murder trial, this was probably the most important order of legal business to cross his desk in months, all the rest having been mundane in comparison. By force of habit, he began to read one of the papers, becoming lost in its content, his visitor now feeling ignored. This was no surprise because he often ignored people, sometimes deliberately, at other times unintentionally, a bad habit that had manifested itself both at work and at home. Anyone who knew him had been subjected to it at least once, and for those who lived with him, more than that.

"Excuse me, are you finished?" asked his visitor, taking off a pair of white gloves and stuffing them into a pocket.

"I'm sorry, let's eat," Dan said, looking up from the paper. "Wait a minute, what are you doing? What the hell do you think you're doing?" he asked before walking around to the front of his desk. "Did you take that from my study? Put it down, let's talk. Nothing is so bad that we can't talk," he said, slowly reaching out his hand. "Wait," he blurted out, looking toward the door. "What are you doing here? What the hell is happening? Please don't, please…"

Dan found himself at the other end of his own gun, the barrel pointed straight at his chest, while at the same time his lunch companion had been interrupted by someone else. Two shots were fired, one bullet to the chest killing Dan instantly while another became lodged in the ceiling above his head only after a struggle for the gun had ensued.

The two callers, one a killer, the other not, glared at each other with icy stares before one of them would let go of the gun and back away, fleeing the office only after grabbing a piece of apple pie with an eager hand. Still tightly holding the grip of the gun, the other would indifferently watch the person make off with the pie before coldly turning back to the victim who lie crumpled on the floor.

"I'd stay for lunch, but you appear to be indisposed," the person coldly remarked, quickly leaving the office too after tucking the gun away.

Dan lay in a pool of his own blood on the floor until Andrew Mink showed up at two o'clock that afternoon to collect the paperwork. Looking down at his dead law partner and friend who stared up at him blankly, his legs twisted in a knot, Mink felt a chill run up his spine. As he looked around the office, now spinning in slow motion, he felt as though he would faint. Mink wanted to flee for his life, his own self-preservation, but he needn't have worried.

The killer had long since vanished, along with the gun, after having murdered the intended target. Dan Biggs never got to eat his leftover fried chicken and apple pie that day, both gone as well without leaving so much as an enticing aroma in the air. Only the crumbs dropped in the elevator would reveal that someone had eaten a piece of apple pie before exiting the building. Mink was in shock as he picked up the receiver to the phone.

"Hello, police? Please hurry," he politely requested in a shaky voice before collapsing into a chair, "I believe there's been a murder."

***

I got home that day at one-thirty, having been on the town green all that time, studying for my history test and enjoying my lunch under the shade of a large tree. Dulcie was in the kitchen preparing a pot of hot tea. She seemed to be calmer, more at peace. I guess her time alone on the beach helped her to come to grips with what had happened between her and my father that morning. I only wondered how she'd handle it. Would she still be leaving us like she wrote in her letter and more importantly, would he let her go?

Only time would tell, I suppose, but for now she went about her business without any indication of her intentions. I felt a little better too, having sat in solitude on the town green to think and breathe deeply, shedding my latest fury over father's conduct toward Dulcie, before studying for my test. The house was quiet, but mother had to be around somewhere, her car visible through the garage window.

"Where's mother?" I asked Dulcie after walking into the kitchen.

"In her bedroom," she said quietly. "I'm about to bring her some tea. She came home from the charity bizarre not feeling too well. After finishing up some business at her desk, and she was in there with the door closed for quite a while, she went upstairs and took to her bed. She's a dedicated woman, your mother."

"I better check on her," I said, placing my empty school lunch bag on the kitchen table, having eaten the fried chicken and apple pie while I was studying.

"Take this tray with you then and be sure to pour the tea out for your mother when you get up there. You know she doesn't like to lift a finger when she's not feeling well."

"I will," I answered, taking the tray from Dulcie before heading up to mother's bedroom.

Upon entering, I could immediately see that mother wasn't well, her face pale and her eyes swollen.

"Hello, mother," I said. "I hear you're not feeling well."

"I guess I've been overworking myself," she said quietly.

"Let me pour you some tea," I said, placing the tray down on her bedside table.

"That would be nice," she said, laying there like a wet rag, the sickest I had seen her since her return from the Eddie debacle.

"Have you called your doctor?" I asked as I poured the tea.

"Oh, there's no need for that, not today. I'll be fine," she said, taking the cup of tea from my hands. I was skeptical.

After handing her the tea I excused myself and went back downstairs to the kitchen. Using the number left on a pad near the telephone, I called mother's doctor and summoned him to the house, Dulcie already having gone off to do the marketing. I went back upstairs and sat with her until he arrived, the first time I had ever wished father were home. After escorting the doctor upstairs, he quickly went to mother's bedside where he took out his stethoscope and listened to her heart.

"I'm not surprised," he said, sadly shaking his head, "given how busy you always are, never letting yourself rest, smoking those damn cigarettes. Have you been taking your medication, Mrs. Biggs?" he asked softly.

"Oh, yes, doctor," she answered in a weak voice, "I've been taking my medication faithfully." The doctor pulled me aside.

"Stay with your mother. I'm going to call an ambulance," he whispered before leaving the room with an urgent gait. I walked back over to mother's bedside and placed a gentle hand on her arm, petting it with a light touch.

"Everything's going to be all right, mother," I said, trying to reassure her.

"Oh, I know it will," she responded weakly. "I know it will." She took my hand and squeezed it as tightly as she could, pressing something hard into my palm. When she let go, I looked down to see a key. I looked at her.

"The key to my top desk drawer," she whispered. My heart began to beat fast.

"Will it tell me where Eddie is, mother?" I asked, hoping that her answer would reveal what I had been longing to hear for months now.

"It will tell you many things," she said mysteriously, her weakness getting the best of her as she closed her eyes. I quickly slipped the key into my pocket.

The doctor came back upstairs and, once again, rushed immediately to mother's bedside. "Ambulance is on its way," he whispered to me. "Where is your father?" he asked.

"At the office," I said, still looking at mother, her breathing becoming shallower now.

"You better give him a call," the doctor instructed, although he didn't insist, before tending to mother again. I wanted to be there with her, absorbed in what was happening. I wasn't going anywhere.

Moving his stethoscope around her chest, he seemed to be searching for a heartbeat that was no longer there. He took her wrist in his hand, feeling for a pulse. He then put two fingers on her neck, searching for a pulse there too. He took the stethoscope out of his ears and looked at me sadly. "I'm sorry, son, she's gone." Poor mother. Poor dead mother.

Before I could even process what the doctor had just said, the doorbell rang. In a fog, I forced myself to go downstairs and answer the door, my feet trudging as though they were made of cement. When I opened it, a police officer stood before me, flashing his badge.

"Does Ellen Biggs live here?" he asked.

"Ellen Biggs is my mother," I answered in a mindless response. The shock was just beginning to set in.

"Is she at home?" the officer inquired.

"My mother is dead," I muttered, my knees about to give way.

"I'm so sorry. May I come in?" he asked gently, closing the door behind him. Just then, the doctor came downstairs.

"The funeral director is on his way, Tom," he told me. "Now all we have to do is get in touch with your father. Hopefully he'll get here quickly." The doctor walked over to the telephone in the front hall and pulled a little black book from his jacket pocket. Picking up the receiver, he began to dial before noticing the police officer standing there. With a surprised look on his face, he immediately hung up the phone. "Oh, I beg your pardon," he began. "I'm Ellen

Biggs' physician. I suppose the funeral director sent you here. What would you like to know?"

"I'm actually here on a matter concerning a Daniel J. Biggs," said the officer. "I came here looking for Ellen Biggs, his wife, but the boy told me…"

"Yes, she is deceased," the doctor confirmed, stepping closer to the policeman. "She had a massive heart attack about five minutes ago."

"Do you suspect foul play?" asked the officer.

"No, of course not," the doctor said. "She had a serious heart condition and died right in front of her boy and me. What's this all about?"

"I'm sorry to hear that because her husband has just been found murdered in his office," the policeman bluntly stated, suddenly remembering that I was standing there. "I'm sorry for your loss, son," he said kindly, his demeanor less brusque as he stepped further into the front hall. The doctor gasped in horror, putting his arm around my shoulders and drawing me near.

Feeling as though I might fall to the floor, he slowly brought me over to the overstuffed chair in the front hall and sat me down gently before he and the police officer walked away to discuss the matter of father's murder in low whispers. Of course, I strained my ears to hear what they were saying.

"You don't find this odd, a husband and wife both dying on the same day?" I could hear the officer ask.

"I don't know what to say about the husband, but I can almost say with certainty that Mrs. Biggs was bound to have a heart attack sooner or later, especially the way she ran herself ragged and continued to smoke like a chimney, all against my orders. Her condition was quite serious," the doctor said honestly, glancing over in my direction, "but she never took it seriously, or ever did anything to help herself as far as I could tell."

"Would you make a formal statement attesting to all that?" the officer requested.

"Of course. It would be one less matter to investigate, isn't that right, officer," commented the doctor, letting out a long sigh. "Mrs. Biggs died of a heart attack, right before our eyes," he repeated sadly, looking over at me. "Let the boy alone for now."

The police officer consented. "Do you have someone to be with you tonight, son?" he asked me.

"Yes, I said," not mentioning Dulcie by name.

"I'll see to it that he's well cared for," said the doctor.

"I'll be back tomorrow," the officer stated, patting me on my shoulder. "Again, I'm sorry for your loss, son." He turned to leave the house only after giving me his card. "If you ever want to get in touch with me for any reason, you just call me at that number." I stared at the card through vacant eyes.

Just as the police officer left the house the funeral director arrived, he and an attendant carefully removing mother's body with the utmost dignity, covering it with a sheet so as to conceal it from the living.

"Why do you think the police officer is coming back tomorrow?" I asked the doctor while staring out of the living room window, watching as they slid mother's shrouded body into a hearse.

"Don't you worry about that," he said, "it's probably just routine. Nonetheless, I'm going to call your father's law partners right now."

Going into father's study, the doctor looked through his rolodex and called Chesterman, Hanson, and Mink who already knew about father's murder, Mink having been the one to discover the body, but were flabbergasted at this latest news regarding mother. They all agreed to be at the house first thing in the morning to help me deal with the police officer and any questions he might ask. The doctor stayed with me until Dulcie arrived back home, for which I was grateful, explaining to her the dreadful circumstances. She grabbed me and hugged me tightly at which time I hugged her back, the first time we had ever made physical contact with each other.

After the doctor left, Dulcie and I wandered around the house in a daze, unable to focus our attention on anything other than aimlessly drifting from room to room. Neither of my parents would be coming home that night or ever again, fate having played a cruel trick, swallowing them up for all eternity. It almost seemed unreal, but deep down inside I knew otherwise. As I continued to ramble around the empty, eerily quiet rooms, I put my hands into my pockets, suddenly stopping short after having forgotten all about the key mother had pressed into the palm of my hand before she died.

There it was, still securely tucked away in the darkness of my pocket, ready to unlock the answers to many questions, especially the one regarding Eddie's whereabouts. "It will tell you many things," mother had said of her top desk drawer, but I would have to wait, and suppress my eagerness, until Dulcie went to bed.

Chapter 11

Under the worst possible circumstances, it was now only Dulcie and me, but I would feel a peculiar sense of solitude without Eddie. Trudging up the stairs, we said goodnight to each other at eleven o'clock, both of us fatigued from pointlessly roaming in and out of rooms like two lost dogs looking for bones. It still seemed so unreal that both mother and father were gone, the shock now starting to set in. My legs were weak and my heart heavy. I couldn't eat dinner either, my stomach too upset to tolerate food. Even the fried chicken and apple pie that I had eaten hours before on the town green were no longer safely settled in my stomach, now churning with crashing waves of extreme anxiety. I didn't know about Dulcie, but my night would be sleepless.

I did lay on my bed for a few minutes, unable to think straight. It was all so surreal. Quick flashes of my parents haunted my thoughts, gruesome images of twisted suffering and gasps for air leaving me horrified. Would I ever be able to think of them in a better light again? I had been demonizing them for so long, ever since they had disposed of Eddie, but now they were no longer just demons, they were dead demons.

Were they burning in hell for what they did? That haunted me too because I was pretty sure they were. I shook off my dreadful thoughts and sat up. I would keep myself busy until I was sure Dulcie was too settled in to come out of her room.

I read, paced, and played with my camera until two o'clock in the morning before slowly opening my bedroom door, the house now dark and quiet, not a sound or flicker of light coming from Dulcie's room. I had stayed in my clothes, mother's top desk drawer key still safe in my pocket, but my feet were bare so as not to make a sound as I quietly crept down the hall.

I decided that if Dulcie were to open her door and question me, I'd simply say that I was on my way to the kitchen for something to eat but that never happened. I made it down the staircase and into father's study without incident, closing the door and locking it from the inside just the way Eddie had done the night of that fateful dinner party.

I tiptoed over to mother's desk and pulled the chain of her lamp which let out a soft glow, just enough for me to see what I was doing but not so overpowering as to light up the entire room. I glanced over at father's desk for only a split second before taking the key mother had given me out of my pocket, her top desk drawer the entire focus of my attention now. Would it tell me where to find Eddie? Would it reveal unexpected secrets? I turned the key over in the palm of my hand several times before carefully putting it into the lock and slowly turning it to the right. Hearing a click, I took in a deep breath before gently pulling the drawer forward.

I looked down and froze, my heart pumping wildly, my hands trembling uncontrollably. There was that familiar jolt, that sudden spike of adrenaline that I always got whenever I saw the gun, the cartridges, and the bottle of potassium chloride capsules in father's desk, only now I was seeing them in mother's. Suddenly, finding Eddie became a secondary concern.

After gathering myself as best I could I slowly lifted the gun out of the drawer with my two trembling hands, the grip clumsily wrapped with a crumpled tissue, and gently placed it on top of the desk, so afraid that it would accidentally go off. It smelled strongly of gunpowder, the way our cap guns used to smell whenever Eddie and I played cowboys and Indians. I threw the crumpled tissue into the wastebasket before removing two cartridges, two less than I usually saw in father's desk drawer, and thoughtfully stared at them in the palm of my hand before slipping them into my pocket.

Had only one of the two missing cartridges been fired from the gun, or both? Clearly empty now I then picked up the bottle that had once contained the potassium chloride capsules. Despite knowing this, I shook the bottle before carefully opening it. Yes, it was empty, every single capsule gone. I shoved that into my pocket too, my instinct telling me that I needed to gather every bit of evidence from the drawer that pointed to something I hadn't yet completely grasped, but what was now slowly dawning on me.

Finally, I picked up two pieces of stationary, one yellow, the other blue, clearly the two love letters that I had seen in father's desk drawer underneath his bank statements. I folded both letters and stuffed them into my other pocket. There were other papers, envelopes, and keys that had nothing to do with

Dulcie and father, so I left them there for another day and quietly closed the drawer, making sure to lock it.

After slipping the key back into my pocket, I carefully lifted the gun off the desk, pulled the chain on the lamp to turn it off, and then left the study. Tiptoeing upstairs and past my bedroom, I ascended the next flight of stairs into the attic, walking over to the bird's nest that Eddie and I had made before he left. Slowly getting down on my hands and knees, I gently placed the gun inside the messy hodgepodge of brush with my two hands where it fit perfectly. I then took the other items out of my pockets, carefully wedging the two cartridges, the empty bottle of potassium chloride capsules, and the two folded love letters between the gun and the dried-up leaves and interwoven twigs, everything now tightly secured inside the nest.

I stared blankly at the grim collection, taking a few minutes to put it all together and whisper it softly out loud. What I had stumbled upon no one must ever find out. It was a secret I'd have to keep forever, even if it haunted me until the day I died. Apparently, I wasn't the only one who liked to snoop inside father's desk, but it was mother's spying that would take a deadly turn.

Everything I had retrieved from her top desk drawer was proof that she knew about father's relationship with Dulcie. She murdered him with his own gun because of it and then killed herself with the potassium chloride capsules, knowing what their affect would be on her unhealthy heart, the Kainor case having taught her that.

I covered up the chilling evidence inside the crude shell of bent sticks with an old, moth-eaten shirt of father's and left it in a dark corner of the attic. I would come back up to retrieve it at first light, determined that no one would ever find out that my mother was a murderess who then, in the end, killed herself, leaving me with the key to her wicked little secrets.

Waiting patiently on my bed, my heart having yet to slow down while my icy cold hands still trembled, I listened for the chirping of the birds, a sure sign that day was about to break. All I needed was the early morning light, however dim, to complete my task, to conceal mother's reprehensible deeds. I slipped into my sneakers as the sky turned from black to gray, a veil of light fog shrouding over the backyard as the birds twittered their morning greeting in unison. I quietly snuck back up into the attic where I grabbed the bird's nest, leaving father's old moth-eaten shirt on the floor.

With the lightest of steps, I sneaked back downstairs and outside into the yard where I brought the nest over to the stream. With my bare hands I mixed together a muddy batter of sand, stones, and water before slopping it into the nest, completely covering mother's incriminating keepsakes, where I then smoothed it over the way Dulcie would before putting a cake in the oven. My hands still muddied and now colder than before, I ran across the yard and climbed up into the treehouse before making my way onto an adjacent branch, steadying myself with one hand while the other now held the heavy bird's nest.

I slowly climbed further up into the tree where a much larger nest had sat for months, securely nestled among the branches, no longer occupied after having been abandoned long ago. I placed my smaller nest inside of it, a perfect fit with room to spare, and then gently twisted, turned, and pressed it down until it had been completely swallowed up by the larger nest of interlocking twigs. It was now snug and immovable inside the larger nest and, most importantly, no longer visible.

I carefully backed my way down the tree, strategically planting my feet on the right branches until I found myself inside the treehouse once again where I could breathe a sigh of relief. I gazed over at the dark house where the lights hadn't been turned on yet, a clear indication that Dulcie was still in bed. I needed to get back inside quickly, though, not relishing the thought of having to invent a reason for being outside so early.

But first, I took my lock box containing all of the incriminating photos of Dulcie and father and brought it a short way into the wooded area behind the house where I hastily buried it under a rock. I then ran to the outside spigot, rinsing my muddy hands as best as I could before going back into the house where I would wash them thoroughly with soap and water in the kitchen sink. Just as I was drying my hands with a paper towel, Dulcie came downstairs.

"You're up early," she said somberly.

"I was just about to make myself some breakfast," I answered, reaching for the cereal in the pantry closet that I didn't really want, my stomach still doing flips.

"How did you sleep?" she asked.

"Oh, on and off I guess," I said quietly, not intending to divulge my nighttime maneuvers to Dulcie or anyone else for that matter. I had secrets to protect, for mother's sake and mine. Only when the dust settled a bit would I be able to go back into her top desk drawer to look for clues that might help me find Eddie.

At nine o'clock sharp, the doorbell rang, Attorneys Chesterman, Hanson, and Mink standing on the front portico. After I let them in, they each, in turn, put their protective arms around me, offering their condolences. Dulcie stood there too, looking on with sadness. She was still in shock.

"So sorry, Tom," said Mink, the partner who found my father and his best friend. "I'm sure yesterday was an ordeal for you, first your mother and then finding out about your father, all too horrible to even comprehend."

"Yes sir," I said quietly.

"Hello, Dulcie," Mink said respectfully, recognizing her too with a sympathetic handshake. The lawyers were well aware of their partner's affair with Dulcie, as was the rest of the town. "I'm sure this was a tragedy for you as well."

"It certainly was," she said in a shaky voice. "Please, let's all sit down in the living room."

We found our way over to various couches and chairs, making ourselves comfortable. There was an awkward silence at first, but after all the sighs and sad looks the partners finally spoke. I felt safe having them there, this group of men who had always been like uncles to Eddie and me since we were little.

"Tom, when the police officer arrives to ask his questions, we'll be here to support you, as your family and your legal representation," said Chesterman. "That goes for you too, Dulcie," he continued. "He might have a few questions for you too."

"Why would he want to question Dulcie and me, anyway?" I asked, starting to get fidgety.

"His job is to find your father's murderer," said Hanson. "Don't take it personally."

"Just be straightforward and honest when answering any questions he might ask, Tom," said Mink. "You might hold the key to solving your father's murder without even knowing it."

"The key?" I asked, swallowing hard while instinctively placing my hand over my pants pocket.

"Yes, something trivial you might have seen or heard that doesn't mean much to you now, but could actually be a significant piece to the puzzle," he said.

"I'll do my best," I said before excusing myself to throw up in the bathroom rather than on the floor in front of father's partners.

"It's been hard on him," said Dulcie who watched me run toward the bathroom.

"On you too, I'm sure," Chesterman said with a touch of scorn before Hanson cleared his throat, a clear indication to his partner that Dulcie shouldn't be derided for her part in the affair.

Just then the doorbell rang, the police officer who had been at the house the day before having returned with his partner. When I came out of the bathroom, they both acknowledged me with heartfelt condolences, shaking my hand and gently patting me on the shoulder.

"Hello, Tom. I'm sure you remember me," said the officer I had already met, addressing me warmly before letting go of my hand. "Again, I'm so sorry for your loss, son. As you might remember from the card I gave you yesterday, I'm Officer Dunnegan and today I've brought my partner, Officer Wertz. We're here to determine if there's anything you or Miss Jackson might know that could help us in our investigation into your father's murder."

"Yes, sir," I said sheepishly.

"We're here to sit in on the conversation if you don't mind," said Mink, introducing himself and the other lawyers. "We're like family to the boy, the only support system he's got right now."

"Not at all," said Officer Dunnegan. "As a matter of fact, I'm glad you're here, counselor," he said, looking through his notepad, "since, according to my notes, you were the one who found the victim yesterday."

"That's correct," said Mink. "I went to the office at around two o'clock to pick up a report Dan had been working on all morning and that's when I found him. Police on the scene questioned me extensively, yesterday."

"Yes, I can see that in my notes," said the officer, still flipping through his notepad. "Quite a terrible thing. Well, why don't we begin. Officer Wertz will speak to Miss Jackson in another room in order to avoid any confusion." The lawyers gave each other a quick glance, knowing the all too familiar game of divide and conquer, as Officer Wertz walked up to Dulcie and shook her hand.

"Why don't we go into the kitchen," she volunteered, pointing the way. I knew she had nothing to hide. Being a mistress wasn't a crime.

"I'll go with you," said Chesterman, following them. Once everyone was settled around the table, he closed the kitchen door.

"Well then, Hanson and I will stay here in the living room with you and Tom," Mink said to Officer Dunnegan.

"Actually, I'd like to go in there," said the officer, pointing to father's study.

"Why?" asked Mink. "We're perfectly comfortable in here."

"I'd like to take a look around, get a sense of the house while we're talking, if that's okay," he said.

"Again, I have to ask why," Mink said curtly. "My partner was murdered at the office, not here at the house. If you're looking for something you'll have to get a warrant."

"Do I need a warrant?" asked Officer Dunnegan.

"Of course not," said Mink. "There's nothing to hide. Please remember, officer, that the boy is a victim of this heinous crime too. He no longer has a father." Mink looked over at me with puppy dog eyes, unaware that father's sudden demise had a greater effect on him than it had on me, although I knew enough to play along and go through all the paces…for mother's sake.

"Let's not get off to a bad start," said Officer Dunnegan calmly, almost apologetically. "I'm not looking for anything. Like I said, I'd like to just take a look around and get a sense of the house while we're talking. Sometimes things unexpectedly present themselves, you know what I mean, counselor?"

Mink conceded that he knew what the officer meant by permitting a faint smile to cross his lips while saying nothing further. "Was that your father's office, son?" I didn't wait for permission to answer, wanting to move this ordeal along.

"Yes, it was," I said, walking toward the study. Officer Dunnegan followed me with Mink and Hanson trailing behind.

We walked into father's study and looked around. It was abandoned now like a ghost town, but I could sense the lingering spirits of both my parents that had yet to find their final resting places, wondering why this room was no longer their own. Ironically, I felt more like an intruder now than I had ever felt when they were alive. A sudden feeling of deference came over me as though this were now a sacred place, just as father had wanted us all to think of his study.

"Let's sit down," said Mink, sitting at father's desk. Hanson sat at mother's desk while Officer Dunnegan and I sat on the small couch. We all seemed to look around for several seconds before the officer began to speak.

"I'm trying to piece together a clear picture of what happened yesterday, Tom. Anything that you can tell me, anything at all, would be helpful," the officer said.

"The boy will do his best," said Mink. "We're here to fully cooperate."

"I appreciate that," Officer Dunnegan said, turning to me. "Did you at any time leave the house yesterday, Tom?" he asked, ready to write down my replies in his notepad.

"Yes, I left the house at around nine o'clock yesterday morning," I answered.

"Was your father still at home?" The officer was now taking notes, making me feel kind of important.

"No, sir, he was already gone," I responded, the question having brought to mind father's argument with Dulcie in the driveway.

"So, he left the house before nine o'clock?" he confirmed.

"Yes, sir," I said.

"Do you know what time he might have left the house?" Officer Dunnegan asked curiously.

"Yes, from my bedroom window I saw him pull out of the driveway at eight fifteen," I answered.

"You seem to be pretty sure of that," he commented, nodding his head.

"Yes, sir, I woke up when I heard his car start. After looking at the clock on my nightstand, I got out of bed and went to the window. It was eight fifteen." Of course, that was a lie, not wanting to tell him that it was actually the loud argument between Dulcie and father that had awakened me. Perhaps I was trying to protect her too.

"Was there anyone else at home when you left the house?" the officer continued.

"No, sir. The house was empty by the time I left," I replied.

"Have you ever heard your father argue or fight with anyone?" he asked.

"No, sir," I said, telling another lie. Not only did he argue with Dulcie that morning, but he often argued with mother too.

"Not ever?" Officer Dunnegan seemed skeptical and rightfully so.

"The boy already answered your question," said Hanson who, up to that point, had been quiet. "What else have you got?" The officer moved on to the next question.

"To your knowledge, had your father ever been threatened by anyone?" he probed.

"No, sir, not to my knowledge," I was quick to say.

"So, you're not aware of any enemies he may have had?" the officer poked further, basically rewording his previous question.

"C'mon, officer," Mink interjected, "how would he know that? He's just a boy."

"It's a fair question," said Officer Dunnegan. "You never know what he's seen or heard regarding his father."

"Go ahead, Tom, answer the question," said an exasperated Mink.

"No, I'm not aware of any enemies my father may have had," I said quietly. Of course, I was certain that there must have been a few disgruntled husbands who despised father, given his bad habit of flirting with other women, but it wasn't a disgruntled husband who killed him. It was a disgruntled wife.

"Tom, you're doing a great job so far," said the officer. "Next, I'm going to ask you a few questions about where you were yesterday, do you mind?" he asked.

"Why do you want to know his whereabouts?" Mink quickly asked before I could reply.

"Is he a suspect?" Hanson interrupted.

"I can assure you both that he is not a suspect," said the officer. "As a matter of fact, we have no suspects at this time. My questions are strictly routine. I'm simply trying to piece together that clear picture I was talking about earlier." I looked at Mink and Hanson in the hopes that they'd allow me to continue. After all, I knew I was innocent, now having only to conceal mother's dirty deed. I just wanted to get this over with.

"Go ahead then," said Mink, "but tread lightly. We'll have to ask you to leave if you badger the boy in any way. He's done nothing wrong."

"I'm sure he hasn't," said Officer Dunnegan, "so let's just move on. The sooner I finish here, the sooner I can leave this poor boy to grieve for both his parents, all right?" Mink nodded in agreement, a signal for the officer to continue. "Where did you go yesterday morning, Tom, when you left the house at nine o'clock?"

"I went to the town green to study for a test," I said.

"And when did you get home?" he asked.

"I got home at about one-thirty," I replied, positive of the time.

"So, you were gone for four and a half hours," confirmed Officer Dunnegan, writing that down in his notepad.

"Yes, sir," I nodded.

"What did you bring with you to the town green?" he inquired.

"I brought my history book, notes from class, and my school lunch bag," I recounted.

"You packed a lunch?" he asked, looking surprised.

"Yes, sir, I did," I verified, wondering why he'd be so astonished by that.

"What did you pack for lunch?" he wished to know. What was going on here? Why was Officer Dunnegan so interested in my lunch? Suddenly, I felt embarrassed.

"Three pieces of fried chicken and a large hunk of the apple pie that Dulcie had made," I said sheepishly, knowing that it sounded like a lot.

"You're making me hungry," Officer Dunnegan laughed. "Did you eat all of that on the town green before you got home?" His laugh put me at ease.

"Yes, sir," I chuckled, feeling more comfortable. "I love fried chicken and apple pie. I ate it all up."

"Good for you!" he laughed again. "Well, I'm not surprised. You're a growing boy!" Officer Dunnegan continued to write feverishly in his notepad. I liked him. He had an easygoing manner and seemed to be playing fair.

"Are we finished yet?" I asked, hoping that we were done.

"Just a few more questions," he said. "Do you recall talking to anyone while you were gone from the house, maybe on your walk down to the town green, or while you sat there, or perhaps on your way back home?"

"No, sir," I said. "I didn't talk to anyone the entire time."

"So, you were completely focused on your studies. Well, that's quite commendable," complimented Officer Dunnegan.

"Thank you, sir." I could feel myself blush a little. I wasn't the great student he was making me out to be.

"Did you see anyone you knew while you were sitting on the town green, or do you think someone might have seen you sitting there all that time?" he asked. "Perhaps someone in one of the shops nearby, or someone who may have been walking past?"

"I didn't see anyone I knew," I answered, "but I suppose someone could have seen me sitting there. I was under that tree for a long time."

"When you left the town green, did you go to your father's office for a visit since it was nearby?"

"No, sir. My father didn't like to be interrupted when he was working," I said seriously, "not ever."

"And when you got home yesterday at one-thirty, who else was there?"

"Dulcie and my mother were at home," I said.

"Yes, your poor mother," Officer Dunnegan said soberly, shaking his head. "I bet you didn't get much sleep last night, did you son?"

"Not much," I confirmed.

"Well, I think I have everything I need, Tom," said the kind officer, patting me on the back. "Now that wasn't so bad, was it?"

"No, sir," I said with a sigh of relief, grateful that it was over.

"Thank you, gentlemen," he said to Mink and Hanson as he stood up, taking one last look around father's study. "I appreciate your cooperation. If you don't mind, I'll wait for my partner outside."

Mink saw Officer Dunnegan to the door. I went to the window and watched as he got into his squad car, immediately opening his notepad to look over his notes. I wondered what he was thinking. He seemed to like me, but did he believe everything I said? In the meantime, Dulcie was still talking to Officer Wertz in the kitchen, while Chesterman sat in as a witness to their conversation.

***

"So, let me get this straight," the officer started, "you went to the beach and sat there the entire time you were gone from the house?"

"Yes, except for the few times I got up to use the bathroom inside the bait and tackle shop," Dulcie said.

"Did you speak with anyone in there?" asked Officer Wertz.

"Yes, I spoke with the owner. We had a delightful conversation about living in New England. His name was Monty something or other," she said, attempting to reach into her memory for his last name. "He reminded me so much of my grandfather. As a matter of fact, I invited him to join me on the beach for lunch so that we could continue our conversation."

"Did he do that? Join you on the beach for lunch?" the officer asked.

"Yes, he did," Dulcie confirmed, "since he had a young man working behind the counter who could watch over the shop while he was gone. He shared his bologna sandwich and fruit salad with me while I shared my fried chicken and apple pie with him. We had a feast, and we ate every last bit of it. It was a lovely time, and he was a wonderful old gentleman." Dulcie gushed, "so kind and full of wisdom. We really enjoyed each other's company. As a matter of fact, we're going to get together again sometime next week for another lunch on the beach, weather permitting."

Officer Wertz was taking copious notes. "Did you come straight home from the beach, or did you stop somewhere else first?"

"No, I didn't stop anywhere else, I came straight home from the beach," Dulcie answered. "I had a lot of housework to do, and I thought Mrs. Biggs might need me."

"What time did you get home?" asked the officer.

"I got home at exactly noon," Dulcie replied, pinpointing her return to the minute.

"Was there anyone else at home when you got there?" Officer Wertz continued.

"No, when I got back to the house it was empty. Mrs. Biggs didn't get home until one o'clock while Tom got home around thirty minutes later. Yes, it was exactly one-thirty when he got home," Dulcie confirmed.

"Did anyone see you pull into the driveway?" the officer asked. "Maybe a neighbor or passerby?"

"Yes, as a matter of fact, I waved to Mrs. Joffrey, our neighbor up the street. She saw me pull into the driveway while she was working in her garden," Dulcie recalled. "We each shouted out a friendly greeting before I went into the house."

"Miss Jackson, I've got to ask," Officer Wertz began, "were you carrying on an affair with Daniel Biggs? That's the word around town."

"Oh, come now, Officer Wertz," Chesterman demurred, rolling his eyes. "Let's not sensationalize my partner's murder."

"I'm sure you've heard of crimes of passion, counselor," the officer countered.

"No, I'd like to answer that question honestly, now that Mrs. Biggs is gone," Dulcie said, interrupting the exchange between the officer and the attorney. "Yes, I was having an affair with Dan," she readily admitted. "I never intended for it to go as far as it did but, yes, we had a romantic relationship."

"Did you ever try to break it off?" questioned the officer.

"Yes, just recently, but nothing ever came of it. I guess he was reluctant to let me go." Dulcie lowered her eyes and pursed her lips.

"Did Mrs. Biggs know about the affair?" Officer Wertz wanted to know.

"No, I don't think so. She never mentioned it to me, and I don't believe she ever confronted her husband about it. I think he would have told me if she had. No, I would have to say she knew nothing about it," Dulcie concluded.

"How could that be?" asked the officer. "No offense, Miss Jackson, but everyone in town seemed to know about it."

"Oh, please," said Chesterman, rolling his eyes again. "Don't tell me that you base your investigations on town gossip."

"Gossip that Miss Jackson has just confirmed to be true," the officer responded quickly. Chesterman shook his head and slapped the table.

"Dulcie, I suggest you say nothing further about it." The attorney was clearly frustrated.

"I have nothing to hide, Mr. Chesterman," Dulcie said. "I'd like to answer the officer's question."

"It's your call," said the attorney, "but I think you're making a mistake."

"It can't be a mistake if I'm being honest," she said.

"Please continue, only if you wish to do so," said Officer Wertz. "I'm not forcing you." Dulcie took in a deep breath as she looked from the officer to Chesterman, and then back again.

"Her entire life was based on her affiliation with high society," Dulcie started, choosing to continue. "It was all about parties, charity events, and working to keep her husband's law firm and its clients happy. She was like a cruise director. Nothing else mattered, so I'm not surprised that she wasn't aware of our affair. Let's just say that Mrs. Biggs was continually preoccupied with her own agenda."

"Did Tom know about the affair?" asked Officer Wertz.

"Unfortunately, yes," Dulcie admitted. "We talked about it several times. He was one of the reasons I wanted to break it off with Dan. The boy needed his father more than I did."

"Were there other reasons?" he asked.

“I simply didn’t want to be responsible for the breakup of his marriage. Mrs. Biggs wouldn’t have deserved that, given all that she did for him. After a while, I was beginning to feel as though he was only using her. He wanted to have his cake and eat it too; you know what I mean?”

“Indeed, I do,” said the officer, still writing down everything that Dulcie said.

“Officer Wertz, I didn’t kill Dan Biggs,” she stated firmly. “I may have wanted to break off our relationship, but I wouldn’t have killed him to do it.”

“I appreciate your honesty, Miss Jackson,” he said. “We’ll be in touch.”

***

Mink saw Officer Wertz to the door, Officer Dunnegan still waiting for him in the squad car, while Chesterman wiped the beads of sweat from his brow with a handkerchief. As their car pulled away, the partners would take their leave of Dulcie and me, arranging to come back the next day not only to see how we were doing, but to continue to advise us and offer legal support. They would also make all the arrangements for mother’s funeral. An autopsy, however, was being performed on father.

Dulcie and I walked into the kitchen, the both of us emotionally drained. At least my appetite was returning, now that Officers Dunnegan and Wertz were gone, but Dulcie had something else on her mind.

“Now, where can that be?” she wondered, talking to herself while looking through the kitchen cabinets.

“What are you looking for?” I asked.

“That picnic basket, the one your mother packed up yesterday with the fried chicken, apple pie, and bottle of wine. She took it with her to some charity bizarre she was going to down the center and I haven’t seen it since. Have you?”

“No, I haven’t,” I answered while making a much-needed salami sandwich. “Why do you need it? Do you plan on having a picnic?”

“Well, sort of,” Dulcie said in a breezy voice. “You see, next week I’m meeting a friend on the beach…oh, where can it be?”

“It’ll turn up,” I assured her, but for all I knew, mother could have left it at the charity bizarre, or in father’s office.

"Come to think of it, I don't recall seeing her walk into the house with it when she got home yesterday," Dulcie remembered. "Oh well, I guess I don't really need it. I can easily pack a nice lunch in a plain old bag too." I looked at her strangely.

With everything that was going on, a picnic on the beach should be the last thing on her mind. She must have read my thoughts. "I guess I'm just trying to divert my attention away from everything that's happened," she said apologetically. "I'm going to take a shower. Shut off the light in the kitchen when you're done with your sandwich." Dulcie sighed loudly as she headed up the stairs. I knew I wouldn't see her for at least an hour.

Following a hunch, I quietly went out to mother's car in the garage and opened the trunk. There it was, the picnic basket that Dulcie had been talking about, the smell hitting me right away. I looked inside to find a couple of pieces of chicken, one slice of apple pie, and an unopened bottle of wine. Why hadn't mother brought this back into the house when she got home yesterday?

I stared at the open trunk for a long time, trying to piece together the significance of the picnic basket. Did it have something to do with father's murder, or did she actually eat an early lunch with the other organizer of the bizarre, the reason for not wanting any breakfast before leaving the house? If that was the case, there wasn't much missing from the basket. It was a mystery.

I quickly took the picnic basket out of the trunk and brought it inside. Seeing that it had been in mother's possession yesterday, I felt as though I should get rid of its contents, just in case they could, somehow, implicate her in father's murder. I had no idea how, or even if, the basket fit into the scheme of things, but I didn't want to take any chances, concealing mother's every move from the day before my top priority.

I placed the unopened bottle of wine back in the wine rack, not seeing any harm in doing that, before cramming the chicken and pie into the garbage disposal. After all its contents had either been put away or pulverized, I took the basket up into the attic where I would stow it inside one of the window seats, covering it over with the same old blanket once used by Dulcie and father.

Running back downstairs and into the garage again, I sprayed the trunk of mother's car with an air freshener that did a pretty good job of covering up the foul odor of spoiled chicken. I looked inside one of the car windows, sadly knowing that she would never sit behind the wheel again, before opening the driver's side door. I could still smell her perfume mixed with the stench of stale tobacco, the odor from the trunk not having wafted into the car, thank goodness.

I swiped a half a pack of cigarettes off the passenger seat before closing the door and walking back inside, stuffing the smokes into my pants pocket. In a final fit of paranoia, I emptied the contents of the garbage disposal into an old container and brought it outside, cleverly dumping the sloppy mess in the wooded area behind the house, close to where I had buried the lock box. Coyotes would lick it up overnight and that would be the end of mother's picnic basket lunch.

Walking back into the house I went upstairs to take a nap, not having slept at all the previous night. Before laying my head down, though, I would have a cigarette, blowing the smoke out of my bedroom window. It was currently a little more than twenty-four hours since all the drama began, but mother's wicked little secrets would remain safe with me along with the key to her top desk drawer, now safely tucked away under my pillow. My dreams would be surprisingly unremarkable, not indicating as of yet the nightmares to follow.

***

In the meantime, Officers Dunnegan and Wertz drove back to the precinct, comparing notes.

"What did you think, Wertz?" Dunnegan asked. "Was she cooperative?"

"Very cooperative," the officer replied, nodding his head. "I believed every word she said. She was honest and forthright about everything which gave me a good feeling about her. I honestly don't think she had anything to do with the murder. How about you? What did you think of the boy?" Dunnegan raised his eyebrows, blowing out a big puff of air as he shook his head.

"I don't know. He was polite, respectful, and answered all of my questions, but..."

"But what?" asked Wertz, surprised that his partner seemed dubious.

"The boy doesn't know that we've been watching the house since last night," Dunnegan indicated. "Was he the one who turned on the light in the victim's office at two o'clock in the morning? And did he take something out of there? I can't help but wonder."

"You can't be sure of either of those things," Wertz cautioned.

"He was outside in the backyard at the break of dawn!" Dunnegan reminded his partner. "I have a feeling he was out there hiding something. You saw him climb up into that tree. He was definitely holding an object in his hand, but I couldn't tell what it was from the car. Suppose it was the murder weapon? Then when he came back down to the ground, he was clutching some sort of box that probably came from inside the treehouse. I couldn't tell exactly what he was up to but there was definitely something fishy going on when he ran that box over to the woods."

"You'd have to convince a judge of that if you want a search warrant. And what are you going to say? That you want to raid the boy's treehouse?" Wertz laughed.

"I'll convince him alright, you wait and see," Dunnegan assured his partner, certain that it was Tom Biggs who murdered his father all along.

***

Chapter 12

Of course, I stayed home from school the next day, missing my history test. Mink and Hanson came by to tell me that mother's funeral would take place on Wednesday morning.

"Is that all right with you, Tom?" Mink asked.

"I suppose so," I said, wondering what choice I had.

"According to your mother's will, she wished to be cremated," said Hanson. "We thought you should know that we followed her instructions. Do you know what it is to be cremated, Tom?"

"I think so," I said, thoughts of mother burning in hell popping into my head again. Father would be next.

"As long as you understand," said Mink, placing a sympathetic hand on my shoulder. "Is there anything else we can do for you today?"

"No, I think Dulcie and I will be fine," I said. "Thanks for stopping by."

"Remember, if the police come back around for any reason you call us immediately," Hanson reminded me. "Don't ever talk to them unless we're present."

"I'll remember," I said, "but why would they want to speak to me again? I already told them everything they wanted to know." I didn't understand why Hanson was so worried about it. Not only was there nothing left to say, but mother's tracks had been perfectly covered as well. And if not, what could they do to a dead woman anyway? I was ready to wash my hands of the entire ordeal.

"Your father's murder hasn't been solved yet, Tom," said Mink, "and as of now they don't have a suspect, so you can be sure that they'll come sniffing around again and again until they have one."

"But why bother me?" I asked. "I didn't kill my father." I was starting to get agitated.

"We know that," said Hanson, patting my head, "but at this point the police are just trying to solve his murder. They're looking for clues and sometimes in cases like this, the best clues are found closest to home. If you recall, I told you not to take it personally. You want them to find the person who killed your father, don't you?"

"Sure, I do," I said, wishing that this was already behind me or, at least, fading from my memory like a bad dream. Mother and father had screwed Eddie and now they were screwing me.

After Mink and Hanson left, I went upstairs to take a shower. As I untied one of my sneakers with one hand, I obsessively lifted the pillow off my bed with the other to take a peek underneath. There it was, the key to mother's top desk drawer, sitting snuggly in the sheets. I thought I might open the drawer today, if Dulcie decided to leave the house but something tugged at the thought, convincing me to wait until after mother's funeral. Perhaps it was for the best. Mother should be buried first before I started to look for Eddie. The information in the drawer would wait, as long as I had the key.

***

Meanwhile, Officers Dunnegan and Wertz were studying Tom and Dulcie's answers from their respective interviews, generating a rudimentary but clear timeline.

"Tom said that no one else was at home when he left the house at nine o'clock that morning, not getting back until one-thirty that afternoon," Dunnegan said, referring to his notes. "He said he didn't speak to anyone while walking down to the town green, sitting there all that time, or walking back home. He didn't see anyone he knew, and he only supposed that someone could have noticed him sitting there, not exactly a convincing alibi. Most importantly, he admitted to packing a large hunk of apple pie in his school lunch bag that morning to bring with him."

"Hmm, it all comes down to the apple pie crumbs we found in the elevator, doesn't it?" said Wertz. "Well, just because he ate apple pie that day doesn't mean he's the murderer," the officer reminded his partner.

"But it means he could be the murderer," Dunnegan countered. "I hear that the funeral for the mother is on Wednesday morning. Between now and then, I'll be down the center interviewing people, talking to shop owners, and showing the boy's picture around town. I'm going to question anyone who works or lives near the law office, and just scope out the area in general. Someone had to see something," the officer concluded. "How about you? Are you still pretty certain that the girl had nothing to do with the murder?"

"I'm reasonably certain," said Wertz. "It's been determined that the victim was murdered at approximately twelve-thirty in the afternoon, correct?"

"Yes, that's the time nailed down by the coroner," Dunnegan confirmed.

"Well, Miss Jackson said she got home at exactly noon and the neighbor from up the street, a Mrs. Joffrey, saw her pull into the driveway. Miss Jackson waved, and they shouted out friendly greetings. There was definite interaction. So, she was supposedly home before the murder took place. I'll have a friendly chat with Mrs. Joffrey, and I'll speak to the owner of the bait and tackle shop too, a Monty something or other. I'll confirm with him that she was present on the beach all that time and that they ate all of the apple pie packed in her bag," Wertz said, smiling at his partner, knowing that Dulcie having packed apple pie for lunch that day too would piss him off. "If they can corroborate Miss Jackson's story, then I'd say she's in the clear."

"Jeez, she had apple pie for lunch that day too?" Dunnegan asked, clearly irritated. He shook his head slowly. "Is this some kind of a joke?"

"Every person in town could have been eating apple pie that day, partner, but we're only interested in the one person who dropped apple pie crumbs in the elevator leading up to Dan Biggs' law office, right?" Wertz slapped his partner on the back. "Don't worry, we'll get the creep."

"Remind me to check the kid's school lunch bag for apple pie crumbs that might be a match to the crumbs we found in the elevator," Dunnegan said.

"We haven't gotten that search warrant yet," said Wertz.

"Oh, we'll get it," Dunnegan promised. "We'll get it."

***

Wednesday morning seemed to arrive quickly, mother's funeral being the sendoff of dreams, one that every affluent person would desire, if not insist upon. Old Windsor Cove high society respectfully descended upon the pretty Saint Matthew's Church which was decorated with white roses, her favorite flower, thanks to Chesterman, Hanson, and Mink. The fragrance emanating from the bouquets that were placed at the end of every pew and all over the alter was intoxicating as it mixed with the exotic perfumes of the rich.

The ladies walked solemnly down the aisle in their black dresses and wide brimmed hats while the dignified gentlemen who accompanied them wore morning suits. The deep and reverent sounds of the organ rose to the rafters, filling the church with the hymns of the dead and the prayers of the living. As the mahogany and gold urn containing the cremated remains sat on a table before the alter, mourners were left to their memories of my deceased mother in better days.

People lightly touched it as they filed past to take their seats, making the sign of the cross while whispering words of grief under their breath and through their tears. The cleric waved his incense burner, God's blessing permeating the air as an all-enveloping earthy aroma.

It was now official. Mother was a member of the faithful departed in the eyes of the Church, but I still wasn't convinced that her soul went to the right place, even with the sacred push she just got from the priest. She would have to answer to God for her many transgressions if she did, in fact, make it to the pearly gates, but if anyone were to ask me, I'd say that mother was shaking hands with the devil right now. Poor mother. Poor diabolical mother.

Dulcie and I sat in the first pew and watched the hallowed proceedings without uttering a single word to each other. I was cool and collected, not a single tear falling from my eyes. Chesterman, Hanson, and Mink sat nearby, ready to support me if I needed it, but if I felt anything at all it was sheer boredom as I awaited the ending to this holy spectacle. I just wanted to get out of the church and into the cemetery where I could bury my mother's remains deep into the ground, hiding them as I did the gun. But when I spotted Officers Dunnegan and Wertz sitting by the door, I couldn't help but think that they were like two cats waiting to pounce…and I was the mouse.

When the church service was over, all of the mourners headed over to the cemetery, a gaping hole in the earth having already been dug, waiting to swallow up what remained of my mother. Eventually, father would go in there too, once his autopsy was complete and the coroner had his say. They would lie together for all eternity, ironical partners in death, this murderess and her victim.

Everyone cried as they said their farewells, mother having died too soon according to many, and threw roses into the burial abyss before turning to leave. I shook a lot of hands while Chesterman, Hanson, and Mink stood close to me and watched as the mourners got into their cars and drove off, or most of them anyway. One car remained, its two occupants leaning against the trunk, arms folded, having taken it all in. Officers Dunnegan and Wertz stood up and began to saunter toward me, looking unusually arrogant. Dulcie was by my side, just as she had been all morning long, and watched as they approached.

"What do you suppose they want?" she asked.

"They probably just want to offer their sympathy," I said. "They were in the church too." But I knew better. A shiver ran down my spine as Chesterman, Hanson, and Mink encircled me.

"Hello, Tom," said Officer Dunnegan. "Tough day."

"Yes, sir," I said quietly, suddenly feeling threatened.

"May we speak to you, son?" asked the officer.

"What's this all about?" asked Mink. "We assumed you were through asking questions when you left the house the other day."

"Just a few more matters to clear up. It's important," Dunnegan said. "We wouldn't bother you today of all days if it weren't essential that we speak again."

"The boy just buried his mother," said Mink, appalled at the intrusion. "Can't this wait?"

"Like I said, it's important," Dunnegan reiterated. "Wertz and I would like it if we could all go back to the house and talk, if that's okay with you, counselor."

"I suppose so," said Mink. "What other choice do we have?" He was clearly annoyed.

"Well, we can go down to the station," said Officer Wertz, smugly chewing on a piece of gum. "It's up to you." Mink looked at the officer and squinted his eyes.

"This better be good. For you to bother the boy today is unconscionable," he said. The officer seemed to soften his stance after seeing the reproachful look on his partner's face.

"It pains us too," Wertz said with a kinder tone, "but please know that your full cooperation, especially on this day, is greatly appreciated."

Mink instructed Dulcie and me to go back to his car. I came to the realization that burying mother wouldn't necessarily put an end to all the questions, giving me an uneasy feeling in the pit of my stomach. My main objective was to keep her wicked little secrets, even in death. I didn't want the world to know what she had done. It was too shameful, too disturbing. If anyone were to ever find out, a black cloud would hang over the Biggs name for all time, altering the way people would look at me for the rest of my life.

I didn't want to be known as the boy whose mother disposed of his brother, murdered his father, and then killed herself. I began to shiver uncontrollably. Had the officers found out what she had done? I was determined to say nothing in regard to my mother, prepared to feign ignorance if I had to. Perhaps then the police would go away and leave me alone.

When we got back to the house the officers were right behind us, both cars pulling into the driveway at once. After we got comfortable in the living room, Mink got blunt.

"All right, what the hell is going on here?" he asked.

"We have a few more questions for Tom, that's all," said Officer Dunnegan. He excused Dulcie, telling her that her presence was no longer required, her story having already been corroborated by Wertz. She left the room after giving me a supportive smile.

"Well, get on with it then. The boy needs to rest after the traumatic morning he's had," Hanson snapped. Chesterman wiped his brow with a handkerchief.

"I'll make it as brief as possible," Dunnegan declared stiffly. "So, Tom, last Saturday you left the house at nine o'clock in the morning and got home at one-thirty in the afternoon, correct?"

"Yes, sir," I said. "I've already told you that."

"Well, we showed your photo to people all around the town green and spoke to most of the shop owners and their employees, asking if any of them had seen you last Saturday between the hours of nine o'clock in the morning and one-thirty in the afternoon. Plenty of folks recognized your picture, you're a popular young man, but no one saw you last Saturday. We were especially interested in speaking to the owner of Jack's Toy Workshop which sits directly across from the town green. He said he's known you and your family since you were little and would often see you walking around the center with your mother and younger brother, but he didn't recall seeing you on the town green last Saturday, or anywhere else down the center for that matter."

"So what?" Mink snapped. "Perhaps he was too busy that day to look out his window!"

"Maybe so," said the officer, "but the point is, we couldn't corroborate Tom's alibi with anybody, not a single soul." Dunnegan flipped through his notepad. "We also talked to the folks at Webster's Soda Fountain, Taylor's Drugstore, The Clock Emporium, Television City, Chamberlain Jewelers, Old Windsor Cove Bank and Trust, Andy's Barber Shop, Dave's Spirits and Tackle Shop, the Town Hall...the list goes on and on. We even had a conversation with Mr. Laskov, the owner of the small supermarket where Tom works. No one saw the boy."

"You said you spoke to most of the shop owners and their employees. Who didn't you speak to?" asked Chesterman.

"Mrs. Plumb's Dress Shop is closed this week, so we haven't spoken to her. Apparently, she's on vacation," said Dunnegan.

"Well, do you plan on speaking to her?" he asked.

"We'll eventually catch up to her," Dunnegan assured him, although he didn't seem to place much importance on what Mrs. Plumb might have to say. "I don't know that she'd be able to tell us anything different from what we've already heard."

"Well, that remains to be seen doesn't it, officer?" Chesterman countered.

"Yes, yes, of course," said Dunnegan, waving off Chesterman's concern about the absent Mrs. Plumb. He immediately changed the subject. "Say, I didn't know you had a younger brother, Tom."

"Yes, sir," I said. "His name is Eddie."

"Where has he been throughout all of this?" asked the officer.

"Eddie has a psychological disorder," Mink quickly interjected. "He's being treated at a medical facility somewhere."

"Somewhere?" Dunnegan had a confused look on his face.

"That's right," said Mink, a little indignant. "I don't know which facility he's in, and neither does Tom. Eddie doesn't even know about his parents yet. We have no way of getting in touch with him."

"Was he already out of town when Attorney Biggs was murdered?" asked Wertz.

"Eddie's been long gone," I said, "and I don't know anything more than that." Of course, I would never tell Dunnegan and Wertz, or Dulcie and the law partners for that matter, that the key to mother's top desk drawer would probably unlock the mystery of Eddie's whereabouts. That would remain my business alone.

"Well, I suppose we can revisit your brother's situation at another time," said Dunnegan. "I have a few more questions pertaining to you, Tom."

"Yes, sir?" I couldn't imagine what they might be.

"When you went to bed last Saturday night, your father having been murdered that afternoon, did you later get up at approximately two o'clock in the morning and go into his office over there," Dunnegan began, pointing toward father's study, "before turning on the light and, perhaps, removing one or more items from the room?"

I froze. How did he know I was in there? Before I could speak, Mink put a heavy hand on my shoulder.

"Has this house been under surveillance?" he asked.

"Let's just say that we're looking for answers by any means we have at our disposal," said Dunnegan.

"I thought you said he wasn't a suspect," Hanson protested.

"There may be a perfectly good explanation as to why he might have been in there at two o'clock in the morning," said the officer, hoping that I'd be allowed to cooperate.

"Well, unless you're ready to charge this boy with something, he has nothing left to say. And by the way, the last time I checked, turning on a light in your own home wasn't a crime," Mink stated emphatically.

"How about going into your backyard at the break of dawn and hiding evidence?" asked Dunnegan. I thought I was going to faint.

"What the hell are you talking about?" Mink thundered.

"Now we can do this nice and easy, or I can go to the judge and get myself that search warrant I've been itching to get. What's it going to be?" Dunnegan folded his muscular arms over his chest and rocked on his heels.

"You go right ahead and get yourself that search warrant," challenged Mink. "We'll be right here when you get back. The boy has nothing to hide."

"Well, maybe that's because he's already hidden whatever needed hiding," Dunnegan said facetiously. "We'll be back as soon as we get that warrant. Don't go too far."

Dunnegan and Wertz left the house quickly without the answers they wanted to hear, their squad car speeding away for affect. Mink paced the length of the living room floor in exasperation while Hanson lit up one cigarette after another. Chesterman simply plopped himself into a chair, wiping the beads of sweat that continually fell from his brow with an already damp handkerchief.

I couldn't believe that the officers actually knew it was me who had gone into father's study and turned on the light at two o'clock in the morning and, what's even worse, saw me out in the backyard at daybreak, hiding the evidence that would prove mother's guilt. I didn't know what would happen next, but one thing I knew for certain was that I'd never divulge mother's wicked little secrets no matter what they did to me. Mink said it was time to come clean and if there was anything I had to say, I better say it now.

"There's nothing to say," I repeated over and over again. "I couldn't sleep, so I was wandering around the house aimlessly from room to room, and that's how I wound up in father's study."

"And what about being in the backyard at the break of dawn? Were you wandering aimlessly then too, or was the officer's allegation correct? Were you actually hiding evidence?" Mink asked with both surprise and disappointment in his voice.

"Like I said, I couldn't sleep so I went outside to mess around," I deceitfully claimed. "I thought it would make me tired. What's wrong with that? Anyway, it's my backyard and I can go out there whenever I want to," I said like a petulant little boy. My eyes welled up with tears, but my lips were sealed. I would never tell the truth, not to the cops, not to Mink, and not to Dulcie. No one would ever know what mother did and they could never pin father's murder on me because I was innocent. I had it all figured out.

Mink suddenly backed down. No matter what the reason was for my turning on the light at two o'clock in the morning or going outside at the break of dawn the partners had to support me, these men who were like my uncles, the only family I had left now besides Eddie and Dulcie. In my private thoughts, I was painstakingly honest, though, asking myself whether they considered me to be more like their nephew...or their client.

For three days I hung around the house, not yet ready to return to school. Chesterman, Hanson, and Mink came over every day and tried to get as much information out of me as they could in preparation for the next visit by law enforcement, but I didn't say anything beyond what I had already told them, my lips remaining sealed. According to Mink, there were many angles and variables that needed to be considered but I just wasn't interested, not having been the one who murdered father.

Dulcie stayed busy cooking and cleaning, having already gotten permission from the partners to permanently remain in the house as my nanny, while I dawdled in the attic, the place where I felt safest. I dare not go outside to climb into my treehouse or even further up into the tree than that, any notion of moving the evidence I had hidden certainly out of the question for fear that I was being watched, not only by the police but by the partners too. I now had the distinct impression that they no longer trusted my word, and rightfully so.

Every day after breakfast, I would go up to the attic to sit on one of the wide window seats and watch the world go by, always on the lookout for spies. I cried more than once, not only because mother and father were both tragically taken from this earth, but because I still didn't know where Eddie was, the information that would help me find him still locked up in mother's top desk drawer. I found it both frustrating and annoying that I was too afraid to even go into the study at this point, never mind open the drawer, for fear that someone was outside watching for lights or looking into the windows.

Perhaps I was just being paranoid, but I couldn't help but think that the attic was now the only room left in the house that wasn't under surveillance. It was a place much like purgatory, though, Dunnegan and Wertz having yet to decide what should become of me. I also felt guilty. Was I prolonging Eddie's absence? I toyed with the idea of giving Mink the key, but later thought better of it. I would have to be the one to bring Eddie home.

After observing the outside world from my window seat for what always seemed to be hours, I would then roll out the rug and hit golf balls into the pie plate at the other end, or look at some of the old family photos from the trunk. I finally understood why Eddie was so captivated whenever he looked at those pictures, the grim black and white world of those long-ago relatives now captivating me too. I even held the photo of dead cousin Leo Biggs in my hand as though it were gold, unable to look away from it, thinking only of Eddie. I realized then and there that if I wanted to find my brother I must safeguard the key to mother's top desk drawer, no telling what the police might do with it if they were to search my room.

That was the day I took it from underneath my pillow and brought it up to the attic, carefully hiding it at the bottom of the trunk of old family photos, the one of Leo Biggs, postmortem, completely covering it. Just as I closed the lid to the trunk, Dulcie came up the attic stairs looking for me.

"You better come downstairs quickly," she said. "Officers Dunnegan and Wertz are here, and this time they brought two other cops with them." I knew this day would arrive, but my legs turned to jelly, nonetheless.

"I'm coming," I said quietly, resigned to whatever was going to happen, the partners there to protect me. My lips would remain sealed.

I went downstairs to find Dunnegan and Wertz standing in the middle of the living room with Chesterman, Hanson, and Mink, the two other officers who I had never met before standing by the front door.

"Hello, Tom," said Dunnegan. "We've come back to take a look around. Your lawyers are holding a legal search warrant that I just obtained from a judge."

"Yes, sir," was all I would croak out, holding back my tears.

"Go right ahead," said Mink. "You won't find anything." He put his arm around my shoulders.

"We'll just see about that, now, won't we?" Dunnegan responded, ordering the other officers into the kitchen where they immediately took possession of my school lunch bag and placed it into a large plastic bag. "Now, head out into the backyard," he ordered. The partners and I followed and would watch from the patio.

Once they were out in the yard, the younger of the two officers who I had never met before immediately climbed up the tree and into my treehouse.

"There's nothing up here!" he shouted down to the others.

"Are you sure about that?" Dunnegan shouted back up.

"I'm positive! The treehouse is empty!" he repeated.

"Then keep climbing!" Dunnegan ordered, confusing the young officer as he stood in the middle of the treehouse, looking up at the branches above him.

"Keep climbing? For what?" he asked in a loud voice. "What am I looking for?"

"Everything and anything!" yelled Dunnegan. "Do it!"

"The only thing I see above me is a bird's nest!" the young officer hollered down.

"Get it! I want to look at it!" Dunnegan demanded.

"But suppose there are birds in it?" the officer asked sheepishly.

"Then shoo them away, damn it! I want that nest down here now!" Dunnegan blustered as the young officer climbed higher into the tree and wrestled the heavy nest from its resting place. "That's it! You've got it! Now bring it down here!"

The young officer carefully backed his way down to the ground, balancing the large bird's nest in one hand, the smaller nest that I had brought up there hidden inside of it.

"Damn, this is heavy," he complained, shaking his aching hand after having carefully placed the double bowl of bent sticks with its mud topping on the ground. My heart sank.

"What the hell do they want with a bird's nest?" Mink asked out loud. "Do you know, Tom?"

"No, I don't," I said, shaking my head, but Mink looked at me suspiciously.

Just as the young officer had placed the nest on the ground, the other officer, along with Wertz, had found my lockbox buried under the rock. They walked it over and placed it down next to the nest.

"Now, look at what we have here," said Dunnegan, nodding his approval. "These have to be the items I saw the boy hiding early that morning." He quickly looked my way before telling the others what to do.

The partners and I watched helplessly as the police carefully broke through the now dried mud that I had slathered over the top of the smaller nest, unpacking the grim contents discovered underneath. Despite the layer of dirt everything was still intact, evidence that I thought would be hidden forever. They placed the gun, cartridges, folded love letters, and empty bottle of potassium chloride capsules into plastic bags before opening the lockbox. They then placed all of my private photos in a bag too, while the lockbox itself was placed in a larger bag of its own. Dunnegan smirked.

"I think we've gathered enough evidence here to arrest the boy," he said to Wertz who reluctantly agreed before glancing over at me.

"On what charge?" asked one of the other officers.

"Suspicion of murder," said Dunnegan, gathering up all of the plastic bags after a long silence among the men. "I regret that I was right, you know," I could hear him say. Wertz apparently understood his partner's pensive sadness, indicating that he felt the same way himself.

"I know how you feel," he said, patting Dunnegan on the shoulder before the two officers began to walk slowly in my direction. I suddenly found myself in hot water. And there wasn't a damn thing the partners could do about it.

Chapter 13

At the police station they put me in a small interrogation room where I sat at a table with three chairs for a good long time, Mink my only company, until Dunnegan walked in with his notepad, closing the door behind him. He sat opposite me looking grave and disappointed, like a teacher whose class I had just failed, or like…my father.

"We have a serious matter here, son," he began with deep concern. "Some of the items taken from your property may very well be linked to your father's murder."

"You don't know that," Mink immediately interjected.

"Ballistics is examining the gun and its cartridges right now, dusting them for prints," the officer told him, "so we'll know soon enough. Forensics is also taking samples from the bottom of your school lunch bag," Dunnegan added after turning back to me.

"Samples? Samples of what?" asked Mink.

"Crumbs or any other food remnants that might be in there," he answered.

"What exactly are you looking for?" Mink inquired, confused as to the importance of whatever might be at the bottom of my school lunch bag.

"There were apple pie crumbs found in the elevator that led up to the victim's law office. Whoever murdered Daniel J. Biggs ate apple pie in that elevator, either going up before the murder or coming down after it, perhaps in celebration," Dunnegan speculated.

"Or maybe someone was just hungry, and the crumbs had nothing to do with the murder," Mink countered immediately. "Look, Tom already told you that he had packed apple pie into his lunch bag that day and ate it on the town green. Of course, you're going to find traces of pie crumbs at the bottom of his bag but that doesn't mean he killed his father," Mink asserted.

"No, it doesn't, in and of itself," Dunnegan began, "but if those traces are an exact match, ingredient for ingredient, to the crumbs that were found in the elevator, then I'd say there's reason to suspect that they both came from the same pie, the one made by Miss Jackson, which points directly to you, Tom. Your nanny has an airtight alibi, but you don't." Dunnegan's stare was intense, but it didn't intimidate me at all. "Were you the one who ate apple pie in the elevator that day, Tom?"

"No, and I didn't kill my father," I said, irritated by the question.

"Then tell me why you stashed the gun and the cartridges up in that tree?" he asked. "You went to painstaking trouble to make certain they were concealed too, covering them over with mud after placing them in a small bird's nest which you later hid inside the larger one that sat above your treehouse."

"I don't know what you're talking about," I said, feigning ignorance.

"Oh, come now," said the officer, sitting back in his chair. "I watched you climb that tree in the early morning hours, so don't try to tell me you didn't hide those things. I saw you do it. And what is the significance of the empty bottle of potassium chloride capsules? How do they fit in?"

"I have no idea how those things got up there, and I know nothing about an empty bottle," I said, lying through my teeth.

"Empty bottle of potassium chloride capsules?" Mink queried, his eyes lighting up as though he remembered something. Something important. Had the Michael Kainor trial come to mind?

"Yes, and a couple of love letters, one written by Miss Jackson, and the other by the boy's father which appears to be unfinished. Why did you hide those things, son?" Dunnegan repeated, his eyes trained on me the entire time as though Mink weren't even in the room.

"I didn't hide those things," I said.

"We're looking at all the photos from the metal box that you buried under that rock too. You knew about your father's affair with Dulcie Jackson, didn't you?" he asked me. "There's no use in denying that. Miss Jackson told Officer Wertz that you knew all about it." I sat silently. "You took many pictures of them together. Their affair made you angry, so you murdered your father."

"I didn't," I said defiantly.

"Then who did?" he asked.

"I wouldn't know," I said, keeping my emotions in check. I wasn't as vulnerable as Dunnegan had hoped I'd be, all of his attempts to crack me like a nut having failed. "You're the one responsible for finding my father's killer, not me."

"Have I found the killer, Tom?" he asked. "Is he sitting across from me right now?"

"That's enough!" Mink said angrily. "You haven't charged the boy with murder, and you have nothing yet that would point to his guilt!"

"Tell me why you hid all of those items in the backyard, Tom," demanded the officer, ignoring Mink.

"I went outside to mess around because I couldn't sleep, thinking it would make me tired," I said, telling him the same exact thing I had told Mink, "but I didn't hide anything."

"I saw you," he said.

"You saw wrong. I don't know what you're talking about." I remained defiant, frustrating Dunnegan in the process. Just then, another officer came into the room and handed him a piece of paper. The officer stood behind Dunnegan and waited.

"Forensics just came back, Tom. When they dusted the gun, two sets of prints clearly appeared. According to the coroner the first set, which was found on the barrel, belonged to your father. That's not surprising, seeing that the gun was registered in his name. My guess is that the second set of prints belongs to your father's killer. Does that second set belong to you, Tom?" he asked me.

"No," I said, knowing that the second set belonged to mother. But wait, I had touched the gun too.

"It's time to fingerprint the boy," Dunnegan ordered the officer who was still standing behind him. I was gently taken by the arm and led out of the room. Mink stayed behind with Dunnegan, having been promised that I'd be brought right back after being fingerprinted.

***

"If the prints are a match, you know I'll have to formally charge him with murder and obstruction of justice for hiding the evidence, counselor," the officer told Mink, but the savvy lawyer sensed that something didn't add up.

"Where does the empty bottle of potassium chloride capsules come in?" asked Mink. "Why would the boy hide those?"

"I'm not sure," said Dunnegan. "I don't get the connection either, but the whole truth will eventually unfold with some good old fashioned detective work." Mink's mind went into overdrive and would remain there.

***

I was finally brought back to the small interrogation room after a long while where the two men were still seated. A preliminary report had just come back from forensics confirming that the traces of pie crumbs found at the bottom of my school lunch bag did, in fact, match the crumbs that were found in the elevator at father's office building. My prints were a match to the second set of prints on the gun too. Where were mother's prints? I was in trouble, and stupid for not having anticipated that the police might see me as the culprit after finding my prints on a murder weapon I was simply trying to hide.

Apparently, my innocence didn't guarantee that they'd let me off the hook immediately, having to pin the murder on someone. Mink and the other partners would have to get me off with a good defense because as far as I was concerned, ratting out my mother was not an option. The only thing I could be glad of, at that point, was that I had taken the picnic basket out of her car and disposed of its contents.

She must have eaten a piece of Dulcie's pie in that elevator which made perfect sense to me now, apple pie being one of the foods I had taken from the basket and crammed into the garbage disposal. No matter. My lips would remain tightly sealed as I was formally charged for the murder of my father.

"Book him," Dunnegan snapped unceremoniously.

Within two hours I was brought to a juvenile detention center where Mink and I would have our final conversation of the day.

"Is there anything at all you can tell me that would help in your defense, Tom?" he asked, letting out a long sigh.

"No, I don't think so," I said, resigned to the circumstances, having to delay bringing Eddie home my only regret.

"I don't understand why you're being so tight-lipped, Tom," Mink said, his frustration obvious. "I don't believe for a minute that you murdered your father, but yet you're being accused of not only murdering him, but hiding the evidence too. And what about that empty bottle of potassium chloride capsules, the love letters, and all those photos? Where do they come in? Help me to understand all of this, Tom. Please." I couldn't be certain of Mink's angle, but if it was an attempt to make me admit to covering up for someone, then I wouldn't take the bait.

"I didn't murder my father or hide any of those things," I told him.

"Then who hid them?" he asked.

"Not me," I repeated.

"You were as good as caught when Dunnegan saw you in the yard," Mink reminded me.

"They're wrong and there's nothing left to say about it," I stated, disregarding Mink's plea for help. He would have to leave without the answers he wanted to hear, obligated, nonetheless, to put up a good defense on my behalf. I was led away in handcuffs to an empty cell, left there with nothing but my own thoughts as to whether or not I was doing the right thing. Lights out plunged me into darkness, and only then did I allow myself to quietly break down, calling for my mother who would never come to me again no matter how hard I cried.

Mink came to the detention center every day to fill me in on my legal defense and try to get me to fess up, making it clear that the district attorney intended to put me on trial.

"You're not helping yourself, Tom," he would repeat day after day, but I made my feelings clear.

"I've told you and the police everything I know." Of course, Mink knew better, recognizing that, for whatever reason, I felt obliged to lie. "Now, it's your job to get me off," I told him in no uncertain terms.

"Are you covering up something, Tom," he asked me time and again, "or, perhaps, protecting someone else?"

"No, sir," I promised, the poor man repeatedly getting nowhere with me.

"I fear that if you're covering up the real truth and, somehow, the DA's office finds out…" he started to say one day before looking away. "I don't even want to consider the consequences. I shudder to think what your father would say," he whispered, his voice cracked with emotion. "Please tell me now what really happened, boy, so we can help you," he pleaded after turning back to look at me.

"There's nothing to tell," I stated emphatically, remaining defiant. "Goodbye for now, Uncle Andrew. Thanks for coming." I boldly stood up that day and walked away from my lawyer, the guard letting me out the door.

As I sat in my cell day after day, Mink and the other partners did business behind the scenes. Father, who had already been buried privately without the fanfare that defined mother's funeral, always said to never underestimate the value of a good private investigator, explaining why the partners hired one immediately.

As a matter of fact, he was the same one who had helped father win an acquittal for Michael Kainor, proving himself then to be a cracker jack sleuth. He interviewed all of the same shop owners and employees that Dunnegan and Wertz had and then some, including Mrs. Plum who had by then returned from vacation. He scoured the area around the town green daily, showing my photo and asking questions while seeking someone, anyone, who could have seen something or, perhaps, recalled a forgotten tidbit.

He went to the law office as well, thoroughly inspecting the space where the murder had occurred, taking measurements, examining the rug on his hands and knees, and opening all of father's desk drawers, before scanning the elevator in search of evidence that might have been missed. He even spoke with my teacher and friends from school.

I wondered what they all thought of me now, the boy accused of murdering his father. I must have been the talk of the town, the only distinction mother ever wanted for herself, but instead of being the darling of high society I was probably the town pariah, my name only as good as the mud used to cover up the gun. In any case, the last I had heard his efforts hadn't scraped up anything as of yet.

The partners did their share of the dirty work too, talking to people in town, retracing my steps, and searching around the house for anything that might assist them in building up a good defense. They went through father's study with a fine-toothed comb and did the same to my bedroom, even looking under the mattress. They checked the backyard again, poking around the wooded area before climbing up into my treehouse. I'm not sure what they were looking for, but they searched anyway, never asking how to get into mother's top desk drawer. I don't think they ever went up into the attic, though, the most important room in the house.

It was the place that preserved the past, offered seclusion, and guarded secrets. It was the place that hid the key. I found it all to be fascinating, given that they were tasked with proving my innocence, but must never discover mother's guilt in the process. I held my breath for the desired outcome every day.

Dulcie visited me at the detention center once a week, bringing me food, warm socks, paper to write on, and other harmless personal effects. There was always someone standing nearby, listening in on our conversations, but I didn't care. I wasn't going to say anything that they could use against me, and Dulcie never wanted to delve too deeply into the situation anyway. Our chats were always innocent and unremarkable, but I looked forward to her visits anyway because she had a way of reassuring me that I'd eventually be able to come home, ending this nightmare. Even the partners couldn't do that.

"Are they treating you all right?" she asked me one day.

"Oh, sure they are," I responded, then filling her in on how I typically spent my days. "The food here is pretty good, but not as good as yours, and I go to classes every morning where they teach us math, science, and history. There's a library near my cell too. I've already read a couple of good books."

"Well, that's positive news. When you come home, you'll be all caught up with your studies, making it easier to go back to school and just pick up where you left off," she said, flashing her beautiful smile, looking on the bright side with a cheery, upbeat attitude. But would it really be that easy?

***

In due time, Chesterman, Hanson, and Mink received a phone call from the district attorney's office which was now looking to strike a deal. A meeting was set up for that afternoon.

"We'll give him twenty years with the possibility of parole after fifteen if he pleads guilty," said the DA. "That's a pretty good deal. I'd take it if I were you."

"No way," said Mink. "He didn't do it. I can feel it in my bones."

"You mean you'd rather go to trial?" The prosecutor was annoyed.

"It might not come to that," Mink stated confidently. "We're still exploring a few strong hunches, so we'll be talking again soon." The fact of the matter was that Mink and the partners had nothing, relentlessly grasping at mere straws while hoping that the private investigator might find that one piece of critical evidence, allowing them to avoid a trial altogether.

"Make it real soon. If you don't take the deal then I'll be looking to move this to trial within the next couple of months," said the DA.

"In the meantime, is there any chance you can get a judge to set bail for the boy?" asked Mink.

"Not a chance in hell. He's being held without bail because the evidence is stacked up against him. That deal must look pretty good right now, doesn't it?" And with that, the DA ended the meeting and walked out of the room, leaving the partners to continue their search for that elusive proof of Tom's innocence.

"Huh," Chesterman grunted as he opened the mail upon their return to the office. "A condolence card from Michael Kainor. Strange."

"What's so strange about that?" asked Hanson.

"It's just that I've been thinking about that empty bottle of potassium chloride capsules the police found with the gun and the love letters," said Chesterman. "Kainor's wife died from a potassium chloride overdose that caused her diseased heart to stop."

"True," Hanson confirmed.

"Well don't you find it funny that Ellen, who also had a diseased heart, died of a heart attack the same day Dan was murdered?" Chesterman questioned his partner.

"What are you saying?" Hanson asked. "Are you saying that someone murdered Ellen that day too, only with potassium chloride?"

"No, I don't think so." Chesterman scrunched up his face as he wiped his sweaty brow with a handkerchief. "Hell, I don't know what I'm saying, but there's got to be a connection. Ellen knew all about the Kainor case and what all that potassium did to the sick wife. Tom knew about it too. Is it possible that..."

As luck would have it, Mrs. Plumb walked into the law office just when Chesterman was struggling to come to some kind of conclusion. The partners were always fond of Mrs. Plumb whose dress shop had been a staple on Kimball Avenue for many years. She was like everyone's grandmother, the oldest shop owner in the neighborhood, a kindly old woman who always kept a batch of homemade cookies on the front counter for customers and anyone else who might want to stop in to say hello. She had been a widow for a long time, although it was rumored that she and Mr. Laskov the grocer were carrying on an affair.

"Hello, my dear Mrs. Plumb," said Mink, gushing over the old woman. "Mr. Chesterman has already spoken to you about Tom Biggs, hasn't he?"

"Oh, yes," she confirmed as she took a seat in front of his desk. "I spoke with Mr. Chesterman, the police, and that nice private investigator."

"Then this is a social call. How nice of you to come by," said Chesterman who was leaning on Mink's desk, smiling at the beloved Mrs. Plumb. "That vacation of yours sure did you a world of good."

"Well, I wouldn't say that this is a social call," she contradicted him, "but you are right about the vacation." Mrs. Plumb appeared to be nervous as she crumpled her hankie, first in one hand, then the other.

"Then what can we do for you today?" asked Hanson jovially who had been quietly filing papers. "I know. You want to try out a new cookie recipe on us," he kidded.

"Not quite," Mrs. Plumb said in a shaky voice. "When I spoke with Mr. Chesterman and the others, I said that I hadn't seen Tom Biggs on that Saturday, but that wasn't the whole truth."

Mink jumped out of his chair. "Do you mean to tell me that you did see Tom that day?" He could hardly contain his excitement.

"Well, no," said Mrs. Plumb, "but I did see his mother."

"You saw Ellen Biggs that day?" Mink asked with surprise. "We were told that before she died that Saturday afternoon, she had attended a charity bizarre somewhere around here, but we couldn't confirm that."

"Well, I don't know anything about a charity bizarre, but she did come into my shop. Oh dear," said Mrs. Plumb, visibly shaken as she wiped her nose with the hankie, "I hope I haven't done anything wrong."

"Now, what makes you say that, dear lady?" asked Mink, placing a box of tissues in front of her. The other partners were now listening intently. "Please proceed."

"Well, she was always such a dear customer of mine. She had ordered so many expensive dresses from me and always paid her bills on time," she said, "so when I heard that her husband had been murdered, well, I didn't want to get her into trouble. Then, of course, she died too, and at that point I was just too frightened to come forward." Mrs. Plumb was emotional, a tear or two falling as she spoke. "Of course, no one ever asked me about her," she added, "only about the boy." The partners looked at each other. Chesterman couldn't help but smile.

"Do tell, Mrs. Plumb. Everything you know," he said, taking her wrinkled hands, still nimble with a sewing needle, into his own. "And you haven't done anything wrong my good woman, so don't you worry about that." Mrs. Plumb cleared her throat before she began.

"You see, Mrs. Biggs came into the shop at around noon that day. I remember the time because I was just about to lock up and start my vacation. Well, she not only paid her bill in full, but she closed her account too which I thought was odd."

"You didn't ask her why she was closing her account?" asked Hanson.

"No, I was too preoccupied with leaving early because I had a train to catch," said Mrs. Plumb. "I was going to Pennsylvania to visit my friend Harriet; oh, she and I go way back to high school…"

"Please tell us more about Ellen Biggs," Chesterman interrupted her in a whisper, placing a gentle hand on Mrs. Plumb's arm.

"Oh, yes, of course, well after she paid her bill and closed her account, she told me that she was going to have lunch with her husband. She had a picnic basket with her," the dressmaker continued.

"Did you ask her what was in the picnic basket?" Mink asked.

"Yes, she told me there was fried chicken, apple pie, and a bottle of wine inside. I can still smell the fried chicken," said the old woman, closing her eyes while breathing in deeply through her nose. "It smelled scrumptious." Mink and Hanson were feverishly writing down Mrs. Plumb's every word.

"Did you say apple pie?" Chesterman confirmed.

"That's right, apple pie," she said. The partners shot each other a quick glance.

"What was she wearing?" Hanson asked as he continued to write.

"Oh, that's easy," said Mrs. Plumb with a melancholy smile, "she was wearing the sky-blue suit I had made for her with a pill box hat. Oh, how I loved the way it looked on her."

"Can you remember anything else?" Chesterman gently pressed as he smiled at the old woman.

"Well, let me see," she said, scratching her chin, "I believe she was wearing the matching shoes I had suggested she buy and, oh yes, a pair of white gloves."

"White gloves?" Chesterman looked at his partners and raised his brow.

"Yes, white gloves with her initials stitched into the material. Well, anyhow, she said goodbye as though she were leaving town, or wouldn't be returning to my dress shop. I found it all to be so strange." Mrs. Plumb became introspective.

"Thank you, my dear," Chesterman said, respectfully kissing the old woman's hand. "You've been a great help."

After seeing the kindly Mrs. Plumb to the door, Chesterman looked over his notes, no longer struggling to come to some kind of conclusion after the dear old woman had unwittingly connected the dots.

"Now I see!" Chesterman exclaimed, unable to contain his glee. "Don't get me wrong. I'm heartbroken over the old woman's account, but I believe it vindicates Tom!"

"Tell me what you're thinking," said Mink, wondering if he had come to the same conclusion. Chesterman paced up and down the office, too excited to stand in one place.

"How could we have been so stupid?" he began. "We've all been so busy concentrating our suspicions on the living, that we've overlooked the culpability of the dead! Don't you see? Ellen came here to the office to, supposedly, have lunch with Dan but her real intention was to kill him, probably because she knew about his affair with Dulcie Jackson. After she murdered her husband, she then went home and killed herself by taking an overdose of potassium chloride, knowing that it would do the job because of her heart condition, something she probably learned from the Michael Kainor murder trial."

Chesterman kept pacing while Hanson and Mink watched, nodding their heads in agreement. "Somehow, Tom knew about all of this, or maybe discovered it, and hid the evidence to protect his mother." The winded lawyer plopped himself into a chair and took in a deep breath before looking at his two partners in earnest. "All we have to do now, gentlemen, is prove it."

"How do you propose we do that?" asked Hanson. "Tom's prints are on the gun not Ellen's, and besides, she's gone," he said, bowing his head. "God rest her soul."

"Yes, but Mrs. Plumb said that she was wearing white gloves. If we could find those gloves, I bet they'd test positive for powder burns. Then there's the picnic basket. If we could find that and have it tested too, I'm sure it would prove that it was Ellen who carried the apple pie into the office, dropping crumbs in the elevator. We have a witness to corroborate all of this, gentlemen. What more do we need?"

"The gloves and the basket," said Mink, ready to get down to work. "I'll call the DA's office, and Dunnegan too. They'll want to meet with Mrs. Plumb. Chesterman, call our private investigator. He'll need to know what's going on. It's time we get Tom Biggs out of that juvenile detention center."

After Mink made his phone calls, he went to the detention center to see Tom and inform him of the latest news. As usual the boy lied, denying any knowledge of the picnic basket or the gloves.

***

"I have no idea where that picnic basket is and as for the gloves, I was never one to keep track of my mother's accessories," Tom said with a faint smile, finding it ironic that he had gone to such great lengths to hide the basket after doing away with the food that was in it, but never considered that his mother's white gloves, the ones she always wore, could give the whole show away. Come to think of it, he never even thought to look for those gloves which could be anywhere in the house. As usual, Mink knew the boy was being less than truthful.

"If the picnic basket has traces of the same apple pie crumbs that were found in the bottom of your school lunch bag and the white gloves test positive for powder burns, then I think the judge will have to reconsider the charges against you," said Mink. "Not only that, but we have a witness who spoke with your mother right before she went to have lunch with your father at the office, only minutes before the murder took place. I'm afraid it's all but over, son. I know you've been protecting your mother, we all know, but it's no use. You can tell me the truth now. Your mother's gone." Tom gave Mink a hard look.

"I have no idea what you're talking about," he said, like he had so many times before.

"Stop trying to be some sort of hero, Tom. The evidence will tell us the truth if you don't," said Mink.

"Then let it. I have nothing to say." Tom's lips would remain sealed.

***

The district attorney found this newest wrinkle in the case to be intriguing, enough to go to a judge for another search warrant.

"Does the nanny know about this?" he asked Mink.

"We didn't tell her and as far as we know, Mrs. Plumb hasn't spoken to anyone else besides us." Mink knew that everything would have to be done by the book in order for Tom to be exonerated and the case dropped.

"What does the boy say about it?" the prosecutor asked.

"Nothing," Mink said. "No wonder he hasn't been talking. He didn't want to give his mother away. Can you blame him?"

"You know, if the kid's mother actually did kill her husband, she might have been savvy enough to dump the basket and the gloves elsewhere," said the prosecutor. "If we don't find them at the house, chances are slim that we're ever going to find them, not soon enough anyhow."

"I just have a hunch," said Mink, "that you'll find them at the house. I'm telling you; Tom Biggs didn't kill his father. I've believed in his innocence since the beginning."

"I hope you're right, for the boy's sake," said the prosecutor. "It's a case I'd be pleased to drop. If I'm compelled to try a fourteen-year-old for murder, it will haunt me."

"I'm already haunted," confided Mink. "Join the club."

While the DA was having a discussion with Mrs. Plumb at her dress shop where she'd be more comfortable, Chesterman never leaving her side, Hanson and Mink remained at the office, pacing the floor and biting their fingernails for a different reason. It was then that Dunnegan and Wertz, along with a team of policeman, were back at the house conducting another search, this time looking for the picnic basket and a pair of white gloves.

Before opening drawers and rummaging through personal belongings Wertz spoke to Dulcie, informing her of what they were hoping to find and why, confident that she would be as truthful with him as she had been in the past. In the meantime, the other officers began their search in earnest.

"I've been looking for that picnic basket too," she said, "but I haven't been able to find it. If Tom's been trying to protect his mother, then, perhaps, he hid it."

"He must have done a decent job of it if you haven't been able to find it all this time," Wertz commented.

“Well, now that I know it’s probably been deliberately hidden, I have a pretty good idea where it might be,” Dulcie said, confidently leading the way. “Follow me.”

Wertz followed Dulcie into the attic. It didn’t take long for the two of them to find the picnic basket that Tom had hidden inside one of the window seats, covered over with the old blanket.

“There it is,” said Dulcie. Wertz looked at it and nodded his head, shouting for Dunnegan to come up and take a look.

“Still giving off an aroma of fried chicken and apple pie,” he said, having breathed in deeply after carefully opening the lid with a gloved hand. “I’m certain that the inside of this basket will have a story to tell.” Wertz carefully picked it up and put it in a large plastic bag. “We’ve got the picnic basket,” he said to Dunnegan who had come up the attic stairs and immediately proceeded to look around.

“Hey, I found a pair of white gloves!” another police officer shouted up to them from downstairs, but Dunnegan would ignore him as he slowly took in the appearance of the incredible attic, intrigued by its wide-plank floors, dark paneling, and incredibly high ceiling.

“Charming,” he whispered, lingering for a few moments to observe everything from the timeworn reminders of the past to the rafters above him. He picked up an old golf club and twirled it in his fingers. “Boy, I’d like to spend more time up here.”

“Sir! Did you hear what I said? I found the gloves!” the officer shouted again. “They were in the pocket of a lady’s suit jacket hanging in the bedroom closet and they have the initials EB stitched into the material! The only white gloves we could find on the premises!” he added.

“I heard you!” Dunnegan answered, reluctantly having to leave the beguiling attic, secretly hoping to return one day.

So, while Mrs. Plumb repeated her story to the district attorney with Chesterman by her side, the police found what they were searching for, Dunnegan and Wertz still having as much control over Tom’s fate as the district attorney’s office and the judge. The picnic basket and the white gloves were sent to forensics for testing, the partners hopeful that Tom’s nightmare, and theirs, would soon end.

All of the players were in constant communication with one another as they awaited the test results, Mink and the others all but certain that not only would the traces of apple pie found in the basket match those that were found in the elevator, but that the gloves would test positive for powder burns, proving that it was Ellen Biggs who had fired the gun that killed her husband. Along with Mrs. Plumb's account, it would all be enough to reconsider the charges against Tom.

"Although I have to say that the judge isn't too thrilled with the boy and the fact that he hasn't been cooperating," the prosecutor mentioned to Mink.

"Well, ironclad evidence doesn't lie," countered the lawyer. "Hopefully, Tom will give up the fight to protect his dead mother once the test results are in."

"Nothing's ever ironclad until the judge says it is," the prosecutor reminded him. "Everything about this case makes me feel uncomfortable."

"I have every confidence that it will all be over soon." Mink was feeling pretty good as he made a note to himself to invite Mrs. Plumb to supper once everything had blown over.

Within a day, the test results were back, the prosecutor notifying Chesterman, Hanson, and Mink immediately. Hanson answered the phone while the partners paced in front of his desk with a nervous energy neither of them could control. The private investigator was there too, but he sat calmly in a chair and gazed out the window, none of this new or exciting to him. He had seen cases like this before. Anything could happen.

"Give it to me straight," said Hanson.

"Well, the pie crumbs were a match," started the prosecutor, "but the white gloves, now get this, tested negative for powder burns."

"You're kidding me," Hanson said, rubbing his forehead.

"The basket isn't enough, I'm afraid," the prosecutor said. "Believe me, I was hoping for a better outcome, but without powder burns on the white gloves or the mother's fingerprints on the gun, or anywhere in the office for that matter, then this case will certainly be moved to trial. Remember, counselor, that it's the boy's prints, not the mother's, that are on the murder weapon."

"But he didn't do it, damn it!" Hanson shouted into the phone. "What about the old lady? Didn't her story count for anything?"

"I'm sorry, counselor," said the prosecutor, "although I think she'll make a pretty good witness for the defense. That deal I offered you is still on the table, otherwise we'll see you in court."

"Wait a minute," said Hanson. "What about the picnic basket?"

“What about it?”

“You know that the basket is potentially exculpatory evidence if we can prove that the mother somehow played into all of this. If it’s not turned over to the court as evidence then that could be grounds for a mistrial.”

“Hold on, counselor. I have every intention of turning it over to the court during discovery just to cover myself,” said the DA, “but I doubt the judge will go for it. There’s nothing to tie it to the murder and someone could have planted those crumbs in there. After all, the nanny led the police to the basket, didn’t she, which the judge will probably find suspect. Trust me, it will only confuse the jury and waste the court’s time.”

Hanson hung up the phone. Chesterman and Mink didn’t have to ask what the prosecutor had told him. It was written all over his face. They had taken a gamble that didn’t pay off. Chesterman brought his fist down on a small table while Mink buried his head in his hands.

“Well, we’re back to square one, gentlemen,” Hanson said with a somber tone of voice, rolling up his sleeves. “It’s time we get back to work.” But something about that picnic basket nagged at Mink who strongly believed that Ellen Biggs played a part in all of this. Nevertheless, the partners had no choice but to, indeed, get back to work in preparation for the murder trial of their young client.

In the meantime, the private investigator lit a cigarette as he continued to sit calmly in his chair and gaze out the window. He wasn’t surprised at all by the disappointing outcome. Nothing surprised him anymore. He now had his work cut out for him too, but he had a few theories of his own.

Chapter 14

The courtroom was packed that day, the town never having seen a murder trial before, let alone that of a young boy. Chesterman, Hanson, and Mink were clearly ready, no longer somber but, rather, exuding in confidence as they put papers in order at the defense table that sat across and to the left of the judge's bench. I had already pleaded not guilty at a pre-trial hearing, but that didn't stop the avalanche of armchair attorneys and back seat reporters from making predictions and drawing conclusions of their own. The spectators in the gallery eagerly awaited the sordid details and explosive testimony that normally emerged from a trial such as this one. It had already made the dailies and television news, throwing me into a spotlight for which I hadn't bargained.

The prosecution felt less than confident and the buzz around town suggested that there was widespread sympathy for me, perhaps more than what had been anticipated. How could they put a child on trial? But the crime was all too heinous, and every lead pointed to me, the obvious suspect, given my prints on a gun that I deliberately concealed. The DA was haunted by it all, though, just as he had predicted.

Apparently, his nights had been sleepless for months, putting together a case that wasn't as impenetrable as he would have liked. Of course, the defense must never be allowed to sense his vulnerability, or the internal conflict with which he struggled, given that he had a son of his own who was just about my age.

The DA would have to get past his own doubts and relentlessly dig his heels into the case, starting with his opening statement for the prosecution. He would portray me as a young boy who had become angry and violent after finding out about my father's affair with my nanny. The affair would cloud my judgment and, according to the evidence, would cause me to go to my father's law office, knowing that he would be there, and kill him in a cold-blooded fit of jealousy and rage.

I would then make the mistake of leaving a trail of apple pie crumbs in the elevator of my father's office building, the same crumbs that would be found at the bottom of my school lunch bag. The other and, perhaps, more significant mistake would be trying to hide the evidence, specifically the murder weapon, two unused gun cartridges, and two love letters proving my father's affair, all of which dusted positive for my fingerprints. The DA claimed that I murdered my father, giving the jury no other choice but to convict me.

In his opening statement for the defense, Mink would portray me as the victim, claiming that the evidence clearly showed how I was being wrongly accused of something I hadn't done or was even capable of doing. He would contend that the facts of the case and those who had come to bear witness would undoubtedly demonstrate that the prosecution couldn't possibly prove my guilt beyond a reasonable doubt; that it hadn't done its due diligence according to the avalanche of evidence that had unfolded before them; and that it was looking to convict me, despite strong indicators that pointed to a contrary conclusion.

The impassioned lead lawyer would further contend that the prosecution's evidence was flimsy at best, all based on innuendo and presumption, making its case weak in the eyes of the law. Mink strongly asserted that I did not murder my father and the jury, after weighing all of the evidence, would come to that same conclusion before finding me innocent. He was like rolling thunder and his bravado deeply impressed me, one who had only ever witnessed such drama on television, but it insulted the prosecutor who had rejected his opening statement at every turn and was now more determined than ever to relentlessly dig his heels into the case. Dominate I sat there, watching and listening, a scared little jackrabbit being hunted down for supper with no other holes in which to jump. This was it. Was it all worth it, putting myself in this serious situation to cover up for a dead woman? I thought so. Despite what she had done to Eddie, I simply couldn't have my mother's name dragged through the mud, the woman who had raised me labeled a murderer for all eternity by the same society in which she had so eagerly endeavored to become prominent. Taking the rap had been painful, but I had every confidence that the partners would get me off.

After all, I was innocent. They couldn't throw the book at someone like me, a mere child sitting at the defense table in my blue suit and loafers, my hair carefully combed back off my forehead with a beeswax gel to highlight the freckles on my face. For added luck, I slipped a penny into the top of each loafer, but my wide frightened eyes should be enough to complete the picture of an innocent youth, the son of a lawyer and a socialite whose only desire now was to go back to being a small-town boy. The prosecution would call its witnesses, Officer Dunnegan being the first.

"On that fateful Saturday afternoon, what time was the victim murdered?" asked the DA.

"At approximately twelve-thirty p.m.," said Officer Dunnegan.

"And at what time did the defendant get home from the town green?"

"He told me that he got home from the town green at one-thirty p.m., approximately one hour after the murder took place," said the officer.

"Did anyone see him while he was down there?" the DA questioned.

"No, we couldn't find any witnesses who might have seen him while he was down there."

"Moving on, did you see the defendant climb the tree in the early morning hours of the day after the murder?" asked the DA, changing his line of questioning.

"Yes, I saw him climb the tree that next morning," established the officer.

"And was he carrying something?" The DA was waving a pencil around as though he were conducting an orchestra.

"Yes, I believe he was carrying a nest up into the tree," said Officer Dunnegan who didn't sound too confident in his answer.

"Objection, Your Honor," said Mink. "Speculation."

"Sustained," the judge agreed.

"Then what happened?" asked the DA.

"I saw the defendant come down from his treehouse with a box in his hand which he ran over to a wooded area behind the house," said the officer.

"Did he bring anything else down besides the box?" the DA inquired.

"I couldn't tell. I could clearly see the box, but it was still too dark to be certain as to whether or not he had brought anything else down," Officer Dunnegan admitted.

"Is this the box you're referring to?" asked the DA, holding up the box I had buried.

"Yes, that's the box," replied the officer, the jury now getting a good look at it.

"Is this the same box that was found buried under the rock in that wooded area behind the house?" asked the DA.

"Yes, it's the same box," the officer confirmed.

"Do you believe that it was the defendant who buried this box under the rock?" questioned the DA.

"Objection," Mink said again. "Asking the witness to speculate."

"Sustained," said the judge.

"When the box was opened what was found inside?" asked the DA.

"There were Polaroid photographs of Dulcie Jackson and the victim hugging, kissing, and engaging in other affectionate gestures, as well as photos of court documents. Besides the photos, the box also contained a pocketknife, a couple of pieces of sea glass, five or six foreign coins, a few rocks, and a rodent skeleton," recounted Officer Dunnegan.

"Do all of the items from inside the box carry the defendant's fingerprints?"

"Yes, they do," confirmed the officer.

"So, the items from inside the box indicate that the defendant knew his father and his nanny were carrying on an affair, is that correct?" the DA asked, attempting to get the question past the defense.

"Objection, Your Honor," said Mink. "The prosecution is leading the witness."

"Let me ask it another way," said the DA. "Did the defendant know that his father and his nanny were carrying on an affair?"

"According to my investigation with Officer Wertz, Miss Jackson stated that Tom Biggs knew about the affair between she and his father," replied the officer.

"Let's talk about the nest," the DA said, changing the subject. "What was found inside of the nest after the other officer had retrieved it from way up in the tree?"

"Underneath the hardened mud was found a gun, two cartridges, two love letters, and an empty bottle of potassium chloride capsules," described Officer Dunnegan.

"Did the gun have the defendant's fingerprints on it?"

"Yes, it did," the officer confirmed.

"Was it the same gun used to kill Dan Biggs?" the DA questioned further.

"Yes, it was the same gun used to kill the victim," the officer corroborated.

"Did all of the other items carry the defendant's fingerprints as well?" The DA was now tapping his pencil in the palm of his other hand.

"Yes, the cartridges, love letters, and empty bottle all dusted positive for the defendant's fingerprints," verified Officer Dunnegan.

"And who wrote the love letters?" asked the DA.

"Dulcie Jackson wrote one of them to Dan Biggs while he wrote the other one back to her, although his letter to Miss Jackson had never been finished, making it unclear at the time as to whether or not he had actually given it to her," said the officer.

"So, do you think Tom Biggs read the letters?" questioned the DA.

"Objection, Your Honor," said Mink. "The prosecution is asking the witness to speculate again."

"Sustained," the judge responded.

"Did Tom Biggs, at one time, hold those letters in his hand?" the DA asked, rewording his question.

"Yes, he did," said Officer Dunnegan. "His prints are on the letters."

"Did you read the letters?" asked the DA.

"Yes, I did," said the officer.

"Did they imply that Dulcie Jackson and Dan Biggs were having an affair?" the DA probed.

"Objection, Your Honor," said Mink. "It's irrelevant what the letters may have implied to the officer. He's basically being asked for his opinion."

"I'll allow it," said the judge.

"They clearly implied that the two were having an affair," the officer firmly stated.

"One final question, Officer Dunnegan. Was Tom Biggs playing in his backyard when you saw him, perhaps to deal with the shock of having just lost both his parents?" the DA inquired.

"No, he wasn't playing," said the officer. "He had a purpose for being out there. He was busy like he was trying to get some sort of job done."

"Thank you, Your Honor, that will be all," the DA said as he sat down. Mink stood up to cross examine the witness.

"Officer Dunnegan, where were you when you were watching Tom Biggs in his backyard during the early morning hours of the day after the murder?" Mink asked.

"I was sitting in an unmarked car parked on the street with Officer Wertz," the officer answered.

"So, you were sitting in an unmarked car parked on the street while Tom Biggs was running around in his backyard behind the house?" Mink continued.

"That is correct," replied the officer.

"Approximately how many feet from the street is the backyard situated?" asked Mink.

"The backyard is situated approximately two hundred feet from the street," the officer calculated.

"That's quite a distance," Mink commented. "Were you using binoculars?"

"Yes, I was," answered Officer Dunnegan confidently.

"The entire time?" Mink wanted to know.

"Much of the time," responded the officer.

"And how much daylight did you have while you were sitting in the car?" asked Mink.

"Daylight was minimal because the sun was just beginning to rise." Officer Dunnegan took a long sip of water.

"So, you were sitting in a car parked two hundred feet away from the backyard when daylight was minimal, using your binoculars only much of the time, not the entire time, is all of that correct?" Mink summarized.

"That is all correct," replied Officer Dunnegan.

"When you saw Tom Biggs climb the tree in his backyard from two hundred feet away in minimal daylight, could you positively identify what he was holding in his hand?" asked Mink.

"No, I couldn't, but based on the evidence I strongly believe it was the bird's nest," replied the officer.

"Given your distance from the house and the minimal daylight in which you were operating," Mink continued, "is it possible that the object Tom Biggs was holding in his hand while climbing the tree could have been an oddly shaped rock, a model airplane, or a toaster?"

"Based on the evidence, it seems unlikely that he was holding any of those things while climbing the tree," the officer stated smugly.

"But you just testified that you couldn't positively identify what Tom Biggs was holding in his hand while climbing the tree. Are you sticking by your testimony?" Mink pressed him.

"Yes, I am." Officer Dunnegan seemed insulted.

"So, I'll ask the question again," Mink continued, his voice a little louder. "Given your distance from the house and the minimal daylight in which you were operating, is it possible that the object Tom Biggs was holding in his hand while climbing the tree could have been an oddly shaped rock, a model airplane, or a toaster?" The jury was now intently staring at Officer Dunnegan, then at the judge.

"Objection, Your Honor," said the DA. "Asked and answered. Look, the defense is just being silly now. None of those objects ever came into play in this case and the defense is asking the witness to speculate. It would all be pure conjecture on the part of the witness!"

"I'm trying to make a point, Your Honor," said Mink.

"Well, you're certainly taking the long way around," said the judge. "If you have a point to make, then make it! I'll allow the question. Please answer it the way it was asked, Officer Dunnegan." The jury turned their attention back on the officer.

"I suppose it's possible that the object could have been any of those things, but we didn't find..."

"Thank you, Officer Dunnegan, you answered the question," said Mink, cutting him off. "So, can you definitively say, then, that Tom Biggs was holding in his hand the bird's nest containing the evidence when you saw him climbing the tree?"

"Yes, I strongly believe that he was holding in his hand the bird's nest containing the evidence when I saw him climbing the tree," the officer said defiantly, drawing Mink's ire.

"You testified that you couldn't positively identify what Tom Biggs was holding in his hand while climbing the tree, and that the object could have been an oddly shaped rock, a model airplane, or a toaster. Is that correct?" Mink reminded the officer, raising his voice.

"Yes, it is," said the officer.

"So can you definitively say, then, that Tom Biggs was holding in his hand the bird's nest containing the evidence when you saw him climbing the tree?!" Mink asked again.

"Objection, Your Honor, the defense is badgering the witness," asserted the DA.

"Overruled. Answer the question the way it was asked, Officer Dunnegan," said the judge. "You're coming dangerously close to contradicting yourself."

"No, I can't definitively say that Tom Biggs was carrying the bird's nest containing the evidence when I saw him climbing the tree," the officer admitted, having raised his voice slightly.

"So, does that mean that someone else could have carried the bird's nest containing the evidence up into the tree?" Mink probed in a lower voice.

"Objection, Your Honor, the defense is asking the witness to speculate."

"Overruled," the judge replied.

"Yes, I suppose it's possible that someone else could have carried it up there," the officer responded stoically. If he had been deflated it didn't show.

"When asked if he had brought anything else down from the tree besides the box, you stated that it was still too dark to be certain as to whether or not he had brought anything else down. Is that correct?" Mink asked.

"Yes, it is," replied Officer Dunnegan, his voice remaining steady.

"So, is it possible, then, that whatever Tom Biggs had carried up into the tree was also carried back down along with the box?" questioned Mink.

"It's possible," said the officer, the exhale through his nose audible. Dunnegan had, in fact, painted himself into a corner, so he had to be mindful of his demeanor, appearing frustrated never an option.

"I'd like to move on to the box," said Mink who, so far, was pleased with the way things were going but I wasn't sure what to make of it all, too young and naïve to fully understand how I had landed this murder charge in the first place. How did I get into such dire straits, a scared little jackrabbit like myself? "Did you see the defendant bury the box under that rock, Officer Dunnegan?"

"No, from my vantage point I couldn't see him bury the box because the house was in my direct line of vision," the officer admitted.

"But you saw him run into the wooded area behind the house with the box?" Mink pressed further.

"Yes, I did," Officer Dunnegan said before taking another sip of water.

"To look at the photos?" Mink asked.

"Objection," said the DA, rolling his eyes. "Leading the witness."

"Sustained," agreed the judge.

"Is it possible that he brought the box into the wooded area, sat on a rock, and opened it to simply look at the photos?" Mink continued, rephrasing his question.

"Objection, Your Honor," the DA protested. "The witness is being asked to speculate."

"I'll allow it," said the judge.

"I don't see why..." Dunnegan began.

"Is it possible, yes or no?" Mink pressed.

"Sure, it's possible, but..."

"So, is it possible then that the defendant left the box on top of the ground before leaving the wooded area after which time it was later buried by someone else?" Mink asked. "Is that possible?"

"It's possible," the officer conceded. There was no use in arguing the point after having already admitted that the house was in his direct line of vision, rendering him incapable of positively identifying me as the one who buried the box. I watched the jury as it took notes before glancing over at the DA who looked none too happy.

"Thank you, Officer Dunnegan," Mink said quickly. "That will be all, your Honor." Feeling both angry and frustrated, the officer left the stand and proceeded to take a seat six rows behind the prosecution's table. Mink had mopped the floor with him.

As Mink sat back down the prosecution called Officer Wertz to the stand, the DA's line of questioning centered solely around Dulcie.

"Officer Wertz, did you interview the defendant's nanny, Miss Dulcie Jackson?" asked the DA. I perked up at the mere mention of Dulcie's name.

"Yes, I did," the officer confirmed.

"Did she admit to having had an affair with the deceased?" the DA inquired.

"Yes, she told me that they had been having an affair." I scowled, causing Mink to lean over and whisper in my ear. I hated that my family's dirty laundry was being aired out in public.

"And did she state whether or not the defendant knew about the affair?" the DA questioned.

"Yes, she stated that the defendant did know about the affair," indicated the officer.

"And that the defendant was angry about the affair?" the DA poked.

"Objection, Your Honor," Mink interrupted. "Leading the witness."

"Sustained," the judge replied quickly.

"Did she state whether or not the defendant was angry about the affair?" the DA asked, rewording his question.

"No, she didn't use the word angry," the officer contradicted. "She just said that they had talked about it several times and that he was one of the reasons she wanted to break it off with the deceased. She said that the boy needed his father more than she did."

"Thank you, Officer Wertz," said the DA after a surprisingly short examination. "That will be all, Your Honor."

"Would the defense like to cross examine this witness?" asked the judge.

"No questions, Your Honor," Mink said as he looked through his notes, allowing the prosecution to call the head of the forensics team to the stand next.

"How many sets of fingerprints did you find on the gun?" asked the DA.

"There were two sets of prints found on the gun, one belonging to the deceased, and the other belonging to Tom Biggs," the scientist answered confidently.

"Were those the only fingerprints you found on the gun?" the DA continued.

"Yes, they were the only detectible prints found on the gun. There were also smudges, but their origins were indiscernible," replied the scientist.

"Now I'd like to ask about the apple pie crumbs," the DA advised the witness. "Were the crumbs found inside the boy's lunch bag a match to the crumbs found in the elevator of the victim's office building?"

"Yes, they were an exact match in terms of ingredients, nutrient and chemical composition, density, and freshness," confirmed the scientist.

"So, did the crumbs come from the same pie?" questioned the DA.

"After our scientific analysis, it was concluded that the crumbs in both the elevator and the school lunch bag came from the same apple pie," the scientist answered.

"Thank you," said the DA. "That will be all, Your Honor."

"Does the Defense have any questions?" asked the judge.

"Yes, thank you, Your Honor," said Mink as he stood up from his chair. "Tell me, do you like apple pie?" he asked.

"Yes, I do," the forensic scientist replied, nodding his head in the affirmative.

"Did your mother ever make it when you were a little boy?" Mink asked lightheartedly.

"I don't recall," the forensic scientist said with a puzzled look.

"My mother used to make apple pie quite often," Mink began, "because our family loved it so much."

"Objection, Your Honor," said the DA. "I don't see the relevance."

"I'll allow it," said the judge, "but get to the point, Mr. Mink."

"My point is that everyone loved my mother's apple pie. Perhaps four or five people would eat off of the same pie. My father would leave crumbs in his car, my brother would leave crumbs at the kitchen table, and I would leave crumbs on the parlor rug. All of those crumbs came from the same pie, but they were dropped by different people. Isn't it possible that someone other than Tom Biggs could have dropped those apple pie crumbs in the elevator, even though they were a match to the crumbs found at the bottom of his school lunch bag?" asked Mink.

"I would say that it's unlikely that the crumbs found in the elevator were dropped by someone other than the defendant," the scientist commented.

"I asked if it was possible," said Mink with a penetrating stare.

"Yes, I suppose there is a slight possibility that someone other than the defendant could have dropped those apple pie crumbs in the elevator as long as that other person had in his or her possession a piece of that same exact apple pie," the forensic scientist responded.

"Objection, Your Honor. Speculation," the DA protested.

"Overruled," said the judge.

"Were the same apple pie crumbs or traces of the same apple pie crumbs found anywhere else?" Mink inquired.

"Yes, traces of the same apple pie crumbs were found in the picnic basket that was taken from the defendant's attic," the scientist confirmed.

"Were they an exact match in terms of ingredients, nutrient and chemical composition, density, and freshness to the crumbs that were found on the bottom of Tom Biggs' school lunch bag?" Mink asked.

"Yes, they were," affirmed the scientist.

"And to those that were found in the elevator?" Mink pressed on.

"Yes, an exact match," the scientist stated, nodding his head.

"So, is it possible, then, that on the day of the murder whoever used the picnic basket could have been the one to drop those apple pie crumbs in the elevator?" Mink asked.

"Objection, Your Honor. The defense is asking the witness to speculate again," the DA protested, knowing full well that Mink was doing a fine job of punching holes in his case.

"I'll allow the question," the judge replied before turning his attention back to the witness.

"Yes, it's possible if on the day of the murder that person was in the elevator with the picnic basket," the forensic scientist admitted.

"Your Honor, may we approach the bench?" the DA requested before he and Mink walked over to the judge. "There is no other evidence to indicate that the picnic basket is material to this murder case," whispered the DA.

"That picnic basket was turned over to the court by you during discovery as potentially exculpatory evidence," the judge whispered back. "That was when the basket and its contents were admitted into evidence by me, according to the law, therefore the defense has every right to bring it up. As a matter of fact, I would say that he has an obligation to bring it up. Don't tell me that you've already forgotten what happened during discovery, or are you telling me that I made a mistake in my interpretation of the law."

"No, Your Honor," said the DA, having tried and failed to get the judge to disregard what he had already admitted into evidence.

"Then stop wasting the court's time and do your job. Now, stand back." Mink couldn't help but to applaud the judge, at least in his mind.

"What the hell were you thinking?" he whispered to the DA as they turned away from the judge. Both men walked back to their respective tables and Mink continued. "Let's move on to the gun then," he said, breezing to another topic. "You mentioned that there were smudges found on the gun. Could those smudges indicate that a third person may have touched the gun?" Mink asked.

"The smudges could certainly indicate that a third person may have touched the gun," said the forensic scientist, "given that those smudges contained skin oils that were different to those that comprised the prints, but again there were only two sets of distinct fingerprints found on the gun. Skin oils alone cannot identify a person," the forensic scientist reminded the defense.

"Were the defendant's fingerprints found on the trigger?" Mink asked.

"No, it's practically impossible to find fingerprints on a trigger," the scientist informed the defense while many of the jurors took copious notes.

"Where were they found then?" Mink probed.

"They were found on the barrel near the victim's prints and on the grip, indicating that the defendant had held the gun, probably with his two hands," said the forensic scientist, holding up both hands to demonstrate what he meant.

"Did you find the grip to be smooth enough to sustain fingerprints?" Mink asked curiously.

"Yes, the grip being made of a bone material was smooth enough in certain areas to sustain the defendant's prints," replied the scientist.

"But does that indicate that my client fired the gun?" Mink wanted to know.

"No, not necessarily," said the scientist, "but it indicates that he held the gun in his two hands."

"Were the defendant's fingerprints found in my law office?" Mink continued.

"No, they were not," the scientist responded.

"Were the defendant's fingerprints found in the elevator?" This was the final question Mink would pose to this witness…for now.

"No, they were not," the forensic scientist would repeat.

"Thank you. That will be all, Your Honor." Mink sat back down and watched as the DA shook his head before calling a ballistics expert.

"How many cartridges were fired from the gun?" asked the DA.

"Two," the expert answered.

"And were those bullets recovered?" the DA inquired.

"Yes, one was extracted from the victim's chest, while the other was extracted from the ceiling of the victim's office," the expert replied.

"And were the cartridge casings that housed those two bullets recovered?" the DA continued.

"Yes, they were both found on the floor of the office," the expert confirmed.

"Were the cartridge casings found on the floor identical to those cartridges found hidden up in the tree by the defendant?" asked the DA.

"Objection, Your Honor," Mink interrupted. "It hasn't been established that my client hid anything up in that tree. Officer Dunnegan stated in his testimony that he couldn't definitively say that the boy was carrying the bird's nest containing the evidence in his hand when he saw him climb the tree," Mink argued. "He admitted that he was sitting too far away, and that there wasn't enough daylight for him to discern what Tom Biggs was carrying. The prosecution is merely speculating that my client hid those cartridges up in the tree."

"Objection sustained. Reword your question," the judge ordered.

"Were the cartridge casings found on the floor identical to those cartridges found hidden up in the tree?" the DA asked again without implicating me.

"Yes, the cartridge casings found on the floor were identical in every way to those cartridges found hidden up in the tree, including the caliber and the manufacturer," established the expert.

"Thank you. That will be all, Your Honor." The DA sat back down, tapping his pencil on the table.

"Would the defense like to cross examine this witness?" asked the judge.

"Yes, thank you, Your Honor," Mink politely responded as he stood up. "You stated that the cartridge casings found on the floor were identical in every way to those cartridges found hidden up in the tree, is that correct?"

"That is correct," answered the ballistics expert.

"Were there fingerprints on the cartridges found up in the tree?" asked Mink.

"Yes, there were two sets of fingerprints on the cartridges found up in the tree, those of both Tom Biggs and the deceased," the expert confirmed.

"But were there fingerprints on the cartridge casings found on the floor of my law office?" Mink asked, scrunching his face with a curious expression.

"No, there were no fingerprints on the casings found on the floor. Any fingerprints that might have been on those brass cartridge casings before the gun was fired were vaporized by the high firing temperature," the expert revealed.

"So, do you still stand by your testimony that the cartridge casings found on the floor were identical in every way to those cartridges found hidden up in the tree?" Mink pressed the ballistics expert.

"I was referring to the stamp that indicates the caliber and manufacturer," he replied in an attempt to clarify his statement.

"But that's not what you said. You said that the cartridge casings found on the floor were identical in every way to those cartridges found hidden up in the tree, isn't that correct?" Mink countered, highlighting the inconsistency.

"Yes, however I was referring to…" Mink would cut him short.

"Yet you are now stating that there were no fingerprints on the casings found on the floor of my law office," he pointed out.

"That is correct, but..." the expert tried to continue.

"That's a hell of a difference between the casings found on the floor of my law office and the cartridges found up in the tree, wouldn't you say?" Mink asked sarcastically.

"Objection, Your Honor," the DA interjected, "the defense is badgering the witness."

"Sustained," the judge agreed.

"Is it even possible then," Mink resumed, "to positively identify the person who may have loaded those cartridges into the gun that killed Dan Biggs?"

"No, that's not possible because spent casings are always devoid of prints," the expert admitted.

"So, is it reasonable to say that my client may not have been the one who loaded the gun that killed Dan Biggs?" Mink asked in earnest.

"Yes, it's reasonable because spent casings in and of themselves cannot implicate anyone, given that any skin oils that may have been on their surface area before firing are always destroyed by the firing temperature," the ballistics expert stated clearly.

"Thank you," said Mink. "That will be all, Your Honor."

"The court will take a fifteen-minute recess," said the judge, the tap of his gavel causing me to flinch. Mink, along with the bailiff, escorted me into a small side room to talk.

Mink felt pretty good, all things considered, after having gotten in some pretty good licks but I was glassy-eyed, the seriousness of it all nearly too much to bear. I always fancied myself a pretty good judge of people, but I was blindsided and hurt when Officer Dunnegan took to the stand to testify against me. What was even more painful was that I had been spied upon by someone who I thought was on my side. It turned out that the officer was actually a skunk who had tricked me into thinking he was looking out for my best interest. A naïve little jackrabbit I was.

"It's not too late to tell me what really happened, Tom," Mink reminded me.

"I don't know what really happened," I said, continuing my charade. Mink let out a long sigh.

"All right, have it your own way but I don't believe you're telling me the truth," he said, wagging a finger at me. "Please understand that if we lose this case, the judge will probably lose whatever tolerance he has left and throw the book at you. He already considers you to be uncooperative." My eyes widened. "Right now, you're innocent until proven guilty, but if they find you culpable of this murder then the consequences will be frightful to say the least. You'll be thrown into some juvenile correctional facility for a very long time. Do you understand all of that, Tom?"

"But I didn't do it," I said.

"It doesn't matter," Mink snapped. "There are plenty of innocent people sitting in jail right now. I'm trying my level best to get you off but as I've told you before there are no guarantees. Are you sure you don't want to change your mind and tell me what you know, or what you think you know, about your mother's involvement in all of this?" Mink was practically begging.

"I don't know anything about that," I said softly before hanging my head. The gravity of the situation was suddenly crashing down all around me with an intensity I hadn't expected.

"Well, do you have any questions then?" Mink asked curtly, finding himself irritated at me.

"What are cartridges?" I asked innocently. Mink relaxed a bit, obviously feeling contrite for his impatience. My tight-lipped approach, however, was taking its toll on him.

"You might refer to them as bullets," he began to explain calmly. "They're little cases that contain the powder and the bullet for a handgun like your father's. When the gun is fired, the bullet comes out of the cartridge casing and either hits or misses its target, while the cartridge casing flies off to the side and down to the ground. Understand?" Mink placed a gentle hand on my shoulder, sensing the fright that had suddenly enveloped me.

"Yes, I understand, Uncle Andrew," I replied, barely able to get the words out.

"Anything else, son?" Mink quietly asked, hoping I'd crack under all the pressure and finally give in. The lawyer could only hope that I would come to my senses and save myself.

"Just one other question. What does culpable mean?" I asked. At that moment, Chesterman walked into the small room.

"The prosecution will be calling Dulcie Jackson to testify next," he said in a breathless voice. "We need to get ready."

"Dulcie? What do they want with her?" I inquired, forgetting all about the question I had asked Mink. "Is she going to betray me the way Officer Dunnegan did?"

"I wanted to talk to you about that, Tom," Mink said, pulling his chair up close to me. "You see, they'll be asking Dulcie about her personal knowledge of all this, her observations while taking care of you, and her interactions with you over the last several years but I'll be asking her questions too."

My face must have shown the great displeasure I felt at the thought of Dulcie up there on that witness stand.

"Don't be angry with Dulcie," Mink advised, "she had no choice in the matter but to testify. I'm telling you, Tom, this isn't a game. I'm always willing to listen to whatever you might want to tell me." My lips quivered as I lowered my eyes, but I refused to crack, Mink quickly giving up after reading my body language. "Very well then," he proceeded, "we've got to get back in there. Remind me to give you the definition of culpable at our next break."

I had the feeling, though, that I already knew what it meant.

The court was back in session within a few minutes, the tap of the judge's gavel causing me to flinch once again. Mink placed a comforting arm around my shoulder, but it was obvious that I couldn't possibly tolerate the day's proceedings much longer. Luckily, Dulcie was the prosecution's last witness, the judge certain to adjourn the session at the conclusion of her testimony.

"Miss Jackson, how do you know the defendant?" asked the DA.

"I've been his nanny for several years," Dulcie stated, obviously uncomfortable with having to testify. I quickly blushed from both excitement and embarrassment upon seeing her.

"How long were you carrying on an affair with the defendant's father, Miss Jackson?" the DA inquired bluntly, coming right to an embarrassing point.

"From the time I moved into his house until the time of his murder," she admitted. I felt my face flush.

"How quickly after you moved in did your relationship with the deceased become serious in nature?" the DA probed further.

"Pretty quickly. I would say within a week after I moved in," Dulcie calculated, "maybe sooner."

"And at what time would you say the defendant became aware of the affair?" questioned the DA.

"He knew about it all along, although he didn't admit that to me until later on. He was aware of his father's intentions toward me before I even moved into the house," Dulcie replied, informing the court of my insight before squirming in her seat.

"Why did Dan Biggs ask you to move into his house?" the DA solicited, regardless of Dulcie's rising embarrassment.

"To help out his sick wife, who would be coming home from the hospital, and to be closer to him," Dulcie conceded, never thinking that she'd be thrown into the middle of such a mess just because she had loved someone.

"I'd like to move on to a different topic, Miss Jackson," the DA informed his witness. "Did the defendant get along with his father?"

"They had a distant relationship." Dulcie was right about that, although I resented her having to say it in a court of law. More of the family's dirty laundry come to light.

"As the affair progressed, did their relationship become even more distant?" the DA questioned further.

"Objection, Your Honor," said Mink. "The witness is being asked to speculate."

"I'll allow it," the judge decided.

"Yes, I believe it did," Dulcie guessed. And again, she was right.

"Miss Jackson, was Tom angry about your liaison with his father, especially after you moved into the house?" I could tell that Dulcie was embarrassed and upset over the upheaval caused by the affair, especially now given that she had no choice but to speak about it publicly.

"Yes, very angry. He had asked me to put an end to it because it was unfair to his mother and to him," she said, locking eyes with me for the first time.

"And did you?" the DA wanted to know.

"I tried. I wrote Dan a letter, but never got a response from him," she replied, unaware of father's unfinished letter.

"Is this the letter you wrote?" asked the DA, holding up Dulcie's love letter that was found inside of the nest up in the tree.

"Yes, that's the letter," she admitted as her face blushed.

"And were you aware that the deceased had no intention of breaking off his relationship with you?" the DA questioned, showing Dulcie my father's unfinished letter.

"No, I had no idea. I never saw that letter," she responded, shaking her head. Her bottom lip appeared to be trembling a bit.

"How do you think the defendant got his hands on these letters?" the DA asked curiously, but of course Mink would have none of it.

"Objection, Your Honor. The witness is being asked to speculate," Mink stated again, only this time he knew that the judge would have to agree.

"Sustained," he answered quickly.

"Did you give the defendant a Polaroid camera, Miss Jackson?" the DA asked, moving forward.

"Yes, I did, after he told me that he wanted to be a photographer when he grew up," Dulcie replied.

"Can you identify these photographs found in the defendant's lock box taken by that same Polaroid camera?" questioned the DA.

"Those are photographs of Dan and me," Dulcie said, visibly shaken after seeing the photos as though they sent a chill up her spine.

"Did anyone else other than the defendant have access to his lock box?" the DA inquired.

"I'm not aware of anyone else having access to his lock box," Dulcie informed the DA. "There was only one key, which he had in his possession, and he kept the box up in his treehouse."

"Did the defendant ever tell you that he'd like to kill his father?" the DA asked frankly, taking Dulcie by surprise.

"Objection, Your Honor," said Mink who had been taking copious notes.

"Overruled. Answer the question, Miss Jackson," the judge ordered.

"Yes, once," she conceded. "We were up in the attic eating Chinese food. That was when he admitted to seeing his father and me flirting, kissing, and holding each other. It was then that he told me he would like to kill his father, but I don't think…"

"Thank you, Miss Jackson, you answered the question," the DA interrupted. "Did the defendant ever tell you that he had a crush on you?"

"No, not in so many words," Dulcie uncomfortably replied.

"I object to the vagueness of the witness's response, Your Honor," said Mink.

"Sustained. Did the defendant ever actually tell you that he had a crush on you, Miss Jackson?" asked the judge who had turned to Dulcie.

"No, Your Honor," she said softly. "He never actually told me that he had a crush on me."

"Did the defendant *appear* to have a crush on you?" the DA continued to probe.

"Objection. The witness is being asked to speculate," Mink said.

"Sustained. Reword your question," the judge directed the DA.

"Did the defendant's behaviors indicate that he had a crush on you?" asked the DA.

"Objection," Mink said again, but this time the prosecution got the question to stick.

"Overruled," the judge said. "I'll allow it."

"Once, I saw him gazing at me with a starry look in his eyes like he was smitten, you know what I mean?" Dulcie asked meekly before glancing in my direction. I was embarrassed and could feel the blood rush to my head.

"Objection, Your Honor," Mink interjected once more.

"Overruled," the judge stated, waving him off.

"On the day of the murder, the defendant said he went to the town green. Did you know that he was going there?" asked the DA.

"No, I had left the house before he did," Dulcie remembered.

"And when the defendant got home at one-thirty p.m., approximately one hour after the murder had taken place, did he tell you what he did while he was gone?"

"No, we didn't discuss anything about his time away from the house that day. Instead, he took a tray straight up to his mother who wasn't feeling well," Dulcie recounted.

"Thank you, Miss Jackson. That will be all, Your Honor," the DA said before sitting back down. He had gotten a few incriminatory statements out of Dulcie, but would they be enough to convict me?

"Would the defense like to cross examine this witness?" asked the judge.

"Yes, thank you, Your Honor," said Mink as he stood up from the defense table.

"Miss Jackson, you stated that Tom Biggs, the defendant, knew about your affair with his father, Dan Biggs, all along, is that correct?" asked Mink.

"Yes, that's correct," Dulcie agreed.

"And that Dan Biggs asked you to move in, in part, to help out his sick wife who would be coming home from the hospital, is that correct?" Mink continued.

"Yes, that's correct," Dulcie agreed again.

"Were you carrying on an affair with Dan Biggs while his wife was in the hospital?" Mink asked incredulously.

"Yes, I was," Dulcie admitted.

"And were you still carrying on an affair with Dan Biggs after his wife got home from the hospital during the period in which she was still recuperating?" Mink persisted, feigning disbelief of such conduct.

"Yes, I was," Dulcie admitted again.

"How dare the boy be angry at that!" Mink shouted sarcastically after turning to the jury.

"Objection, Your Honor!" the DA called out, protesting Mink's sudden mockery.

"Sustained! Repress your sarcasm, counselor," rebuked the judge before ordering a sidebar. Mink and the DA approached the bench. "One more stunt like that and I'll find you in contempt. Understood? Now, step back," the judge sternly instructed without waiting for a response.

"Yes, Your Honor," Mink replied anyway before walking back to his table, not at all sorry for the sarcastic comment, although he would appear contrite for good measure.

"The jury will disregard the defense's last remark," ordered the judge before allowing Mink to continue.

"Miss Jackson, when the defendant told you that he'd like to kill his father, did he say it in jest?" Mink asked.

"Objection," Your Honor. "The witness is being asked to speculate," alleged the DA.

"I'll allow it," said the judge. "Please answer the question, Miss Jackson."

"Yes, I strongly believe that he said it in jest," Dulcie replied, nodding her head.

"Did you think at any time that the defendant was intent on killing his father?" Mink asked.

"No, I never thought that Tom was intent on killing his father," Dulcie answered, slowly shaking her head back and forth. "Never." The DA smirked.

"Let's talk about the day of the murder," Mink specified before changing his line of questioning. "When the defendant got home from the town green at one-thirty p.m., did you notice anything strange or unusual about his behavior?"

"No, I didn't notice anything strange or unusual," Dulcie affirmed.

"Was the defendant shaking, or appear to be agitated or upset?" Mink questioned.

"Objection, Your Honor. Asked and answered," challenged the DA.

"Overruled," the judge answered before looking back at Dulcie.

"No, his demeanor was the same as usual," she recalled.

"Did you see any blood on the defendant's clothing or on his hands?" Mink continued.

"Objection," the DA uttered, the bags under his eyes, unnoticed by me until now, causing him to appear weary.

"Overruled," the judge responded, his chin in the palm of his hand. He seemed to be fatigued as well by the day's proceedings.

"No, I did not," Dulcie stated clearly.

"Did the defendant say anything that concerned you, Miss Jackson?" Mink solicited, this being his final inquiry.

"No, he did not," Dulcie repeated.

"Thank you, Miss Jackson. That will be all, Your Honor," Mink said, turning from the judge before letting out a long, silent breath. After sitting back down at the defense table he loosened his tie a bit while jotting down a few notes. At this point I was feeling fidgety and most likely overtired as mother used to call it.

After Dulcie's testimony, the prosecution rested its case and court was mercifully adjourned for the day. I couldn't help but feel betrayed by Officer Dunnegan, Dulcie, even my mother. Was I a fool for not telling Mink about the key that she had pressed into my hand, leading me to unlock her wicked little secrets? Had this all gone too far?

It was getting harder and harder to keep my lips sealed but I didn't see how telling the truth now would exonerate me anyway. I had dug a hole so deep for myself that, regardless of any acquittal, even the judge might be inclined to keep me down there and pack it with dirt so as to bury me once and for all.

Back at the detention center that evening, I was mentally drained and physically weak from nervous exhaustion, unable to keep my eyes open for long. I fell into a deep sleep and would remain there for the next ten hours, at no time stirring during the night. I was quickly engulfed by my dreams, fuzzy and vague for the most part until they eventually evolved into vivid disturbances just prior to the guard's early morning wake up call.

Thank goodness that as I emerged from sleep, the electric chair before me quickly faded away while the noose around my neck became a mere loose fitting pajama top that had been hiked up and twisted by the talons of my tormenting hallucinations. Clutching my throat, I sat up and gasped for air, nonetheless, before taking a good look around to confirm that it had only been my mind playing tricks and conjuring up fears, sending them twirling around me like a thorny cyclone. And yet, the nightmare of the new day's proceedings awaited me still. Today, the defense would call up its own witnesses, but I had to wonder if I actually had a chance in hell of getting off the hook…this scared little jackrabbit.

Chapter 15

The partners were just about finished gathering up the last of their paperwork critical to the direct examination of their witnesses before leaving for court.

"Naturally, we'll make a motion to dismiss the charges and if that fails, we'll call Mrs. Plumb to the stand first," said Chesterman who was armed with a briefcase full of notes that he had taken, not only during the dear lady's visit to their law office, but also throughout her discussion with the district attorney.

"The judge didn't think much of her story, not enough to stop the trial anyway," Mink reminded Chesterman, "given that there were no powder burns on Ellen's white gloves and her fingerprints were nowhere to be found on either the gun or in the office."

"Yes, but there's still the picnic basket with its matching apple pie crumbs. All we need to do is sow a seed of doubt about Tom's guilt into the minds of the jurors and that should be enough to get him acquitted. Besides, I don't think the prosecution made their case," Chesterman concluded.

"Maybe not, but Mrs. Plumb's testimony will open up a Pandora's box. After she tells her little story on the stand, the DA will poke all sorts of holes into it by bringing up Ellen's clean white gloves and missing fingerprints with the forensic scientist," surmised Mink who didn't see any advantage at all to putting Mrs. Plumb on the witness stand. But Chesterman was optimistic.

"Trust me Andrew, her testimony coupled with your effective cross examination of the prosecution's witnesses will sway the jury in our direction, you mark my words," Chesterman said confidently. "Look how we reacted after Mrs. Plumb told us about Ellen's plans to have lunch with her husband only minutes before he was murdered, especially after she mentioned that there was apple pie inside the picnic basket! After listening to the dear lady's story, I was so sure that it was Ellen who had killed Dan and I still say that she's, somehow, connected to his homicide."

“Do you really think that the jury will acquit the boy?” asked Mink, who had started to second guess himself. His worry over losing the case was considerable, not only because of a certain loyalty he had to his dead partner, but because the thought of a fourteen-year-old boy being found guilty of murdering his own father sickened him.

“He’ll be acquitted, don’t you worry,” said Chesterman. “The jury will come to the conclusion that a young boy like Tom could’ve never pulled off such a murder anyway.” Hanson, who had been quietly organizing papers for court, strongly concurred with his partner.

“Yeah, Chesterman is right. A kid like Tom could’ve never committed a murder like Dan’s, not in a million years,” he said skeptically, shaking his head while stuffing documents into his own briefcase. The private investigator who had been working on the case for months suddenly breezed through the office door unannounced.

“I wouldn’t be too sure about that,” he said, contradicting both lawyers who abruptly stopped what they were doing, having been rendered motionless by the statement.

“What do you mean?” said an already uneasy Mink, who had stood up from his desk.

“I have some news,” he informed the partners. “You’ll all want to sit down for this.” He lit a cigarette and took a long drag before relaying his findings to Chesterman, Hanson, and Mink who listened in disbelief.

What he had found was an improbable twist in the case that no one could have anticipated. How it would all shake out in the end was anybody’s guess but for now, it was time to contact the district attorney’s office. The judge would certainly put a stop to the trial, at least for several days, in order to give both sides a chance to regroup and properly prepare themselves for what was to come, namely new witnesses and a left turn into the bizarre.

“I’m not happy,” the judge said with a scowl on his face. “Why wasn’t this evidence brought to my attention sooner and why weren’t these witnesses on the original list? The trial is half over, for Christ’s sake!”

The private investigator sat in his chair, unmoved by the judge’s bluster. He was known in the business for seizing upon opportunities that might change the trajectory of court cases and this one was a perfect example. Given the outlandish development that had presented itself, after some good old fashioned detective work, he had no choice but to throw a monkey wrench into the trial and no irritable judge would ever intimidate or detour him. His answer was stock and a bit blasé.

"It's new information, Your Honor," he said before taking a long drag off his cigarette.

"I can assure you, Your Honor, that if we had been in possession of this evidence or had known about these witnesses prior to the start of the trial, then we would have by all means made a full disclosure to the court," said Mink, more willing to explain the situation to the judge. The DA sat with his elbow propped up on a side table, his cheek cradled in the palm of his open hand. He already knew that a whole new ball game awaited him. "Therefore, in light of these new developments, Your Honor," Mink continued, "I respectfully ask that you put a temporary halt to the trial, allowing both sides several days to interview new witnesses, cross-check testimony, and consider new evidence."

"The proposed testimony and accompanying evidence are substantial to the case, Your Honor," Chesterman interjected, "and, if allowed, will address the main issue at hand here which is the murder of Daniel Biggs. Their importance to the defense is immeasurable and could very well exonerate our client."

"And what are your thoughts on all of this?" the judge asked the DA.

"I don't believe we have any other choice but to allow the new testimony and admit the additional evidence," he conceded. "The boy was seen entering and exiting the building at the time of the murder by a witness who will attest to that in court, while another can positively identify the newly discovered physical evidence."

"Including the fingerprint that ended up being a match to…" began the private investigator before being waved off by the judge who was loath to listen to his nonchalant tone of voice any further.

"Yes, yes, understood. The trial needs to be temporarily halted," he said, none too pleased about it. "All right, I'll give both sides four days to interview new witnesses, cross-check testimony, and consider new evidence, ample time I would say. Court will reconvene next Monday at which time the defense will begin to call its witnesses. Now, if you gentlemen will excuse me it's time for my daily tonic which awaits me at the Old Windsor Cove Country Club."

After a collective thanks to the judge, both sides got down to business. Such surprises were rarely seen in the relatively mundane world of lawyering, common only to television and dime store novels. This crazy new slant in the case would sell newspapers and remain the topic of town gossip for months to come.

The private investigator had undoubtedly exceeded all expectations, he himself astonished by the speed at which everything had fallen into place once he got the ball rolling. Perhaps it was simply dame fortune, but he knew better than that. There was more to his job than sheer luck. What did Dan Biggs always say?

"Never underestimate the value of a good private investigator. He's a lawyer's best friend." But unlike a best friend time would slip away, never to be recaptured. Monday morning arrived quickly.

***

"Your Honor, the defense asks for a motion to dismiss the charges against our client. The prosecution has failed to prove its case," Mink stated in this obligatory motion, rarely granted by a judge, before beginning his defense.

"Motion denied," said the judge, the rejection fully expected by the partners. "Bring in the jury after which time the defense will call its first witness," he instructed after a tap of his gavel. I only winced this time, finally getting used to the sound. The partners had effectively placed Mrs. Plumb and the picnic basket on a back burner, their necessity to the case having now become moot, while their alternate witness would bring a smile to my face and a yearning for a bacon-wrapped fig or crab cake.

"The defense would like to call as its first witness the head chef from the Epicurean Castle, Your Honor," said Mink. The man who had both befriended me and kept my father from thrashing Eddie on the night he ruined our mother's dinner party took to the stand, having previously spoken to the private investigator about someone he saw on the day of the murder. "Please tell the court where you were and what you saw at approximately twelve-fifteen p.m. on the Saturday afternoon that Daniel Biggs was murdered," directed Mink.

"Well, I was coming out of the bank on Kimball Avenue when I saw a young boy walking into the building where your law office is situated," said the chef. My ears perked up.

"Can you describe the boy?" asked Mink.

"He was young, a little heavy, and had dirty blonde hair. He was also disheveled and pretty dirty looking, like he hadn't had a bath in a long time. To me, he looked as though he were homeless," concluded the chef.

"What was the boy wearing?" Mink inquired.

"He was wearing blue jeans, a black t-shirt, black sneakers, and a pair of gray woolen gloves, the kind without the tips on the fingers," the chef recalled.

"Are these the gloves he was wearing?" asked Mink, holding up a pair of gray gloves without fingertips.

"Yes, those are the gloves," said the chef, making a positive identification.

"Is the boy you saw walking into the building on that day sitting in this courtroom today?" questioned Mink.

"No, he is not," the chef replied.

"Is this the boy you saw walking into the building on that day?" Mink questioned further, holding up a photograph.

"Yes, that's the boy I saw," answered the chef.

"Thank you. That will be all, Your Honor," said Mink as he sat back down at the defense table.

"Would the prosecution like to cross examine this witness?" asked the judge.

"Yes, thank you, Your Honor," said the DA. "Are you absolutely certain that the boy you just identified in the photograph is the same boy that you saw enter the office building where the law office is situated at twelve-fifteen p.m. on the Saturday afternoon that Dan Biggs was murdered?" asked the DA.

"Yes, I'm certain," said the chef.

"And how far away from him were you when you saw him?" the DA inquired.

"Well, I was coming out of the bank, so I was approximately twenty feet away," the chef estimated.

"Do those glasses that you're wearing help you with your distance vision?" the DA asked curiously.

"Yes, they do," the chef confirmed.

"Were you wearing them on that day?" the DA probed.

"No, I wasn't, not on that particular day. I had left them in my car," the chef recalled.

"So, can you normally see twenty feet away without your glasses?" the DA probed further.

"It usually depends on the situation," began the head chef, "but that particular day was sunny and bright, allowing me to get a good look at the boy as he entered the building. The boy in the photograph is definitely the same boy I saw enter the building that afternoon."

"Would you mind removing your glasses?" asked the DA at which time the chef complied.

"Objection, Your Honor," said Mink. "What is the point of asking the witness to remove his glasses? The question was asked and answered by the witness who was confident when he identified the boy in the photograph as being the same boy he saw enter our building at around the time of the murder."

"The court will realize my point in a minute, Your Honor," the DA promised. "I can assure you of its relevance because it will demonstrate the witness's visual acuity when attempting to identify someone at a distance without his glasses."

"I'll allow it, counselor, but get on with it," said the leery judge who sometimes found the DA's tactics to be questionable.

"Thank you, Your Honor," he said before turning back to the witness. "So, tell the court again, was this the boy you saw go into the office building at approximately twelve-fifteen on the afternoon of the murder?" the DA asked the chef after backing up twenty feet from the witness stand while holding up a large photograph of his own son.

"I think so," said the chef, squinting to see the photograph.

"Objection, Your Honor!" shouted Mink. "The prosecution is attempting to trick the witness with false evidence, namely the photograph he is holding up which was not the photograph entered into evidence by this court."

"Sustained," the judge said angrily.

"I am merely trying to show, Your Honor, that this gentleman cannot see twenty feet away without his glasses," explained the DA who knew he had crossed the line. The jury knew it too, but they got his point. I had to suppress a giggle.

"The jury will disregard the prosecution's last question and the witness's answer to that question," ordered the judge who was outraged at the DA's desperate maneuver, especially after the chef had already described the person he had seen in such detail, proof that his glasses weren't necessary at that particular time. "What the hell was that?" he whispered to the DA after ordering the lawyers from both sides to approach the bench. "Are you looking to be held in contempt? Or perhaps you wish to have an ethics charge filed against you."

"Like I said, Your Honor, I was merely trying to show…" started the DA.

"I don't care what you were trying to show. No more circus tricks," the judge instructed through clenched teeth before telling the lawyers to step back. "Now, will there be anything else?" he asked the prosecution.

"That will be all, Your Honor," said the DA as he walked back to his table, struggling to stifle a grin. The incident had tickled Mink's funny bone too but, of course, he couldn't show that in court. It probably would have been a slam dunk for the prosecution if the judge had allowed the DA's silliness to continue, the chef obviously unable to clearly see the large photograph that had been held up at a distance of twenty feet away. Actually, I needed a little bit of silliness right about then, particularly after having seen the sobering photograph of the boy who, according to the chef, had entered father's office building on the day of his murder.

"Then the defense may call its next witness," the judge ordered before taking in a deep breath and a long sip of water. The DA had rattled him.

"The defense calls Monty Kravitz, owner of the Bait and Tackle Shop located on the cove, Your Honor," Mink said, watching as the old gentleman made his way over to the witness stand before swearing to tell the truth. "Mr. Kravitz, please tell the court what you saw two months ago when you looked out onto the beach from your store window."

"I saw a young boy coming out of the old shack on the beach," answered the elderly gentleman, a timeworn fixture on the cove for decades. "He strolled down to the surf where he washed his hands and face in the saltwater before walking off the beach and heading toward town."

"Can you describe the boy, Mr. Kravitz?" asked Mink.

"Oh, he seemed kind of young, a bit stocky and had greasy blonde hair. He looked as though he hadn't had a mother's care in a long time. I told myself that if the boy ever returned to the shack I would notify the authorities, but I never saw him again." I sat at the table, mesmerized by the testimony which had dumbfounded me to say the least.

"What was the boy wearing on the day you saw him, sir?" Mink inquired.

"He was wearing blue jeans, a black t-shirt, and black sneakers," said the old gentleman.

"And after the boy walked off the beach and headed toward town what did you do then?" Mink continued.

"I strolled over to the shack and poked around inside," the owner of the shop admitted, appearing embarrassed that he had invaded the boy's privacy. "It looked as though he had been living there for a while."

"Can you describe what you saw inside the shack?" Mink inquired.

"I saw an old tarp, a few empty food containers, a flashlight, and a book of matches. Oh, and I saw a pair of gray woolen gloves without the fingertips," said Mr. Kravitz.

"Are these the gloves you saw in the shack?" asked Mink, holding up the same gray gloves he had shown to the chef.

"Yes, those are the gloves all right," confirmed the old gentleman.

"Let the record show, Your Honor, that the gloves positively identified by Mr. Kravitz as having been the ones he saw in the shack on the beach are the same gloves positively identified by the chef as having been the ones worn by the boy he saw enter the office building at twelve-fifteen p.m. on the Saturday afternoon that Dan Biggs was murdered," Mink stated carefully.

"Duly noted, counselor," said the judge.

"Is this the flashlight you saw?" Mink continued, holding it up for the witness.

"Yes, I believe it is," confirmed Mr. Kravitz.

"Is the boy you saw coming out of the old shack on the beach sitting in this courtroom today, sir?" Mink asked.

"No, I don't see him here today, said the old gentleman, shaking his head."

"Is this the boy you saw coming out of the old shack on the beach?" Mink questioned, holding up the same photograph he had shown the chef.

"That's him," Mr. Kravitz verified eagerly, pointing to the photo. "That's the boy I saw coming out of the shack."

"Let the record show, Your Honor, that the boy in the photograph, who has just been positively identified by Mr. Kravitz as having been the one he saw coming out of the old shack on the beach, is the same boy who was positively identified by the chef as having been the one he saw enter the office building at twelve-fifteen p.m. on the Saturday afternoon that Dan Biggs was murdered," Mink stated.

"Duly noted, counselor," said the judge.

"That will be all, Your Honor," said Mink, taking a long drink of water after he sat down. He seemed as though he could jump out of his skin, knowing that the defense had stumbled onto something big. I stared straight ahead in disbelief, never uttering a word or asking a question.

"Would the prosecution like to cross examine this witness?" asked the judge, secretly holding his breath.

"Yes, Your Honor," said the DA. "Did you find any weapons in the shack, Mr. Kravitz?"

"No, I didn't," the old gentleman stated clearly.

"When you saw the boy come out of the shack, did he appear to be carrying a weapon?" asked the DA.

"I didn't see him carrying a weapon," the shop owner replied.

"Could he have had a weapon in his pocket?" the DA probed.

"Objection, Your Honor," said Mink. "The witness is being asked to speculate."

"Sustained," the judge responded in agreement.

"Did the boy appear to have blood stains on his clothing?" the DA prodded further.

"Objection, Your Honor. Mr. Kravitz would not have been able to detect the existence of blood stains on the boy's dark colored clothing given the distance from his shop window to the beach, therefore he's being asked to speculate again," Mink concluded.

"I'll allow it," said the judge. "Did the boy appear to have blood stains on his clothing, Mr. Kravitz?" the judge asked after turning to the witness.

"Not that I could see, Your Honor," said the old gentleman. Mink smirked before slightly shaking his head.

"And finally, Mr. Kravitz," began the DA, "did you notice any blood stains inside or outside of the shack?"

"No, I didn't notice any blood stains either inside or outside of the shack," the old gentleman answered confidently.

"So, you're saying it was spotless both inside and out, is that correct?" the DA asked, looking for further confirmation.

"Objection, Your Honor," said Mink. "The prosecution is leading the witness."

"Overruled," said the judge. "You may answer the question."

"I wouldn't call it spotless. The inside of the shack was certainly dirty, but I've gutted enough fish in my day to know blood when I see it and I tell you I didn't see any blood stains inside or outside of that shack," the witness repeated adamantly. Mink lowered his eyes and jotted down a few notes, appearing slightly perturbed.

"That will be all, Your Honor," the DA said with a slight grin, finally eliciting eyewitness testimony that could possibly play in his favor later on, although the winds had already shifted toward the defense. Mink could sense that the judge was relieved at the conclusion of the DA's cross examination.

"The defense will call its next witness," he instructed.

"The defense would like to recall to the stand the head of the forensics team, Your Honor," said Mink, rallying his enthusiasm once again. I blanched and felt as though I would be sick, although I was angry too. It didn't look as though mother, for whom I'd been taking the rap all along, had killed father after all. Could it be? Was it possible? I was stunned.

"There were several fibers taken from the rug in Dan Biggs' office and one taken from the elevator," Mink began. "Do all of those fibers match each other?"

"Yes, they do," said the forensic scientist. "They're all the same color and are made of the same woolen material."

"Are the fibers found in Dan Biggs' office and the one found in the elevator a match to the fibers that make up the gray wool gloves found inside the shack; the same wool gloves worn by the boy who was seen entering the office building at twelve-fifteen p.m. on the Saturday afternoon that Dan Biggs was murdered?" Mink asked.

"Yes, an exact match," confirmed the scientist.

"So, are you telling me then that the fibers definitely came from these gloves?" Mink asked further, once again holding up the infamous gray gloves without the fingertips.

"Yes, the fibers came from those same gloves," verified the forensic scientist who was now highlighting the fiber similarities on a big screen in the courtroom for the benefit of the jury.

"Did the gloves test positive for powder burns?" Mink inquired.

"Yes, they tested positive for powder burns," the forensic scientist certified, once again highlighting on a big screen the different areas on the gloves that were clearly blackened by gunpowder while the jury took notes.

"Can you tell the jury in basic terms what those powder burns indicate?" requested Mink.

"Yes, the powder burns indicate that while wearing those gloves the person also fired off a gun," the scientist simply explained.

"Besides the powder burns, did the gloves test positive for anything else?" Mink asked.

"Yes, the gloves were found to contain traces of pie crumbs as well," the forensic scientist confirmed. The courtroom was hushed. Mink intently stared at the witness and nodded before moving on.

"Was the one fingerprint that had been found in an odd location inside the law office on the day of the murder a match to any of the fingerprints found inside the shack?" he asked.

"Yes, it was an exact match to one of the fingerprints found inside the shack," the scientist corroborated.

"And was that one fingerprint found to be an exact match anywhere else?" Mink probed further.

"Yes, that one fingerprint was found to be an exact match to a fingerprint that was part of a set on file in Baton Rouge, Louisiana," responded the forensic scientist.

"And to whom does that set of fingerprints on file in Baton Rouge, Louisiana belong?" Mink questioned.

"To a petty thief by the name of Eddie Biggs," the scientist revealed. Sudden murmuring throughout the courtroom caused the judge to tap his gavel several times.

"So, would you conclude that Eddie Biggs, who had been charged with petty theft in Baton Rouge, Louisiana, was inside of Dan Biggs' office at twelve-fifteen p.m. on the Saturday afternoon that he was murdered?" Mink loudly inquired before taking a sip of water. I nearly jumped out of my chair, Chesterman having to keep a hand on my arm.

"Objection, Your Honor!" slammed the DA. "Eddie Biggs is not on trial here!"

"Overruled!" the judge answered quickly. "Sit down, counselor!"

"Yes, I would make that conclusion," the forensic scientist conceded.

"Sir, do you recognize the person in this photograph?" Mink asked, holding up the same photo he had shown to the head chef from the Epicurean Castle and to Monty Kravitz, the owner of the Bait and Tackle Shop on the cove.

"Yes, that person in the photograph is Eddie Biggs," the forensic scientist confirmed after having recognized my brother.

"And how is it that you're able to positively identify the person in this photograph as Eddie Biggs?" Mink asked curiously.

"When I went down to Baton Rouge last week to analyze his fingerprints, his mug shot was made available to me as a part of his file," explained the forensic scientist.

"Let the record show, Your Honor, that the boy in the photograph, who has just been positively identified by the forensic scientist as Eddie Biggs, is the same boy who was positively identified by Mr. Kravitz as having been the one he saw coming out of the old shack on the beach, and by the chef as having been the one he saw enter the office building at twelve-fifteen p.m. on the Saturday afternoon that Dan Biggs was murdered."

"Duly noted, counselor," the judge said.

"That will be all, Your Honor," said Mink as he sat down, placing a hand on my shoulder while Chesterman wiped his sweaty brow with a handkerchief. I visibly shook, my fists clenched underneath the table.

"Would the prosecution like to cross examine this witness?" asked the judge.

"Thank you, Your Honor," said the DA. "Approximately how long after the murder of Daniel Biggs took place was the fingerprint found inside of his law office?"

"The fingerprint was found by my forensics team when it dusted for prints approximately two hours after the murder took place," said the forensic scientist.

"Can you please explain to the court why that fingerprint was not entered into evidence at the start of the trial," requested the DA.

"Yes, the fingerprint was found in an out of the way place in the office and was considered at the time to be irrelevant to the case by both sides so, therefore, was never admitted into evidence by the court," spelled out the scientist.

"And what about the three woolen fibers, two found in the office, one found in the elevator?" the DA continued. "Weren't those considered to be irrelevant to the case as well?"

"Yes, they were considered to be irrelevant to the case by both sides as well so, therefore, were never admitted into evidence by the court," repeated the forensic scientist. "It was felt at the time that the lone fingerprint and the three fibers would add nothing of substance to the case, only serving to confuse the jury."

"Where have these so-called irrelevant items been stored all this time?" asked the DA.

"They were catalogued on the day of the murder and have been safely stored by the forensics laboratory ever since in order to keep them safe from contamination and alteration."

"Don't you think it's unusual, sir, that this forensic evidence, which was previously considered to be irrelevant to the case, has all of a sudden become magically relevant to the defense team so late into this trial?" asked the DA.

"Objection, Your Honor," fired Mink. "He is questioning the workings of this court."

"Overruled," said the judge.

"No, it isn't unusual at all. Actually, it's more common than you think," began the forensic scientist. "When new witnesses come forward, as they did in this case, then everything formerly collected at the crime scene must be reconsidered and reexamined. That's why nothing is ever thrown out or destroyed, even if it's not initially entered into evidence."

"Thank you. That will be all, Your Honor," said the DA, clearly frustrated when he sat down.

"Your Honor, may we have a short recess?" requested Mink, doubtful that he'd be able to subdue my agitation any longer which been prompted by the chilling turn of events.

"The court will take a fifteen-minute recess after which time the defense will call its next witness," said the judge before a light tap of the gavel. The partners, along with the bailiff, escorted me into the small side room where we could talk. I was quick to vent my anger.

"When you told me that Eddie was somewhere in the area, I didn't believe you!" I shrieked. "Then when you said you had evidence of Eddie's involvement in father's murder, I figured you made it all up just to get me off! What's going on here? I don't understand!" I bawled. "I don't understand!"

"It's not made up, Tom, I can assure you of that," said Mink, placing a hand on my shoulder. I put my head down and cried, not only because I had been sitting in jail for months to protect my mother's reputation, but because I had done it for nothing, the brother I was so committed to finding and bringing home having already betrayed us all. I felt as though I had been punched in the gut. "This new information, placing your brother at the scene of the crime, will hinder the prosecution's case once and for all."

"I don't understand!" I cried again without lifting my head.

"You see, Tom, he can no longer prove beyond a reasonable doubt that you were the one who murdered your father," explained Mink, "by virtue of the fact that we now have new eyewitness testimony and hard evidence that point to the contrary."

"That it was Eddie who killed father?" I asked through tears after finally lifting my head.

"That will be for another jury to decide," Mink answered quietly.

"Is there a chance he didn't do it?" I asked.

"There's always a chance, but our responsibility is to you right now," replied the unrelenting lead attorney who was ready to get on with the trial, knowing that he was within striking distance of an acquittal. On some strange level I understood that Mink had to villainize Eddie in order to get me exonerated. I wouldn't mind that so much if Eddie were the actual culprit, but if he was just being used as a sacrificial lamb, as a pawn in this game of courtroom chess, then I would have to denounce Mink's strategy. Eddie had been through enough. Besides, why was it mother who was in possession of the gun? Nothing made sense anymore.

"And all this time I thought it was…" I began, a sudden urge to tell the truth prompting me to speak before Mink placed a quick hand on my arm, giving it a gentle squeeze.

"It no longer matters, boy," he whispered. "I don't need to know." I quickly fell silent.

"All right, Uncle Andrew," I said. "I understand."

Once court was back in session, Mink called a frail but determined Louise Bartlett to the stand.

"Mrs. Bartlett, can you identify the person in this photograph?" he asked.

"Yes, that's Eddie Biggs," she answered. "He lived with me for a while before running away."

"And can you identify these gloves?" Mink asked.

"Yes, those are my gloves," Mrs. Bartlett confirmed. "I used them to do yard work and various other chores. Eddie took a liking to them and removed them from the shed, wearing them from time to time. Once he disappeared, I never saw the gloves again until now."

"Can you tell the court why Eddie ran away?" questioned Mink.

"Well about a year and a half ago now, Eddie stole a bicycle from a sporting goods store. He was caught and arrested by the police. He spent about three weeks in a juvenile detention center before I could pay the fine and get him out. At around that same time I came down with cancer, the doctors telling me I would need an operation and months of treatment afterward. I wrote to Eddie's mother several times, telling her that I was sick and could no longer take care of Eddie, that his money had run out, and that she needed to come and get him," recounted Mrs. Bartlett.

"Did you tell her about the arrest too, ma'am?" Mink inquired.

"Yes, I told her everything," she replied.

"Then what happened, Mrs. Bartlett?" Mink continued.

"I never heard back from her. In the meantime, I got sicker and sicker. I told Eddie, along with another boy I had been taking care of named Richard, that I would have to make him a ward of the state due to my circumstances," she revealed in a shaky voice.

"What did they do after you told them that?" Mink probed.

"They stole my car and headed north with Richard at the wheel. Unfortunately, he drove the car into a lake in North Carolina," the woman recalled sadly. "I felt horrible, and so guilty."

"Would you please tell the court the result of that tragic accident," Mink instructed.

"Richard was killed. His body was found inside the car which had sunk to the bottom of the lake." Mrs. Bartlett wiped her teary eyes with a handkerchief.

"And Eddie? What happened to Eddie, ma'am?" Mink probed further.

"His body was never found," she responded regretfully, shaking her head. "The authorities searched in and around that lake for months with no luck. It was a real mystery. I kept writing the boy's mother, but she never wrote back. I decided to go about my business, finally having my operation and post operative treatments after having worried about the boy's fate for so long instead of my own. I had all but forgotten about Eddie until several weeks ago when the private investigator knocked on my door." Mrs. Bartlett wiped her nose with the handkerchief before being told to step down, the DA declining to cross examine her.

It was obvious that she had been seriously ill but her determination to speak about Eddie in person, given that her testimony might eventually lead to his whereabouts, was admirable to all those who watched her struggle to get in and out of the witness stand, even with the help of the bailiff. I was dumbstruck while my mind raced with dizzying speed as I thought about my mother, my brother, and this frail woman who had at one time been such an important part of Eddie's life. It was all so mind boggling, but at least I knew that I would no longer have to search for Eddie. The authorities would do that.

The last person recalled to the stand before the defense would rest its case was Dulcie. According to Mink her final testimony wasn't really necessary, but he saw it as an insurance policy. He wanted to show the jury one more time that it was definitely my brother who had been seen in the area by eyewitnesses before being positively identified by both the forensic scientist and Mrs. Bartlett. One more positive identification could only serve to cinch his case.

"Miss Jackson, can you identify the boy in this photograph?" asked Mink, holding up the same photo of Eddie that he had held up to all the other witnesses.

"Yes, that's Eddie Biggs," Dulcie confirmed.

"And how is it that you're able to positively identify the person in this photograph as Eddie Biggs?" Mink continued.

"I was his nanny," Dulcie responded. "I know what Eddie Biggs looks like."

"Let the record show, Your Honor, that the boy in the photograph who has just been positively identified by Miss Jackson as Eddie Biggs is the same boy who was positively identified as Eddie Biggs by both the forensic scientist and Mrs. Bartlett. He is also the same boy who was positively identified by Mr. Kravitz as having been the one who came out of the old shack on the beach, and by the chef as having been the one who entered the office building at twelve-fifteen p.m. on the Saturday afternoon that Dan Biggs was murdered."

"Duly noted, counselor," said the judge.

"Thank you, Your Honor. The defense rests its case." Mink sat down at the table and let out a long, silent breath.

Closing arguments by both sides would be brief. The prosecution had been deflated by the last set of eyewitnesses and the hard physical evidence that placed Eddie at the scene of the crime. It had seemingly not proven my guilt beyond a reasonable doubt but another motion by the defense to dismiss the charges against me was denied, forcing each side to present its summation.

The DA would argue that I murdered my father in a cold-blooded fit of rage and jealousy after finding out about his affair with Dulcie, the nanny on whom I had a secret, adolescent crush. After arriving back home after the murder, I would place the murder weapon, two unused gun cartridges, and two love letters proving my father's affair inside of a bird's nest, later bringing said nest up into a tree in my backyard for the purpose of hiding it, this having been witnessed by a police officer. All of the evidence inside the nest would later dust positive for my fingerprints, making me the obvious culprit. He would also contend that I was the one who left the trail of apple pie crumbs in the elevator of my father's office building, the same crumbs that had been found at the bottom of my school lunch bag.

According to the DA, all of this damning evidence, coupled with the fact that I had flat out told Dulcie that I would like to kill my father, clearly paved the way for the jury to return a guilty verdict. It was apparent, however, that the private investigator's bombshell findings, even though late to the game, would make this argument a tired one and the DA knew it.

Mink, on the other hand, would argue that I was clearly innocent of my father's murder, that the prosecution had the wrong person in custody, and that it was looking to convict an innocent boy despite powerful eyewitness testimony and hard evidence that strongly pointed to someone else. He would contend that the district attorney's office hadn't done its due diligence, nor did it prove my guilt beyond a reasonable doubt, despite what the police officer thought he saw from his car parked two hundred feet away from my backyard while using binoculars only much of the time, not the entire time, when daylight was minimal at best. Mink would further contend that my fingerprints were never found on the trigger of the gun, in the law office, or in the elevator.

Then there were the gray gloves. He would repeat that the prosecution's evidence was based on innuendo and presumption, making its case weak in the eyes of the law. He would state emphatically that I did not murder my father and that the jury, after weighing all of the evidence, would come to that same inevitable conclusion and find me innocent.

The partners and I sat in the side room waiting for a verdict. I was nervous and obviously worried.

"Uncle Andrew, what will happen to me if the jury finds me guilty?" I asked, my eyes pooling with tears as my hands shook uncontrollably.

"They have to find you innocent, Tom," he said, confidently nodding his head. "Juries can surprise you sometimes and go the other way but in this case, I think we've definitely won." The fact of the matter was that he wasn't all that sure, putting on a brave face solely for my benefit.

Mink lit one cigarette after another as he paced the floor while Chesterman incessantly wiped the sweat from his brow, jotting down useless notes on a legal pad to keep busy. Hanson tried to distract me by eliciting my help on a crossword puzzle that he had found in a copy of yesterday's newspaper. We were all absorbed in our own diversions while the jury deliberated, taking only three hours to reach a verdict. The partners glanced at each other with trepidation, wary of the swift decision. It could mean, though, that the seven men and six women overwhelmingly agreed with Mink and that the prosecution fell woefully short of proving my guilt beyond a reasonable doubt, given the latest evidence that pointed to someone else entirely.

But it could also mean that they agreed with the DA, citing all of the evidence he had against me, including my own damning words to Dulcie expressing a desire to kill my father. Either way, someone had made a mighty convincing argument. With both heavy hearts and butterflies in our stomachs, the partners and I went back into the courtroom where we would all face the moment of truth. I was able to stand, but only barely, requiring Mink's support.

"Have you reached a verdict on the charge of murder?" the judge asked the jury.

"We have, Your Honor," answered the foreman.

"What say you?" asked the judge. I now felt as though I would faint.

"We the jury find the defendant, Thomas Biggs, not guilty of the charge of murder." The partners grabbed me and hugged me in turn. I hadn't heard the verdict through the buzzing in my ears and never saw the jury, my vision having turned fuzzy and blue.

"Have you reached a verdict on the charge of obstruction of justice?" the judge asked the jury.

"We have, Your Honor," the foreman repeated.

"What say you?" the judge asked again. The partners held their collective breath.

"We the jury find the defendant, Thomas Biggs, not guilty of the charge of obstruction of justice." The partners had done it, they had gotten me off...at Eddie's expense.

"I'd like to thank the jury for its service. The defendant is free to go. Court is adjourned," concluded the judge with a tap of his gavel, but I was oblivious this time to its sound, my ears still buzzing.

The partners whisked me away as quickly as possible, although everything around me seemed to be moving at a snail's pace, and I would stay with Mink until it was decided what would be best for me. Dulcie went back to the house, figuring that she'd begin to pack up her things. There would be no way she could remain there now, especially after her testimony, but I had mixed feelings about her after all was said and done. I certainly resented the affair that she had with my father, along with everything she was forced to say in court, but I actually felt sorry for her too, having been put in such an awkward position by the prosecution.

In any case, I looked at Dulcie differently now, having no desire for things to go back to the way they were, of that I was certain. Even though I would vaguely think about her in the hours following my acquittal, my overriding thoughts were with Eddie now. Where was he and would I ever see him again? It would remain to be seen...but not for long.

Chapter 16

At Mink's house I could finally breathe but it took some time for me to unwind. Being away from the juvenile detention center, a place I had lived in for so long, felt strange and a bit surreal. Uncle Andrew put me up in his guest room which was comfortable and plush, the mattress thick and the bedding warm, yet I tossed and turned for several days, unable to sleep or get used to my new surroundings. I was safe, warm, and free but I wasn't relaxed. I was still haunted by what could have happened to me if the partners hadn't gotten me off and I couldn't stop thinking about Eddie. Where was he? If he was, indeed, the one who had killed father, the private investigator's surprising evidence certainly making it look that way, would he come for me next? Every little noise, every car that passed, every person who walked by Mink's house was my brother come to kill me.

A television was placed in my room for entertainment and distraction while Mrs. Mink cooked me the most delicious meals, anything I desired, including all of the burgers, fries, and ice cream I could eat. I didn't go anywhere or see anyone for a week except for Chesterman and Hanson who had every right to check up on me and even gloat a little. I owed them my life.

After about a week had passed, there was discussion about my education and when I should return to school. Before I could even consider that, though, I wanted to meet with the private investigator to learn more about how he had found my brother. What he uncovered left me spellbound in court, fascinated and speechless over every little detail of Eddie's whereabouts and his improbable journey back home. I could have never unearthed all of the information that he did about Eddie's other life, even though it was always my plan to find my brother and bring him home after mother had taken him away.

More importantly, I felt that if I knew the details of his investigation, the particulars about a brother who I hadn't seen in so long, then perhaps I could begin to unwind, stop looking over my shoulder, and live my life again without wondering if and when I'd be ambushed by the elusive Eddie. Mink felt badly about my mental anguish, understandable, he said, after what I had been through, and was willing to do anything he could to alleviate my fears.

"I want to speak with the private investigator, Uncle Andrew," I told him. "I want to know everything."

"I don't know that he'll tell you everything, Tom. He certainly won't give away the tricks of his trade, but all right, I'll have him over to the house," Mink agreed. "You can ask him whatever you want but whether or not he chooses to answer you is strictly up to him."

"Thank you, Uncle Andrew," I said softly. "I appreciate it. Another matter, if you don't mind, is that at some point I'd like to go back to the house and maybe stay for a few days. I know Dulcie's over there and we do have a few loose ends to tie up. Besides, I want to take a good look around and gather some of my belongings."

"I understand," he replied kindly. "Let me give that some thought, but first things first. Mrs. Mink and I will have the private investigator over for lunch tomorrow. He's always up for a free meal and, besides, the sooner you talk with him, the better you'll feel about your safety. I can assure you, Tom, that I will never let anyone hurt you, not your brother, not anyone. Your nightmare is over, boy, all right?"

"Yes, Uncle Andrew," I said with a nod, but my insides were twisted. A sudden clap of thunder would send me scrambling to my bedroom. I dove under the covers and would remain there until morning, but Mink was true to his word, having invited a special guest for lunch that very afternoon.

"Sure, kid. What do you want to know?" the private investigator uttered through a mouthful of food. I was grateful that he was open to a conversation about Eddie.

"Well, how in the world did you know about my brother?" I asked candidly without waiting for an answer. "How did you follow his footsteps into father's law office on the day of the murder and then trace him back to the shack on the beach? And how did you find out about Mrs. Bartlett? My brother has been gone for such a long time and mother kept his whereabouts a strict secret, even from father who never knew where she had dumped Eddie, nor did he ever want to know." The private investigator continued to chew, his eyes looking back and forth between Mink and me. He finally raised a brow and put his sandwich down.

"Well, now that's a lot to unwrap," he said with a slow grin, "but I suppose I can start at the beginning. You know that your trial got a lot of press. People were interested. Well, more like morbidly curious," he snickered with a dry grin, "you know what I mean?"

"I suppose," I answered, just trying to focus and keep up.

"Well, I started receiving these anonymous phone calls about a strange little boy who used to live at the Biggs house. That would be Eddie, of course. He had gotten himself into some kind of trouble at home and, because of that, was sent far away. Mink and the others filled me in on what had happened, your father having admitted to the dinner party fiasco before he was murdered. Anyway, I was told by one of those tipsters that the banished boy could have come back to murder his father."

"At first, I figured that your younger brother making it back up here was improbable, but the thought of it kept gnawing at me. Finally, I decided to investigate the credibility of such a notion, hitting the road and flashing his photo to all kinds of folks up and down the coast in an effort to sniff out leads. Before I knew it, people who had claimed to see Eddie were coming out of the woodwork. Are you following me, kid? Am I going too fast?"

"No, I can follow you just fine," I said, leaning in toward the private investigator as a show of interest, but also to help my concentration.

"As luck would have it, I actually found several people down south who recognized the photo of your brother, two of them having helped him make his way back home," he revealed before taking another bite of his sandwich.

"Who are they," I asked excitedly, "and how did they come to help Eddie? Would it be possible for me to talk to them?"

"Oh, I absolutely cannot tell you who they are, kid," he said, shaking his head back and forth, "because they wish to remain anonymous, you understand. They didn't want to be called to testify and they certainly wouldn't want to talk to you. They're unsavory characters, kid, you get my drift?" he asked dryly.

"I get it, I guess," I answered, still feeling dejected.

"Don't take it personally, kid," he directed. "That's how the detective game works. You tell me what you know, and I'll slip you a few bucks and keep your name a secret. You follow me?"

"Sure, I follow you," I said, ready to hear the rest.

"Well, one of those people let Eddie stow away in the back of his truck for the distance of three states, flipping him a couple of greasy burgers and one or two gas station hot dogs along the way. After he took your brother as far as he could, another guy in an old van picked him up after finding him on a road headed north with his thumb out. He was the one who drove Eddie the rest of the way up here, dropping him off only one town over from Old Windsor Cove before turning around and driving back home."

"Hitch hiking? Eddie? I would never have guessed that he knew how to do that!" I exclaimed in disbelief.

"Oh, Eddie not only knew how to hitch hike, but he also knew how to fish food out of dumpsters and restaurant garbage cans too," the private investigator informed me while shoving the last bit of a roast beef sandwich into his mouth.

"That's disgusting," I commented.

"That's survival, kid," he said, lighting a cigarette while Mrs. Mink poured him another cup of coffee, "and your brother got damn good at it."

"Well, what about Mrs. Bartlett?" I asked. "How did you find out about her?"

"The most helpful tattletale of all was the one who told me about Mrs. Bartlett," acknowledged the private investigator, nodding his head in approval of the tipster. "I hightailed myself over to Baton Rouge so fast you'd a thought my ass was on fire." Mrs. Mink uncomfortably cleared her throat, but the comment made me giggle, something I hadn't done in a long time. "She told me Eddie's tale, basically what you heard on the stand, and it confirmed my suspicions. If Eddie was scrappy enough to survive that car crash into the lake and make himself disappear, then what would have prevented him from traveling back to his hometown without being detected by the authorities. He's a clever little runt, all right."

"Then what did you do?" I asked, enraptured by his account.

"I came back up here and started to poke around Old Windsor Cove in earnest," he continued. "I talked to everyone who knew Eddie—his teachers, classmates, people on Kimball Avenue, and the nanny, what's her name?"

"Dulcie," I said in a whisper, mesmerized by how easily his words flowed.

"Yeah, right, Dulcie," he said, pointing a finger in recognition. "Well, it all somehow led me to the beach where I spoke with the owner of the bait and tackle shop. Turned out he recognized Eddie's photo as the kid who'd been living in the old shack on the cove. From there he stole food, begged money and, as far as I could tell, followed your mother around town."

"Mother? Did she know he was following her?" I asked.

"I believe she did, I believe she knew he was up here," the private investigator stated. "A woman fitting her description left food at the shack once, but she simply couldn't bring herself to acknowledge the mistake she'd made in sending him away until the day of the murder when she got up the nerve to confront your father, demanding that Eddie be allowed to return home, or else. And yes, kid, I'm figuring she had the gun hidden in her picnic basket."

While eating the piece of chocolate cake Mrs. Mink had placed on the table before him, the private investigator continued my brother's saga. As for me, I couldn't eat another bite for fear of throwing up. "According to the chef from the Epicurean Castle, Eddie followed your mother into your father's office building. Let's just say that your father objected to Eddie's presence, some sort of scuffle ensued, and your brother got a hold of the gun, shooting it off twice, killing your father."

"Maybe your mother tried to stop him, maybe she didn't. After the murder, a scared, starving kid grabbed a piece of pie out of the picnic basket and ran. He's the one who dropped the apple pie crumbs in the elevator while the powder burns on his gloves clinched him as the murderer. How he ever got all that evidence up into the tree we'll never know. End of story," he said with a wink, licking the chocolate off his fork.

"End of story!" I said, exasperated by his flippant attitude. I wasn't about to admit that I had found the gun in mother's top desk drawer, a secret I had kept all along, but I wanted to scream that I knew there was more to the story than what he was telling me, that mother had played some sort of role in father's murder. He wasn't even there so how could he be so certain as to what really happened? "I don't know. That sounds like a pretty fantastic story to me," was all I could get out.

"That's the point, kid, it's just a story, but a believable one," he said. "Who knows? Maybe we hit the nail on the head! You have to admit, your brother had a motive, having been sent away like that."

"Or maybe you simply created a good example of realistic fiction," I countered.

"Exactly!" the private investigator confirmed, pleased that I had finally understood the meaning of good legal strategizing. "The important thing is that we got the jury to accept it, winning you an acquittal," he said proudly before asking for another cup of coffee. "Let's face it, kid, there was no way the jury could find you guilty beyond a reasonable doubt—once your brother became a part of the mix."

"You mean you lied," I said to him, suddenly feeling sorry for Eddie, "at my brother's expense."

"I wouldn't say that. We used everything at our disposal, including hard evidence, eyewitness testimony and forensic science to put together a hell of a case. Now, whether or not the law decides to go after Eddie is up to them." My bewilderment silenced me for a minute, keeping me from asking another question. "Remember, your brother does have a criminal record, at least making his guilt plausible, if not true," he threw in for good measure before I could find my tongue and speak up again.

"Where is Eddie now?" I pressed on, almost afraid to hear the answer.

"Who knows?" The private investigator said dismissively, shrugging his shoulders. "I no longer need to chase after that elusive little runt." My heart began to beat fast. Suppose Eddie was stalking me right now. Whatever pity I felt for my brother had been brief. I was back to being downright scared of him.

"The boy needs some assurances that his brother has left town," Mink joined in, having let me steer the conversation up to that point. "We did such a good job in making Eddie out to be the real murderer that now Tom is fearful that his brother will come after him next."

"I can't promise you that he won't, kid," the private investigator said honestly, "but that's pretty farfetched, don't you think? Enjoy your freedom and forget about your brother. Let the authorities handle it. You'll be okay," he concluded before tousling my hair. I wasn't so sure.

After he left, I was more scared than ever, having heard nothing that would alleviate my fear of Eddie. If anything, the private investigator had fueled my paranoia. I really wanted to go home now to the security I had been missing for so long, to the familiarity of that special place where no one would bother me, no one would find me.

I longed for its memorable dark embrace, the taste of mustiness that would settle on my lips as soon as I ascended the stairs, and the tall imposing windows that looked down upon the world without judgement. I needed to hit a few golf balls, open the old trunk, look at a few photos, and retrieve the key to mother's top desk drawer that I had hidden underneath the photo of Leo Biggs, postmortem. All I had to do was convince Mink. It was time to go back to the attic.

"Uncle Andrew," I started tentatively, "I think it's time I return to the house."

"Well, I don't know, boy," he said, slowly shaking his head. "I've been thinking about it. Do you really think you should do that? I mean, why would you want to dredge up all those bad memories?"

"I have some good memories too," I assured him, suddenly feeling sad again over all I had lost.

"I know you do, Tom. I don't mean to imply that all of your memories are bad ones. I'm sure you can recall a number of good times you had growing up in that house with your parents and brother. I suppose those are the memories you need to hold onto, but do you really think you can go back now without being traumatized all over again by recent events?" Mink asked, his face creased with obvious concern. He let out a long sigh. "I would hate to see you hurt all over again. You're vulnerable right now, not quite back on your feet yet."

"At some point I'll have to face whatever awaits me there, Uncle Andrew," I stated, this scared little jackrabbit ready to tie up those loose ends, Eddie or no Eddie. "Please, Uncle Andrew, bring me to the house."

"Well, all right, but there's no way I can let you sleep there," he stated adamantly.

"Why not?" I asked, surprised by his response. "I'm certainly old enough, but Dulcie is over there anyway. She'll keep an eye on things."

"Are you sure you want to speak with her?" Mink questioned. "I don't know if I can approve of the arrangement."

"Has she suddenly become a threat?" I asked in reply, finding his trepidation puzzling. "Besides, it's my house. Why is it that she can be there, but I can't?" Mink became reflective.

"Okay, tell you what. I'll advise Dulcie that we'll be over tonight and that you'll be staying for a few days as long as she's there to keep an eye on things. You can take a look around, gather your belongings, make your peace with her…and then…say goodbye to the house," he directed awkwardly before his voice trailed off. It seemed as though he had a plan about which he had yet to inform me.

"What do you mean?" I asked. "You're making it sound so final. I don't want to say goodbye to the house. That's my house. I'll be living there again one day, won't I?"

"To tell you the truth, Tom, I intend to sell the house," Mink admitted.

"Sell it! What right do you have to do that?" I asked, feeling the blood surge to my head, turning my cheeks a bright red. "How come you haven't mentioned that to me until now? Shouldn't I have had a say in the matter?"

"It's the only option, Tom. You can't live there on your own because you're far too young. Besides, the maintenance and taxes alone would be astronomical, a lot of money to spend on a vacant house. As your lawyer and guardian, I must advise you to sell it and bank the money for future use. You'll always have a home with me," Mink promised, placing a protective arm around my shoulder. "I'm sure your parents would want it this way too. I hope you can understand my position." Mink was gentle but firm. The house would go up for sale as soon as possible.

"I suppose," I answered reluctantly, my eyes pooling with tears, "but for now I just want to go home and pretend that things are back to normal, if only for a few days." I felt vulnerable, just like Mink said, and a little nervous about seeing Dulcie again. I hoped that sleeping in my own bed would give me some peace, and being in familiar surroundings would restore a small sense of order to my life. Perhaps I'd even be able to think more objectively about Eddie. One could hope, if only for a few days.

Mink drove me over to the house that night after he had spoken to Dulcie.

"Are you sure you don't want me to go in with you, Tom?" he asked.

"No, Uncle Andrew," I said, "I'll be fine. Don't you worry about me."

"I don't want you to be disappointed," he said. "Things will never really be back to normal, no matter how hard you pretend."

"I know," I agreed in a soft voice. "I know."

"Call me if you need anything," he instructed before I slid out of the passenger seat and closed the door. I stared at the house before me. After all this time I was home…really home.

Dulcie greeted me at the front door with arms open wide. I had no choice but to hug her, making it a quick one, lingering no more than a few seconds before breezing past her and into the front hall where Tinker awaited me too. I scooped him up, letting him lick my face before he wriggled out of my arms and scampered off into the living room. He looked happy, Dulcie having taken good care of him.

"I made your favorite dinner," she said straight off, sensing my discomfort. I assumed it wasn't fried chicken and apple pie.

"Smells delicious," I acknowledged. "What is it?"

"Beef stew with biscuits and gravy," she smiled. I didn't recall that ever being my favorite dish, but anything was better than prison food. Mrs. Mink had been feeding me well since the acquittal and now Dulcie had fussed for me too.

"Sounds good," I said quietly. "If you don't mind, I'm going to head up to my bedroom and get settled." I walked up the stairs without waiting for an answer.

"Dinner is in an hour," she called after me. I merely waved my hand before walking into my room and closing the door. I threw the few belongings I had with me on the floor and laid down on my bed, the old familiar mattress conforming to my body and welcoming me like an old friend. As the light turned to purple, I dozed off and dreamed of irrelevant and unrecognizable things, my sleep peaceful and without nightmarish undertones until Eddie stepped forward from a sudden mist, leaning over me with a gun, pointing it straight at my chest. He grinned from ear to ear before taking careful aim, laughing an evil laugh before pulling the trigger.

I sat up quickly, flailing my arms and gasping for air as I continued to swim up from a deep sleep. I clutched the blanket and yanked it hard before the fog lifted, bringing my bedroom into sharp focus where I could plainly see that it was free of intrusion. There was no Eddie and no gun. Dulcie walked in after a light rap on the door.

"Are you okay?" she asked. "It's time to eat."

"I'm fine," I said. "Just had a bad dream." She reached over and turned on the lamp beside my bed the way mother used to whenever I had an uneasy sleep.

"Dinner's on the table. Come down soon," she smiled. Dulcie acted as though no time had passed, as though mother, father, and Eddie were downstairs waiting for me, as though things were the same between us. Her long, dark brown curly hair still bounced while her strikingly beautiful green eyes penetrated my soul even now, yet I had no desire to be in her company other than to get a few things off my chest and tie up those loose ends. I was hungry but wasn't looking forward to dinner.

"I was surprised to see you in court," I started after Dulcie had dished up my plate.

"I had no choice," she said. "I was compelled to testify by the DA's office."

"Whose side were you on, anyway?" I asked, dipping my biscuit in the brown gravy. "It was hard to tell." I was determined to put her on the spot as I had done several times before today.

"Why, yours of course, silly," Dulcie said smiling. "Look, I tried to wiggle out of it, you can even ask Mink, but I couldn't. I knew you were innocent the whole time, but all I could do was put my faith in the partners that everything would turn out all right and it did," she said, shrugging her shoulders. It seemed as though Dulcie was trying to make light of it and wanted to change the subject. For me, it wasn't that simple.

"Do you really think everything turned out all right, Dulcie?" I asked rhetorically. "Just switch out the older Biggs brother for the younger one and you have the potential for another messy court case, maybe even worse than mine!" I said, raising my voice as I gathered up the carrots and celery on my plate with the rest of my biscuit. "Who the hell knows what will happen to Eddie or where he'll end up?" My agitation gave my anxiety away. In my mind, Eddie lurked around every corner.

"I don't think Eddie murdered your father," she remarked casually, ladling out another plate of stew for herself, her demeanor calm, almost disinterested, now that the trial was over.

"Then who did?" I asked, genuinely keen to hear her opinion.

"I wouldn't want to venture a guess," Dulcie said, holding back her thoughts, but I was always under the impression that she blamed mother for the murder just as I did. "Would you like some more stew?" she asked.

"No thanks, I'm full," I acknowledged, waving her off with my hand. "Well, in any case, it's over. I just want you to know that I'm not angry with you for testifying but I think it best that we make a clean break of it and part ways. You're moving out and I'm going back to Mink's house, so I guess this is goodbye."

"We can still be friends," Dulcie said, surprised by my abruptness.

"No, we can't," I answered without regret. "You had an affair with my father and made a mess of our lives. It all played out in public, and I resent you for that." Even I was surprised by my candor.

"You can't possibly blame me…"

"I can and I do…for everything," I said once and for all. It was true. I blamed her for father, for mother, and for Eddie. "After we leave here, I don't think we should ever see each other again," I announced as I got up from the table. "Thanks for dinner. I'm going up to the attic. Please don't follow me," I requested over my shoulder before disappearing from the kitchen. Dulcie never said a word, but I could sense that her jaw had dropped while her strikingly beautiful green eyes burned a hole in the back of my head.

I said what I had come home to say. My next demon to conquer would be Eddie and, perhaps, after that I could then begin to heal and move on. Mink was right. Things will never really be back to normal, no matter how hard I pretend.

I walked up into the attic, the warmth and security emanating from the dark wood slowly enveloping me like a blanket from childhood, washed and stitched many times over, as I climbed each step. Overpowered by the smell of days gone by, I was carried back to the many hours I spent up here with Eddie. Pulling the chain that dangled from the overhead light, I walked over to one of the windows and timidly peeked out onto the street as though I were hiding, afraid to show my face, reluctant to let the world know that I was free.

Perhaps I was a little hesitant, but for now I wanted to remain in this blanket where Eddie would never find me and no one would dare intrude, not even Dulcie. Only Tinker would follow me up here.

I stood back and took it all in—the old clothes still draped over wire hangers that dangled from the metal garment rack; the dresser, time worn with its scratches and coffee-stained wood; the chairs and couch, faded and threadbare, that had outlived their usefulness; father's first set of golf clubs nestled safely inside the worn leather bag; and the stuffed head of a deer that he had once shot and killed, during a long-ago hunting trip. I walked from one end of the attic to the other and then back again, touching everything I passed as though I were shaking hands with old friends come to greet me.

I laid out the rug, still rolled up, and eagerly placed the dirty pie plate at one end as though I had done it only yesterday. After hitting a few golf balls into the plate, I made my way over to the trunk of old family photos where the checkers game, neatly packed away in its box, had been precariously balanced upon the rounded, hinged lid.

Apprehensive at first, I would finally grab the box and toss it to the floor before slowly lifting the heavy lid, waiting perhaps for something sinister to jump out at me. I shuffled through numerous black and white images of forgotten relatives who were now lost to time before putting them aside to dig deeper, feeling around for the real reason my hands were in the trunk. Before I knew it, I had almost reached the bottom.

With a gripping anticipation I swept my hands from side to side until I came upon the key to mother's top desk drawer, sitting right where I had left it. I grasped it tightly and fished it out of the trunk, slipping it into my pocket where it would remain until morning. I then dug deep into the now disheveled photos one last time, clutching the one that had sat on top of the key before bringing it up slowly.

I looked at it with a reverence that only Eddie would understand. I whispered a quiet word of thanks to Leo Biggs, postmortem for protecting mother's key in my absence before placing the morbid image on top of the old dresser. There it would finally escape the darkness of the trunk, a right that I felt this distant cousin had earned.

I was ready to go downstairs, pleased with my accomplishments so far, having tied up those loose ends with Dulcie and now retrieving the key to mother's top desk drawer. Tomorrow, I would unlock it and its residual secrets, if only to satisfy my own curiosity and answer a few lingering questions, before climbing into my treehouse for old times' sake. There I would decide what to pack up before returning to Mink's house. I knew he wanted me back soon so that I could return to school but I had to finish here first, putting both the past and Eddie behind me. Just then, a bird flew overhead.

I rushed to one of the tall windows and opened it wide, the feathered creature making a hasty exit into the night. Maybe it was Eddie, saying goodbye. I would pull the chain that dangled from the overhead light before going back downstairs to bed where new dreams awaited me. I could only hope that they'd be pleasant enough, leaving Eddie out of the picture.

The success of my trip back home, thus far, had lent itself to a contented night's sleep. I awakened to the aroma of toast and coffee, remembering after a bit of early morning confusion or, perhaps, just wishful thinking that it wasn't mother who was down in the kitchen. Nonetheless, I jumped out of bed and threw on my clothes, finally ready to open her top desk drawer with the key I had triumphantly concealed all this time. I would smoke a quick cigarette before going downstairs to breakfast, unsure of how I should greet Dulcie.

I would certainly be civil, perhaps even cheerful, but any interference or even mild curiosity on her part would be most unwelcome once I entered father's study. For now, I would conduct myself with a bounce and a whistle, all the while keeping a protective hand in my pants pocket so as to cradle the key.

"Good morning!" Dulcie said cheerily as though our conversation the night before hadn't taken place. "How would you like your eggs?"

"You don't have to make me eggs," I answered. "Plain old toast is just fine."

"Nonsense. I told Mink that I would take care of you as long as you're here and that's exactly what I'm going to do." Dulcie was adamant.

"If you insist, then I'll have scrambled eggs," I said appreciatively before buttering a piece of toast. "Actually, I'm starving." My remark was pleasant, and it appeared that any ice between us had already melted. But I was determined to remain detached.

"Scrambled eggs coming up," she said, bringing a full plate to the table quickly. I practically inhaled them, anxious to get to the study, although I savored every bite, nonetheless.

"I'm glad you liked your eggs," she said after collecting my plate, clearly sniffing the air around me. "Do I smell cigarettes?" she asked.

"Thanks for breakfast, Dulcie," I said, getting up from the table quickly. "I have something important I need to do right now, so please excuse me." I left the kitchen without responding to her question, no longer feeling obligated to explain myself.

"Is there anything I can do to help?" she called out as I walked into father's study, locking the door behind me. My silence would serve as the only reply.

It felt strange to be in father's study again, this ghost town, voices from the past echoing in my ears and long-ago conversations piercing the eerie quiet, if only in my head. I slowly walked over to his desk, surveying everything on top before opening the drawers just as I had done in the past. Now that the gun and its cartridges were gone there was nothing of interest, nothing to give me that jolt.

I no longer cared about father's personal papers or court documents, leaving them for Mink to eventually sift through and discard. I dragged out the large jar of coins from underneath the desk and placed it by the door as a reminder to take it with me when I left the room, choosing to leave behind the drawer of now stale chocolate bars.

Fingering the key in my pocket, I then walked over to mother's desk. I was apprehensive, almost frightened to open the drawer and finally read the correspondence that had been locked away for all those months, probably having everything to do with Eddie. After hearing reports about my brother, both at trial and from the private investigator—I expected no surprises, but took the key out of my pocket with trepidation, nonetheless. I gently pushed it into the lock of the top desk drawer before slowly turning it to the right until I heard a click. My heart pounded as I pulled the drawer toward me, the papers, envelopes and keys that I had left for another day still there, waiting to be examined.

Much as I had anticipated, I picked up a letter from Louise Bartlett regarding Eddie, a sort of update on his progress at home and in school. It seemed as though he was happy with her at first, well-adjusted and thriving, until subsequent letters indicated that his behavior had become reckless, eventually leading to his arrest. There were four unopened letters without return addresses, post marked in Mississippi, all written by Louise as well.

Initially, they were a polite notification of her inability to care for Eddie any longer, given her cancer diagnosis, but they then became progressively frantic and desperate, pleading for a response from mother. She wrote about how Eddie's money had run out, how mother would have to come pick him up as soon as possible, and how she would have to make Eddie a ward of the state if mother continued to ignore her letters.

Father's affair with Dulcie may have distracted mother beyond reason, rendering her incapable of dealing with Eddie any longer or, perhaps, she was simply unwilling, thinking it best to erase him as though unopened letters could do that. In any case, other than the keys to a PO box that I never knew existed, there was nothing else of interest, the correspondence from Louise Bartlett confirming what I already knew about my brother.

Feeling around the back of the drawer one last time for something I might have missed, I found my fingers fumbling over a photograph. Pulling it out I stared at it long and hard, a recent picture of Eddie, unkempt and scruffy, standing in front of the old shack on the cove. The private investigator was right. Mother did know that Eddie was up here, sending a chill down my spine. Stuffing all of the letters and the picture into my pants pocket, I closed the drawer and locked it, grabbing the small photo of my parents snapped by Dulcie so long ago at mother's insistence off the top of the desk, before slowly walking away.

After taking one last look around the abandoned room, the hub of my parents' existence where monumental decisions were made, I found it ironic that all it could give me was a jar of change, a photo of my parents and, of course, a drawer full of mother's secrets. I had but a few good memories of father's study, yet it was essential that I come back here and face it alone, unlocking mother's top desk drawer a priority, another goal that I needed to accomplish before I could move on with my life. Now, what to do with those secrets.

I closed the door behind me after leaving father's study for the last time and went straight to my bedroom, in no mood to talk to Dulcie. After turning the lock, I placed the large jar of coins on my desk, never before having so much money in my possession while, at the same time, feeling destitute, deprived of all that was really important. I sat on my bed and smoked another cigarette, but it wouldn't take long before I would bring Louise Bartlett's letters and the photo of Eddie outside, away from the house so as not to be seen by Dulcie, where I would light them on fire. Giving me closure and a strange sense of satisfaction, it was another order of business that I could check off my list.

I counted change for the rest of the morning, Tinker at my feet, before poking around Eddie's bedroom. I halfheartedly decided to keep the toy airplane that had been sitting on his desk all this time, pangs of guilt forcing me to preserve a reminder of Eddie in happier days when he was my little brother, not our father's murderer. I still cringed at the thought of him now, lurking nearby, ready to come after me next. Seeing the photo in mother's desk burned his image into my brain, a dirty little animal, lying in wait while watching my every move. Suddenly, after finding me alone, he would draw his weapon and…

"Hey, I made you lunch," Dulcie said as she stood in the doorway to Eddie's bedroom, nearly causing me to jump out of my skin. "I didn't mean to startle you. By the way, I noticed that you were in your father's study for a long time. What were you doing in there?" I took the toy airplane off of Eddie's desk and walked toward the door, prompting Dulcie to move aside.

"If you don't mind, I'd like to eat my lunch in the treehouse," I stated without responding to, yet, another one of Dulcie's questions, refusing to divulge my business any longer. I breezed past her and went into my bedroom, Eddie's toy plane under my arm. I placed it alongside the large jar of coins and the photo of my parents, another memento headed for Mink's house.

I sat in the treehouse for a couple of hours with the breeze on my face, eating the bologna and cheese sandwich Dulcie had made me as I contemplated many things. I looked above my head to where I had hidden the nest, no longer afraid that I was being watched by the authorities. But even if I was, no matter.

After the trial, Mink had explained to me the meaning of double jeopardy, assuring me that under the law, I could never again be charged with the murder of my father. Blinking hard I dismissed all thoughts of that conversation, replacing them with pleasant memories of the many contented days spent in my treehouse, another private place I would miss.

I closed my eyes and listened for mother's voice on the breeze calling me for dinner, father's whistle, Eddie's laugh. I thought I had heard them all and, perhaps, I had. I looked down at the house, the backyard, and the neighborhood out front, knowing that I would never return to this place. I watched the silver ribbons of light that danced on the waters of the stream near the woods, the frogs free to hop around now that Eddie was no longer there to harm them, before Dulcie called me into the house. Mink was on the phone.

"Sure, Uncle Andrew. I'll be ready tomorrow night, seven o'clock. Yes, that will give me plenty of time. Everything's fine. I'll see you then." After hanging up the phone, I went into the kitchen to see Dulcie. "I'll be leaving tomorrow night after dinner."

"Okay, I'll make you something really special," she gushed.

"I don't want you to go to any trouble," I told her, hoping that I could just slip out of here without a contrived sendoff.

"Oh, it won't be any trouble," she said, "and as a favor to me you can take those maddening birds in the attic with you." She wasn't joking.

"Birds?"

"Yes, don't you hear them?" she asked. We both fell silent, the unmistakable flapping of wings clearly heard through the kitchen vents. "They drive me crazy, especially when I'm in my bedroom trying to sleep. I know I won't be living here much longer, but even one night without having to listen to their incessant fluttering would be a welcome relief."

"That's funny. I opened one of the windows in the attic last night to let a bird fly out," I said, puzzled as to how they were getting in. "I'll go see if I can figure out what's happening."

Eddie was always fascinated by birds in the attic, the reason we built that nest together in the first place before mother took him away, but they scared me then and they scare me still. Nevertheless, I climbed up the attic steps in a stooped position before pulling the chain that dangled from the overhead light. There were two birds flying around up there this time, clearly familiar with the high rafters, the intimacy of the dark wood, and the many places on which to perch.

I ran to one window and opened it wide before running to the other and doing the same. I gazed overhead at the high peaked roof. How were the birds getting in? While carefully looking around, I noticed a gaping hole in the dark paneling behind the metal garment rack before Dulcie suddenly appeared.

"Do you know how that hole got there?" I asked her curiously. "I never noticed it before today."

"Your mother told me shortly before she died that she had hired an electrician to do some work behind the paneling," Dulcie replied, the first time I had ever heard that story. "You probably never noticed the hole because the garment rack sits in front of it."

Still, I thought it odd, always having assumed that I knew every nook and cranny of the attic intimately. Shrugging my shoulders, I walked behind the metal garment rack with the intention of sticking my head into the hole, but the two birds caught my eye first, having found their way over to the open windows that would allow them to escape into the late afternoon sky. I let out a sigh of relief and decided that I'd had enough for one day.

"I think I'm going to go back downstairs," I informed Dulcie, wanting to save my last goodbye to the attic for tomorrow when I'd be alone and could take my time. It would be there that I'd spend my final hours, wrapped in its warm embrace, this place that I'd never forget. For now, I'd pack up some things and ponder my life in this house while waiting for dinner, meat loaf and potato pancakes in front of the television set.

My heart felt much lighter, most of my goals having already been accomplished. The only matter remaining was my fear of Eddie. I had to banish him from my nightmares and remember all the times when he himself was vulnerable and scared, when he was just a little boy, my little brother. That would be my final achievement, the last order of business to check off the list before moving on without the trepidation that gripped me…without Eddie.

Chapter 17

I woke up the next morning to a large clap of thunder, its accompanying flashes of lightning slicing through the darkness and rain outside my window. I sat on the edge of my familiar childhood bed for the last time, rubbing my eyes, and decided to leave my pajamas on a little longer than usual. The dreariness of the day called for a bit of lounging but my last hours in this house would also be a time for goodbyes. I looked around the room before packing up the rest of my belongings, things I didn't want to leave behind. I easily managed to arrange a small collection of personal effects in an orderly fashion by the bed, ready to be packed into Mink's car. There wasn't much but it was all I wanted, all I needed in order to walk out the door never to look back. The large jar of coins and a small photo of my parents, my football and a favorite sweatshirt, Eddie's airplane, a book of Edgar Allen Poe stories, and one of mother's decks of cards ordered specially from Toller's Stationary rounded out the collection for now, the camera Dulcie had given me having already been disposed of in the bedroom trash can.

Upon today's final departure from the attic, I would also take father's boyhood checkers game and the photograph of his long-ago cousin, Leo Biggs, postmortem. It saddened me to think that all of these items, so important to me now, could one day become as insignificant as the camera. Only time would tell.

I suddenly heard the flapping of wings overhead. There were birds in the attic again and this time they were large in number. I listened carefully to the incessant fluttering as Dulcie had called it, knowing that I would have to once again clear out these flying pests before I could say my final goodbyes to the most treasured room in the whole house. As I looked for shoes to put on my feet, Dulcie knocked on the bedroom door.

"French toast and sausage for breakfast," she announced.

"I'll be down in a bit," I said. "I was just headed to the attic."

"Don't tell me there are birds up there again," she said, disappointed at the thought.

"I'm afraid there are," I answered, slipping into the comfortable slippers Mrs. Mink had bought me after the trial. "I won't be long. I want the attic to be free of them when I'm up there after breakfast, spending some time and saying goodbye."

"Would you like me to go up there with you?" Dulcie asked.

"That won't be necessary. All I have to do is open the windows," I said.

"No, I mean when you're up there after breakfast, you know, spending some time. Maybe you and I can play a game of checkers, for old time's sake," she suggested. She appeared hopeful that I'd say yes.

"No thanks, Dulcie," I said, shaking my head. "I'd rather be alone." No longer concerned about her feelings I brusquely walked past her and climbed the attic stairs, my eyes staring straight ahead. Dulcie and I…we were through.

The attic was dark and gloomy, the torrential rain that pelted the windows quickly dripping down like beads of sweat on a hot day. I could sense the presence of the birds, but they were eerily silent, probably perched in the rafters, waiting to swoop down and pull at my hair or pluck out my eyes. I quickly reached up to pull the chain dangling from the overhead light, but the bulb popped, leaving the attic to its gloom. Intermittent flashes of lightning would brighten the room for only seconds at a time, not enough for me to make my way over to the windows comfortably.

The thought of having to go back downstairs for a new lightbulb aggravated me as lightning temporarily illuminated the attic yet again, this time revealing the rapid approach of a single bird. Quickly covering my head with both arms, I could feel the draft on my face as it plunged nearby only to taunt me, leaving a single black feather aimlessly floating in its wake before flying back to the rafters. The attic fell into silent darkness once more.

While carefully making my way back toward the attic stairs I became frightened by a rustling noise and stopped dead in my tracks. Unable to move, I imagined a mortal presence other than my own, my eyes darting nervously around the dark room while the appearance of goosebumps signaled the sudden chill that had made me shudder. I whispered Dulcie's name but was met with silence before looking up toward the dark rafters, imagining that the birds must be watching.

I drew in a deep breath and let it out again, now feeling silly after having stood there like a statue which only served to scare me even more. I cautiously shuffled forward in the darkness, the attic stairs in my sight, until a dirty hand came from behind and covered my mouth. I couldn't move or scream but I could hear the pounding of my heart along with a familiar laugh in my ear.

"Did I scare you, Tom?" My eyes, wide with fright, quickly narrowed to slits. I broke free and spun around, having recognized the sound of my brother's voice.

"What the hell are you doing here?" I asked, taking a few steps back. There was Eddie, disheveled and reeking for lack of a recent bath, his build now taller and heavier than mine.

"Aren't you happy to see me, Tom? Where's Dulcie? She'll be happy to see me," he stated casually, shrugging his shoulders. I stood there guarded, my body flooding with a sudden adrenaline rush. Ready to defend myself if I had to, I was desperately trying to get a read on my brother. Was he there to kill me?

"How did you get in the attic?" I demanded to know. He quickly pointed to the hole in the paneling behind the metal garment rack.

"A tunnel! A secret tunnel, Tom!" Eddie shouted with delight. Breathing hard I walked over to the gaping hole and took a peek into the darkness. "It runs down to the cellar near the old coal chute!" my brother informed me.

"What old coal chute?" I asked, never before having heard of such a thing.

"The one mother told me about," Eddie bragged.

"Mother never said anything to me about an old coal chute," I said, astonished that Eddie knew something about the house that I didn't. "When did she tell you about that?"

"When she came to see me at the shack. She told me to come home where I'd be warm, to come in through the old coal chute by the chimney and follow the tunnel behind the furnace to the attic. She said that father would never know I was up here. And guess what? He never did know!" Eddie took pleasure in telling me his little story while I could only stare at him in disbelief. It took me a few seconds to find my tongue.

"So, mother *did* go to see you at the shack," I managed to whisper in amazement, the hair on the back of my neck standing straight on end.

"Only once," Eddie confirmed, "but she warned me that father must never know."

"I realize you hated father, and I don't blame you, but did you have to kill him?" Eddie appeared to be pathetically removed from reality, almost delirious, given his vacant eyes. But actually, he was perfectly lucid.

"What are you talking about?" he asked me, suddenly scrunching his face and furrowing his eyebrows. "I didn't kill father. Mother did that."

"Everyone knows that you were in father's office the day he was murdered," I informed my brother, "and besides, your gray gloves tested positive for powder burns which means you're the one who shot off the gun!" My heart was pounding in my ears.

"I was wondering what happened to those gloves, Tom!" said Eddie with a laugh, totally missing my point. "I guess after taking them off, I left them in the shack!" He looked around the attic with a bright smile, obviously happy to be there. "Want to play checkers, Tom?" I finally got up the nerve and lunged at my brother, grabbing him by the shirt collar with both hands before giving him a shake.

"Why did you kill father?" I asked angrily, no longer afraid that Eddie was coming for me next. He was the same boy he had always been.

"I told you I didn't do it," he insisted, wriggling out of my grip, "mother did."

"Explain," I seethed through clenched teeth, still not convinced that my brother was telling the truth. Eddie sat on top of the trunk of old family photos and began his story.

"Mother told me she was going to see father that day, so I waited in the alley between his office building and Chamberlain Jewelers. When I finally saw her enter father's building I followed her," Eddie recounted.

"Whatever for?" I asked.

"Mother was going to tell father that I needed to come back home once and for all," said my brother, "and I wanted to be there when she said it. I finally got up the nerve to face him again, Tom! Besides, I couldn't go back to Baton Rouge." Eddie shrugged his shoulders as though he had been making ordinary small talk.

"Go on," I said impatiently, although my heartbeat had become more measured.

"Well, by the time I got up to father's office, mother had a gun pointed right at his chest!" Eddie shouted with excitement, almost glee. "Hey, I'm hungry, Tom," he said, suddenly changing the subject, "can you get me something to eat?"

"Finish explaining," I said, grabbing Eddie by the shirt again. Flashes of lightning lit up the attic along with my brother's face.

"Okay, okay," he said, freeing himself of my hold on him once more. "Before I knew it, mother had shot father in the chest, and he immediately dropped to the floor. I rushed over to her and tried to grab the gun from her hand, but she wouldn't let go. We struggled and the gun went off again, the bullet firing into the ceiling I think." Damn that private detective. He *was* wrong about Eddie being the killer while my suspicions had been right all along. Poor mother. Poor murderous mother.

"That's when your gloves, along with the crumpled tissue, wiped mother's prints off the gun, leaving only smudges," I thought out loud. "Didn't father try to stop her before she shot him?"

"It all happened so fast. Look, I'm really hungry, Tom," my brother repeated. "Can you please get me something to eat?" At this point, Eddie was begging.

"Finish the story first," I demanded.

"There's not much else to say. Once I realized that I couldn't get mother to let go of the gun I backed away and ran," my brother conceded. "I went back to the shack on the beach and stayed there for the night, but I left the next morning and never returned. I guess that's when I accidentally forgot to take the gloves with me." My mouth hung open as Eddie told his story.

"Did you happen to grab a piece of apple pie out of mother's picnic basket first before you ran out of father's office?" I was finally able to ask.

"How did you know that, Tom!" Eddie's eyes got big. He was mystified as though I had just seen the past in some magic crystal ball.

"It came out at my trial that there were apple pie crumbs in the elevator that led up to father's law office. I knew I hadn't dropped them there, so at first I thought it was mother, but then the private investigator, in corroboration with the forensic scientist, figured out that it was you," I informed him.

"I read about that trial in an old newspaper I found near the beach," Eddie admitted, shrugging his shoulders again. "Too bad."

"Too bad? Is that all you can say? You're crazy!" My brother's nonchalant attitude had me fuming. Just then, five birds swooped down from the darkness of the rafters and flew overhead while flashes of lightning continued to brighten the attic at intervals. “Wait here,” I barked, giving Eddie a look of disgust before going downstairs, my breathing now under control.

Running into the kitchen I made my brother a peanut butter and jelly sandwich before grabbing a new lightbulb from the pantry. All the while, Dulcie sat at the table and watched me, wondering what was going on before she spoke up.

“What are you doing?” she asked. “Breakfast has been ready for nearly half an hour and it’s getting cold. Why do you need a peanut butter and jelly sandwich, for god’s sake?” She was irritated and insulted after having cooked specially for me.

“Keep breakfast warm if you can,” I said. “I have birds to tend to in the attic. I’m starving so I’ll just eat this sandwich in the meantime.” Dulcie stood up from her chair, ready to follow me. “No, stay there,” I ordered. “I’ll be right back.”

“But maybe I can help!” she shouted after me.

“No, thanks!” I called back, quickly running up the kitchen stairs to the second floor where I then rushed to the attic, only to find Eddie standing by one of the windows holding a bird. He seemed to be mesmerized as he stared at it intently, unaware of my presence.

I finally made myself known after clearing my throat. Eddie snapped out of his hypnotic state, hastily throwing the bird he had been holding up toward the darkness of the rafters before grabbing the sandwich from my hands. A few black feathers would remain suspended in the air above our heads as I stood on a chair to change the burnt-out lightbulb.

Upon pulling the chain, I got a good look at my brother who was devouring the peanut butter and jelly sandwich like an animal. I quickly jumped off the chair and hurried to the windows, throwing them both open, hoping the birds would find their way out soon. Before I could turn around, Eddie had me in a choke hold.

“Where’s the nest we made together, Tom?” he whispered in my ear. “The birds have nowhere to rest.” As Eddie let out a laugh I gave him an elbow to the gut, causing him to let go of me and stumble a few steps back. I spun around to face my unpredictable brother.

“Mother’s dead too. Did you know that?” I asked bitterly, furious with Eddie for the emotional rollercoaster I had been riding for months on end, due in large part to him as well as Dulcie. I so wanted to get off.

"Yes, I heard. Poor mother," Eddie lamented. "Are you sure you don't want to play checkers, Tom? Look, one bird left!" he suddenly shouted, pointing up to the rafters. My brother's mind was obviously in a twisted state.

"Is that all you care about? The damn birds?" I asked.

"Sure. What else is there?" Eddie shrugged his shoulders as though nothing else mattered.

"You need help," I stated emphatically, "and you're not going to get it up here in the attic. The authorities are probably looking for you right now. Go and tell them everything that you told me, that you didn't kill father. They'll believe you," I pleaded.

"Did they believe you?" Eddie replied with a surprisingly astute rhetorical question. "To think that they put you on trial for murdering father. Boy, did they get that wrong!" Eddie laughed.

"Well, then why didn't you go to Mink or the police and tell them so?" I asked. "You were an eyewitness! You could have gotten me off the hook a lot sooner!" I shouted, my fury building.

"Me? Who would have believed me? All I wanted to do was come home," Eddie admitted, looking up at the one bird still flying around the rafters. He pointed and laughed, indifferent to what I had endured. "Birds sure do like it up here in the attic, same as I do. Well, anyway, I'm home and there's no one to tell me I can't stay, right, Tom?"

My brother walked toward the attic stairs like he had done so many times before, ready to breeze back into his old life as though the past had been erased, as though mother would be downstairs sitting at the kitchen table while Dulcie would be standing nearby, waiting to take him to Dairy Delight.

"Hold on, Eddie," I said quickly, taking a few steps in his direction. "I can't let you go down there. As a matter of fact, I'm here to tell you that...you can't stay." Eddie's eyes grew wide.

"You can't tell me that," my brother said defiantly.

"Oh, yes, I can. You need help, Eddie, and you owe a lot of people an explanation. Besides, Mink is selling this house now that mother and father are gone." I was blunt, hoping that my brother would understand.

In the meantime, the last bird in the attic had finally flown down to the window seat and perched itself, ready to fly into the dreariness of the rain-soaked day at any moment. Still, I felt it my duty to hasten its departure. As I slowly walked over to the feathered creature to shoo it out the open window

Eddie followed from behind, putting me in another choke hold, this time with a knife to my throat. The startled bird flew back up into the rafters.

"You're not going to tell me I can't stay here. Nobody can tell me that, not even Mink," Eddie contended in spitting words of anger.

"Take it easy, Eddie," I said as he rocked the blade of the knife back and forth across my throat. Flashes of lightning continued to brighten the attic at intervals while drops of heavy rain pelted the top pane of the open window before dripping inside, soaking the window seat.

"Tell me I can stay," Eddie demanded.

"Take the knife off my neck and we'll talk," I said, standing perfectly still. As though a switch had been thrown, my heart was pounding in my ears again.

"Hell, no. Tell me I can stay, or I'll slit your throat right now," Eddie threatened. To make good on his intention he pressed the blade of the knife into my skin, eliciting a trickle of blood that stained my shirt collar. I could only wince, my feet cemented to the floor.

"Okay, okay, you can stay," I agreed after feeling the stream of wetness drip down my neck. Eddie quickly backed off and laughed. My relief was slow in coming. This couldn't be happening.

"I knew you'd let me stay, Tom! I just knew it!" he exclaimed, folding the knife before slipping it into his shirt pocket. I placed a hand on my bloody neck. "Hey, take a look at this! Hello, Leo Biggs, postmortem!" my brother shouted with delight before picking up the photo I had placed on the dresser. "I can't tell you how many times I've thought about you, old cousin!"

Now the blood began to ooze through my fingers while Eddie intently stared at the photo before stuffing it into his shirt pocket alongside the knife. I stood there and watched him, unable to make any sudden moves. "I have to go back to the woods to get my stuff, Tom," he said abruptly as I pressed harder on my wound.

"Woods? What woods?" I asked, slowly realizing that my brother was fixing to leave again, although that didn't stop my heart from pounding.

"You know, Tom! The woods behind the railroad tracks on the edge of town. I have a few belongings stashed there behind an old woodpile. I'm going to go get my things and I'll be right back, okay Tom?" Eddie assured me.

"Yeah, sure. You go get your things," I said, looking at the blood all over my hand. "I'll be here when you get back." Was I going into shock?

"You should put a bandage on that, Tom," Eddie instructed before letting out a giggle, proud of the damage he had done, but his attention toward me would be short lived. "Oh, look! The bird is sitting on the window seat again. Shoo! Shoo!" Eddie shouted as he ran toward the window, lunging at the bird as it flew out into the rainy grayness. "Fly away!" my brother cried, waving his arms, the distraction of the bird having stopped him from leaving.

"Didn't you say you had to go back to the woods to get your stuff?" I reminded him. Eddie's eyes lit up.

"Yes, I did, Tom!" he remembered. "I'll be right back! Wait until Dulcie sees me!" he whooped excitedly before running behind the garment rack and disappearing into the darkness of the hole in the paneling. I watched him go before looking at my hand again, now covered in a deep red film of dry blood, the oozing from the cut on my neck having stopped. I closed my eyes and took in a deep breath, gathering myself quickly.

I hurried down the attic stairs and went straight to my bedroom window where I watched Eddie run across the driveway and up the street through the pouring rain. Before rushing to the basement where I'd look for the old coal chute, I stopped in front of the mirror that hung in the hallway to inspect my bloody neck, a gruesome image that sent me straight to the bathroom sink where I'd rinse off before tiptoeing downstairs. Slipping past Dulcie and into the pantry where the basement door was located wasn't difficult and neither was finding the chute, even in the faint light.

Located by the chimney just like Eddie said, it was a square opening that looked out onto the driveway, its wooden door that, at one time, securely closed it off now forced ajar. Large enough for a person to fit through, I could see how my brother, and the birds, easily got in. Using all of my might, I pushed a nearby metal cabinet in front of the old coal chute, permanently blocking Eddie's reentry. I wondered, though, if he would try to get into the house any other way.

Walking behind the furnace I then saw the tunnel. I climbed into the dark opening that meandered upward behind the walls of the house until it reached the attic. Lined with torn cobwebs and electrical wires it wasn't difficult to navigate, this unknown passage that would secretly usher Eddie into the world of checkers and Leo Biggs whenever he wanted.

Before I knew it, I was walking through the hole in the paneling behind the metal garment rack. I made the trip back and forth several times and wondered all the while how Eddie had managed to remain silent and undetected while snaking his way behind the walls of our house. As much as I hated to admit it, his cunning impressed me.

I quickly walked back down the attic stairs to the second floor where I opened the door to mother's bedroom. It looked the same as the day she died and evoked powerful memories from what seemed a lifetime ago. I could unmistakably smell her perfume and hear her voice, asking me to fetch her slippers and take her robe out of the closet; see her sitting up in bed, telephone in one hand, cigarette in the other; watch her at her vanity table once more, applying her makeup and brushing her hair; taste the lemongrass tea she allowed me to sip from her cup before gently taking it from my hands to drink it herself. Poor mother. Poor beautiful mother. I had scant time to spend on memories though, quickly picking up the telephone that still sat on the nightstand to call Mink.

"Uncle Andrew, it's Tom," I said, trying to catch my breath. "I don't have much time to explain but Eddie's on his way to the woods behind the railroad tracks on the edge of town. As a matter of fact, he might already be there. His plan is to gather a few belongings he has stashed behind an old woodpile and then come back here to the house. Yes, sir, the house. I thought you should know. Don't worry, I'll wait here." I hung up the phone so that Mink could call the police before rushing over. All I could do was maintain my composure and wait.

I changed into a shirt that covered the already scabbed over slit on my neck before going down to the kitchen. I calmly sat at the table where Dulcie put a dish of cold French toast and sausage in front of me. I picked up a fork and began to eat.

"Where have you been?" she asked.

"Clearing out the birds in the attic," I said casually. "This is really very good. Thanks for making breakfast."

"It's stone cold! You could have cleared out the birds after breakfast, you know!" Dulcie was annoyed and I guess I didn't blame her. I began to tremble inside.

"That's true," I said in agreement, "but I wanted to get it over with. Anyway, the birds are gone, and breakfast is still delicious." I picked up the morning paper on the table and perused the front page so as to avoid any further discussion, but I realized quickly that Dulcie would have to be told what happened in the attic. She had a right to know and besides, Mink would be here soon.

"Well, I'm glad the birds are gone but your breakfast was meant to be eaten hot," Dulcie pouted as she cleared the table. I decided to come clean before she could even walk the dishes over to the kitchen sink. My nerves were now rattling, causing me to shiver, but I kept my shaking hands under the kitchen table.

"Dulcie, can you sit for a few minutes?" I asked in my best grown up tone of voice. "I have something to tell you." My heart had wasted no time in beating quickly again. Just then the doorbell rang.

"I'll get that," she said, putting the dishes back down on the table.

"No, let me," I insisted as I got up, struggling now to maintain my rapidly slipping composure. Mink had gotten here much sooner than I expected but upon opening the door I could see that I was wrong about that.

My neck still throbbed as Dulcie and I escorted Officer Dunnegan into the kitchen, a person I never thought I'd see again, not today, not ever. He said he had some bad news about Eddie as if there could ever be good news about my brother. I would listen to what he had to say, although I knew that Eddie's return had been ill-fated all along. The three of us sat down at the kitchen table, awkward in each other's company.

"Would you like a cup of coffee?" Dulcie asked the officer with a stiff politeness.

"Oh, no thank you, Miss Jackson," Dunnegan said, taking a pad out of his jacket pocket, the same pocket that had held the large pocketknife and the old photograph.

"I'm expecting Mink," I said flatly. "As a matter of fact, I thought when the doorbell rang…"

"He's the one who called me, Tom. I'm sure he'll be here shortly." Dunnegan took in a deep breath before putting his head down, loath to tell me what I already knew. "Like I said, I have some bad news about your brother."

"Get on with it, Officer Dunnegan," I said impatiently. "Mink doesn't have to be here for you to give me news about Eddie."

"I'm afraid we found your brother's body in the woods behind the railroad tracks on the edge of town," he said delicately, exuding uncharacteristic compassion. But there was no need for that. I was numb, unable to feel anything other than the throbbing in my neck. Dulcie gasped, putting her hands to her mouth.

"How did he die?" I asked, incapable of summoning any emotion at all about yet another death, my entire family now gone.

"It appears that he was running through the woods and slipped on the wet terrain, falling to the ground before hitting his head on a rock. I'm so sorry, Tom," said the sympathetic officer. "You've been through a lot. You didn't deserve this." I found it ironic that Eddie, who was somehow embedded in every family tragedy that had befallen us like dominoes, had died by sheer accident, the most tragic way of all. Dulcie put an arm around my shoulder, but I shrugged it off.

"Thanks," was all I could say before Dunnegan handed me Eddie's pocketknife and the photograph of Leo Biggs, postmortem. I put my hand up to my neck again just as the doorbell rang. Mink was finally here.

"What's going on, Dunnegan?" he asked anxiously as he walked into the kitchen, Dulcie having let him in. I'm sure the look on her face gave it away, but he asked anyway. "Any news about Eddie?"

"My brother's dead, Uncle Andrew," I blurted out before the officer proceeded to fill him in on everything.

"Call me tomorrow for a police report, counselor, but it was an accident, pure and simple. Again, I'm sorry, Tom," said Dunnegan, shaking my hand. "I don't believe there's any reason for us to see each other again."

"Does that mean you won't be parked outside of my house tonight watching everything I do?" I asked, impassive but unable to tolerate Dunnegan's presence any longer.

"No hard feelings, Tom. I was just doing my job," he said before walking toward the front door. Dulcie followed and let him out while Mink looked at me with a soft yet sorrowful expression. He had been through plenty too.

"C'mon boy, let's go home," he said in a whisper, gently tousling my hair. I had a lot to tell him, but I wasn't ready.

"I need a few hours, Uncle Andrew," I said, trying to muster even the faintest of smiles. "Please come back then." He appeared to understand, nodding his head in agreement. I still needed to say my farewells to the attic, but first...I had to throw up.

Ascending the attic stairs for the final time felt surprisingly hollow after my encounter with Eddie, causing me to ask myself if I really needed to go up there again. What drew me to this place now, this attic so darkly stained with deceit? What could I do that hadn't been done before, or think that hadn't been thought? The only thing left was to quickly say my goodbyes and leave. But it wouldn't be that simple.

Surrounded by the aura of my brother's treachery, his long shadow still towering over me, I put my hand to my neck again before drifting over to one of the window seats where I would look out onto the world from this place for the very last time. I could still feel Eddie's presence darkly shrouding everything around me, the weight of his memory holding me hostage as I glanced up at the empty rafters and then over at the hole in the paneling behind the metal garment rack.

All was quiet and still except for the sound of Eddie's voice, ringing in my ear. I sadly looked around at the clothing, the furniture, father's first set of golf clubs, and the stuffed head of a deer that he had once shot and killed during a long-ago hunting trip. My gaze lingered on the trunk of old family photos upon which we played our checkers games and ate our lunches. And then there was the nest that Eddie and I had made together, left to a far corner of the attic as a gift for the birds, eventually reclaimed by me for my own deceitful purposes. I could still see father and Dulcie under the old blanket, and picture myself hiding mother's picnic basket inside the very window seat where I now sat, covering it over with that same old blanket.

I could smell Eddie's dirty hand over my mouth and feel the cold blade of his knife at my throat. I blinked hard and shook my head as if to banish the painful memories, but nothing could ever do that. It was woefully obvious that the attic would never again hold the same charms for me, given all that had happened here, but that wouldn't lessen the ache I felt at the thought of having to leave this place. I began to cry.

Rain still trickled down the glass pane before me, my vision mixing it with my own tears, as I called out for mother. I felt alone and frightened, just as I had during my detention, unsure of how my future would unfold. Sitting on the hard window seat, my salty tears falling into my lap, I realized that I was saying goodbye to much more than just the attic.

Closing my eyes tightly, I held my breath and buried all unholy thoughts of mother and father before talking to Eddie. I told him I forgave him and hoped he'd rest easy for all eternity. I had to say that, not for Eddie's sake but for mine. Perhaps he was with mother and father again, driving them crazy in the afterlife. I managed to chuckle at the thought, regaining my composure as I considered the way poetic justice works sometimes.

I wiped away my tears and stood up straight and tall, my goodbyes just about over. Ready to leave, I retrieved the old checkers game and picked up one of father's golf balls, playfully tossing it into the air and catching it again before stuffing it into my pocket. No longer afraid that Eddie was lurking around every dark corner, I confidently walked toward the attic stairs with the checkers game securely tucked under my arm, remembering the words of the private investigator who told me to enjoy my freedom and forget about my brother. I would certainly enjoy my freedom, but could never forget about Eddie…even if I tried.

I changed into my jeans and brought my belongings down to the front hall, placing everything near the door. Mink would be here any time now and I wanted to be ready. It was all there, whatever was personally important to me or held a fond memory, neatly stacked, my whole life defined by a large jar of coins and a small photo of my parents, my football and a favorite sweatshirt, Eddie's airplane, a book of Edgar Allen Poe stories, and one of mother's decks of cards ordered specially from Toller's Stationary. Also included were the old checkers game and the golf ball, mementos that reminded me of father in his younger days as much as they did my beloved attic. Dulcie quietly walked into the front hall.

"You left these on the kitchen table," she said, handing me Eddie's large pocketknife and the photograph of Leo Biggs, postmortem.

"Thanks," I said quietly, placing the photograph in my shirt pocket. I stared at the knife long and hard, turning it over and over again in the palm of my hand. I unfolded it, surprised by the cleanliness of the blade. I put a hand to my neck again. "Here you go, Dulcie," I managed to say, handing her the knife. "Something to remember Eddie by." Her expression revealed both surprise and humility.

"Oh, no, I couldn't," she said. "This knife belonged to Eddie. You should keep it."

"No, he'd want you to have it," I responded quickly before walking away as though it weren't a big deal, leaving her no choice but to accept the knife that had sliced my throat. I attentively looked over my belongings so as to make sure I hadn't forgotten anything, but also to avoid a sentimental goodbye between Dulcie and me. Still, a friendly parting was in order. "Well, it's been nice knowing you," I said awkwardly. "Take care of yourself."

For the first time ever, her dark brown curly hair and strikingly beautiful green eyes repulsed me.

"You too," she said warmly, reaching out to hug me. I thrust out my hand and we shook on it instead. "I wish you all the luck in the world and a life filled with happiness," Dulcie added, clearing her throat in an effort to diminish the severity of the clumsy moment.

"Thanks. You too," I responded obligingly, but my grin was disingenuous. Just then, the doorbell rang. Dulcie opened the door for Mink.

"Hi Tom! Are you ready?" he asked, only as cheerful as decorum would allow given Eddie's death mere hours ago.

"Yes, Uncle Andrew," I said. "I'm ready."

"Is this everything then?" he asked, looking over my belongings neatly stacked near the front door.

"Just about," I said before running into the living room to scoop Tinker up into my arms. I returned to the front hall with my dog, ready to walk out for good, all of my goodbyes having been said. I would leave Dulcie behind, finally out of my heart and, as of today, out of my life. "Now I have everything."

As the two of us drove away, Mink explained how he and his wife were looking forward to having me live with them permanently and that they were both eager, not only to provide me with a good education but to watch me grow up to be a fine man someday as well. He said that they would do everything in their power to make me happy and hoped that I would always feel comfortable enough to come to them with a problem. I listened passively while staring out the car window while Tinker sat in my lap, the shock of everything starting to set in.

"Perhaps you'll even go to law school and take over the firm one day," Mink projected. "The key is to always be honest, not only with us but with yourself, you know what I mean, Tom? It's an easy recipe for contentment and a clear conscience, the only way to live."

"Yes, Uncle Andrew," I agreed. "Is this about the trial?"

"No, Tom. That's all in the past," he assured me. "You'll never have to rehash the trial with us, or anyone else, ever again. Today, we start fresh, all right?" he said, slapping me on the knee.

"All right, Uncle Andrew," I began, "then I have something to show you straight off."

"Show me? What is it, Tom?" Mink asked curiously. I pulled down my shirt collar, causing him to gasp in horror before pulling off to the side of the road. "What the hell happened to you?" His face was draped in shock as he collapsed onto the steering wheel, unable to take his eyes off my throat.

"Drive me to a doctor, Uncle Andrew, and I'll fill you in on the way," I told him, my neck now throbbing more than ever.

Mink was right. He'd been right all along. The key was to always be honest, something I hadn't been for a long time, having come from a house of deceit where I was surrounded by the web of lies we were all guilty of spinning, all except Eddie. He was guilty of many things but lying wasn't one of them. Father, mother, and I paid a heavy price for our lies, but for different reasons, I pitied Eddie the most.

Perhaps, one day, when all of this is nothing more than a distant memory and I've attained the contentment that Mink talked about, I'll think of Eddie and smile. Perhaps. For now, though, I found it difficult to believe in the possibility of coming to terms with my past. Yes, I had made my peace in the attic, but would I really be strong enough to move on from there, to block Eddie, and my parents for that matter, from haunting me ever again? I shuddered, overwhelmed by the thought, as we sped off toward the hospital. But Mink would make me a promise.

"We're going to get you all the help you need, Tom," he assured me, the urgency in his voice telling me that I required more than just a few stitches.

"Thank you, Uncle Andrew," I said gratefully, staring out the car window again as I let go of my tears, hoping that all my wounds could be mended. Perhaps then, I'd learn how to accept my past, remember all of the good times and confront the bad ones head on, including today when Eddie came home and ominously walked…into the attic darkly.

Made in United States
North Haven, CT
08 July 2024

W

Y

ABOUT THE AUTHORS

Richard S. MacAlpine was born in Geneva, New York, but was raised in New Jersey. He graduated from Transylvania University in Lexington, Kentucky, and did graduate work at Colgate University in Hamilton, New York. For thirty-three years, Rich taught European and American history at Oneida High School in Oneida, New York. During that time, he developed an interest in researching family history, which started his relationship with the Yates County History Center in Penn Yan back when

Richard MacAlpine (left) and Charles Mitchell (right).

it was widely known just as "the Oliver House." After retiring from teaching in 2001, he and his wife, Jeanie, moved to a home on Keuka Lake, where he became more than just a researcher at the history center. He has served on its board of directors since 2006 and has served as editor of its bimonthly publication, *Yates Past*, since 2008. Starting in 2004, Rich has researched and written over one hundred articles on various aspects of Yates County history. Twenty-two of those articles appear in his book *Yates County Chronicles*, which was published in 2014 by The History Press. Rich and Jeanie have three adult children and nine grandchildren.

Charles R. Mitchell, after a tour in the U.S. Army in Germany and graduation from Elmira College, worked at Corning Inc. for eighteen years. After that, he bought the Photographic Center in Penn Yan, utilizing his photographic and framing skills. He began volunteering at the Oliver House Museum organizing the photo archives. This led to employment as curator when that position became available. In the last twelve years as curator, he has scanned and digitally enhanced over six thousand images, including those in this book. He has authored three books: *Keuka Lake*, *Penn Yan and Keuka Lake* and *Hammondsport and Keuka Lake*. He has coauthored seven: *Glenn Curtiss*, *Flying High*, *Women in Aviation*, *Corning*, *Bath*, *Watkins Glen* and *Finger Lake Postcards*. All ten books were with Arcadia Publishing in its Images of America series. His program on Keuka Lake steamboats has been presented to many audiences over the years.

Visit us at
www.historypress.net

This title is also available as an e-book

CPSIA information can be obtained
at www.ICGtesting.com
Printed in the USA
LVHW081407280122
709435LV00011B/444